WAR BREAKER

Michael O'Connell was dismissed from the CIA because he knew too much. The former agent had helped Pakistan turn a fleet of B-50s into nearly undetectable nuclear bombers. And now, with Pakistan and India on the verge of war, the agency is demanding O'Connell's expertise for one last assignment—to get the bombers back.

In a desperate attempt to save the world from utter annihilation, O'Connell must dodge the bullets of frantic foreign agents and fight off an arms trader willing to pay a pretty penny for just one of the bombers. Only then can he restore the balance to a world which teeters on the brink of destruction.

JIM DeFELICE

WAR BREAKER

LEISURE BOOKS **NEW YORK CITY**

A LEISURE BOOK®

July 1996

Published by

Dorchester Publishing Co., Inc.
276 Fifth Avenue
New York, NY 10001

Printed in the United States of America.

Looking into the future gives a writer certain luxuries. Though technically feasible, some of the devices and facilities included here (notably the air force bunker in Islamabad and the Snow Leopard) do not yet exist in South Asia. But the intelligence and ingenuity of Pakistani scientists and engineers is not my invention.

One thing I wish were an invention is the presence of nuclear arms on the Indian subcontinent. India has exploded nuclear devices and has a range of delivery systems, including missiles, capable of hitting several neighboring countries. Though as of this writing the Pakistanis have not exploded an atomic weapon, reliable authorities estimate that they possess at least half a dozen. Depending on the configuration of the weapons and the planes, their F-16s and perhaps some of their older jets would be capable of delivering them.

As I finished the final draft, skirmishes had once more erupted in Kashmir, and religious riots were erupting in northern India.

Jim DeFelice

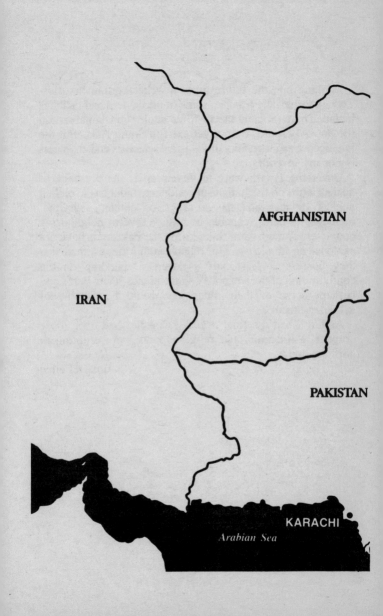

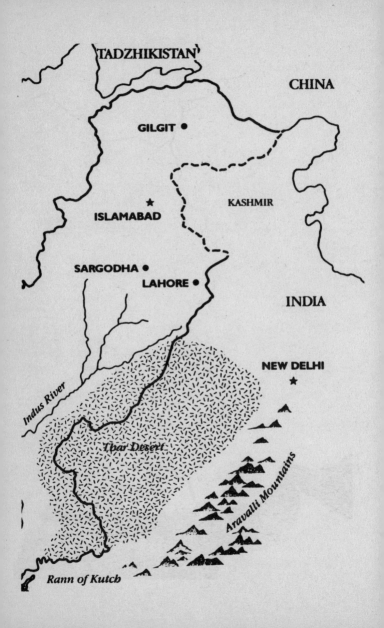

WAR BREAKER

TUESDAY, SEPT. 16, 1997

Upstate New York. Apx. 9 A.M.

It was spontaneous, as if his will suddenly collapsed.

Whatever had held Michael O'Connell together over the last few weeks—months, two years—disappeared suddenly, without warning, and he slid slowly to his knees, alone in the middle of his office.

The room was nearly empty, its few valuable contents sold at auction early this morning. All that remained of O'Connell's Helicopters & Tours besides its president were a desk and a few chairs; the furniture had come with the office and was too battered for anyone really to want. Sinking down in front of the desk, pulled down not so much by gravity as internal inertia, the thirty-eight-year-old O'Connell began to do something he hadn't done in nearly twenty years: He began to pray.

"Our Father," he started, real reverence in his voice. The Jesuits who had raised him would have loved the sincerity. The Our Father was a perfect prayer. Short, simple, it covered all the basics—acknowledgment of the deity, eternity, man's role in God's plan. There was a plea for temporal as well as spiritual sustenance; a reminder of the need and power of grace, and humility.

The words spilled from his mouth, a torrential surrender. Even his hands were clasped: not in the pointed, symmetrical way the priests instructed, but a more natural, more dire grip, each finger hard against the other. It took only a few seconds to finish the prayer. O'Connell remained kneeling two minutes more, his mind a complete blank. And then, finally, the loathing returned, steeled him, and he stood.

Praying? Father Fran would love it. His prodigal son was returning.

O'Connell practically spit at the thought. Silently, he went back and sat at his desk, which didn't even have a telephone on it anymore. He still had the office only because he'd paid the five-year lease in advance. That was almost two years ago, when things were still optimistic.

He had no plan for the rest of the day, let alone for the rest of his life. It wasn't that he'd been avoiding reality, or that he'd felt by ignoring the inevitable he could escape it. Nor could he say that he'd been overcome by events—after the initial excitement of opening wore off, it had become obvious he wasn't going to make it. The tip he'd gotten about plans to legalize casino gambling in the Catskills had proved groundless. The lucrative private charters had failed to materialize, and even the gigs checking power lines were a losing proposition. He'd gotten in way over his head from the start, leasing too many helicopters and signing too many IOUs. But it had taken a long time to work through the bank credit line and the savings he'd used to stake the company. There'd been plenty of time to plan. He just hadn't.

Maybe he could get a job flying a traffic helicopter somewhere. Maybe somebody would walk into the office and hand him a million dollars, just for the hell of it.

Maybe one of the Jesuits had kicked, and left him an inheritance.

O'Connell laughed perversely, then slid his chair forward and reached into the bottom of the desk, lifting out a bottle of Jack Daniel's. Jimmy, his last employee, had brought it in on his final day of work three weeks ago, along with two double-shot glasses. Poor little guy. One of the best helicopter mechanics O'Connell had ever met, and he'd had to go back to Minnesota and live with his sister and brother-in-law, working on cars at a nearby garage.

O'Connell hated the taste of bourbon—hated all booze. Alcohol was the reason he'd been orphaned and sent to the home. His father and mother had died in a car crash when he was three, and the smell of liquor generally turned his stomach. But it was better than praying.

Consider it penance. Penance for having wasted two years, and seven before that. A sacrifice, so he could get on to the future, whatever that was.

O'Connell filled the glass to the first line and recapped the bottle. He brought it to eye level and stared at the amber liquid, pushed it into his mouth, practically gagging as it burned its way to his stomach.

The Jesuits were all heavy drinkers. They would have been disappointed.

Good.

O'Connell put the glass back in the drawer without cleaning it and leaned back in the chair again. He stayed that way for a half hour or more, his mind ruminating uselessly on the past, until there was a knock on the door.

"Yeah?" He could see the shadow of a man, maybe two, through the glass. Just his luck—his first customers in months, and no helicopter. "Come on in."

He knew right away they weren't customers. It wasn't just the Sears suits: the two young men, barely into their twenties, were too stiff to be anything but government employees. He owed so much money to the IRS they probably figured they could recoup some of it by using him as a training exercise.

"You want to be talking to my attorney, Len Zimmer," O'Connell told them. "He's in charge of everything. Let's see if I got his card." He pulled open his top drawer and began fishing through the collection of papers. He wasn't sure whether he had any more of Lenny's cards, but it was worth the effort to look—the cards had a pacifying effect, especially on tax people. "Your agent was at the auction, Jerry what's-his-name. Nice guy for a taxman," said O'Connell, digging deeper into the drawer. "Anyway, Lenny's handling everything."

"We came to talk to you," said the shorter of the two men. They were a classic Mutt-and-Jeff team. The short one was a little fat, with a thick brush of a mustache beneath his nose. His partner, tall and thin, had a face so white it looked as if it had been painted on.

"I'm afraid my attorney's the boss," said O'Connell, continuing his search. Reaching deep into the drawer, he brushed aside his old Browning pistol, one more relic from the past, and found one last, crinkled card. "Here we go," said O'Connell, retrieving it and then trying to straighten out the wrinkles.

"Mike," said the tall man. "We're here to see you."

O'Connell looked up and realized they weren't tax collectors at all.

"No one calls me Mike," he said, the slightest hint of a Boston accent drifting below the subdued anger. "My name is Michael."

Both men took CIA identification cards from their jacket pockets. The tall one's name was John Fashona; Shorty was William Baright. O'Connell stared past the small, plastic-coated cards and their bright new leather holders, into the faces of the men. They had a naive, untested hue to them— new agents, fresh off the farm.

"The DDO wants to talk to you," said Baright.

"Has to be a mistake," said O'Connell. "I don't work for the Company anymore."

"The DDO wants to see you," echoed Fashona. The DDO was the CIA's deputy director of operations—number three man in the agency, directly responsible for all covert operations. He had been O'Connell's last boss, the man who fired him in disgrace. "We're here to escort you."

"What if I don't want to go?"

"That may not be up to you," said the man.

"I think it is," said O'Connell. He put his hands back on the desk drawer, intending to close it.

"Don't," said Shorty. As he spoke, his partner took a step back, his hand reaching around to the back of his trousers.

O'Connell smiled and pushed the drawer closed.

"I haven't had bullets in that gun in two years," he said. "I'm not even sure it works anymore." He stood, put out his hand, deciding it might be part of his penance to seem almost friendly. The men hesitated.

"You can shake my hand," he said. "I'm not contagious."

Fashona took it first, weakly. Baright followed, a little more firmly.

"Drink?" he asked.

They shook their heads.

"Good," said O'Connell. "The stuff makes me sick. What'd they tell you about me?"

They shrugged together. If things in the agency didn't work out for them, they could always work up a comedy routine.

"I got kicked out," O'Connell said. "For overstepping my authority and diverting arms to the Pakistani government. That's the official story. The real story is, I got shafted for following orders."

They looked a bit skeptical. The media had done up the Pakistan arms shipments big, overly righteous that weapons intended for rebels in Afghanistan were given to nonrebels in Pakistan. Even if the affair wasn't talked about on the Farm—and O'Connell suspected he was a whole chapter in somebody's "don't do this" textbook—both of these kids had probably read all about it in the papers just about the time they were trying to decide what to do when they got out of college.

"Real-life lesson number one," said O'Connell, playing the grizzled veteran for them. "The agency will screw you if it gets a chance. No matter who you are or what you do, eventually you will get it in the back."

They were somber, but not overly impressed. He wouldn't have been impressed either.

He could shock them by telling the whole story, what he'd

15

really helped the Paks do, but what was the point? They wouldn't care. And if they went home and told their keepers what he'd said, he could have real problems. If the agency thought he might suddenly become talkative—if the DDO or someone else started seeing him as a liability—he was in big trouble.

Maybe they did already. Maybe that's why the two Boy Scouts had been sent after him.

"What's this all about?" O'Connell asked.

"The DDO wants to see you," said Baright.

"About what?"

"We need you to come to Langley with us," said Fashona, referring to the CIA's headquarters in Virginia. "We'd like you to come now."

"What if I have something better to do?"

"Like what?"

O'Connell looked around the office. They had a point.

"We have time to stop at your house and pack a few things," said Fashona.

"No problem," he replied, deciding he might as well go along while there was still some pretense that it was voluntary. "My suitcase is by the door. The lease on my apartment ran out last week."

CIA Headquarters. Apx. Noon

O'Connell tried to stretch out the crease in his back as they drove up to Langley's Dolly Madison gate. The agency must be cutting back on travel allowances—both the car in New York and the one they'd taken out from National Airport were barely compacts. But then domestic operations were always on a shoestring; it was only overseas that officers and bureau chiefs got chauffeured Mercedes and Land-Rovers.

The guard checked their credentials and waved them into the CIA complex. The weather had turned cold, and stepping from the car O'Connell pulled on his jacket, the soft leather folding over his cotton shirt. As they walked toward the building, he noticed a group of people coming out to their cars, laughing. These would be office workers, analysts, people who could afford to take a leisurely lunch. To them, the agency was only a job. They were overt CIA—drudges as far as O'Connell was concerned.

He wasn't even inside the door, and already he was slipping into his old mind-set. Silently he cursed himself for letting his guard down. These people screwed you, he reminded himself. You're only here to find out what the hell is going on. And then to laugh in their faces.

But the old patterns were too easy. The security officer at the front desk handed him an ID badge and motioned him to a terminal. Though the apparatus was brand new, O'Connell didn't need to be told how to use it. Neither his two escorts nor the officer said anything as he punched in his old code and then placed his hand on the palm scanner. The machine beeped, and flashed some green letters on the screen: Someone had restored his clearance.

O'Connell clipped his badge over the side of his jacket. It was impossible not to feel like a case officer returning from an extended overseas assignment. Following Fashona and Baright down the hall, he forced himself to remember the last time he'd walked here. Then, too, he had been escorted; then, too, he had an appointment with the DDO. But at least then he knew what to expect.

"Michael?"

On the flight to D.C. he'd realized he might run into her, and in fact had almost used that possibility as an excuse to turn around and go back to New York. But it could just as easily have been a reason to come.

O'Connell stopped, closed his eyes, saw her before he turned around to look. Short—barely five-two—with a rounded face and the well-muscled body of someone who spent nearly two hours every day working out. Long trains of tight black curls cascaded around her face, highlighting her penetrating eyes.

"Michael?"

For nearly two years he'd struggled to consign Morena Kelso to a back corner of his mind. At first, it had been torture, but as time went on and his other troubles mounted, the woman he'd had an affair with for nearly three years, the only woman he'd really loved in his life, had faded. Every so often he'd look at some of the old photos. More and more, the face in the photos had become strange to him, pretty instead of haunting.

But it was vivid now when he turned around, flushed with the emotion he himself was trying to deny.

O'Connell's arms jerked out involuntarily, as if to reach for her. He quickly pulled them back. Morena began walking down the hall toward him. She seemed absolutely as he remembered her, though her hair was now shorter and her clothes brighter than she would have worn in sexually repressed Pakistan. He could even smell her French perfume, her one outright concession to vanity.

Not that she was a nun.

Mercifully, the elevator arrived while she was still a good twenty feet away. His handlers stepped in immediately. O'Connell took a second more, barely managed the step backwards. The door snapped closed, and O'Connell caught a glimpse of Morena's face clouding with a familiar scowl. But she said nothing.

"You know her?" asked Fashona. His two handlers had turned out to be relatively congenial, filling him in on recent agency lore on the way down.

"Sure I know her," said O'Connell. "I know everybody."

"She's deputy head of South Asia," said Baright, with more than a hint of awe.

"Head of South Asia?" sputtered O'Connell.

"Deputy head."

Morena's primary job in Pakistan had been to act as access agent, making contacts and fingering potential sources of information and spies. She'd been good at that, extremely good. She'd run a couple of people herself, and had helped the agency out of some difficult spots. There was no question about her potential or intelligence. Still, O'Connell couldn't believe she'd risen so fast. She was barely thirty. And a woman. Even now, that would bother a lot of people, no matter what other assets she had.

"She's got a hell of a set of lungs on her," said Baright, who was just about her height.

"Great legs, too," said Fashona.

"She could snap your neck in two seconds with one of them," said O'Connell. The kids laughed, though the last thing he meant was to make a joke.

She'd never called, or gotten word to him. He'd been the one who tried, in those long, angry days right after Stockman gave him the short list of alternatives. Morena had ignored him.

Wise for her career. Cut all ties with the scapegoat, especially if you'd been sleeping with him.

The scapegoat stepped from the elevator, following the two rookies down the hallway. This was a big deal for them, running a personal chore for the agency's top spook. No doubt they'd be rewarded with decent postings, be the envy of their graduating class.

O'Connell had missed all that, bypassed the politics and the ass-kissing. He'd come over from the army to do some specific jobs, and then drifted into the middle of the action. Pakistan had been one the agency's biggest stations as the Cold War ground down. By some measures it was the Company's biggest, larger and more important than even Moscow. The war in Afghanistan had established its importance; after that, its proximity to the Middle East as well as China and the remains of the Soviet Union put it at an important crossroads. Anyone with ability could get on there. And O'Connell, his most recent business experience to the contrary, was a man of great and varied abilities.

His memory, for example. He knew Stockman's secretary's name was Marsha, and that she had two children, Paul and Tricia, both of whom would be in elementary school now. But he merely nodded when she greeted them. "He's expecting you, Mr. O'Connell," she said, gesturing toward the dark gray security door that led to the inner office.

Mr. O'Connell. She addressed him, not the two neophytes. They were still outsiders. He was the one who'd put in his dues, taken the risks. Gotten the shaft.

Stockman was sitting at his desk, a walnut boat that went well with the paneling. Nothing had changed here, least of all Stockman, whose dark blue suit had the same wrinkles O'Connell had noted the last time they'd met. He sat upright at his desk, frosty, his large body tightly wound. His shoulders still hinted at the physical strength that had gotten him out of so many jams and helped earn him his nickname during his salad days: the Abominable Snowman.

"Thank you, gentlemen," said the DDO. The two men mumbled responses and left with cautious grins on their faces.

O'Connell stood by the edge of the desk, didn't bother to shake the deputy director's hand when he offered it.

"So why am I here?" he said bluntly.

"How are you, Michael?"

O'Connell shrugged, said nothing.

"Business isn't that good, I suppose."

Not for the first time O'Connell considered the possibility that the agency had purposely sabotaged him.

"Business is dead," he said. "What is it you want?"

"Relax. Sit down," said the Snowman, trying to sound uncharacteristically warm and friendly.

"I prefer to stand," O'Connell said.

Stockman smiled as if he were an indulgent father. Two of his front teeth wore gold caps; legend had it that they'd been busted in a brawl in Saigon in the early seventies.

"Drink?"

"I don't drink."

"Oh, yes, that's right," said Stockman, going to the sideboard and retrieving a bottle of bourbon—Jack Daniel's again. "Afraid you'll dull the edge."

"You canned me two years ago, Carl. I don't owe you a thing."

"I don't know about that," said Stockman, his voice starting to chill. Apparently he'd made his stab at being Mr. Congeniality. "There could have been a trial."

"I'm sure you would have loved the headlines when I told them what really happened."

"It would have come down on your head," answered the

Snowman, returning to his desk.

"You seem to have done a pretty good job sweeping it all under the rug. That must be why the new administration kept you on—they don't know, do they?"

"It was the director's project," said Stockman. "Not only wasn't I DDO at the time, but none of us on the review committee were informed. You know how Woolsley operated."

"You never saw the intelligence estimate predicting the Chinese would help them if we didn't?"

"Neither I nor anyone else in this building was briefed on your mission."

It was a perfect setup—O'Connell had dealt directly with CIA Director Richard Woolsley, and the director had died several months before O'Connell was recalled from Pakistan. If everyone agreed they didn't know about the project, who could contradict them?

"Don't run the deniability game with me, Carl. I know how this place works."

"You don't know anything about the way this place runs, Michael," said Stockman, his voice even but his eyes flaring. "You don't know anything about this place at all. I've always respected your abilities. You can fly helicopters with your eyes closed and speak more languages than half the UN. Your memory's a goddamn photocopy machine. But you don't know this place. You still think everything works like the army."

O'Connell watched as the DDO turned his attention to his drink. The outburst was as emotional as Stockman ever got. Even in a culture that regularly operated at thirty-two degrees Fahrenheit, the Snowman was especially cool.

"Something had to be done to protect the agency," said Stockman.

"Somebody had to be screwed, you mean."

"Perhaps I didn't handle it as well as it could have been handled," offered Stockman. "Had the Senate gotten involved, we would have had another Iraq on our hands."

Even if Stockman's version were correct, O'Connell should have been taken care of. The agency owed him; he'd been following the director's orders. As DDO, it was the Snowman's job to watch out for him, no matter what the situation was. Besides, what did Father Fran used to say? *Me invito* or *me auctore*, it doesn't matter on the receiving end. Whether something happens "against my will" or "at my suggestion," you still get screwed.

Damn Jesuits again. They'd also said *nil sine numine*— "nothing without the divine will"—the motto of the state of Colorado.

"Why don't you sit down?" Stockman said.

Momentarily brooding on the fact that he seemed unable to stop any of his old nemeses from haunting him, O'Connell slid into the chair.

"These are different times," continued Stockman, trying to sound expansive. "New president, our third director in three years."

"Same DDO."

"There've been a lot of changes around here."

"Yeah, like Morena Kelso number two on South Asia."

"She has a lot of abilities," Stockman said, practically winking. "Did you get a chance to speak to her?"

"Why would I want to?"

"Have you been following this business between Pakistan and India?"

"Oh sure. It's the only thing I think about."

"A war is about to break out in the Kashmir. There have been Muslim riots, and the Indians have moved troops in. I'm getting satellite and eavesdropping intelligence on it every half hour."

"A war is always going to break out in Kashmir."

"This time it's going to be different. Kashmir will only be a diversion. The Indians are preparing an attack across the Thar Desert in the southern Punjab. If they succeed, they'll cut Pakistan in half."

"It'll be a cakewalk," said O'Connell. "They'll be through in a week and a half, if that."

"Exactly."

O'Connell said nothing for a moment, his gaze tacking along the clear brown surface of the Snowman's desk. He'd sat in this office only once before—the day he'd been canned—but it was hauntingly familiar, as if he'd spent most of his life here.

Stockman reached down and unbuttoned his jacket, slid back in the chair and took another long sip of the bourbon. "We've lost the planes you helped them build," said the DDO. "We thought they were still at Kahuta, but we were wrong. I sent a team in two weeks ago, and they came up empty. I have satellites photographing every inch of the damn country, and we still can't find them."

"What's the big deal about three long-range bombers?" But O'Connell knew what the big deal was even before he asked. A hole had opened in his chest, sucking air out of his lungs. "You think they held back nukes," he said in a low voice.

"Don't you?"

Yes, O'Connell did. He had brought up that possibility with the director when he was assigned to help build the planes. Woolsley's response was an almost off-hand dismissal, a bland assertion that it wasn't possible, followed by an assurance that even if it happened, the agency would be able to "monitor and control" the situation. In any event, it would be much more dangerous, he said, if the Chinese were involved.

The assignment that had led to O'Connell's dismissal began just a few months after the UN succeeded in getting all of the countries in South Asia to sign a treaty banning nuclear weapons. In the case of Pakistan and India, this involved destroying missiles that had already been built and were in fact already pointed at each other. Extensive inspection provisions were added to the pact to make sure that each side remained honest. On-site inspectors manned stations in nuclear plants, research facilities and military installations around the clock.

As a practical matter, the treaty relied heavily on secret American assistance. Satellite coverage ensured that no missiles capable of delivering the weapons were deployed in either country. Airplanes, of course, were a special problem. Pakistan still had fifty-odd F-16s left over from the early days of the Reagan administration. All were capable of carrying weapons roughly the size of those the Pakistanis had destroyed under the treaty, though the bombs were relatively primitive and awkwardly bulky. For their part, the Indians had manufactured a bomb small enough to be carried by either their Mirage 2000s or perhaps MiG-27 swing-wing fighter-bombers.

UN observers kept track of the planes at their bases, but since they were flying in and out all the time, there was an additional safeguard: Specially developed U.S. satellites monitored the fighter-bombers from space. Tuned to special tamperproof transponders on each plane—as well as their exhaust patterns—the satellites made sure they didn't go anywhere the UN monitors couldn't see. The elaborate treaty protocols actually allowed both sides to use their planes for warfare; it was only nuclear devices that were proscribed.

Because all of the planes concerned would need at least some modifications to carry nuclear weapons, the arrangement was almost foolproof; they could never get out of sight long enough to be fitted for the weapons. In theory, the two countries—never exactly friendly—could continue at each other's throats without the world having to worry they would irradiate each other.

The banning of large surface-to-surface missiles on the subcontinent put the Pakistanis at a severe disadvantage in any conventional war with India. At best, Pakistan's F-16s had a 600-mile combat range; even if they had been tweaked and improved, as most observers believed, much of India lay far beyond their reach. Before the disarmament treaty had even been signed, the Pakistanis began looking around for a way to change that. America, obviously, wasn't about to sell them any B-1 or B-2 bombers, and the historic enmity between the Pakistanis and the Russians precluded any deals there. Besides, Indian satellite surveillance was so good that any delivery of bombers would immediately be noted.

So they came up with an innovative solution—they would find older planes, ones that would attract no attention from the Indians when purchased. That was where O'Connell, who at the director's orders had given up most of his more adventurous assignments to help the Pakistanis with armament and technology purchases, got involved. He managed to locate three old B-50 bombers, lumbering American planes dating from the early fifties. Last used for weather patrols in Southeast Asia, they had originally been designed as heavy bombers, but no one in their right mind would conclude that the aging planes were to be used in an offensive capacity. Besides, they were bought by a commercial company, which promptly "lost" one in an accident and sold the other two for scrap.

On paper. What really happened was that the planes were taken to Kahuta and put through an extensive retrofit program. Using Pakistan's own technology, a team of twenty men painstakingly upgraded and modified the B-50s: First to make them more difficult to detect, and then, if found, to duplicate the signature of a harmless civilian plane. The modified B-50s absorbed radar signals and fed out fake ones. The fuselage of the planes had been layered with a black polymer radar-absorbing material. Each had a gold-plated hump on top of the fuselage, where the fake signals were created, amplified and transmitted. In the hot Pakistani sun the gold seemed to shimmer, giving the top of the plane an artificial luster—Golden Bears, they called them.

"It is as if God kissed them," a Pak engineer had once told O'Connell, so reverently that the agent shuddered.

Besides the planes, O'Connell had arranged for several purchases of semiconductors and technical equipment critical for the radar masking system. He was not easily dazzled, but he was amazed by the capabilities of the small band of Pakistani engineers and scientists who worked on the project. The devices worked very well. O'Connell had no doubt the program was as advanced as any in the world.

He also came to increasingly suspect that the planes were not going to be used for just dropping conventional weapons. For one thing, Kahuta was not an air force facility; plane development was generally done at the Pakistan Aeronautical Complex in Kamra. Further, the project was so highly compartmentalized that none of his contacts in the air force seemed to be aware of it.

More ominously, as he grew more familiar with the men on the project, he learned that most worked for the Pakistani Institute for Nuclear Science and Technology, the people who had run the country's nuclear program.

Armed with nuclear weapons, the bombers could be used as "war breakers"—potent, desperation weapons launched to stem the tide of an otherwise unstoppable invasion.

At least that's what the Pakistanis would think. Perhaps it was what the director thought, for surely he knew what they were capable of. The reality, O'Connell realized, would be very different—with their own cities devastated, the Indians would fight back with everything they had. There would never be peace; the whole world might be drawn into the conflict—Russia was still a very close ally to India, and the Chinese would be anxious to jump in if the Russians got involved.

"I'm extrapolating from intercepts," said Stockman, breaking the long silence, "but I think my conclusions are sound. Our analysts and the desk haven't even reached that conclusion, but they don't know about the planes. I want you to go back, Michael," added the DDO. "I want you to find the planes and disable them."

"How?"

"Blow them up. We can't let them fly," said Stockman. "Millions of people will die in India. And that will be just the beginning."

"You should have thought about this two years ago," O'Connell said. "When I worked for you."

"We thought we knew where they were. Obviously, your information was wrong."

"Those planes were there when I left."

"They're not now. They don't seem to be anywhere." The DDO took a set of satellite photos from his drawer. "These are all within the last week."

O'Connell looked at the photos of the Pakistan Air Force's air bases. But there was no way the Pakistanis would put the planes there—the Indians' satellite coverage was every bit as extensive as the Americans'. Why build an undetectable airplane and put it in something as obvious as a reinforced hangar?

Better to put them in someplace *really* obvious. That was the real genius of the Golden Bears. They were right out in the open.

"These are the bunkers they built for their F-16s," said O'Connell, sliding the photos back. "They're not for Golden Bears. The base is up north."

A little piece of Stockman's ice chipped off his face. "These *are* up north. And they're the only bunkers in the country."

"They're not there," said O'Connell.

He'd been to the real base. It was an old airplane junkyard up near Gilgit, seemingly abandoned. There would be only enough people at the isolated mountain base to fly and maintain the planes—anything else would attract attention. A second installation nearby contained a larger security contingent, but even this one appeared to be a dusty boneyard.

You didn't need anything else. The area was so desolate, the only paved road within a hundred miles was a two-lane highway, easily controlled much farther down the valley. And the airspace, being relatively close to Kashmir, was heavily patrolled. Any military craft in the vicinity would be shot first, challenged later—no matter its markings or nationality.

The bombers sat there, covered with dirt and plastic overlays that made them look like derelicts. The CIA analysts, like their Indian counterparts, saw them every day, and every day checked them off as ghosts in a cemetery.

Why go to all that trouble for conventional bombers? O'Connell had known what was up from the very beginning, whether he wanted to admit it or not.

"Where are they, Michael?"

Something perverse in him kept him from saying anything. He was enjoying the fact that Stockman's steel facade was slowly melting away.

"If I did know and I told you," said O'Connell, "you'd lose your deniability."

"I'm not screwing around." Stockman caught himself, realized he'd been baited. He glanced at his drink, still half full; when his gaze returned to O'Connell he was back in full, icy control. "Will they launch if we violate their airspace?"

O'Connell shrugged. He honestly didn't know the answer, though he suspected that they'd be ready to leave at a moment's notice. But he also suspected that Stockman was reluctant to call the Air Force in because then he'd have to explain that the CIA had helped build the planes.

"We have to disable them. You've done more difficult things than this. Tehran, for instance. That was ten times as hard as this."

"That was when I was still young and naive," said O'Connell. The DDO was referring to one of his first jobs as an agent, a kidnapping operation in the Iranian capital that O'Connell had pulled off with minimal assistance.

Stockman gathered his photos together. "Things aren't going too well for you. This could change your luck."

"How's that?"

"You'll be paid pretty well," said Stockman. "A quarter of a million when you're done."

"A quarter of a million dollars is pretty cheap, especially since I'd never get out to collect it."

"Sure you would. You could talk your way into hell without a hiccup. Harvey Westlake headed the team that went into Kahuta; he'll work with you. Him and Paul Smith. They have some locals—"

"I work alone."

"Not on something like this. I have a dozen people waiting to brief you."

"Is Kelso one of them?"

"She could be, if you want."

"I don't want," O'Connell said quickly.

Stockman shrugged, as if to say, suit yourself. "No one here knows the whole layout, so when you talk to them—"

"Why am I going to talk to them?"

"You have a responsibility here. You helped them."

"I did what I was told."

"You didn't object, did you?"

O'Connell didn't answer. After his first conversation with the director, he'd kept his mouth shut, even about the connection with the Pakistani Nuclear Institute.

"The agency needs you," said Stockman. "And the country needs you."

O'Connell stuck his hands into his jacket pockets and slid his legs forward in the chair. Appealing to his patriotism? Stockman was on thin enough ice with his conscience.

The rocky flats and the abrupt gray mountainsides surrounding the base loomed before him. The strip where the bombers would be was bare, with only two or three buildings at the very end of the packed-dirt runway. They'd have to move quickly, very, very quickly.

How do you get away, though? A helicopter would have limited range and be too easy for them to shoot down; besides, every interceptor in Pakistan would be looking for it.

Take one of the planes. The radar defenses would work as well against the Paks as the Indians.

O'Connell shook his head. Was he deciding to do it? Why? Did he feel guilty? Were the planes and their bombs his responsibility, his sin?

He'd left the world of sin and penance behind years ago. But he was going to do it. Why?

For the money, the quarter of a million. He didn't like being broke.

No, it wasn't the money. It was the adventure. He missed the adrenaline rush.

It would be suicidal, even with Westlake, who was Stockman's personal troubleshooter and already something of a legend. But that was part of the attraction.

"I'd need a helicopter," said O'Connell.

Stockman didn't even smile, as if he'd already assumed O'Connell was going back. Bastard.

"That may be difficult, if the war starts," said the DDO. "Obviously, we can't borrow one from the military, and there are rumors they'll nationalize the few civilian aircraft."

"Contact Blossom," said O'Connell.

"God, Blossom is the last one we want involved. We've been trying to distance ourselves."

"I'm not going to involve her," said O'Connell. "But she could supply a helicopter very easily."

Blossom was the code name for one of the agency's most deeply covered operatives, a member of the Pakistani government with her own political party and militia, as well as a network of agents, informers and saboteurs. O'Connell didn't trust her, but it wouldn't be necessary to.

"All right," said Stockman without hesitating. "I'll arrange a meeting in Karachi."

"I want something else. A pilot who's flown B-50s."

"How the hell am I going to do that?"

"The easiest way off the base will be in one of the planes. Get the air force to give me a list; I'll find him myself."

"We don't have much time on this, Michael; I want you in Pakistan tomorrow, the day after at the latest."

"Tomorrow?"

"Once they're invaded, they'll use the weapons within a week."

"If I can't find someone in twenty-four hours, I'll come up with a different plan."

"Harvey—"

"He doesn't know the whole situation, does he?"

Stockman looked doubtful, though he nevertheless jotted down a note on the yellow pad he habitually kept near the phone.

"So where is the base?" Stockman asked.

"I told you, it's up north. Near Gilgit."

"Are you sure?"

"Sure enough. If I tell you where it is, you'll screw me again, won't you?"

Stockman remained quiet. This was part of the dance, O'Connell thought—Stockman didn't really want to know where the base was. He wanted as much deniability as possible.

O'Connell wasn't going to tell him anyway. It was a bit of leverage, at least for the moment.

"How much do you remember about the technical details of the weapons they destroyed under the treaty?" Stockman asked.

O'Connell shook his head. But as soon as he did he realized he remembered quite a bit. Now he saw a book of schematics in front of him, an air force weapons expert giving him a rundown at the director's orders.

The man called the bomb a "gadget," and later, laughing, a "joint."

"I have someone downstairs who will give you a full briefing," Stockman was saying. "He was on the team that supervised the disassembly of the six they had at the treaty. Hopefully, things haven't changed too much."

O'Connell nodded.

"The SatInt people are standing by if you need them. These are two backgrounders on the military situation." Stockman passed two thick binders over the desk. "Dr. Jablonski will update you on the politics. The circle on this," Stockman added, "is very small. The people who are going to talk to you don't know about the planes, the bombs, or the operation."

And didn't want to. Stockman's main concern in all of this was protecting the agency's butt. He might not even care if the nukes were used, O'Connell thought skeptically, as long as they weren't dropped from planes that could be traced to the CIA.

The DDO reached into his drawer and took out a large manila envelope. "Personal papers, plastic, and your passport kit. There are four blanks, besides yours. I think you'll appreciate the photo."

The cynic's voice inside O'Connell's head tried one last time. Get up and walk out, it told him. This is payback. They cut you loose, flushed your career, flushed you. Now it's your turn. These hot shots don't even know where the damn base is. And they don't care about you; if something goes wrong, they'll leave you on the line to dry.

And yet something kept him there, staring at the DDO's emotionless face. O'Connell focused on a scar, a small piece of skin tucked in midway back on Stockman's left jaw, a stitch gone bad years ago.

"Your quarter of a million is just a start," said Stockman, seeming to sense he was wavering. "You could use it to arrange for a new helicopter. With some agency contracts, your financial picture would brighten considerably. You did want to be a businessman, didn't you?"

Could he even succeed? Even if he were right about where the base was, there was no guarantee the Pakistanis had gone ahead with the rest of their plan. It might be as heavily guarded as a SAC missile site.

Leave, Michael. Pick your bones up and get the hell out. Tell them what you know about the base and let them bomb it. That would screw Stockman—he'd have to tell the air force what they were bombing, and why.

An air force raid would never work. The planes would be put in the air, and it'd be impossible to find them. They'd use the weapons now, instead of waiting for O'Connell to get there and undo what he'd done.

Father Fran, his old theology teacher and guidance counselor, whispered in his ear. You're too impulsive, Michael. You jump into things without thinking. You have a volcano for a heart and a computer for a brain, and they don't always connect.

There was a buzz on one of Stockman's secure phones. The DDO picked it up slowly, his eyes still fixed on O'Connell. "Yes?" the Snowman asked the receiver softly. He said nothing for a minute or two, listening. Then he hung up the phone.

"We have an intercept indicating an invasion order has been given," Stockman said as he hung up the phone. "The tanks are on their way now."

O'Connell felt a chill run through his body. "Give me the damn passports," he told his boss.

East of Kashmir. Apx. 5:30 A.M.

Captain Syyid "Rocket" Khan slipped his Falcon to the right of the squadron commander's plane, waiting for his wingmate to catch up and fill out the pattern as the Pakistani F-16s began their early morning patrol of the Kashmir frontier. As soon as Lieutenant Tariq ''Tark'' Yusuf caught up, the four planes would slide into fluid twos and approach the arbitrary line that split the province of Kashmir into Indian and Pakistani halves. At that point, Khan and his wingmate would swing south, shadowing the border, ready to pounce on anything from a flight of Indian MiGs to an overly aggressive hawk. The wing commander, Lt. Col. Shahid Haq—''Possum,'' as he liked to be called—and his wingmate Lieutenant Zia would head north in what was by now a familiar routine.

Each F-16 carried four short-range Sidewinder AIM-9Ls, heat-seeking or IR (for infrared) missiles, loaded in double racks on the wingtips. The American-built planes also carried two midrange French Matra Super radar-guided missiles. The original avionics systems of the planes had been replaced and the missiles tweaked so that they could be used as fire-and-forget weapons once launched.

Necessity had goaded the Pakistanis into great creativity. The vagaries of international politics closed and opened the flow of weapons into the small country on no predictable schedule. Feeling overshadowed and often threatened by India, its large neighbor to the south, the Pakistanis had developed an efficient aftermarket acquisition network, as well as a considerable capacity for improving what they bought. The planes flying the air defense alert patrol this morning, for example, weren't just carrying missiles considered too advanced for most of their F-16A counterparts. The Pakistani aircraft plant in Kamra had strengthened and reshaped the planes' wings, added composite maneuvering fins, and rebuilt the engines on these and four other models, making the eight Falcons assigned to Squadron 11 roughly the equivalent of the never-deployed American AFTI variants. Aided by a subtle shift in the plane's center of gravity, the new designs had improved the Falcon's already substantial handling characteristics at both high and low speeds.

With typical fighter-jock chauvinism, Khan saw them as the equal of any plane flying. He wouldn't have hesitated to take his plane against two American F-16s, let alone an Indian MiG. But then he'd done pretty well with the American loaner, an F-16C he'd been given on his last advanced training assignment in the States. Not only had he scored among the top pilots in the Southeast Open Air competition, but he'd been a star at the American Red Flag exercise at Nellis. Sliding almost effortlessly between CAP and OCA missions (combat air patrol—escort—and offensive counter-air, or intercept), he had built a reputation as a balls-out jock who could handle anything thrown at him. He'd also learned the difference between being a good pilot and a hot dog. At twenty-five, the youngest member of the Khan clan was growing up.

Which was a bit more than could be said for Tark, who did a barrel roll as he found his spot in the formation.

"Damn it, Tark," Khan grumbled, but he kept his mike switch off, hoping the colonel wouldn't catch it. Yesterday, the Possum had treated them to a half-hour dissertation on the tensions between India and Pakistan, all because Tark had buzzed an observation plane on the way back to the base.

It wasn't that Tark was a bad pilot, Khan noted as he watched his wingmate ease his plane into position; he just failed to appreciate the importance of discipline when trouble wasn't staring him in the face.

The colonel either missed Tark's display or was too preoccupied to comment. The squadron leader had to make contact with *Eyes One,* a two-engined turboprop Fokker F-27 that acted as a long-range radar operator for the patrol. The Fokker's interior had been gutted and packed with an array of radar equipment to look over the border. Though more far-reaching than the Falcon's units, the Fokker's sensors were nowhere near the equal of those on American AWACS planes. Nevertheless, its function was roughly similar. It was connected with the flight through a telemetry hookup that could automatically provide threat information to the F-16s' computers and tracking systems.

The Fokker droned along above the mountains, twenty miles inside Pakistan territory, tilting its radar-swelled belly toward Kashmir. It was accompanied by a Mirage IIIP from Squadron 5, a dedicated reconnaissance-type that could be dispatched for quick "look-and-see" missions. If that happened, Khan and his squadron would be giddied up to provide cover.

While the air above Kashmir had been as silent as ever during the past few weeks, tensions on the ground had been mounting. Khan expected that there would be at least one or two border incidents before tempers cooled. There had been many since partition split the Muslims and Hindus in 1947. The pilot's uncle in the foreign ministry—like many other air force pilots, Khan had relatives in several important government positions, including a second cousin who headed the air marshal's general staff—explained that the tensions now were primarily due to India's turbulent interior politics and not any real disagreement with Pakistan. Still, Pakistan's support for Muslim rebels in the Indian half of Kashmir had caused problems for years.

Khan craned his neck around to check the sky, scanning carefully to make sure nothing had snuck in under his radar. As difficult as that would be, it was not impossible. The most potent weapon in modern warfare remained old-fashioned surprise, and the Pakistani pilot did not intend to be speared by it, especially today. This was scheduled to be his last flight with the alert squadron.

Tomorrow he was joining a newly created group whose mission would combine deep penetration interception with ground attack. It was an honor to be chosen for the new group, which would pair two Falcons with four Mirage attack planes, and Khan couldn't help but be excited by the new assignment. He'd be flying with one of the PAF's best fighter pilots, Colonel Teru "John" Benzair, one of his mentors. Even so, Khan felt a bit sad to be leaving behind his friends, especially Tark. Though he would still be stationed at the same air base, Sargodha, he knew that eventually his unit would be rotated elsewhere. Besides, he would be transferred to the Third Wing; this afternoon he was to shift his quarters to the apartments maintained by his new command.

"Two minutes to split point," said Possum over the discrete messaging system. The DMS packaged communications in small laser bursts which made them almost impossible to intercept. Even so, in the interest of good form the other pilots acknowledged with a visual thumbs up and a waggle of their wings.

The pilots used English almost exclusively for their squadron communications, rather than Urdu, their national but by no means universal language. As members of the country's educated class, they spoke English well; most, like Khan, had gone to college in the States. The language simplified things, since not all of the pilots had Urdu as their first language; the variations in the different tongues used in the country could be fatal during a battle. Besides, using English psychologically reinforced their connection with the American air force, which the Pakistani pilots uniformly admired. To say that their service was modeled on that of the Western superpower would have been to understate the importance of the U.S. influence on their tactics, slang and attitudes. Change the insignias, remove the quotes from the Koran pasted on the dashes of Pakistani jets, and it would take an expert to discern that these were not American jocks.

The sun was below and in front of them, rising up out of the Himalayas as a majestic disk of purplish red. Its rays painted the mountains and the wispy clouds that melted before Khan as he flew. The pilot looked at the sun for a moment, wondering at its majesty, then swept his eyes down across his instrumentation, noting the course readout on the right CRT display and pausing briefly to double-check the altitude on the dial to its left before returning his gaze to the clear sky before him. The heads-up display floated his flight data in ghostly white letters and lines on the windshield. The four planes were flying at 28,000 feet, only a thousand feet above the mountains. They were cruising at 380 knots indicated, conserving fuel despite the large belly drop tanks they carried.

Khan could change the HUD's display mode by flicking his thumb on the stick he gripped to his right. It was currently in long-distance scan. The radar, an improved (and smaller) clone of the Hughes units used in larger American planes, sent its pulse-Doppler signals out far ahead, looking for motion as much as a hundred miles away. The powerful unit was like a warning beacon, easily detected by sophisticated aircraft, but at the moment Squadron 11 had no reason not to let the curious know they were there.

The planes they were most likely to meet here—MiG-21s, or perhaps MiG-27s adapted for recon missions—were unable to detect or defeat the radar at long-range. India had a dozen or so MiG-29s in its hangars, but none had ever been spotted this far north. The Fulcrums were serious meat, capable not only of good close combat but also equipped with a first-rate passive threat detection system. According to Pakistani intelligence, the only thing the Indians lacked were the Russians' advanced Alamo missiles.

Not that it mattered. Khan's squadron had trained extensively against a variety of simulated threats, and to a man would have agreed they could take out even Alamo-equipped planes without much of a fuss.

"Angel flight this is Angel leader. Thirty seconds to break."

Khan turned to his right and watched Tark begin dropping back, easing off his speed so he could hold an inside position when the two planes turned. Khan relaxed, checking his instruments once more. If they wished to be more discreet, he could punch a button on the up-front control (UFC) panel just below the HUD and switch to the passive systems, whose sensors were contained in the pods fitted to the Falcons' ribs. The German manufactured infrared search-and-track (IRST) gear homed in on heat in the cold mountain air. Unfortunately, this equipment was not nearly as efficient as the rest of the plane, or even the gear on the MiG-29s. Khan had once watched in dismay as it failed to get a lock on a mock aggressor within visual range, less than two miles away. And unlike the frontline systems in America and Russia, the French Supers could not be slaved to the IRST; the main radar had to be activated to use the medium-range weapons. This was a bad fit, since the detectable radar was initially intended to give a long-range, standoff punch on the theory that an attacker would still be too far away to do anything serious when you fired. But it would be a problem only against MiG-29s, and in theory they would have similar difficulties.

Khan wondered what new expression the Possum would use as a signal for them to begin their maneuver. The colonel was continually trying to invent new slang, usually by flubbing things he'd heard from Americans. The turn-off point was his favorite occasion. Yesterday, he had said it was "Time to watch TV," an improvement over his all-time howler: "We're pregnant."

Khan flexed his arm muscles. They would be giving the cease-fire line a two-mile buffer. He checked the mountains preparing to turn. The only things down there—and from here they were too small to see—were some markhor goats.

The white haze covering the farthest peaks formed a barrier to the known world. Though the F-16s could easily fly over them and on into China, there seemed no point—from here it was easy to imagine that there was nothing at all beyond that line. The Falcons toed along the quiet edge of the earth, where not even Allah cared to go.

The pilot had tried to describe the feeling of this silence to his fiancée while they sat together in her father's living room two nights before. Like so many times before, her large brown eyes scanned his face as his tongue stumbled. Hir Ranjha had a way of looking into his soul and understanding without his needing to say things. It was an unworldly power; occasionally it scared him.

"Break out the song and dance," said the flight commander. Khan could practically hear Tark hooting in his cockpit as they swung the fighter jets in an easy turn to the south. The two planes tilted their wings together exactly twenty-seven degrees and brought their noses smoothly across the centerline, picking up speed to complete the turn. The maneuver was executed with the precision of an acrobatic team; the planes could have started a foot apart and they would not have touched, so practiced were the pilots.

"Float five," said Khan, using the squadron's term (actually, another of Possum's) for one of their standard border flight paths. The pilot eased his power up and began a climb to 40,000 feet. He would fly lead, with Tark sitting at approximately 30,000 feet about a quarter mile back and to the west. The two planes would crisscross several times as they ran along the border before circling back to the point where they had split with their mates. The pairs would then pass each other and duplicate the maneuver on the other side. When they returned to the rendezvous spot, Possum would order another swing, this one at low altitude, with the pilots looking for anything unusual in the mountains. Their tracks here were a bit peppery—just over Mach .90—but still well under the F-16s' capabilities.

"I'm floating along, as free as a song," said Tark.

"No unnecessary communications, Angel four," said Colonel Haq tersely.

The lieutenant undoubtedly had a retort for that, but wisely didn't share it. That was fortunate, for at that moment *Eyes One* broke in. The warning burned Khan's ears, as if it had come from the devil himself.

"I have bandits approaching. One-five-zero klicks from the border and closing. Map coordinate one-five-zero. No IDs, a lot of planes."

Khan touched his hand to his helmet, as if there were a short in the radio system. Planes coming out of Indian territory toward them?

The Falcon had received the telemetry from the Fokker already and plotted it on the map that flashed in the right CRT. The Indian planes were flying very low, shielded by the complex geography of the mountains. Khan swung his eyes up from the CRT in the direction of Kashmir, involuntarily trying for a visual sighting of a group of planes about ninety miles away.

"Go to passive systems," barked the Possum. "Fluid intercept."

Khan switched to the IRST. His first thought was that this was a drill. But they were right on the border, too close to India.

Tark was already turning behind him as Khan released his centerline drop tank and felt the Falcon jump upward, glad to be free of the drag. The pilot leaned the stick to the left and brought the slippery Falcon around in a twisting dive toward the mountaintops, slicing directly toward the valley where the Indians had been spotted.

The Fokker would be turning off now to a safer position—running away, basically, since it was a slow, lumbering target. While the Pakistanis believed that neither the Indians nor the rest of the world knew of the recon plane's capabilities, they couldn't afford to take chances—there were only two such planes in the entire air force. The Mirage would escort the plane back, and Khan knew that its pilot had orders to sacrifice himself rather than allow the Fokker to be shot down.

It couldn't be a drill, but it could be a screwup. There had been false alerts before.

Khan eased himself lower, gliding now between the tallest peaks. The mountains were barriers to his sensors; he might not get any readings at all until he was almost in visual range. He tucked back west, figuring to swing around ahead of the Indian planes and take a quick dash toward them. He could then duck their Doppler radars by cutting off to the right—a quick ninety-degree turn defeated the radars most fighters carried, especially at long-range. Then he'd have a shot at dropping in off the side or coming up the rear as the Indians crossed the border.

Assuming, of course, they were there.

The squadron's briefed intercept procedure called for the four F-16s to make their own way to an attack at the Indian border, Khan and Tark from the south, Possum and Zia from the north. Angel flight's rules of engagement presumed that they were free to attack if the Indians showed an intention of crossing. While in the past there had been an emphasis on restraint, the colonel had been very clear this morning that anything that looked as if it had the potential to cross was to be severely punished.

Khan felt his stomach tighten as he approached the area where the planes had been headed. He was a hell of a pilot in the simulations, but this wasn't going to be an exercise.

Tark was following, tracking in farther east. Though Khan had a rough idea of where he was, he couldn't see him. Once more the passive detection system wasn't worth a damn—the IRST couldn't even flag his wingmate.

If there were Indians there, he wanted to get a fix on them well before the border. The Supers could be reliably fired from twenty-five miles off.

No signals. Might not be anything. Might be the whole Indian air force.

The Falcon was doing Mach 1.2 now, fast going this close to the mountaintops. But the speed forced him to focus, and that in turn relaxed him. Khan lined up a diagonal valley to the east and decided to slice into it, hunkering down between rocks spit up ages before man was even a thought in the mind of God.

And holy God, there were all sorts of planes coming his way. The IRST had a cloud of signals, off to the left, hugging the far side of this very pass. But the gear refused to lock on any one of them.

His bing box—the radar detector—was silent. Khan groped closer to the mountainside, harder to find. He had to keep surprise on his side.

Several quick swipes at the red buttons that worked the IRST controls on the dash failed to coax a definitive read, not even on the distance: the HUD indicator read ten miles, but it was obviously a false reading. It stayed there, stuck, when it should be counting down as they closed.

They weren't using any radar, apparently trying to tiptoe in quietly.

Unless there were MiG-29s with them, scanning with their own IRSTs. He wouldn't know about it until his system picked up a missile. He'd be dead meat here, huddled against the mountains.

Khan hung in for another few seconds, waiting for the detector to give him more information. Now it started counting down—nine miles, but still nothing he could use to fire missiles.

If it was really nine miles, he had maybe twenty seconds before visual range—in other words, twenty seconds to get out of sight and regroup for an attack. Khan braced himself, then picked up his left wing and flattened his head around a mountaintop, the Falcon spinning as neatly as horse in a carousel. The plane pulled 6 g's as it cranked through the half circle, and Khan felt himself pushed sideways in the seat, the bladders in his pressure suit puffing as he let the Falcon's left wing back down to complete the one-eighty. He was now flying in the same direction as the Indian planes. His targets had disappeared from the IRST, the equipment once more confused by the mountains.

Leveling off in the gap, he craned his head back as he turned to see if Tark was behind him. He also wanted to make sure he hadn't just flashed into the sights of another flight of planes. If the Indians were smart, they would have split their forces, given each a different valley.

No Indians, but no Tark either. Hopefully, he'd found another crevice to hide in.

Khan turned his head back just in time. There were no other Indian planes in the valley he had just turned into because it wasn't a valley at all. He was flying straight into a mountain.

Only the F-16's quick acceleration and maneuvering ability saved him. He twisted off to the left, barely missing the slope, then snatched the wings back and came up again, diving down the other side of the mountain to keep his head down. He was momentarily dazed, unsure of where he was or what he needed to do. If he were jumped now, he'd be dead.

"Take it easy," he told himself. "They don't see you."

He twisted his head—quickly this time—and saw that he was alone in the valley, which was running away from the Indian planes. He checked his breathing (nice and deep, though not exactly easy) and spun the Falcon up and around. Hopping through a canyon, he saw a clear way back out to the canyon the Indian planes were flying down, their probable route still marked out on his CRT's map. He spotted a gap where his path would intersect theirs three miles or so ahead, and as he goosed the jet forward he realized he'd be in a perfect position—as long as he hadn't outrun them.

No problem: he shot up over the mountaintop and saw the enemy planes running about two miles ahead, oblivious to his presence. Khan took a deep breath and counted the Indian planes. He had fourteen: attack planes in a triple diamond, three fours right behind one another. Two other planes were flying as outriggers, probably a low-altitude CAP.

Definitely a bombing mission, tearing toward Khan's home.

Skimming low over the terrain, the Indian planes had their wings swept back against bulky rectangular fuselages that flared into a huge tail area—late-model MiG-23s or MiG-27s. The Mikoyan-Gurevich attack jets had restricted cockpit views and limited defense radars that kept them from seeing the F-16 tiptoeing in off their left tail fins. The two other planes were both much smaller, and appeared to be MiG-21s. If they were flying escort, Khan knew there must be a total of at least four; that was the way the Indians grouped their flights. He didn't like the fact that he could only spot half, but he couldn't worry about that now. The bombers were easy targets, as long as he didn't get too cocky.

Khan quickly worked out a plan: Turn the radar missiles on, lock two of the planes in the first diamond and let them off. Then he'd hit the gas and swing into the trailing group, using his Sidewinders and cannon to take out as many MiGs as he could. Khan didn't expect them to make things easy by continuing blithely along while he shot them down, but if his luck held he'd have both radar missiles off and be homing in on his third target before they quite realized what was going on. By that time, his mates ought to be jumping in.

He would ignore the escorts as long as possible. The MiG-21s didn't pose a serious threat except in very close combat, and the bombers were much more important targets.

Who the hell did these bastards think they were, flying in to bomb his home?

Hir would be just getting up, making tea for her father before getting ready to leave for her teaching job in the exclusive private school not far from her home in Lahore.

Khan's finger touched the radar switch. The rest of his body worked mechanically, its actions marked by the display on the HUD. Click, click. Missiles up. Super One, lock and go. Super Two, lock and go.

The Falcon shook as the missiles rocketed from its wings. It was a bold, proud bird on the attack.

"Angel flight, complete intercept," said the Possum, his voice shaking in Khan's ears and momentarily breaking his concentration.

There was Tark, crossing above him. Probably had been on his one-eighty for at least a mile—good thing he hadn't been a MiG.

Remember your checks, captain. This isn't a drill.

Khan caught the flash of a missile taking off from his wingmate's plane. The other two F-16s jumped in from the other side, small bursts of flame and smoke flashing beneath their wings as their weapons launched.

"Those are mine on the left," said Khan, his mind reengaging. He practically jumped forward in his seat, pushing the plane into the fight. His equipment was going crazy. The MiGs hit their afterburners and now everybody was moving incredibly fast. The MiG-27s had some speed, but weighed down with their stores they couldn't climb. He looked for his next victim.

The bing box. Somebody's missile was coming at him. *Flares and chaff, flares and chaff. Turn, Khan, turn, give it 9 g's if you have to.*

Warning bells were ringing all over the cockpit. Don't push yourself too fast, the plane turns better than you do.

The targeting square had a huge gray shadow in it. He'd pulled a MiG right into his sights.

Sidewinder.

Pull up.

Khan's plane became a tiny steel ball, hurtling through a burst of debris. He came around a little too quick, felt the blackness dragging on the sides of his face. He was going too fast, pulling over 7 g's, too many for a man though well below what the plane could do. And now as he corrected and fell flat there was a bogey on his tail, bullets all around, one of the attack planes trying to shift to the fighter role.

The g fog cleared as tracer rounds popped off to his left.

The MiG-27s could go like all hell, but they couldn't turn, and Khan shook the one behind him with literally a flick of the wrist, the F-16 responding quickly to the stick. He expected the Flogger pilot to send off a heat-seeking missile, but none came; the attack plane was too loaded down with bombs to carry air-to-air.

Khan's maneuver put him head-on into a MiG-21, its sharpened nose a spear that screamed for revenge. The older Indian fighter was no match performance-wise for the Falcon, but its missiles were respectable—Khan watched an Aphid catch fire under the wing and stutter toward him.

It was a dumb move, born of panic or inexperience. The missile was a good short-range weapon, but head-on this close it was child's play to kick past it. Khan did so and then followed the MiG into a shallow dive to his right, careful not to overcommit, rolling the avionics over to gun mode as he pitched downward. He squeezed the trigger as the Fishbed pilot began banking to the left, running out of altitude. The 20-mm rounds from the M61 tucked behind Khan's left arm perforated the Indian plane's wing and it abruptly began a hard tumble toward the rocks.

The F-16s had succeeded in shattering the enemy formation, and the Indians scattered haphazardly through the mountain air, trying to get away. Khan took a turn across the valley and caught a Flogger in front of him with its wings popped forward. The configuration was meant to give the MiG more maneuverability, but it also showed Khan that its airspeed had dropped and it was low in the essential energy needed to outdance an opponent. He fired his second Sidewinder and turned to find another target, watching out of the corner of his eye as the Flogger sucked in a missile enema. He caught a MiG that had dropped its ordnance and was swinging its wings back to run away. Khan took a swipe with the cannon, his plane rocking with the recoil, but turned off before he got a hit, reluctant to spend ammunition on a plane that had already taken itself out of the fight.

Just as he turned, Khan saw a speck disappearing toward the west. It took a second for his brain to translate the image: One of the fighter-bombers had slipped past the defenders and was flying unscathed into Pakistan. Khan swung back around and hit the throttle so hard for afterburners it almost came out of the console.

He was a flash of light streaming through the valley, a silver gleam of speed and will. But the enemy was gone.

Even fully loaded, the MiG-27 was speedy. Khan knew the odds of finding the Indian before the Falcon began running low on fuel were slim, but he didn't think logically; he didn't think. He flew out of the mountains toward his homeland, hurtling toward the enemy as a great bolt of lightning.

His screen was completely blank, the sky empty and open. His whole body was a roar, a fluttering thunder of rapidly burning kerosene. Khan's eyes focused on the HUD screen, looking for an image and ignoring the flight data. He didn't need to know how fast he was going, how high he was or how much fuel he was burning. He was going as fast as he could. Faster.

He'd left the pilot who'd been momentarily flustered far behind.

But there was no way he could catch the MiG. His search radar would be a warning beacon, a signal that he was coming. The MiG pilot would see him, duck down, get away somehow.

Surprise was the only important weapon.

Captain Syyid "Rocket" Khan reached over and turned the radar off. He tilted the Falcon's wings about fifteen degrees to the left, believing that it gave a slightly better angle to look ahead from.

He'd quickly run out of fuel at this rate. The Falcon gobbled it at an incredible pace, its Pakistani-altered G.E. power plants absolutely ravenous for fuel at high speeds.

A hawk tackling its prey relaxed at the last second. It was an act of faith, a leap into instinct. It had its plan, it knew the outcome; there was no need for tension. Just act.

Khan closed his eyes briefly, relaxing, calling on Allah and his pilot's intuition to help.

When he opened them, the MiG was there ahead of him, framed out against the ground by the IRST, running deep into Pakistan with a full load of bombs beneath its wings. Ten miles. Eight miles. Five.

Khan had him. His last two Sidewinders jumped from his wings.

But the Indian pilot had intuition of his own, and somehow saw him coming. As soon as the missiles were underway, the MiG cranked upwards, some of its bombs falling away with the force of the maneuver.

No, he hadn't lost them—he'd released flares to confuse Khan's missiles. The ruse worked; one Sidewinder shot out wildly to the east; the other tracked down toward the ground.

Stubbornly, the Indian pilot held onto his bombs, slowing his climb. Khan, his throttle out to the firewall, decided the best thing to do was come right at him, gun blazing. He threw a steel girder of bullets across the MiG's flight path and then pulled off, sliding the Falcon around to get a better angle of attack. Climb after the bastard, he thought, but the sky in front of him was empty.

Just as Khan realized where the Hindu was a storm broke above him, the MiG slashing down with its guns blazing. The Falcon miraculously escaped the diving attack unharmed, Khan pushing it off quickly to the right. He let the nose tip straight down, then put everything to work, snapping around and once more almost blanking out from the rush of g-forces.

He ought to be on the tail of the MiG now, but damn this guy was better than he'd expected. He was coming back already.

The MiG had begun running out of energy—his wings were stuttering forward, desperate for anything to keep him up. All those fins and Kamra's fancy artistry paid off: Khan pushed the Falcon around and cut off the turn, gave the gun a long burst, hugging it, not minding the bounce as each bullet made its way into the soft metal of the MiG, right up the fuselage, through the glass, across the infidel scum's body.

Washington, D.C. Apx. 8 P.M.

CIA South Asia Deputy Chief Morena Kelso sipped her wine and watched as the agency's deputy director of operations sliced the round piece of foie gras into twelve equal triangles and began ladling the surrounding raspberry sauce over them. Carl Stockman's weakness for the rich French appetizer was undoubtedly a major reason for his steadily growing paunch. Morena and Stockman had eaten in the exclusive restaurant a half-dozen times in the past two years, and the white-haired covert operations chief always ordered it.

Stockman had suggested they come here because he wanted to talk to her, but Morena suspected he wanted something besides dinner and table talk. While she thought he was an excellent DDO, she resented his barely disguised attempts to seduce her. Morena was tempted, as Stockman's hand strayed from his napkin, to grab it and yank it from its socket. Then she would rise and pour the bottle of Léo-ville-Las-Cases—a perfect Medoc, Stockman gushed as he ordered it—over his grimacing face.

Instead, she calmly slipped her hand down to meet his. As she had done nearly every time they'd dined together, she patted it politely and then retrieved it gently but firmly from the hem of her dress. Stockman let her bring it to the table, then gave her a smile that implied he was only doing his duty. She ignored it, turning her eyes across the heavily draped room to a painting of George Washington and his first cabinet.

"I guess you're wondering what I want to talk about," said the DDO.

"Why didn't we just talk at the office?"

Stockman gave her a reproachful glance, as if she had asked why the world wasn't flat. "I have to be at the situation room for the Security Council meeting by nine-thirty."

"You've told me that three times already, Carl. What is this all about?"

Morena expected that Stockman was either going to confirm the rumor that they were losing another two agents off her desk, or transfer her. She wouldn't mind being transferred back out into the field, if the assignment were right. Washington was boring.

But Stockman surprised her. "This is back channel," he said curtly. "Absolutely."

Stockman was always working "back channel." The whole agency worked that way. There were the official lines, the chartable organization and responsibilities, and there was reality, the small cabal that made all the real decisions and undertook all the important tasks. Part of it was for efficiency—there were so many congressional and institutional checks on things that it could take weeks to get everybody on board even if all you wanted to do was blow your nose. But the shell games and conspiracies were also an outgrowth of the agency culture. There was an innate need for insiders and outsiders.

It was his tone, not the words, that were significant. The sharpness in his voice was reserved for very critical business.

"What is it?" asked Morena, but Stockman had turned his attention back to his dish as the waiter approached their table. Morena waited impatiently as the young man refilled her wine glass. He was hovering a bit more than was necessary, and it crossed Morena's mind that, given his vantage point, he might be trying for a better glimpse of cleavage.

"Do you need something?" she asked in a way that made the young man's face flush. Twenty-one or -two, he was good-looking despite a large nose.

"I, ah—does Monsieur or Mademoiselle require anything?"

Mademoiselle was tempted to ask in rapid-fire French how long he wanted to keep his job. (Among her father's many CIA posts was a lengthy counterintelligence stint in the embassy in Paris; Morena had attended a French grammar school and still spoke with the accent of a native.) She shook her head, allowing the boy to escape with a stiff bow.

Stockman, meanwhile, narrowed his eyes and began contemplating epicurean nirvana. He didn't chew the appetizer, he mashed it into his tongue.

"What does this have to do with Michael O'Connell?" Morena asked.

Stockman's eyes betrayed a slight surprise.

"I saw him in the hallway this afternoon," she said as the DDO finished the last bit of his fancy appetizer.

He gave her one of his you-don't-really-know-everything smiles, his cheeks puffing and his eyes squinting. Morena felt it was a condescension reserved for women and children; a man would have smacked it off his face.

"Still hung up on him?" the DDO asked.

"Of course not."

Another condescending smile to show that he didn't quite believe her. He pushed his plate away. "What do you know about Golden Bear?"

"What is it?"

"The Pakistanis have a way around the disarmament treaty. They've managed to build some bombs. Maybe a half dozen. Golden Bear is a way of delivering them."

"What?"

"They're radar-masking airplanes, practically invisible once they're off. Michael O'Connell helped build them."

A quiver started in her throat. Morena had to put her hand to her neck to contain it, rubbing nonchalantly on the outside while inside a tremor ran straight through her stomach. She felt for a moment as she had two years before, when O'Connell had been kicked out. Stockman himself had shown her the evidence, the tracks of money in Israel and France, the diverted shipments. She'd stared speechlessly at the papers, listening to him lay it out, unable to do more than simply breathe.

"Pepper, miss?"

Morena looked up to find the waiter looming over her, a large pepper mill in his hands. Her entree had just been placed down by an assistant.

"Yes," she said softly.

She was not naive. There were an infinite number of agents she would have believed capable of violating the agency's trust for personal gain. But not Michael. Even with all his dark, brooding moods, he was the one man she thought could resist any temptation thrown at him. The sense that he was different from the others was a large part of her attraction to him. It brought an intellectual edge, a justification, to the raw passion that consumed her when they made love.

To be wrong about that—it had almost broken her.

Morena nodded at the waiter when he stopped working the grinder, then forced herself to give him a look, a ferocious glance that came from the cold pit of her stomach and sent him scurrying for the kitchen.

"Why wasn't that in the estimate I just signed?" Morena asked coolly.

"Be realistic."

"What does it have to do with me?" she said.

"I need you to go to Pakistan. I need you to contact Blossom."

"Blossom?"

"O'Connell is going in to scuttle the planes. I have Harvey and Paul Smith in Rawalpindi. He asked for help."

"I can't believe Michael would have done that. Not on his own."

Stockman said nothing.

"He didn't, did he? I know he met with the director at least once when he was coming back here—"

"Morena, keep your voice down."

"He was set up, wasn't he? You lied to me."

"I took care of a difficult situation."

"But if Woolsley told him to do it—"

"He's dead now, Morena; it's easy for O'Connell to blame him."

"God, Carl, you were supposed to be different. And this—this isn't just breaking the law."

"What law was broken?"

"It's more than law. If we helped them build the bombs—"

"We helped them build airplanes. It was a miscalculation, and I had nothing to do with it. I just inherited the mess."

"This could start a world war."

"Enough," said Stockman. "Jesus, Morena, just because we sweep the place doesn't mean people are deaf."

She slipped her thumbnail against her forefinger. Focus

on something physical, her father used to tell her. Get your control back.

"Only a dozen people in the agency know about the weapons, and even less about the planes," Stockman said. "If this war continues for more than a week, we're sure they'll be used."

"Michael was the scapegoat, wasn't he?" Morena said in a tight, clipped tone. Ideally, she wanted her words to sound neutral, not to hint that she no longer believed anything Stockman said. It was difficult though; the DDO gave her a reproachful look before answering.

"This wasn't the only thing he did."

The money trail could easily have been concocted. Even if it weren't, there had never been anything that showed explicitly that he was stuffing bills in his pocket. ("Too smart for that," Stockman had said. And like a fool she'd nodded her head.) Something on this scale—Michael would never do this on his own. Not for money.

"See if you can get Blossom to give him a helicopter, without getting her entangled. Harvey has his own spear carriers, but you know O'Connell; he likes to think he's on his own. He'll be at the Imperial in Karachi no later than Thursday; he has to hook up with Harvey by Saturday morning. I doubt we've got more than a week to stop them."

"What if I don't want to get involved?"

"What you want is irrelevant. You know Pakistan and Blossom better than anyone else here, and you're one of the few people I trust."

"To keep my mouth shut?"

"To get things done, Morena."

"You expect to keep this secret?"

"Do you have any idea of the repercussions if this gets out? They'll think we built the bombs."

"Are you sure we didn't?"

"Millions of people will die, Morena."

She looked down at her plate. The gold border seemed for a moment to trace out a bombsight.

"Michael doesn't know you're going. I had a feeling that if I said anything about you, he might change his mind."

She couldn't blame him, could she?

"Where are the planes?"

"They're somewhere in the far northeast corner of the country, near Gilgit. He wouldn't say."

"He wouldn't say?"

"He thinks he needs leverage."

"You didn't press him too hard, did you? The less you know, the better."

"Don't be ridiculous," answered Stockman. "I don't play those games. There was no reason to press him. He's going, he'll work with Harvey—and you—and you'll take care of it."

"What about our backup?"

"I'll leave that to Harvey. I expect a coded message on the base location before they go in; otherwise it's his call. You don't have to be part of the assault, Morena," he added patronizingly.

"I can handle myself, thank you."

"Suit yourself."

"You trust Michael?" asked Morena.

"I have to."

He trusted him because he hadn't gone bad in the first place. They'd set him up. And she'd been completely fooled. Worse, she'd deserted him.

"I want you to leave tonight," Stockman said. "We'll give you some cover excuse at the office."

"Carl—"

Stockman patted her hand, which was lying on the table. "This won't hurt your career, believe me."

About an hour after Morena had lost her appetite for French food, Michael O'Connell pulled into the parking lot of a McDonald's in suburban Virginia. Before locking his rented Ford, he patted the inside pocket of his faded black leather jacket, making sure his maps and the addresses of the B-50 pilots the air force had supplied were still there. Then he looked over the roadway and parking lot and headed into the restaurant.

Stockman would send a tail along with him when he traveled overseas; that was standard security. But someone following him now meant he wasn't trusted. The agent worked at his nonchalance as he studied the row of cars from the corner of his eye. For all the ease of jumping back in, he was rusty; he wasn't quite sure he could pick up a shadow.

Cheeseburger, large fries and strawberry shake—as he finished his order he realized he was still thinking like a businessman in the throes of bankruptcy. Hell, he'd just checked into a Super Eight motel.

You're a government employee again, he told himself. Should have at least gone for a Big Mac.

"It's all I got," O'Connell apologized as he handed the clerk one of the hundred dollar bills Stockman had given him. The Snowman had also supplied an American Express Platinum Card in O'Connell's own name; the DDO's ability to arrange that, given the agent's dismal credit rating, impressed him more than any story of the Snowman's exploits in Vietnam.

O'Connell wasn't supposed to use the card in America. Stockman obviously wanted to make sure there was nothing putting him in Washington—and linking him to the agency—in case things went sour. He'd been given a Visa card with phony ID for plane tickets, the car rental and the Washington hotel. Those could be traced to the agency, but not him specifically.

"I'm gonna have to give you a bunch a ones," said the counterman.

O'Connell shrugged, sticking a straw in the shake as he waited for the change.

Why the American Express card in his name? And the passport? He'd be leaving an easily traced trail directly into Pakistan.

"Here ya go," said the kid. O'Connell took the bills and wadded them into his jacket pocket, picked up his tray and walked around the side of the restaurant. The front booths had been commandeered for a nine-year-old's birthday party, so he headed to the back. The last thing he wanted to do was have some elementary school kids running by his table.

No, the last thing he wanted to do was go to South Asia. The burst of enthusiasm he'd felt in Stockman's office was gone.

So why was he going?

I need the money, he told himself as he unwrapped the cheeseburger. I'll get back on my feet, and this time I won't make any mistakes.

But it wasn't only that. The challenge had seduced him.

Stockman was counting on that. He bribed him with excitement, reaching for the buttons. He'd even tried guilt, the old Jesuit tactic. You ought to feel guilty for helping them, Stockman had said.

God, he'd been set up *again*.

If they didn't succeed in blowing up the planes, the agency would simply pin their existence on him. What more proof would they need besides the fact that O'Connell was back in the country at the time of the attack? Stockman might even want the operation to fail—there was no way of knowing what sort of geopolitical maneuvering was going on.

Rather than going to Pakistan, he ought to find an attorney and start talking to the congressional oversight committee. That would pay the bastards back.

He stuffed a handful of french fries in his mouth, wiped his fingers on a napkin and retrieved the printout with the pilots' addresses from his jacket pocket. Was this a setup, too? It hadn't taken long to prepare; he'd had it before he left Langley.

O'Connell stirred the straw in the milk shake, crunching the frozen slush at the bottom. He had to remember how to separate healthy suspicion from paranoia. He was getting too far-out here, seeing conspiracies behind every tree. Next he'd think there was a bug in the burger.

Stockman had only been humoring him with the list of pilots. He'd practically said as much, saying to forget about working out a plan himself; Harvey Westlake would take care of things. Harvey was a loudmouthed blowhard who would tell you ten times in five minutes that he came from Cherokee blood. He *was* good; even O'Connell had to admit that, though his knowledge of the special op's achievements was only secondhand. Still, the idea of Westlake as the new fair-haired boy annoyed O'Connell as much as anything, made him stubbornly insist on his own plan.

O'Connell unfolded his maps of Virginia and Maryland and began examining the list of pilots. The B-50 had last flown operationally in the mid-sixties and these were all old men now. O'Connell crossed out anyone born before 1926—seventy years old. Was he crazy? Another round of cuts at 1932—sixty-five, retirement age.

How the hell am I going to talk somebody that old into going halfway around the world, O'Connell wondered. Even for the hundred thousand bucks Stockman had said he could offer?

The ten-page printout included men from states all along the Eastern seaboard; O'Connell made another cut, losing people from Maine, Pennsylvania, Georgia and a considerable contingent from Florida, New York and New Jersey. When he was done, there were five names left. Two he had to cross out because he couldn't find their towns on the map. That left three: Charles Allison Hoyt, Peter Olafsen and James Greeley.

O'Connell studied the addresses. Hoyt and Olafsen lived in Virginia, obscure towns he'd never heard of, though he spotted them easily enough. Greeley's address was 8 Halcyon Court, in Minisink, Maryland, just on the edge of the Greenbelt. Probably one of those garish monstrosities shoehorned into an end lot on a cul-de-sac. And within forty minutes of three major airports. Its owner would be a fatcat pilot who'd spent his life after the service in the second-floor sauna between hops to Europe.

Save him for last. Go with Olafsen first—Scandinavians were always the most adventurous. Call them from the hotel? No, better to talk to them in person. They'd never believe what he said over the phone.

Maybe he didn't need someone with experience on the B-50 to fly the plane. Granted, it was a big plane, but if he could find someone used to flying under pressure, maybe a smuggler or something, he could take the chance.

That or rely on Westlake.

O'Connell stirred the milk shake again. If you took too long finishing these things, they started to separate.

He could get Renard in Iran to dig him up one of his pilots. The arms dealer probably knew twenty people who would take the job without even a shrug.

Renard. O'Connell alone had given him enough business to pay for the massive castle he'd built in southern Iran. The expatriate Frenchman would be curious about this, real curious. What would he pay for an A-bomb, O'Connell wondered. Couple of million? Ten, twenty million? He could name whatever price he wanted.

The damn french fries were cold. O'Connell shoved the list and maps back into his pocket and got up from the table. Outside, the air had a faintly damp smell to it, as if rain were approaching. Once more he scanned the line of cars and the street as he walked, looking for a shadow.

If Stockman trusted him, perhaps he could trust Stockman.

As he walked from the restaurant, O'Connell noticed a commotion not far from his car. Two young men were hassling an older man, obviously looking to rob him.

"Hey," O'Connell called out. "What's going on?"

The words had a salutary effect on the muggers—one took a swing at the man.

Without thinking, O'Connell ran at them. "Hey," he yelled, "leave him alone."

He was almost on top of them when the young man nearest to him swung around. A knife flashed in his hand.

"I said, leave him alone," said O'Connell, though he had enough sense to jerk to a stop.

"Why should we?" said the young man with the knife. He was in his late twenties, short, thin, dark-complexioned though not black. So was his companion and their victim.

O'Connell's overriding obsession with his mission suddenly made him think they were all Pakistani.

For a moment it hung there, tense and nervous in a suburban parking lot thousands of miles from everything that mattered. It was a long moment, and O'Connell had time to curse himself. He should have minded his own business.

Once more he'd jumped in impulsively, not thought it out—his fatal flaw.

And then the man with the knife lunged, and O'Connell's reflexes took over. He grabbed the underside of the oncoming arm and pulled it forward. The knife fell harmlessly to the ground, dislodged by a sharp blow to the assailant's wrist. O'Connell gave him another hard punch to the side of the head, sending him reeling to the ground.

The agent turned and saw the other mugger pulling up a gun. Without thinking, O'Connell ducked his head and ran straight into him, pounding his head like a battering ram against his chest. The weapon and the mugger tumbled to the ground.

O'Connell kicked the gun away with his left foot but missed the man with his right. The mugger knocked him off balance with a glancing blow and O'Connell drew back, wishing now that Stockman had put a shadow on him. At least he'd have some help here. But just as he took a step forward to see how tough this little guy really was, someone came out of the restaurant yelling. The muggers turned and ran.

A burly black youth in a McDonald's uniform asked him if he was all right.

"Yeah," replied O'Connell. "Better check the old guy out, though. I think they clobbered him."

"What old guy?"

The man was gone.

That's gratitude for you, O'Connell thought as he got in his car. Served him right for getting involved.

Morena picked up the glass of ginger ale and surveyed her small Alexandria apartment. From where she stood in the bedroom she could see into every room. They were pale, dim, almost sad. Even the kitchen, with its overly cheerful red tiles set between the counter and cabinets, had a depressed pall to it.

The rooms were wearing the forboding feeling that had crept up her spine during dinner. Standing in front of the half-packed suitcase, she analyzed her unease, broke it into its components as her father had taught her. Part of it was the unpredictable variables of dealing with Blossom, whom she hadn't spoken to in nearly a year. Part of it was the difficult nature of the mission, and the fact that, despite her determination and her angry words to Stockman, covert nasties had never been her strong suit.

But another part, a large part, was the fact that her faith in the agency had been shaken. Up until now, she had trusted Stockman to tell her the truth, or at least a reasonable approximation, and to basically do what was right—and legal. But Golden Bear was proof that she'd been wrong.

Morena had seen herself as one of the new, young officers who was changing the Company, taking it out of the bad old days and making it respectable, ethical, a force for good. Stockman was supposed to be one of the leaders of that revolution. He'd been appointed DDO three years before as the agency searched for new directions, and he'd been kept on by the new president. The pundits called him a perfect counterpoint to Walter Jablow, the CIA director whom President D'Amici had appointed shortly after taking office. A well-respected former senator, Jablow was Mr. Outside to Stockman's Mr. Inside. Together, they were supposed to take the agency into the new century.

The new century looked a lot like the old one.

The ginger ale, warm now and a little flat, tasted bitter. Morena eyed the suitcase—in two hours she was going to catch a flight to Greece, and make connections from there. She toyed with the idea of calling her father. He was retired from government service, living in New Jersey and, as he put it, occasionally boring political science students at Princeton. Their talks generally had a calming effect. But she couldn't call him; there was no way she could talk about what she had to do—no way he'd let her.

What could he say, anyway? Buck up, Kelso—you knew what you were getting into.

No, he'd be horrified. Her father had helped Stockman advance when he was younger. He'd sent him a telegram of congratulations when he was appointed, and told her "that young man" would restore morality to the agency.

Morena put the glass down on the dresser and opened her bottom drawer, retrieving two pairs of baggy khaki pants to slide into the suitcase. She went to the bureau and took out some long scarves. Pakistan was a Muslim country, and it was best to dress modestly there, inconspicuously. She wouldn't need the fancy camisole her fingers grazed as she pulled out a scarf.

She hadn't worn it in awhile. O'Connell had given it to her, in Islamabad.

How would she deal with him? She'd cut him off completely, mad at herself as well as him.

She lifted the silky top out, remembering how well it fit her body.

She could feel the tug back. It was dangerous. Even if he'd merely followed orders, he had still been involved in something he should have known was wrong. He should have refused, should have done what was right.

He should have talked to her about it. Morena put the lingerie back in the drawer, closed her suitcase, and went to look for the cat.

Sargodha Air Base, Pakistan. 6:30 A.M.

All this pounding was starting to hurt. Khan put his hands up. "Enough," he shouted. "I surrender!"

That only made the ground crew press closer. His victory was their victory, and they were savoring it. "Six planes, Captain. Six!" shouted little Armi, the mechanic who worked on the avionics and weapons systems. "A fantastic performance," said Ali, the crew chief. "A great triumph. Your cousin will be very proud."

"There's our hero," said Tark, walking out onto the tarmac where Khan had been ambushed by the crew. "Rocket Khan."

"We all did well," said Khan as they finally let him go. "How many planes did you shoot down?"

"I only had two," said Tark. He laughed. "If you had left me a few, I would have done better."

Khan smiled, then kneeled down to say a short prayer of thanksgiving to Allah. As he rose, three Mirage fighter-bombers screamed off the runway, past a thin column of dark smoke on the southern horizon. The base itself had come under missile attack while the Falcons had been away; fortunately, the only serious casualty was a small storage building that had been destroyed.

Khan, sobered by the reminders of war, started around his aircraft for the customary postflight check.

"The Possum wants to see you in his office," said Tark.

"Why?"

"Maybe he's jealous of your success."

Khan frowned. Colonel Haq was not so petty as that. He passed behind the plane's gray-colored tail fin, inspecting the empty flare and chaff holds. There were some singes from the missile firings; otherwise the Falcon was unblemished. "You shouldn't make fun of the colonel," said Khan.

"Don't go shooting off, Rocket," said Tark. The lieutenant said something in his native Siraki, the language of his home in southwest Punjab. "I give the devil his due," Tark translated roughly, "but I don't go to work for him."

Yesterday, Khan would have run back and grabbed his friend around the neck for a good-natured wrestling match. But the roar of another bomb-laden Mirage leaving the runway emphasized for the young captain how terribly serious things had become. He said nothing, silently walking toward his commander's office.

His mood was not lifted by the dour expression on Colonel Haq's face when he entered his small room. The walls were crowded with photographs of the colonel at his various commands. Haq had flown in nearly every plane in the Pakistan Air Force, and often spoke lovingly of such elderly citizens as the T-33, a 1950s-era American jet that until recently had remained in the Pakistan inventory for photographic assignments. But his expression said there would be no ice-breaking reminiscence today.

"Come in, Captain," said Haq, rising. The colonel, influenced by American informality, might have offered Khan a "high five" had his mood been lighter; instead, he merely gestured him into a chair. "Congratulations on your flying."

"Thank you sir. God was with me."

"Yes," said Haq, turning away. "It calls for a celebration." He bent over a side cabinet and returned with a bottle of Macallan and two glasses. "This is very fine Scotch whiskey," said the commander, pouring a small bit in each glass.

The Scotch surprised the pilot. Not so much because of the religious laws prohibiting it—alcohol was a common vice among the country's privileged—but because he had never seen Haq drink before, not even in America. Offering the Scotch was a gesture of intimacy that went far beyond hospitality.

Even so, the colonel's voice and manner remained uncharacteristically stiff as he handed the glass to Khan and toasted his victories. Khan, whose drinking experiences were mainly limited to beer consumed during his college days and visits to the U.S., took a half mouthful of the Scotch and felt his throat burning as he swallowed. He was coughing by the time the liquor hit his stomach.

The colonel smiled. "Scotch is an acquired taste."

"Yes, sir."

"I would offer another toast to your wedding, but I'm not sure you'd survive it."

Khan's wedding—their plans would have to be changed now. The pilot pictured Hir Ranjha in her wedding dress, a luxurious silky red with golden-edged scarves. Her face would have a slightly quizzical look during the ceremony, weighed down by the seriousness of the event, and all the extra jewelry. A special jeweled loop would be hung across her face, linking to a clasp in her nose—she had told him several times how strange it felt.

"No more for me either," said Haq, putting down his empty shot glass. "We fly again in two hours."

Khan nodded. Amusement passed from the colonel's face as he studied the young pilot intently. There were furrows along Haq's forehead, and his cheeks had grown heavier since this morning's preflight briefing.

"I have bad news," said Haq. "Colonel Benzair was shot down. His unit engaged a group of Indian fighters about the same time we did, in the sector near Kotli.''

Khan felt the small amount of Scotch that had made it to his stomach burn a hole completely through to his flight suit.

Benzair was a superb flier, one of the best in the air force. He had been Khan's instructor in his bootstrap fighter maneuvers class; the two men had immediately formed a tight bond. He had chosen Khan as his wingman in the elite mixed attack-interceptor squadron that was to have become operational tomorrow.

"I know that you were close to him," Haq continued softly. "It is a great loss to us all."

"Yes," managed Khan. "How, sir, how did it happen?"

The colonel gave him a hopeless, baffled shrug. "I do not know the details. But it is confirmed."

"His chute?"

Haq shook his head ever so gently, as if hesitating to disturb the dead man's memory. "You will have to carry on, son. You're to command the squadron now."

"Me?"

"There will be a promotion, of course," said the colonel. "Effective immediately. And you will choose another interceptor pilot to join you—a Falcon pilot, obviously."

"My wingmate, Lieutenant Yusuf," said Khan immediately.

The colonel hesitated. "I suspected you would want him. You have to be careful, Syyid."

"Tark and I have been flying together for almost a year, sir. He's a good pilot."

"Yes, he is," admitted Haq, picking his next words carefully. "His skills are excellent. But his temperament—he does not always make the careful choice."

"I've seen him use excellent judgment. He's young— he'll grow up," said Khan, not considering that Tark was a year older than he was.

"It's all up to the individual, Major. With all the training that the commander can give, with all the best examples and doctrine, it comes down to the individual pilot." Haq eyed his empty shot glass, then stole a wistful glance toward one of the pictures on the wall near Khan. "A leader can do many things, but he cannot do the job for his men."

The younger man, his thoughts returning to his dead mentor, nodded absently.

"This will be a difficult war," continued Haq. "There have been ground skirmishes in Kashmir already, and India has struck across the Thar Desert." The colonel's voice trailed off. With great effort, he tried to lighten his tone, though the frown on his face betrayed him. "I saw two of your kills myself. And I've heard all about the MiG that had escaped. That was a fine piece of work, to catch him."

"Thank you."

"Good luck with your new command," said Haq, standing. The colonel's stare, dark round eyes set deep in an ashen face, stopped him from responding. "Take care, Syyid."

Pakistan Border, on the Great Indian Desert. 8:15 A.M.

Lt. Gen. Arjun Singh, commander of the Indian Third Army Group, got out of his battered jeep and walked up the road a few yards. The crisp morning air felt sweet in his mouth, and already the sun warmed his nose and cheeks in a way that foretold a beautiful day. The meteorologists had promised good weather through the end of the week, and the general took the clarity of the sky as one more omen that things would go as he had planned.

Better than he had planned.

Arjun stopped at a point where a huge break in the road's macadam began. For the next fifty yards, the asphalt pitched and weaved like waves in a river, dirt and tar churned by an invisible current. The torrent that had caused this destruction was made of steel; barely two hours ago an entire division of Arjun's Vijayanta tanks had passed through this sector, galloping out of the night to cross the Indian-Pakistani border and rush on toward the Indus River, deep in Pakistan. The armor spearhead had met such little resistance that its units had already traveled nearly forty miles.

The invaders' surprise was so complete that helicopter assault troops that had attacked towns on the northern bank of the Indus in the first hour of battle were already being regrouped for assaults on strategic sites in the Sulaiman foothills originally designated second- or third-day targets.

Stroking his beard, the general turned toward his jeep and beckoned to his driver, a short fellow Sikh who served as Arjun's valet, secretary and occasional sounding board. Sergeant Ajit Singh Teg often displayed an ability to read his commander's mind, though it did not take much intuition now to realize that Arjun wanted his binoculars. The general nodded at his sergeant as he took them, momentarily adjusted his black turban, and then brought the glasses silently to his eyes, savoring the moment as he surveyed the territory he had so easily won.

Meanwhile, men had begun to stir from the convoy of staff vehicles and trucks accompanying them. A tall, skinny figure emerged from one of the Land-Rovers and walked toward the general.

"There were buffalo here once," said the man, a brigadier general. He stood next to his commander. "This was once a lush plain. Now it is covered by sand spilled from the hourglass of time."

Arjun merely grunted, continuing to sweep his eyes over the dunes that obscured whatever might remain of the dead Vedic civilization. He was used to General Shastri by now.

Sattua Shastri, a Hindu of the Kshatriyas caste, was second in command of the battle group Arjun had assembled. As a soldier, he was slow and cautious, a distinct counter to Arjun's instinctive nature. His real skill was as an organizer; if the attack had been Arjun's plan, Shastri had been essential to getting the men in place to carry it out. Still, while Arjun valued his ability, the Hindu's personal airs grated on him. Shastri pretended to be a scholar and poet. Arjun would not have kept him as second-in-command except for pressure from the general staff, which was suspicious of the brilliant lieutenant general because he was a Sikh. Shastri's patrons obviously did not fully comprehend his negative opinions of them.

"Has it ever surprised you, General," said Shastri, "that the word for war in the Rig Veda is *gavisthi*—a search for cows? The disappearance of those buffalo had a large impact on history."

"I hadn't thought of it," said Arjun, turning toward the jeep.

"War was linked to immediate results in those days," said Shastri, following. "Not politics."

"My objective, General, is to strike across the Indus River," responded Arjun testily. "I do not care whether I find cows there, or politicians."

"I'm sure we'll find both," said Shastri as they reached the general's vehicle.

"We're ahead of schedule," said the general.

"I am well prepared," answered the brigadier, his philosophic tone melting into more bureaucratic cadences. "I would suggest again, however, that we not move our forward headquarters into the enemy's territory for at least twenty-four hours. That would still be a day ahead of schedule."

"The schedule was too conservative," said Arjun, slamming the jeep door behind him as he wedged himself in. He could have had any car he wanted, but chose the battered jeep. What he lost in comfort he more than made up in symbolic value. "I have to be as close to the front as possible."

"We have excellent divisional commanders," said Shastri. "You trained many of them yourself."

"Your objections have been noted, General. Let's go."

"I recall a story about Shiva," started Shastri.

"One Shiv was born, one died, and one was born again," said Arjun, quoting a passage from Sikh scripture that exposed the shallowness of the Hindu myths. "From dust they sprouted, to dust they returned."

Shastri smiled indulgently, but at least Arjun's citation had its desired effect—forestalling more Hindu claptrap. The brigadier was forever trotting out some religious commonplace about this or that god to bolster his opinion—a rather easy thing to do in India, given the vast pantheon of deities, half-deities and their myriad incarnations. As a Sikh, Arjun knew there was only one God. While he must permit his men—and his superiors—their superstitions, there was no need for him to waste his time listening to their misguided fables, especially when they stood in his way.

Though he would never discuss it with non-Sikhs, Arjun saw his mission largely in religious terms. His ultimate objective was Lahore, over six hundred miles away at the northern tip of the great Punjab plain. Lahore had been the ancient capital of the Sikhs, stolen from them by the Muslims with the Hindus' connivance at the Partition (the great splitting of India and Pakistan upon independence from the British in 1947.) That was the real reason for this war, or at least for Arjun's participation. Before it was over, he would walk through the streets his ancestors had ruled, a liberator, a lion, a true soldier of the *panth*.

First he needed to lead his troops across the Indus, and onto the highways on the other side of the Pakistani river. By nightfall, before nightfall, he would split southern Pakistan in half. Tomorrow, his troops would push up the valley toward the Bolan Pass, completing the dissection. Then, as two divisions of his army squeezed off Hyderabad and Karachi from communication with the north, Arjun's armored units would re-form for a second lightning attack, a pincer that would streak up the Indus valley. The Muslims would either surrender or be pushed back to the hills and mountains in the north, where they could stay forever, as far as Arjun was concerned, as long as the Punjab was reunited under Sikh rule.

"How seductive war is when you fight Ravana," said Shastri, referring to yet another mythic character, this one a demon.

"What?"

"I am just thinking how easy it is for us to push the Pakistanis back," said the brigadier general. "As if we were Vishnu or Ramma, or perhaps Shiva the Destroyer, chasing devils from the earth. I shall have to make a note of this."

"Just make sure our tanks have plenty of petrol," said Arjun. "Then you can write whatever you want."

Washington, D.C. 11 P.M.

John Grasso pulled his jacket forward, closer to his chest, trying to keep warm as he waited inside the State Department vestibule for the television interview to begin. He was wearing his brown suit, a color that his personal assistant said made him look like Humpty Dumpty on camera, but that couldn't be helped—there simply wasn't enough time for the secretary of state to change before heading for his flight to New Delhi. Besides, Tracy couldn't have meant the Humpty Dumpty crack; she wasn't the kind of woman who would sleep with anyone she laughed at.

His hands were ice. He wanted some hot coffee, but he'd been temporarily abandoned by his staff, most of whom were either scurrying to their homes to pick up suitcases or were still back at the National Security Council session trying to prevent a last-minute attempt by the president's chief of staff to bring the Russians into the negotiations as "co-facilitators."

Let Fomichov earn his own goddamn Nobel Peace Prize, thought Grasso. He detested his Russian counterpart, who had a penchant for upstaging him at joint press conferences. Fomichov would never be caught dead in a brown suit. He probably owned nothing but blue ones, tailored to hide his spare tire.

Grasso stomped his feet impatiently on the thin red hallway carpet. The CNN correspondent who'd arranged the interview, Kevin Kalm, had gone outside to get his camera crew fifteen minutes ago.

Grasso didn't like Kalm. Seven or eight years before, the reporter had been one of his graduate students at Columbia—an overachieving underachiever, which perhaps explained why he had done so well in television. Grasso had given him a C+, and distinctly remembered that the approaching Christmas season had played a key role in his grading.

The secretary had agreed to do the exclusive interview tonight because the live satellite feed would be seen in Islamabad and New Delhi, the capitals of Pakistan and India respectively. They knew he was coming, of course—the Pakistani president had practically begged him to—but Grasso wanted to use the opportunity to reinforce the idea of a quick cease-fire.

Besides, with the president's polls starting to slip and stories hinting that the honeymoon was over for the new administration, positive publicity like this wasn't something Jack D'Amici would forget.

Thank God the last administration had gotten rid of all the nuclear weapons on the subcontinent, Grasso thought. If they hadn't, the damn Pakistanis would have their hands on the trigger already. Not that he blamed them—if he didn't get a cease-fire in place soon, the only territory the Pakistanis would control would be in Afghanistan.

For some reason the CIA had brought up the nuclear issue this evening at the National Security Council meeting, with the agency's deputy director of operations suggesting that one or both of the countries might have been able to find a way around the disarmament treaties. But the director himself—as well as the other intelligence agencies—pooh-poohed that, and Grasso figured that the DDO was trying to underline his presence at the session. Carl Stockman was an ambitious son of a bitch, and his ambitions went beyond the CIA. Grasso—who'd gotten his job largely because he was in the same Sons of Italy chapter in New York as the president—knew a politicking move when he saw one.

"Where the hell is Kalm?" Grasso said to the empty hallway. He took a step forward to open the door and was almost flattened as it swung into him.

"Gee, I'm sorry, John," said Bill Schenck, the secretary's security director. "Are you all right?"

"Yeah," said Grasso, smiling weakly at his linebacker-sized assistant. His wrist felt as if it had been snapped in half but he shook it bravely.

"Your hand's not broken, is it?"

"No, no," said Grasso, who wouldn't have admitted if it were. He was barely five-feet-four, so he had to look up at practically everyone, but his head went back nearly ninety degrees to see Schenck, six-five in his stocking feet. "Nothing like what Washington did to Bauer in last week's game against the Giants."

"Right," said Schenck. "Is Tracy Su-Jan on your flight?"

"Yes, Tracy is coming."

"Just making sure," said Schenck.

Grasso couldn't tell whether the security chief's voice had a wink to it or not. The door opened again, the cold air raising goose pimples on the back of his neck.

"We're all set, Professor," said Kalm, stepping inside. "You can come on out any time you want."

"Outside?"

"We thought it might be more dramatic if we had the White House in the background."

"The White House?"

"We're all set up."

"The White House is five blocks away."

"Not on the lawn itself," said the correspondent. "Just in front. We'll play with the telephoto and have the White House way off in the background. Talk about your visuals."

"Damn it—"

Kalm looked hurt. "You said you would give us the interview because you wanted impact, and so I worked to get you a good image—"

"All right, all right," said Grasso, unimpressed. Kalm had probably misinformed his crew about where he had scheduled the interview, and was afraid to order the men to move. "We'll meet you there. Come on, Bill."

"Righto."

The gust of air as Schenck opened the door practically knocked Grasso over. He didn't have an overcoat or even a sweater—would the fact that his face was purple help or hurt his chances for the Peace Prize?

"Uh, Professor, would it be possible to hitch a ride with you? My crew had to go back to get ready for us."

Grasso contemplated leaving Kalm to walk back over to the White House in the cold, but that would only further delay things.

70

"All right, what the hell." The secretary slid into the backseat as Schenck held the door open. "You better remember you owe me one."

Even compared to the other television people who covered State, thought Grasso, Kalm was a bit of a bozo. His only qualifications for the job—besides having known the secretary, which Kalm had undoubtedly played up to his bosses at the network—were a perfect soupy smile, a youthful face, and a lot of luck. He'd somehow managed to be in Romania a week before the 1994 revolution, had been traveling in Argentina when their president was assassinated in 1995, and was on vacation in Hawaii when the earthquake struck last year.

Considering all these calamities, Grasso realized that maybe Kalm didn't have good luck at all. Maybe a way ought to be found to keep him out of India, or at least off the secretary's plane.

"What sort of questions would you like me to ask?" Kalm said as the driver spun the limo into a U-turn on Constitutional Avenue.

Grasso took the correspondent's obsequiousness in stride. "I suppose you could ask how important a cease-fire would be, and whether other countries will back it."

"And what will you say?"

"It's very important, and of course they'll back it."

"Sounds good to me," said Kalm, looking out the window.

"I have to sound balanced," Grasso explained, suddenly feeling like a college professor again, with a duty to explain even to a slow student. "We naturally have a tilt toward Pakistan, but the idea is to come across to the Indians as evenhanded. We believe that the invasion is almost entirely predicated on their internal politics. In fact, our intelligence indicates that there's a power struggle going on right now. If we can come in as neutral parties, we'll end up encouraging the forces that want peace, and we'll have a cease-fire quickly. This is really an internal thing with India."

"Uh-huh," answered Kalm, still staring out the window.

"This is on background, of course," said Grasso.

71

"Excuse me?"

"This is all off-the-record." He gave the correspondent's leg a friendly tap. "For a past student."

"Oh sure," said Kalm. "Say, you think that guy over there is taking a leak, or what?"

A small portable stage had been erected at the base of the ellipse in front of the White House gates. Grasso got out of the car and took a few steps toward it when he was assaulted by two men. One grabbed his jacket and hooked a microphone to it; the other puffed his face with makeup.

"Ready!" shouted someone near the van, and Grasso was literally lifted onto the stage by the producer, a woman who stood about five-ten and had biceps nearly as large as Schenck's. Kalm sidled up next to him, putting his arm on the secretary's shoulder in what was meant to be a reassuring gesture.

"Just like we rehearsed it, OK, Professor?"

"Sure," said Grasso. The wind picked up, and Grasso realized that if he stayed out here for more than ten minutes, he would turn into one of those cryogenic animals museums used for wildlife displays.

"Damn. They had to go to a commercial break. Two minutes," shouted the disembodied voice by the van.

It was more like fifteen. Of some consolation was the fact that a flunkie left and returned with coffee for Grasso in the meantime. The secretary practically tore off the top to take a gulp when it was handed to him. He realized belatedly that the liquid was extremely hot. Grasso was spitting it out of his mouth as Kalm began telling the world how serious the crisis in Pakistan was, and how one of the highest-ranking officials in the U.S. government was about to embark on an historic peacekeeping mission whose ramifications would be felt for decades to come.

"The secretary has allotted us a few seconds before he leaves to answer some questions," said Kalm, taking a step backward and looking at Grasso, who hurriedly tossed the coffee cup and its contents over the side. "Mr. Secretary?"

"Yes, Kevin," started Grasso, his tongue still stinging. "As you said, the situation in Pakistan and India is very serious. While we understand that—''

''Would you agree that there has been a decided American tilt toward Pakistan?'' interrupted Kalm.

Grasso grimaced.

''Well, no, not a tilt. We're honest brokers here, a neutral party—''

''Playing both ends toward the middle?''

''No, I wouldn't say that at all,'' answered Grasso. ''We believe that we can respect the views of both sides.''

''You don't think India initiated this war?''

As Kalm spoke, he put his arm behind Grasso's back. The secretary's first thought was that he was trying to steal his wallet.

''Well, I wouldn't want—''

''A little closer,'' whispered Kalm.

''We're not taking sides in this conflict,'' said Grasso tersely, taking an awkward step forward. At least he wasn't cold anymore. In fact, his body temperature was rising nicely. ''We are neutral.''

''It's been said around the State Department that the Indians started this war for internal reasons, Mr. Secretary, and that the outcome has more to do with their politics than with Pakistani transgressions. Do you agree?''

Grasso cursed himself for not flunking Kalm and scuttling his career when he had a chance.

''I have to keep an open mind,'' said Grasso. ''The administration is keeping an open mind.''

''But that's really what's going on, isn't it? The Indians started this mess.''

''I won't know what the hell is going on until I get there, will I?''

''It's been a long day,'' Kalm told the camera.

''The president, in consultation with the UN secretary general, has asked me to undertake a shuttle mission to the capitals of Pakistan and India, in the hopes that we can avert war,'' said Grasso as calmly as possible. As he spoke, he slid his arm around and checked to make sure his wallet was still in his back pocket. ''We have already received assurances from both sides that we will be taken seriously.''

"But Mr. Secretary, isn't it a bit late to avert war? They're already fighting."

"We hope to get a cease-fire in place," said Grasso.

Kalm had put his hand to his ear. He frowned, then began speaking hurriedly to the camera. "Thank you very much, Mr. Secretary. We're going to go now to New Delhi, where an hysterical Hindu mob has just set fire to a car outside the American embassy. . . ."

WEDNESDAY, SEPT. 17, 1997

Suburban Maryland. Apx. 3 P.M.

For Michael O'Connell, the day started optimistically enough. The motel was cheap but its beds were comfortable, and he slept better than he had in weeks. When he woke, his old confidence had been magically restored. He felt even better when he heard a news report saying the American secretary of state was on his way to Pakistan and a cease-fire was expected. That would keep the airport at Karachi where he was to meet Blossom open to commercial flights, enabling him to fly there directly. And it would remove the ticking clock from the operation.

But the agent's optimism began fading as soon as he noticed that the mailbox in front of what was supposed to be Olafsen's house said "Smith." Sure enough, Olafsen had died three years before.

The address the air force listed for Hoyt actually belonged to an abandoned sausage factory. Which left Greeley and his Halcyon Court lair—an unlikely taker, even if he did live there. As O'Connell drove, he once more considered where he would get another pilot. Here it would be better not to count on Blossom. While commandos could always be rounded up, pilots were a precious commodity in Pakistan and it would be too chancy to arrive in the country without one.

Renard, the French arms dealer based in southern Iran, was his most convenient and likely source. Officially, Renard was on the agency's red list—which was supposed to mean avoid at all costs. But there was a difference between "supposed to" and reality; Westlake of all people wouldn't squawk.

Besides, what could Stockman do? Can him again?

Renard would want to know why he wanted a pilot, even if O'Connell didn't specify someone who could fly an old crate like the B-50.

Hell, just tell him it's for a bomb. Split the proceeds—what's one worth?

"And lead us not into temptation," the agent muttered to himself as he glanced at the map folded open on the seat next to him. O'Connell made a turn past a small shopping center and drove down a road that seemed like something out of *Country Living*. Stone walls bordered long, steep driveways lined with foliage just starting to redden with the approach of autumn. The weather was still relatively warm, and O'Connell leaned his arm out the open window, propping his head and trying to calculate the real estate values of the houses he passed as a diversion. He nearly missed the small signpost that announced Lilac Boulevard, the connecting road that would take him to Greeley's house.

Why even bother, thought O'Connell as he backed up the car after overshooting the street.

The roadway changed from asphalt to packed dirt about a quarter mile in. Another half mile and the stone walls disappeared. O'Connell continued down the road, wondering if he'd misread the map, when he saw a sign for Halcyon Court.

It was a trailer park. Number eight was at the end of the first row, a sad-looking green affair, probably dating from the mid-sixties.

It was his own damn fault. When the two farmhands showed up, he should have refused to go with them. He should have taken his bag and headed south. Like to Antarctica.

The man who had once been the CIA's most important covert operative in South Asia stopped his car in the middle of the gravel roadway in front of a trailer that looked to be worth more for salvage than as a home—though even then it wouldn't do more than buy a fair dinner. O'Connell studied the address for a moment before crumpling the paper and tossing it to the side. He retrieved the cup of coffee he'd stuck between the dashboard and the window an hour ago. Cold, the bitter liquid had lost any charm it might have had when he bought it—just the thing to motivate him to get out of the car, spitting the mouthful out as he walked toward the trailer.

The graying wooden stairs creaked heavily as he walked up them to knock on the door. The screen in the storm door looked brittle. He had to stoop down to get at the metal part.

O'Connell knocked twice. No answer.

He'd already begun to turn away, his mood sinking to new depths, when the door opened. A tall, graying black man dressed in a pair of pajama bottoms and an undershirt stood in the doorway behind the screen.

''Yeah?'' asked the man.

O'Connell turned back and almost laughed in self-derision. Why did he always jump into things?

''What can I do for you?''

''I'm sorry,'' said O'Connell. ''I'm looking for a James Greeley.''

''So?''

''The guy I'm looking for was in the air force during Korea. He was a captain in the service.''

''I left the air force as a major,'' said the man gruffly. ''And I missed most of Korea. What is it you want?''

O'Connell studied him a second. He was around the right age, maybe even a little younger, in decent shape.

''Can I come in?''

The man silently swung the screen door open. O'Connell

followed him inside, wiping his feet on a woven welcome mat before stepping onto the bright yellow and brown shag carpet of the small living room.

The inside of the trailer was in considerably better shape than the outside. Tidy and clean, it was furnished simply but comfortably. It also stunk of alcohol. O'Connell's stomach turned with his first step indoors.

Greeley motioned him over to the kitchen area. A bottle of Jim Beam, about a third empty, sat in the middle of the small table, a narrow water glass next to it.

"Want a drink?" asked Greeley, sitting on one of the two linoleum-covered chairs.

"No thanks."

"I got beer in the fridge."

"No," said O'Connell.

"You a teetotaler?"

"I just don't drink that much."

"OK with me," said Greeley, pouring himself out a drink. "I like bourbon," he added. "Warms the mouth."

"I'll bet," said O'Connell. The fumes sent a fresh wave of nausea through him.

Greeley took a gulp from the glass as if it were orange juice. His arm muscles bulged as he held up the glass; there was steel left in his body at least. The bleached fabric of the old T-shirt bulged around his chest, and his neck looked like a bough hewn from a chestnut tree. But his eyes hung in his face like balloons with the air run out, their centers dilated by the booze and the smoke from a cigarette burning in the ashtray.

"So what do you want?" the black man asked.

"You used to fly B-50s?"

"What about it?"

"I'm looking for a pilot."

Greeley frowned at his drink. "So?"

Even if this guy had been a pilot thirty-odd years ago, there was no way he was still flying. This much drinking— must be how he'd washed out and landed here.

O'Connell almost got up to go. But then he realized this was exactly the kind of person he was going to have to settle for—someone so down that a half-baked scheme would look like a golden opportunity.

Somebody like himself.

"I might have a job for the right person," O'Connell said. "I have to admit, I'm a little surprised."

"What, because I'm black?" Greeley bristled.

"No."

"Not the right color for a pilot?"

"How come you live in a trailer?"

"What about it?"

"I thought maybe you'd work for an airline."

"Oh, I worked for an airline all right," Greeley laughed bitterly. "Made me a goddamn mechanic. Didn't keep that job too very long."

The last thing O'Connell wanted was a lecture on race relations. "You don't look old enough to be the right guy," he said. "These were big planes—first jet bombers, right?"

"Screw you. They were based on B-29s, and when they became obsolete because of things like the B-52, they refit them as tankers, used them as weather planes, and even sent a few over Russia to test the defenses. You want to know the takeoff speed?"

O'Connell shrugged.

"One-twenty. Now you got to watch the way you load the sucker, because they got a tendency to—"

"Thanks."

"Here," said Greeley, jumping up and taking two quick steps into the living room. He yanked a framed photo from an end table, sending several others to the floor. "This look like a jet to you?"

A small clump of men stood in front of a shiny silver plane; a young black man with an officer's cap stood second from the left, his mouth cocked open in a confident smile.

"I was a lot slimmer then," said Greeley, looking over his shoulder. "And dumber."

"I need someone who's flown a B-50," said O'Connell handing him the photo back. "Somebody who can keep his mouth shut."

"Yeah?"

"And who wants a hundred thousand dollars."

Once more, Greeley surprised him. This was obviously a man to whom $100,000 was a considerable sum. Yet he made no reaction.

"I'm working on something that needs a little traveling," added O'Connell. "You interested?"

"Travel where?"

"Pakistan. We go there, we pick up the plane, we come home."

"Pakistan? That's on the other side the world."

"Just about."

"This here's a real B-50?"

O'Connell nodded.

"B-50's a special kind of plane," said Greeley. The wariness in his voice had been softened, and gradually was transformed into a kind of nostalgic wonder. "It was obsolete, more or less, as soon as it flew. Jets killed it. But a hell of a plane. Best thing I was ever in. Better than the B-47, ten times. Saw a bunch of those lined up on an airfield in Florida used as target drones, and I said, good riddance. But I didn't think there were any B-50s left. Hell—they'd be thirty years old."

"There's at least three, that I know of."

"This about drugs?"

O'Connell smiled and shook his head. "I'm working for the government. Kind of an independent contractor."

He was dangling at the point of no return. Did he want this guy to go with him? He was old, an amateur, and had a chip on his shoulder. Plus he was a drinker. The only thing he had going for him was that he had flown a B-50 years before.

Still, something had happened to his face when O'Connell mentioned the plane. His eyes weren't so puffy anymore.

"I used to be a CIA agent," said O'Connell. "They want me to get the plane."

"Yeah, right," laughed Greeley. "Where's your trench coat?"

"Sorry for wasting your time," said O'Connell, standing up. Greeley reached across the table and caught his arm. It was a strong grasp, stronger than he'd imagined.

"Tell me more."

His eyes weren't puffy at all. They were as hard and firm as the young man's in the picture, just as determined.

"It's just an in-and-out thing," said O'Connell, who wouldn't have told even a fellow agent much more. "We get in, the plane's ready, we fly it out."

"They just handing it to us, or what?"

"I'll take care of that end. You'll be part of a team."

"A team? We stealing this plane?"

He wouldn't tell him the whole story, but he wouldn't lie. "As a matter of fact, we are."

"Shit," said Greeley, shaking his head and picking up the bottle of whiskey.

"The rough stuff'll be over in five minutes."

"Five minutes, shit—this plane going to be gassed up?"

"It'll be set up and ready to go at a moment's notice. We're just substituting you for the regular pilot."

Greeley was making some mental calculations. "It's going to take more than five minutes," he said. "Takes a long time to get down the flight list. You got to have the engines all warmed up and everything. And then there's the loading—has to be done perfect, because there's a special balance to the plane."

"They've thought of all that."

"You're really with the CIA?"

O'Connell walked to the telephone hanging on the wall next to the refrigerator. He dialed the DDO's private line—a special phone hookup that gave twenty-four-hour access to Stockman.

Assuming it hadn't been changed. And that he remembered it correctly. He'd been given the number three years ago, and never actually used it.

"How long has it been since you've flown?" O'Connell asked as he dialed.

"Long time," Greeley admitted. "A very long time. But I could close my eyes and see myself in the cockpit right now. You go through it enough—it isn't something I'd be likely to forget."

O'Connell heard the line connect and handed the phone to the old man. "Tell him you were on the list. He'll know what you're talking about."

Greeley took the phone doubtfully and held it to his ear. *Some pizza parlor in a suburban mall answers and I'll be going to Pakistan alone,* O'Connell thought. *That or Greeley would make him drink the rest of the Jim Beam.*

"Hello? My name is James Greeley. I got a guy named—"

"Michael O'Connell."

"Michael O'Connell in my kitchen. See, he's telling me this thing about—"

Greeley shut up as Stockman began talking on the other end. O'Connell walked over to the living room. He reached down to the floor and picked up the photos that had fallen, rearranging them on the end table. They were snapshots of kids, probably grandchildren. A formal photograph of Greeley and a silver-haired woman hung on the wall.

O'Connell looked back and saw Greeley nodding at him. "Do you want to talk—" he started, but once more Stockman said something to cut him off. Greeley nodded and hung up the phone. "All right," he told O'Connell. "What do we got to do?"

"First off, we stop drinking. I need somebody who's going to be sober the whole way through."

"Don't worry about that."

O'Connell frowned. "That your wife?" he asked, pointing to the picture on the wall.

"Yeah," Greeley answered.

"You have to discuss this with her?"

"I buried her last Friday."

Over the Atlantic. Apx. 11 P.M.

James Greeley leaned across the aisle of the Air France 747 as the stewardess passed.

"Another Coke, Mr. Greeley?"

"If you could."

What he really wanted was one of those little whiskey bottles she'd had earlier, before the cabin was darkened and the movie began. But he'd promised O'Connell he wasn't going to drink, and for a hundred thousand, he wouldn't.

And for a chance to fly the old Fifty.

But it was tough with this much temptation. How many times had he made that same promise to Olissa?

"You probably been to Paris a lot, huh?" Greeley asked O'Connell, leaning over the empty seat between them.

"You ought to try and get some sleep." O'Connell's eyes remained closed, his head sunk deep into his pillow.

"I'm OK."

"I don't want you falling asleep on me later."

"I'm watching the movie," lied Greeley. "Interesting."

"Uh-huh."

"You ever been to the Louvre?"

"We're not even going into the city."

"Me and Olissa were in Paris, back in '63. I had a whole month off, and we—"

"Go to sleep."

Greeley frowned. O'Connell didn't rank among the most sociable people he'd ever met. He wasn't Greeley's idea of a CIA agent either—not exactly Arnold Schwarzenegger, though he seemed confident enough. He had dark hair, a freckled face—weren't these guys supposed to be blond WASPs? With upper crust accents. Erudite, that was the word. Not that O'Connell was dumb—he'd said something in French to one of the cabin crew, and he'd grabbed a copy of the *New York Times* while they were waiting in the terminal. But O'Connell didn't talk like an Ivy League type.

He seemed sour, pissed off at the world. Guy like this— CIA, young, white—ought to have the world by the balls.

Greeley shifted in his seat and reached his hand down, fumbling for his earphones. He didn't care for the movie, or the seven channels of saccharine pop music the stereo offered, but he was afraid to sleep. Last night had been a jumble of memories of his wife. And they weren't the good ones, either. It seemed that his brain had stored up every argument, every fight, and waited to spring them on him when she died. His perspiration had soaked the bed sheets; he woke to find them dripping with water, raveled tightly around his body, as if they'd meant to strangle him.

Greeley had only hit his wife once: a mistake, a real mistake, when he was a little drunk and angry and mostly frustrated, having been laid off from yet another job because he was the last one in. Hit her with the back of his hand, a slap that stunned him as much as her.

"If you touch me once more, James Greeley, you'll never see me again." She didn't sleep in their bed for two weeks, even after he'd apologized, groveled—sincerely, for he really loved her, had just temporarily lost his mind, the pressure too much.

His one real transgression, his only major sin—never cheated on her, never even thought of cheating—and that was what his mind replayed, again and again.

"Mr. Greeley?"

"Thank you, Miss," said Greeley, smiling at the young woman who leaned down to pour the contents of the small Coke can into his plastic cup. She had a small bottle of Johnnie Walker Red in the same hand as the Coke can, and for a moment Greeley thought she had made a mistake and was going to pour the Scotch in with the soda. He wouldn't object; that kind of thing was almost like fate.

But she didn't. She smiled politely and went to bring the Scotch to another passenger.

Greeley didn't consider himself a real drinker. He averaged only three or four beers a night. He didn't drink liquor except on weekends, or if something set him off.

Olissa's last night in the hospital. Even the kids asked him to stop, but it was too much, a plunge deep into a sticky, humid night, with no way out.

Until the CIA agent appeared. As if Olissa had gone up to St. Peter, explained the situation, and asked if he could straighten everything out. Give him the chance to do the one thing he always felt cheated out of, and he'd be all right.

Greeley wondered how they'd gotten his name. Just like the air force to screw something like that up. They'd never gotten anything straight, not even his birth date—though he'd been responsible for that bit of deception himself—after taking him as a junior college graduate and lining him right into a special showcase "Negro" program.

That was his last break. He was supposed to have become a pilot. He tested high enough to be a pilot. It was right when the service was really starting to integrate. He was on the cusp. Monday, everything was set; Tuesday, no more showcase program. He ended up a navigator instead of a pilot. They gave him a load of b.s. about shortages of trained navigators, tried to sweet talk him about his intelligence. "You got navigational aptitudes, boy."

Boy. Exactly.

If you were black, you got sent to the rear of the bus. Support personnel. Important, but not quite that important. Crucial, but not in command.

For James Greeley, integration was a crock. At least he would've been a pilot if the units were still segregated. He'd take all that other crap in a second, if only they let him have his dream.

After the service he got a job with an airline—on a ground crew, as mechanic. Jobs were short and he could work his way up. Bull. Oh, they gave him a taxi license and he hung with it, until eventually he couldn't take being turned down anymore, turned down and turned back, even from being a navigator or a flight engineer. He got in trouble for mouthing off, or maybe drinking; it was so long ago now he couldn't remember. By then it was just an excuse anyway; even he wanted out.

What did they expect? He'd never really had his chance, the one thing he wanted to do, the one thing he wanted to prove. Nobody let him fly.

So he'd flown in his kitchen. It started as a joke between him and his wife, and then it became an obsession. Sitting at the table, back from his job as foreman of the Durso Metal Shop (thank God the owner was a vet, and black), he'd rock back and forth in the chair, pulling the levers and switches. He loved to explain the plane to Olissa, how the wheel worked, when to lift the landing gear, the delicate balance when the big bomber was fully loaded.

She was a patient woman, to hear that story so many times. To laugh with him. She loved to laugh.

He'd sat in the real seat plenty of times, a captain's favor to a loyal navigator. (A damn good navigator, who'd saved the pilot's butt on several occasions. And a good pilot, too, a white guy you could actually trust, who paid you back.) But he'd never actually flown a full mission himself. Done a takeoff, some level flight, even helped out with one landing when the copilot was under the weather, but never the whole thing together, not on his own.

Oh, but he could. He'd done it so many times in his head, in his kitchen.

Laughing with Olissa.

Sargodha Air Base, Pakistan. 4:30 A.M.

Newly promoted Major Syyid Khan pushed himself back against the F-16's black ejection seat, snuggling into the plane in a preflight ritual he had followed since the first time he soloed. He began moving his upper body in a circular motion, flexing and rotating his muscles. When each had been stretched, the commander of Special Attack Squadron 103 extended his hands and said the short prayer from the Koran his first flight instructor had urged on him years before: "Oh ye who believe. Shall I guide you to a pursuit that will save you from eternal punishment? Believe in Allah and his Apostle and make war in the way of God."

His canopy still open, Khan gazed out across the runway after completing his prayer. It was not quite dawn, but there was enough light to see across the runway as a large bird tried to make headway against the crosswind. It moved its wings deliberately a few strokes, then glided off course. It flapped again, strenuously pulling back toward its goal. The creature took nearly a half minute to cross, and Khan stared the whole time, impressed by its determination.

"Good luck, Major."

Startled, Khan turned to the side and saw Sergeant Ali, his old crew chief, leaning into the cockpit.

"I came over to make sure things were well," said the sergeant, whose duties had been assumed by a Squadron 5 crew member. "Don't want my Rocket taking off unprepared."

"Thank you, Sergeant."

"It's Ali, you rascal," said the chief, patting the top of his helmet and then reaching over to tighten the straps that held the pilot in the reclined ACES II ejector seat. "Show respect to someone old enough to be your grandfather."

Khan laughed.

"Get your men back in one piece," said the sergeant. "And I'll tell you about your cousin the general's first mission in command when you get home."

"Is it a good story?"

"It has its points," said Ali, laughing. The sergeant had served as Nur's chief and had a vast store of tales about Khan's older relative. There was still a strong bond between the two men, and Khan thought it likely his cousin had talked the chief out of retiring just so he could watch over his plane. "Button up now, and take care of that Tark!"

Khan took one last glance at his watch before hitting the starter. The Falcon thought about it a second, shook once or twice, and then bucked with power as the engine rumbled to life. Moving the plane into position with its top still up, Khan craned his neck to watch as the first of his Mirages started down the runway, its delta wings weighed down with bombs. The tailless plane wobbled slightly as it picked up speed, straining but finally pushing itself up off the concrete. A second followed, then a third, before Khan lowered his canopy. He completed a last-second check of his equipment as the fog on the windshield cleared away, then moved ahead to his position at the end of the runway. Tark and his Falcon were right behind him, and the two F-16s strode into the sky together.

The clouds to the east were just beginning to warm with a pink tinge as the fighter escorts caught up with the Mirages. They set a course west of Lahore, preparing to skim down through a weak spot in the Indian border defense.

Their plan was as simple as it was dangerous. They would

drop down to approximately five hundred feet as they crossed the border, and then slip even lower as they approached Bhatinda in India, where there was a formidable radar setup. Taking a right turn to dodge its beams and those from another installation deeper into the Punjab, Khan's Hawk flight would make a sideways V across northern India, heading for its target near Sambhar. There the Mirages would hit two buildings believed to house chemical weapons.

The Indians had placed the buildings close to a residential area, and on a briefing map this morning the intelligence officer had marked out a school about a thousand yards from the targets.

Properly executed, there was no risk of hitting any children and creating a propaganda coup for the Indians; they would be dropping their weapons well before anyone arrived to ring the bell for class. Still, the proximity of civilians was an unfortunate reminder of how serious their business was.

Khan was more worried about getting his Mirages across and back safely than hitting children. With the zags necessary to avoid the air defense, the French-built planes would be flying at the outside limit of their range. Stock-built, the Falcons were even more limited, but the Pakistani improvements had lengthened their legs to the point that they had considerably more margin for error than the Mirages. Not that he intended on lingering any longer than necessary.

''Saddle up, Hawks,'' said Khan over the open radio as he climbed into his lead position. They would use two different communications systems on the mission. Only the two Falcons were equipped with discrete messaging, which was virtually undetectable. Talking to the Mirages meant using the conventional radio; conversations would be kept to an absolute minimum after crossing the border.

Khan watched the Mirages slip alongside him, fanning out in the sky in the spread formation they would use to the border. Tark was playing sheepdog, hanging back to make sure nobody got lost—and no MiG tried to sneak up from behind.

The French fighter-bombers, though at one time promoted

as interceptors, were useless in anything like close air combat; speed bled off their wings so quickly during maneuvers that their best bet was just to run away if attacked. Khan and Tark were both guiding them past the heavy defenses and running interference. Neither the F-16s nor the Mirages were carrying any ground suppression weapons; they were counting on being able to tiptoe in and cut around the radars without being seen.

Khan carefully ran his eyes over his cockpit instruments, then looked outside, inspecting each inch of space around him, trying to remember everything anyone had ever told him. He strove to emulate the best of every commander he'd ever had.

The last thing he looked at before returning his eyes to the HUD was the bright yellow pull handle for the ejector tucked down between his legs.

"OK," he said as the flight reached the first waypoint programmed into the INS flight computer. His right CRT gave a little beep—they were right on course, exactly on time.

The six pilots put their planes into shallow dives and followed the leader. Their altimeters ratcheted downward as they gingerly felt for the ground and the shield it provided to prying radar defenses. Khan flipped his radar off, letting the IRST scan for trouble. The right CRT, keeping track of the preprogrammed mission flight plan, blinked at him.

There was a time not long ago when a fighter pilot would keep track of his course with the help of a paper map clipped to a kneeboard. The black and blue "thought panel" above Khan's right knee was an infinite improvement. When in map mode, the CRT could show his course with as much detail as any map a navigator might study. More importantly, the computer kept track of his position automatically, checking against the laser-ring gyro that clocked each mile to the inch. Preprogrammed with the flight plan and potential alternative routes, it was as efficient as a well-trained secretary. And he could still keep half an eye out ahead as he glanced down at it.

The border.

Khan felt his seat creak as he shifted his weight and leaned the Falcon to his right. He took it still lower, then skidded across into India with a sharp left turn. The pilot glanced through the clear canopy toward the ground below, still darkened with the shadows of night. It was impossible to tell from the air which of the empty fields below belonged to a Muslim, and which to a Hindu.

Safely across, the Pakistani raiders came up a little, flying away from the radar at Bhatinda. Khan's IRST was quiet, and so were the wheat fields below, caring more about the flow of water in their irrigation ditches than the passage of the enemy planes. Though the Indians had ostensibly blacked out their northern cities, there was a glow of lights visible far off to the southeast.

Perhaps it was the huge city of Delhi, Khan thought. Tark's family had escaped from there during the chaos of 1947. The lieutenant still had distant relatives in the metropolis, people he'd never seen: every time riots were reported in the city, he asked Khan if he thought the Sikhs had killed any of his cousins.

Hawk flight took another sharp cut to the east, making for a dead area in the defense coverage between Bhatinda and Hisar. The pre-flight intelligence had been perfect; the Falcons and their Mirages proceeded without a peep from the Indians, swinging back to the west and then correcting south, one more precautionary jink and then a straight run to Sambhar. The Mirages assumed a box-four pattern, separated by about a half mile. As they neared their targets, the attack planes would pull together and close in pairs, one for each target. Each pair leader's plane was equipped with a jamming pod; the gear would be activated before they popped up to hit the buildings, confusing ground defenses.

"You awake back there?" called Khan to Tark over the discrete messaging system. His position indicator gave them ninety seconds to the way-point that marked the start of the last dash to attack.

"Acknowledged," Tark replied.

Khan was just glancing down to recheck his course position when the IRST flickered up a contact. For a brief second two shadows etched a dull line on the corner of his screen, then nothing.

Ordinarily, he'd dismiss it. But his head was tingling; some sort of extrasensory alarm had been set off.

A second later everything in the Falcon's cockpit flashed at once. The six Pakistani planes were being whacked by an enormous ground radar.

A full minute ahead of schedule—the first flaw in their intelligence.

"Beam it and drop," said Khan, giving the prescribed counter-maneuver. ("Beam" meant to turn at a ninety-degree angle to the source, making it difficult for a Doppler-pulse radar to detect the planes.) The Pakistanis pitched their wings and cut sharply to the east. Assuming another radar hadn't been added to the defenses, the repositioning might make their job easier. They'd just slip around the edge here and—

Launch warning—missile on its way.

Not from the ground—it was a plane-launched missile, coming at him from twelve miles away. The warning system could hardly hold it, and there was no trace of a radar painting the target for it.

Somewhere in Khan's brain a file implanted during a now-forgotten training session opened. The missile must be a Russian Alamo AA-10, configured as a long-legged IR device. The missiles came in semiactive and IR varieties. Heat-seekers were usually deadlier, since they didn't need any help once they were launched.

It could only have come from a MiG-29 Fulcrum. The Indians weren't supposed to have the advanced interceptor missiles on the planes, but that was all it could be.

"Take them to the target," Khan told Tark, goosing his plane and pulling hard to his starboard to find the plane that had fired on them. He was surprised to see Tark streaking ahead on a parallel route.

His wingmate should have moved his position forward to meet anything between the Mirages and their targets. Hadn't Khan told him specifically to do that if they encountered any Fulcrums?

He had—and Tark had argued that it would be easier for him to respond if the threat came from the rear. Nevertheless, Khan insisted it was his call—and he had just made it.

He couldn't do much more than grind his teeth. The Mirages would go on their own, and he had the interceptors' missiles to contend with—one of them was heading right for him.

The HUD drew it in crisp outline, the missile driving in like a baseball lined to centerfield. Khan counted off, steady and cool, waited until it was big and fat, then pulled up quickly, tucking the F-16 toward the stars and hitting the flares. The missile scratched its head and then took a course straight for the ground.

Clear, Khan swung back to the south. He switched on the radar and thumbed it to velocity scan, the long-range setting. It ought to be sparkling like a firecracker—the Indians would have gotten relatively close to fire—but the screen remained blank.

Beads of perspiration ran down the sides of his face. It wasn't the tension—the AC had malfunctioned. Though it was still blowing air, the thermostat seemed to have stuck at eighty-five degrees Fahrenheit.

That was the least of his troubles. Tark's F-16 streaked across in front of him as Khan's radar tried desperately to find the enemy planes.

"What the hell are you doing?" said Khan. "Go cover the Mirages."

No response. He didn't have time to repeat the message as his radar finally started earning its keep, automatically flipping through tracking modes to draw a tight box around two MiG-29s. They were approximately sixty miles away, turning back from their evasive maneuvers to make another attack.

Khan watched helplessly as the French Supers launched from his wingmate's plane.

"Tark!"

He'd fired at the first "lock" signal—a good way to guarantee a miss. The weapons were notoriously optimistic.

"These are Fulcrums, Tark," said Khan. "You've wasted

your missiles." Tark did not reply. Khan switched to the open radio, in case something was obscuring the laser communications of the DMS. "They're carrying Alamos. Watch out for a radar lock—they get two missiles apiece, and I'll bet one's IR and one's radar."

The Indians came on a second or two more, then apparently saw Tark's missiles. They fired one each of their own—radar homers, sure enough—and took hard turns away. The Mikoyan designs accelerated, trying to beam the approaching missiles.

Tark banked to the east, pursued by the Indian Alamos. The lieutenant ought to be able to get away from the radar weapons, thought Khan, if he kept his head.

Meanwhile, he went to work on his own shooting solution. With the Indian MiGs concentrating on his wingmate, Khan swung north, hugging the earth, hoping to close unseen. Twenty seconds and he had the two Fulcrums running into his HUD at about fifteen miles out. He wasn't sure whether they could spot him in the clutter or not, but he turned to parallel their course.

"Super One," he said to himself, preparing to launch. The computer had an easy lock and the semiactive radar missile stumbled just a second and then burst away, confident, hurling itself toward the fuselage of the lead MiG. The Indian pilot didn't realize he'd been tagged; Khan detected no evasive maneuvers as he leaned the Falcon to his right, tailing the second MiG.

Accelerating, he fired the second radar missile. Both MiGs suddenly put everything they had into a pair of rolling dives, but it was way too late—the lead plane disappeared from Khan's screen.

The second was still there, barely, the ground clutter and now chaff or something confusing Khan's radar systems. The upshot was clear, though: The second Super had missed.

He couldn't get a fix; the MiG seemed to be spinning back—running away? Khan's helmet nearly touched the cockpit glass as he pushed the Falcon over and screamed toward the Indian plane, trying to spot it visually. But the MiG wasn't running away, it was drawing him in: he was trying to get the F-16 to overcommit, fly by him and take a couple of heat-seekers in the back.

Khan dropped his right wing in the direction he figured the MiG would fly into, and as he pulled up on his stick, there it was.

Just as the two Sidewinders left his wing, Khan's detectors flashed a warning: He was a lock on someone else's scope. The warning didn't flash off as the MiG in front of him exploded; there were more interceptors up here somewhere.

Khan leaned himself into a turn and now the ECM said a radar homer was after him. He struggled to get the missile on his three-nine, perpendicular to his wing, then let go with his chaff and pulled toward it as hard as he could.

The contact disappeared; he braced himself, and in the next moment realized he was still there and the missile had fallen harmlessly away.

Everything was crazy now, bells and buzzers going off indiscriminately. There were three more MiGs in the west, far off, turning.

Khan, quickly scanning the horizon, saw Tark heading toward them.

"Pull off," Khan warned. "They're too much together."

But Tark kept straight at them. What the hell are you doing, Tark? He was hitting his afterburner and then turning to the north, jinking.

Had he just given up? There was no need to make himself a sacrificial lamb—the Mirages should be almost at their targets now.

It took another moment for Khan to finally realize what was happening. Tark was pursued by a missile that had snuck up on him. Somehow he'd let his guard down.

A brilliant red fireball filled the sky where his friend's plane had been. For a moment, it was as if Khan had been hit himself, his head fogged and weightless. Everything was a freaked-out jumble, so many planes coming at him, the ground defense radars snapping on. His body was awash in a salty, rubbery sea. His eyes jumped from the HUD to the multi-purpose showing his location, back and forth, unsure where to concentrate.

Get back to the Mirages, said a voice deep inside his chest. That's what your job is.

Khan's head cleared as he started back toward his flight, flicking up the afterburner finger lifts and kicking the throttle several notches into the avionics bay. The radar flashed on several targets coming out of the north—the Mirages.

No, these weren't Mirages—the Mirages were farther ahead, climbing to start their bombing runs.

Small planes. MiG-21s ready to pounce on the twos in pod formation. The attack planes were dead meat.

"No!" screamed Khan, and the Falcon seemed to hear him, bolting forward as he got a shoot cue on the HUD for the closest MiG. He let loose with a Sidewinder, then punched up the cannon and started firing wildly.

His frenzied attack distracted the MiGs. They broke formation and he followed through, just clearing the debris of the Fishbed his heat-seeker had destroyed. He clicked his HUD back and let off another missile, then banked sharply and went to make sure neither of the other two Indians had continued in on his planes.

His radar detectors were ringing off the hook and the ECM jammed like a madman. The air was a complete magnetic fuzz. But his head was clear.

There was a small puff on the ground back to his right, then another. Suddenly there was a huge column of smoke behind him. The Mirages were streaking past their targets, already looking to saddle up and head back to Sargodha.

Khan drove on the tail end of a MiG and let off his last Sidewinder. There was a satisfying crunch as the missile hit home. Turning to find his planes, he found the tail pipe of another Fishbed trying to steal away. Khan let the Falcon feel its oats as he accelerated to catch up, the belly of the Indian plane swelling in his HUD.

No need for fancy electronics now. Wait until you can read the numbers of the enemy plane, Colonel Benzair had told him long ago. It was an old but sure discipline.

The Indian pilot tried taking Khan farther down on the

deck, but he'd run low on inspiration. The Falcon's M61 punched a huge slot in the cigar-shaped fuselage, a slot that quickly filled with puffs of black smoke. Khan pulled off as the MiG skidded to a flaming end.

"Hawk flight, this is Hawk leader," he said over the mike. "Get on back home. I'll catch up."

"Acknowledged," said Yahya Jamaat, flying the lead Mirage.

"Take them back, Captain," Khan told him as he swooped farther west.

He was out of missiles and had, at most, a half burst of cannon bullets left; if he weren't the leader, Khan would just crank back to his base, outrun anything that took an interest in him. The Fulcrums couldn't be toyed with. But he had to keep his attack planes safe, even if that meant making himself a target. Khan made a slow arc toward the area where he had last seen the planes, his radar beam skipping out ahead but coming back empty.

Was it his fault Tark had been shot down? Shouldn't he have done something more to protect him? Even if he'd pulled a bonehead move, a good commander was responsible for his men.

A warning flashed on the board and Khan tapped his right multi-purpose for an explanation. One of the hydraulic accumulators that helped move the tail control surfaces was malfunctioning. Just what he needed.

He was, however, starting to feel a bit cooler. The air conditioner seemed to be working again.

A few zigs told him the plane was still capable of twisting itself around a pretzel, and for the first time since crossing the border, he let himself relax. The MiGs were probably on the ground by now. He flipped off the Hughes; no need to make himself a target.

Thirty seconds later, his ECM caught an AA-10 missile coming at him. It was almost too late. It took a full second for Khan to react, plunging the plane downward in desperation. The blue sky ran away from the bubble-top canopy, replaced by the dark, unfriendly brown of the earth. Khan had a second of indecision before rolling right. As the sky returned there was a loud snap in his ears, as if the ground had reached up and tried to take a bite of the fuselage.

The explosion rattled him, but he could deal with that. The rudder was a bit loose, but otherwise the electric fly-by-wire controls were compensating perfectly for whatever shortcomings there were in the hydraulics.

As he regained control of the plane, he realized another missile was coming in. Khan dove again, and let off the last of his flares and chaff. This time the explosion was so close that his teeth chattered and he almost lost the plane, the Falcon's nose slipping as he struggled to pull away from the dirt waiting to make his grave below.

When he finally got his nose up, he found himself driving right into a mine field of hanging cannon fire. Khan accelerated blindly, as close to panicking as he had come in an airplane. Explosions bracketed his wings.

A Fulcrum had snuck in off the side at about seven o'clock, and now it was Khan's turn to jink and jive as the two planes played chicken at just under five hundred miles an hour. He wanted to break off but the MiG wouldn't let him, and on the last shift back Khan felt something give behind him as he rolled the plane onto its spine. He quickly pulled out, and though he hadn't planned it, the maneuver enabled him to slip behind the MiG-29.

But this wasn't a Fishbed he was fighting, and after a wink that emptied Khan's gun, the Indian pilot swung back fast enough so that the two planes fell into a harmless orbit—a flat luftberry, in pilot's parlance. The MiG pilot tried to tuck it in, but Khan's hopped-up F-16 was more than a match for him, and he was able to maintain the stalemate while looking for an out.

Khan took two turns before finding a chance to make a break. He lifted the gates and hit the afterburner as the Indian came around heading away from him, going toward the southwest. The PAF pilot struggled to get distance between his plane and the MiG before the Indian could slide into a good position to fire his short-range missiles.

His advantage was barely a breath, and once he heard the launch indicator, there wasn't much Khan could do. The engine behind him was swallowing fuel with abandon, but the pair of Russian-made air-to-air missiles, smaller and lighter, gained quickly.

Don't give up, Khan thought. He pitched the Falcon's nose downward, hoping to gain some speed and maybe lose the missiles in the dust. He didn't have any more flares.

These would probably be Aphids, short-range heat-seekers comparable to the Sidewinders. He'd practiced against them millions of times, but that was small consolation. There were certain situations in which they were practically unbeatable.

This was one of them.

They kept coming. He sunk lower, almost touching the top of the banyan trees lining the fields.

Wasn't going to outrun them.

It was light now, the sun rising. Khan could see the long strands of brown grass and wheat waving in the wind.

"Don't give up!" he told himself. The words were loud and vibrated the whole plane; Khan was screaming into his mask.

He yanked back on the stick a half second before he thought the missiles would hit. The increased angle of attack practically stalled the plane, slowed it down like all hell, almost sent it stuttering to the ground.

But he held it, thank God. One of the missiles, unable to adjust, passed off to the left. The other—

The other exploded under his right side.

"Go!" Khan yelled at his plane. "Just go."

In the long second of silence that followed, the pilot cleared his mind and looked at the words written in English on the yellow handle between his legs: PULL TO EJECT.

If he hesitated too long, there would be no chance. He was very, very low. If the plane spun, he'd lose it, and it would be too late to hit the ball: the ejector would send him twenty feet into the ground. Even as it was, he might not have enough altitude for the chute to work properly.

Pull to eject, Khan.

Come on, Falcon. Come on.

For another long second the plane fluttered there, a bird

winged by a hunter's shot. It shook violently, the engine trying desperately to supply the lift the damaged wing lacked. And then it was as if Allah himself had put a hand to the plane, and righted it—the Falcon leveled out and shot forward, steady, heading back toward the Pakistan border, unpursued.

Islamabad, Pakistan. 7 A.M.

Princess Ghazzala Hussian Raziyya Ali Nizam stood up from the heavy mahogany table she was using as a desk and surveyed the piles of documents littering the library of her house in Islamabad, the Pakistan capital. Twenty-four hours ago, the papers had been in carefully arranged piles, prioritized and segregated by issue and geographic area. Now their jumble reflected the disarray of the last day, sharply contrasting with the well-organized walls of books that surrounded the antique table and the two simple chairs that were the room's only furnishings.

Not that Nizam herself was disorganized. Pakistan's first woman interior minister owed much of her success to her ability to keep track of myriad details. Even now, she knew precisely where each paper she needed was.

More important than her organizational abilities, the forty-two-year-old heir to an ancient line of Mogul princes was adept at turning crises to her advantage. And she saw more potential in this crisis than any she had used over the last ten years to climb to a position of power.

Nizam's goal was not personal aggrandizement. She had no vision of ruling Pakistan, and certainly did not want to follow Benazir Bhutto to become the Muslim country's second female prime minister. On the contrary. Educated at Oxford and the best English public schools, she had too firm a grip on history and politics to have such ambitions.

Her aim was at once simpler and more complicated. Nizam wanted to restore her family's tribal homeland in the hills north of Karachi on the western end of the country. Less than fifty years before, her family had governed the land with wisdom and patience still remembered and praised by the inhabitants; if she could maneuver the government into ceding self-control to the region, her family's restoration was assured.

It would begin very democratically, of course. That's why she had established her political party—a party that during the last election had garnered nearly 80 percent of the votes from the Baluchistan and lower Sind districts her great-grandfather had ruled.

"The cabinet meeting is in fifteen minutes, Princess," said Murwan, entering the room.

"Yes," Nizam told her aide. Murwan had come to work for her family as a boy running errands for her grandfather. As a young girl, she had a crush on the handsome man who gradually became her father's closest confidant. Such feelings had died long ago, but Nizam tended to treat the sixty-year-old aide more as a brother than a retainer. For his part, Murwan was always careful to observe the proper etiquette.

"I would like to suggest again, Princess, that you return to Karachi after the meeting."

"If I see a need."

"If the Indians cut the country in two, you will be stranded here."

"Last night you said they would need three days to do so."

"This morning the reports are much more pessimistic, even the military's," said the aide. "General Chenab has spent all night with Commander Fazal discussing the possibilities of an American cease-fire."

Chenab was the army chief of staff, and a member of the cabinet. But he was merely a puppet for Fazal, the army leader who held the cabinet and government in sway.

"India will certainly accept a cease-fire if its government falls," said Nizam. She had devoted a large part of the night to personal conversations with her Indian contacts. The princess's network in the south was helped immensely by ties with the families there that once ruled the princely states; even the non-Muslims sympathized with her cause. That was natural enough, for if she were to succeed, they too might be able to relive the glory of their ancestors.

"It is difficult to tell if the government will fall or not," answered Murwan. "In any event, we should not take the chance. Here you are cut off from your resources."

Nizam's gut feeling was that the American offer to mediate would be seized by the Indians as well as the Pakistanis. The invasion had more to do with a Sikh power struggle in the military than any actual grievances or even political plans, and this would provide an easy way out.

But an American-brokered cease-fire presented problems for her. Not only did it mean that her country's army would be taken off the hook before it was sufficiently weakened, but it would introduce the Americans as players in any Pakistani power struggle. Her own influence with the Americans was very much on the wane. Only a month ago, the ambassador himself had told her flatly that his country could never back any arrangement "smacking of monarchy." It had taken all of her concentration not to slap the arrogant bastard across the face.

"For the moment, I think it is best to stay here," said Nizam. "It gives me a vantage point for working on the military. We must praise the tower even as we undermine its foundation."

Her aide's answer to the ancient maxim was interrupted by the ringing of a phone. He bowed and walked from the room. Contemplating the difficulties of the situation, she stood to leave for the morning cabinet session. Her clothes—a light blue *salwar kameez,* the traditional long tunic over baggy pants—were perfect; she needed to cut a conservative figure today.

"Princess," said Murwan from the small office directly across from the library. "Could you come here, please?"

"I have to get to the meeting early," Nizam said, stepping from the room. She glanced down the hall and saw her two bodyguards waiting.

"You will want to take this call," said Murwan, holding out the phone.

Nizam sighed and walked into the office.

"I wonder if you could have one of your people meet me

in Karachi tonight,'' said the voice on the other end of the line.

"How are you?'' said Nizam, surprised. Her manner immediately changed; she made her voice more open, welcoming the caller as if it were an old friend from school. "We haven't spoken in so long.''

"The agency is interested in some special assistance. Perhaps Murwan could meet me at the Imperial.''

"But Murwan is here in Islamabad,'' said Nizam. "It is getting difficult to travel back and forth. Still, I suppose something could be arranged. You're coming?''

"I'm in Athens right now.''

"This must be very important.''

"It's crucial.''

"I see,'' said Nizam. "Perhaps I could meet you myself.''

"You?''

"I was planning on returning home this afternoon,'' said Nizam, glancing at her aide. "I don't want to be cut off from my people. You haven't contacted me in so long.''

"The money has always been deposited.''

"Well, yes,'' said Nizam. The insulting reference to the commercial aspects of their arrangement was unintended, and she let it pass. "But there are many facets to our relationship, and money is an unimportant one.''

"I'll be at the Imperial tonight.''

"What is it you need? Information?''

"No. Just a helicopter.''

"Of course, Morena. I am always happy to help the CIA.''

"I have to go.''

Nizam nodded at the phone. "Tonight,'' she said. "I will come myself.'' The connection clicked off at the other end.

"So you've changed your mind?'' Murwan asked as she hung up the phone.

"For the time being. Your argument was a good one.''

Charles de Gaulle Airport, Paris. 8 A.M.

O'Connell unbuckled his seat belt as the airliner rolled down the runway toward the split oval terminal at de Gaulle. His legs were starting to ache. They needed to be in motion. His whole body, his mind, needed the reassurance of movement, something to work off the adrenaline eating away his ligaments and tendons, corroding his muscles and nerve cells. He hated waiting. Waiting made him brood.

One good thing came of the eight hours he spent worrying through different possibilities as they flew over the Atlantic. He realized it would be best not to fly straight into Karachi. Even if the airport remained open, the officials there would be extra cautious. While the odds on getting hung up were not overwhelming, it would be safer to sneak in. And the easiest and quickest way to do that was through southern Iran, which meant dealing with Renard.

Was it just convenience that made him think of the outlaw arms dealer? Or did he want to be tempted once more by the bribes and offers of partnership the expatriate Frenchman would make? Did he subconsciously want to prove to himself that he wasn't the embezzling swine the agency had accused him of being?

Or did he secretly want to give in to temptation? If he didn't believe in the agency anymore, if he didn't believe in his government, what stopped him?

At least the arms dealer would not have kicked him out with phony charges in disgrace if something went sour. His solution would have been much simpler.

O'Connell chuckled perversely.

"What's so funny?"

"I always laugh when I come to Paris," O'Connell told Greeley. He ignored his puzzled look, turning back to the window to watch the plane roll toward the terminal.

Temptation or not, Renard would provide the easiest access to Pakistan. But you didn't just walk in on Renard. O'Connell would have to meet one of his people in Paris to arrange a visit.

Stockman had put a man on the plane to follow them. He was supposed to be deep cover, theoretically unspottable even by O'Connell, but you'd have to be brain-dead not to smell this spook a couple of miles away. Literally—he was wearing the sort of expensive cologne pitched in magazines with photos of men in jockey shorts and legends like, Bring Home Dinner Tonight.

O'Connell watched from the corner of his eye and saw his shadow turn for the thousandth time and give him a casual glance right out of Purposeful Gaze 101. It took a great deal of restraint for O'Connell not to laugh.

It was standard practice to provide covered escort to make sure an agent got where he was going, without interference. The backups—there were generally two—would know nothing about the agent's mission, only that they were to tag along. They were, in fact, on his side. Still, this guy irked O'Connell, especially since he was so clearly incompetent. O'Connell decided to ditch him, partly because he was afraid the bumbler would spook Renard's men when he made contact. It was also possible that Stockman had told him to intercept O'Connell if he deviated from the plan, which called for them to make a connection to Greece.

Besides, it was better on general principles to hide any contact with Renard from Stockman.

Greeley had tossed aside his lap belt the second the plane's wheels touched the ground and was halfway into the aisle as soon as the plane stopped. "Relax," said O'Connell, poking him in the shoulder, "let's hang back a minute."

"Don't we have to make a connection?"

"We have time."

They watched as passengers began filing politely from their seats toward the front exit. A pair of small boys who'd slept through most of the flight stumbled out across the aisle from O'Connell, and for a second the ex-agent's mood lifted: they reminded him of a pair of friends he'd had, brothers, when he'd first come to the orphanage.

The moment evaporated abruptly as Mr. Perfume shot him a glance right out of "Get Smart." When this was over, O'Connell resolved, he'd have Stockman can this guy.

Only when everyone else was in the aisle did O'Connell nod to Greeley. They stood and joined the rear of the procession making its way to the bus that had attached itself to the cabin. A large, seatless coach, the body of the vehicle was attached to its chassis via a set of long scissors that gently lowered it as it eased away from the plane. Staring at the reflection of the interior in the glass, O'Connell noticed a short, mousy woman eyeing them from the corner of the bus—must be the other shadow. She glanced into the reflection in the window and then slipped behind a fat man, away from O'Connell's view, as the bus began moving toward the terminal.

That cinched it.

Last on meant first off, and O'Connell darted through the door as the bus's door whooshed open. "Stick close to me," he hissed at Greeley.

"This part of the plan?"

"Just stick with me," said O'Connell. At the end of the hallway he walked up to one of the customs agents, nodded, and in a French carefully tainted with a Parisian accent, said that he and his companion were traveling on a diplomatic passport. He reached into his left jacket pocket and pulled it out lazily. This was not the standard issue document Stockman had provided. This was an older passport, glommed by O'Connell during a previous tour and infinitely more powerful. Had he considered the matter, the officer might have wondered why the name on the passport—Kevin Daley, an old *nom de guerre*—did not match any on the passenger manifest. But his confidence in the apathy of the French customs office was well founded; the officer gave him a glance, frowned at his stubble and rumpled leather jacket, then waved them both to a door a few feet away.

O'Connell saw the mousy woman grimacing. She and her comrade were well back, and would have to choose between waiting out the line or blowing their covers to pursue him. Either way, he had enough of a lead to lose them.

"Where are we going?" Greeley huffed, barely keeping up.

"To get a car," said O'Connell as he led him into the main area of the airport. He pushed his companion through a door that led to a staircase and started jogging down the double flight of steps.

"What about our next flight?"

"You wanted to see Paris, didn't you?"

"But you said—"

"I changed my mind," said O'Connell, looking over Greeley as he reached the landing. "Tuck your shirt in. The French put a lot of stock in appearances."

"What about our bags?"

"The luggage can go on to Athens without us. It'll confuse them a bit."

"Confuse who?"

"We're being followed," said O'Connell. "That's why we came down here."

Greeley turned and looked toward the top of the stairs.

"It's just agency people. But I don't like working with somebody looking over my shoulder."

"When do we get our bags back?"

"We don't."

"But my only picture of my wife—"

"Don't worry about it," said O'Connell. He spoke louder than he intended, and his voice echoed in the stairwell.

"Don't worry about it?"

"You're telling me you don't have other pictures of your wife?" Though he tried to sound conciliatory, there was a noticeable edge in O'Connell's voice.

"No."

"What about the picture I saw on your wall?"

"That's the one I took. I got that, and I got the one in my wallet."

"Can't be helped," said O'Connell, sincere apology mixing with disgust that much of their lead was being frittered away. His Browning, infinitely more valuable than the photo, was also going to be lost, but that was the way things had to be. *Quod scripsi scripsi.* What I have written, I have written.

O'Connell pushed Greeley through the double doors before he had time to formulate a new protest. The car rental booths were on the left, but there was a line in front of all three.

For a second he considered going straight to the garage and just taking a car, but dismissed that as too risky. O'Connell took a few steps down the hallway, scanning the line to see which one was shortest.

"*Pardon, Monsieur*—can I help you?"

"Sure," said Greeley, who was standing in front of the booth where the woman had just opened a window. "We'd like a car. Right, Mike?"

"What type, please?"

"Oh, a nice big one," said Greeley. "With air conditioning."

"*Nous aurons le plus petit possible, s'il vous plaît,*" O'Connell told the woman, asking for the smallest they had. The smaller the car, the easier it would be to get through the streets.

"How do you wish to pay?"

"American Express," said O'Connell, pulling the Platinum card out of his wallet. He reached into his jacket and took out the passport Stockman had supplied. "*Voila,*" he said to the girl, who smiled indulgently and continued filling out the form, speaking English even after he answered several questions in what he knew was perfect French. Her thin, freckled face bulged with the insincere smile of a Parisian indulging a foolish foreigner.

It took awhile to finish the form, and with each new question O'Connell's impatience grew. He nearly went cross-eyed trying to watch for their CIA tails and appear nonchalant at the same time.

"It's a gray Fiat on level B, at the end of our marked parking area," said the woman, reading from the printout when the paperwork was done. "If there are any problems, please come back here and I will assist you."

"There's no way we can get the suitcases back?" Greeley asked O'Connell as the woman handed him the keys.

"You have a problem with your luggage?"

"No," said O'Connell.

"We changed our plans," said Greeley, ignoring O'Connell's tug. "We wanted to do a little sight-seeing."

"Oh, the airline will retrieve them for you," said the young woman. "I'm sure that they wouldn't have put them on the other plane if you did not check in. You didn't check in, did you?"

Greeley shook his head.

"Here—let me get the service desk for you," said the young woman. She looked up at O'Connell as her thin fingers danced over the numbers. There was a slight trace of a smile on her lips.

"What was your flight number?" she asked.

"Seventeen-thirty."

"And your name, sir?"

"James Greeley. And Mike O'Connell."

As O'Connell reached his hand to hang up the receiver, the mousy woman rounded the corner. Too late now. He'd have to lose them in Paris.

The Browning would be handy, at least—particularly if Greeley didn't learn to keep his mouth shut.

"Michael O'Connell," O'Connell said, correcting Greeley. He listened as the woman spoke in rapid French over the phone. Was she just a typical French clerk or an agency plant? It was awful coincidental that the station had opened up just when they needed it.

Or maybe Greeley was the agency plant.

If you look for the devil, you will find him.

That was straight from Father Fran. But had he meant it as a warning against paranoia? No way—the Jesuits didn't go around wearing rosary beads for nothing.

"Ah," said the woman, hanging up the phone. "They have the bags and will deliver them here," she told Greeley. "The computer noticed that you did not check in for the connecting flight, and they were routed right to the desk. It is quite a sophisticated system."

"Great," said O'Connell.

"Is something wrong, sir?" the woman asked him.

"No," he said as Mr. Perfume passed by. "Everything's dandy."

"Pardon me," said Greeley. "Is there a restroom around here?"

"Oh yes," said the woman, pointing down the hallway.

"Be right back," said Greeley.

O'Connell took him by the elbow and steered him out of the woman's earshot. "Listen, from here on out, you sit

108

quiet and let me do the talking. We're not dealing with girl scouts, all right?''

''But—''

''No buts,'' said O'Connell. ''Do what I say, OK?''

''OK, OK,'' said Greeley. ''Can I take a leak or what?''

O'Connell returned to the rental desk, where the woman was now helping a middle-aged Englishman in a faded overcoat. His French was horrible, but she nodded politely and played along, speaking French slowly so he could understand.

The mousy female spook, meanwhile, was standing a few booths down, ordering up her own car. From the frown on her face, you'd think the agency was making her pay for it out of her own pocket.

''So, we moving out or what?'' said Greeley, suddenly materializing next to him. He had both of their bags.

O'Connell took his suitcase and silently led the way down the corridor. The decor and architecture on this level were much more overtly institutional than upstairs, with its wider spaces and open ceiling, but de Gaulle always reminded him of a World's Fair exhibition he had visited as a child. There was an early-sixties feel of optimism and faith in the perfectibility of man to the sleekly polished walls and their bright speckles of color.

Greeley clambered into the elevator behind him, his big shoes clopping and scraping along, as if he were a two-legged Clydesdale. A businessman trotted up just as the door closed; Greeley saw him and stuck his hand in the door, holding the elevator for him. O'Connell frowned, but it was too late to say anything. The man, an American who looked like he was already suffering a severe case of jet lag, punched the same button O'Connell had, then stood against the wall, rubbing his eyes as the elevator descended.

''Couldn't sleep on the plane. This is only my second trip to France,'' said the man, a skinny fellow about O'Connell's height in his mid-thirties. His rumpled suit was perfectly tailored, and he had an expensive-looking overcoat under one arm. ''Level B's where the rentals are, right?''

O'Connell nodded.

"What do you do?" Greeley asked him.

Good going, Greeley, thought O'Connell. How the hell are you going to answer when he asks us the same question?

"We have a big thermostat contract with Groupe Bulle," said the man, widening his eyes in one last desperate attempt to drag himself to full consciousness. "I'm with Freeman Thermocontrols. Ever hear of us? Biggest company in Highland, New York."

Much to O'Connell's relief, the elevator stopped and opened its doors, ending the conversation.

"Wait a second," said O'Connell, grabbing Greeley's sleeve as the door opened on Level B. Their companion ignored them, shuffling out of the elevator toward his rental car. "Don't go starting conversations with everybody, for cryin' out loud."

"Just trying to be sociable."

"The cars are over there. We go straight for them, OK? Quietly. Remember that we're being watched."

Greeley nodded. Starting down the aisle of cars, they quickly caught up to their elevator mate. Obviously still bleary-eyed, he walked half-bent over as he checked plates against the key in his hand.

"That's got to be ours," said O'Connell, pointing Greeley toward the gray Fiat two cars from the end of the row. He took a few steps toward it and then felt himself diving toward the ground, his reflexes a whole second ahead of the conscious part of his brain.

"Down," he yelled as the bullets flew into the cars around them.

Near the Indus River, Pakistan. 11:45 A.M.

Lt. Gen. Arjun Singh stepped out of the house trailer he was using as his forward headquarters and began walking toward the jeep parked on the road 150 yards away. He was in a foul mood, and even his sergeant stayed well back as the general stormed up the incline toward the vehicle.

Arjun had just gotten off the phone with Brigadier General Shastri, the poet-philosopher masquerading as his second-in-command. Shastri had devoted much of the conversation to suggestions that they take a defensive position and await a Pakistani counterattack. Arjun had exploded, telling him to follow his orders, the most important being to make sure there was enough petrol for the Fifth Armor's rapid advance.

General Arjun had once more changed his plan, adapting himself to circumstances. He wanted to slash westward immediately, passing up the few northern objectives that had not yet been achieved. The Pakistanis had foolishly assumed that he was preparing to attack Karachi, and were busy concentrating their troops to the southeast of his salient. Meanwhile, troops in the northern and western ends of the country were rushing to Kashmir to deal with the assaults there. The road to Lahore was open.

"New Delhi predicts a cease-fire by tomorrow night," Shastri had said weakly.

"Exactly," replied Argun, slamming down the phone. Exactly, he repeated to himself now as he reached the roadway and got into the jeep. There was no way he could get to Lahore by tomorrow. But if the cease-fire didn't stop him, he could take Multan before they had set up a serious defensive line. Once that was accomplished, it would take only a few hours to cut Lahore off.

If he moved quickly, he would be in a position to take the ancient capital of the Sikhs early next week.

Multan was more than 200 miles away. Could Arjun get there in a day? Two days? Securely?

How much of his force could he spare? How bold could he be without being foolish? The two airborne units were already en route to staging areas. He could throw everything up the Indus River valley but the infantry reserve. He'd bring them across to assume the defensive positions on the Karachi side. The Muslims would undoubtedly attempt a counterattack there once they realized what was going on, but if his forces moved fast enough, it would be irrelevant. His defensive lines could fall back, trailing his advance. The territory he had here he wasn't interested in keeping.

"Sergeant Teg, let's go!" thundered Arjun. "I need to be at Eighth Division. Now, Sergeant!"

His aide said nothing as he trudged up the hill. Arjun continued to work out a plan of attack in his mind, trying to decide how weak he could leave his northern flank as he turned to run up the river valley.

If he were in charge of the Pakistani army, he would mount a sweeping counterblow from the south, striking the underbelly of the Indian advance. But the Pakistanis had neither the imagination nor the logistics to undertake such a bold move.

The damn cease-fire would get in the way. He had to do his best to present the politicians with a fait accompli.

Arjun had just returned his impatient glare toward Sergeant Teg when the heavy sound of jet engines began shaking the ground. It took another moment for the general to compute their direction and realize they were not his.

The two Sikhs dove for the ground as a triple-A battery began firing. Arjun, cursing as he crawled toward the back of his vehicle, wondered why he hadn't heard the whoosh of the mobile SAMs parked nearby. Sensing what the target of the attack was, he rose from the dust and started toward the trailer. Sergeant Teg rose rose as well, futilely hoping to restrain his commander. "Get out," the general yelled to the people inside. "Take cover."

Arjun had taken two steps down the embankment when he saw the blur streaking out of the sky. In the next quarter of a second he understood that he was throwing his body down; in the next, that he was bracing for an explosion. The third quarter of a second was a silent, peaceful pause; the fourth, too, was silent, though it was so heavy with anticipation that it could hardly be called peaceful. The fifth was all tension, still silent. And the sixth, the sixth finally was a huge rush of air, a foot kicking him in the back and scooping him up the hill, rubbing his face in the dirt along the way.

He rolled on the macadam, tumbling across the roadway like a child at play.

The sound of the explosion, the loud, crashing cough of a 500-pound bomb igniting, didn't come for another second or so. When it did it was muffled. Fortuitously for the general, the bomb exploded behind the rear of the trailer, and not the front. The miss—the pilot had been aiming for the exact middle of the structure—was insignificant as far as the building and its occupants were concerned, but it made all the difference to Arjun, though he was in no position to appreciate it.

Stretched out on the highway, his lower body flaming with pain, the general screamed at the air force and the SAMs that were supposed to protect his men. Lying on his back, he watched the attack continue, jets streaking above, triple-A flailing about without visible effect. The sector was being hit by a full squadron of planes in a coordinated, well-organized strike. The general twisted around to get a glimpse of the trailer. Smoke was pouring from one end.

My people, he thought. I've got to help them.

There was a loud buzz in his ears, a hiss like a steam shower. Arjun rolled over onto his stomach, stood and immediately fell. He couldn't get his hands out in front to break his fall, and his chin took a tremendous bounce off the pavement.

Groaning, he struggled to get his arms under him and tried once more to stand. This time he fell down the hill, skidding on his side and then rolling for a few yards.

The steam grew louder, drowning out the other sounds. He began crawling on his hands and knees, desperate to rescue his people. A few yards from the door, the heat began to sear his face. His head burned with its own fever, and his eyes and sinus passages felt as if they would boil away.

The general struggled to his knees, then reached up to open the door.

The knob was white hot. His hand melted to it.

Incredible, piercing pain. But then nothing, as if his brain had stepped back from his body, become an observer shouting instructions from afar. Still gripping the door, Arjun looked down and realized his legs were riddled with metal. A trail of blood led back up the hill.

It took all of his strength to pull his hand away from the

door. When finally it came off he lost his balance and fell backward to the ground.

By now the hiss had grown unbearably loud. Arjun heard the screams not of his men, but of millions of souls long dead.

For what seemed like hours he was aware of nothing. Then he sensed that people were standing above him, and he was being lifted gently, placed in the back of a truck.

Charles de Gaulle Airport, Garage Level B. 8:50 A.M.

Rolling on the pavement as bullets splattered through the parking garage, the first thing O'Connell thought was that it was a good thing he'd let Greeley take a leak. Otherwise the old man would be swimming in piss right now, and he'd have to smell that the whole way to Paris.

O'Connell got to his knees behind the front of the car, trying to figure out where the gunfire was coming from. The bullets were from one gun, an automatic weapon.

The funny thing was, this was the first time he'd ever been fired on while in the CIA.

Greeley was hunched under the car a few feet away. "Stay down," O'Connell told him.

"No shit."

Another long burst. The shooting was coming from two rows over, across a diagonal. The poor bastard who'd been looking for his car was moaning on the ground. There was a scream from the other end of the garage, and the sound of heels running away, but whoever had fired at them hadn't moved.

"Don't shoot unless you have a clear shot at him," said O'Connell loudly as he leaped from behind one car to another, trying to see their attacker.

Greeley was either too scared or smart enough not to say anything back. The ruse worked, in a way. Another burst of gunfire raked the cars.

"Stay down," yelled O'Connell as an alarm sounded.

"I ain't getting up," grunted Greeley. A car began

screeching down the lane in front of them.

"Over the barrier, quick," said O'Connell, realizing that whoever was shooting at them would have a better angle once in the roadway. As he spoke he flipped himself back over the small concrete wall that separated the rows of parked cars. Greeley hesitated a second, then got up and dove over, his arms spreading out in front of him as the gunman let off another burst. He landed with the soft squash of a tomato hitting the pavement, but seemed OK.

There were more screams and shouts from the direction of the stairwell. A Peugeot sped down their aisle; O'Connell caught a glimpse of a figure leaning out its window, then ducked as another burst of bullets sprayed the cars around him. By the time he raised his head again, the Peugeot was speeding toward the exit.

His CIA tails had been assigned to do more than just follow him. O'Connell could taste the venom in his mouth—Stockman had set him up again. He didn't want the planes destroyed. He wanted the only person who could tie their existence to the CIA eliminated.

O'Connell's rage was almost uncontrollable. He saw the Snowman in his lair, laughing now, laughing at how clever he had been to maneuver O'Connell out of the country where he could be killed with no possibility of a Senate inquiry. It would cost the life of another innocent victim—Greeley, the pilot—but what was one more?

Two more—the man who'd gotten into the elevator with them was lying across the aisle from their car, a large puddle of blood forming beneath him.

O'Connell was paralyzed by his anger. His eyes were open but everything around him was black, as if someone had put a hood over his head.

"Mike—we better get the hell out of here," shouted Greeley.

The alarm was ringing through the garage. The machine-gun toting militiamen who patrolled the airport upstairs would arrive any second.

"Don't call me Mike," said O'Connell, jumping up. "My name's Michael. I hate Mike."

He grabbed the baggage and threw it in the backseat, plunging into the car to yank Greeley's side open. As he straightened up he slid the key into the ignition, started the car, then cranked the Fiat out of the parking space with one leg still hanging out the side.

"Jesus, I'm getting all banged up here," said Greeley, crashing against the dashboard as O'Connell stepped on the gas. "Look at my arm."

"The scrape on your face is bigger," answered O'Connell, wheeling the car through a turn, watching for another ambush.

The little Fiat's four-cylinder engine groaned as he revved it over 7,000 RPM before slapping it from first to second. The car whined, the front end bobbing with the surge of power to the wheels.

"Don't *you* kill us," said Greeley as he was thrown against the door by a sharp turn.

"Put your seat belt on."

"That guy dead?"

O'Connell didn't answer.

"They after him or us?"

"What do you think?" he said sharply. Greeley bristled but said nothing.

The Peugeot had crashed through the parking attendant's barrier. O'Connell figured there was no reason not to follow the precedent. He saluted as he crossed out onto the roadway, following the sign for the A1 and Paris. Greeley remained silent as O'Connell muscled his way into the traffic, accelerating and dodging into the far lane as quickly as he could find an opening. The Peugeot was nowhere to be seen.

The late summer fields lining the highway were filled with the bright yellow heads of sunflowers, millions of them turning their faces toward the sun, oblivious to the stream of midmorning traffic. They gave a placid, rural air to the approach to France's largest urban center, an army of green soldiers silently greeting visitors. The pastoral scene belied the very technology that had made it possible; it was possible to look at the plants and believe you were back in the preindustrial age. A little daydreaming and a series of rustic huts might appear, with a castle in the distance.

O'Connell didn't have time to gaze at the scenery. The little car couldn't go fast enough and the traffic he was weaving through was too ragged for O'Connell to feel secure. Every time a vehicle approached he cringed.

The one thing he figured they had going for them was the fact that they'd deviated from the plan. Stockman had probably wanted the hit to take place in Pakistan, and couldn't have provided more than a token backup at the airport. Nor did the people he was using seem like first-string.

"You think they're still behind us?"

"They got to be around somewhere," said O'Connell. "And they may have somebody else tagging along."

"Who are they?"

"I don't know."

Greeley raised his eyebrow as if to indicate that he knew O'Connell was lying, but said nothing. O'Connell, meanwhile, spotted a green BMW several cars back in the middle lane that seemed to be shadowing his movements.

He was a sitting duck on the highway. They could pick their spot.

"So?"

"So what, Greeley?"

"You see them or what?"

"I can't tell."

"What we ought to do is pull off the side of the road," said his companion. "Make them commit."

O'Connell glanced at him as if he were crazy, annoyed that an amateur was daring to give him advice. But Greeley might be right—it would force their shadows to make a decision. Either hit them right away, or pull off the road ahead and wait.

If he got them to pass him and then pull off the road, at least he'd know who was after them.

And if they pulled off behind him with their machine guns going?

Better to see it coming.

"Reach back into my suitcase," said O'Connell, putting his right hand on Greeley's shoulder. "There's a gun at the top of my bag. See if you can get it without making it too obvious.''

Greeley slithered down in his seat and slid his left arm back behind O'Connell's seat. It took awhile, but he managed to fish out the pistol.

''What we're going to do is stop by the side of the road, like we're getting something out of the trunk. I want you to stay on the right side of the car. Got it?''

''Uh-huh.''

''If there's any trouble,'' said O'Connell, ''you dive for the ground and get into those sunflower fields.''

A large green truck filled O'Connell's mirror as he brought the Fiat to the shoulder of the road. O'Connell's chest tightened to a slate. His heart bounced off it like a Spalding against the stoop of the orphanage where he'd played after lessons. Then the truck passed, and O'Connell could see that no one had followed them to the shoulder.

''Let's see how this goes,'' he said, practically leaping out of the car. Once out, he walked slowly, deliberately, making as if he'd left something in the trunk. He kept one eye toward the traffic, his pulse racing. Beneath his jacket he switched the gun to his right hand, and there was just enough moisture on his fingers to make them glide across the stock, his forefinger slipping into the trigger ring.

''What do you think?'' said Greeley, walking back toward him. His lip trembled a little. For some reason that seemed vaguely reassuring; he was scared, but at least capable of keeping his guts together.

''They may wait for us up ahead,'' said O'Connell. ''I'm not sure how many people are after us.''

''Who is it who's gunning for us?''

''You wouldn't believe it if I told you.''

''Try me.''

''Might as well throw our bags back here.''

''Who is it?''

If he told him it was the CIA, how would Greeley react? The guy had been in the air force, and probably a part of the reason he'd come along was that he thought he was doing his patriotic duty. Amateurs were like that—they thought the agency was apple pie and George Washington.

On the one hand, O'Connell ought to just cut Greeley loose; he needed maximum flexibility now. On the other, there was no reason he wouldn't still be valuable. Maybe more valuable.

He'd have to deal with Renard. It was the only way to come out of this alive.

And rich. But you'd have to be rich to survive.

"It's the Russians," O'Connell told Greeley, opening the trunk while still scanning the traffic. "They must have got wind of all this somehow."

"Jesus, the Russians?"

"We'll go into Paris and make sure we've ducked these guys, and then I'll get you a ticket to go home."

"Go home? What makes you think they'll let me?"

O'Connell gave him a half shrug. The trunk popped open with a sudden snap that momentarily diverted his attention from the road. He quickly turned back, then began putting the bags in with one hand, keeping the other on the gun. He had to face away from Greeley as he kept his eyes focused on the roadway—so much the better for dramatic effect.

"What are you going to do?" Greeley asked.

"Make new travel arrangements. We're getting shot at. You didn't sign on for that."

"Yeah, but—who are you going to get to fly the plane?"

O'Connell's shrug this time was almost too nonchalant. "I don't know. Probably just find a pilot somewhere."

"It's going to be impossible if he hasn't flown the plane before," said Greeley. "Believe me, you need someone with experience."

"Yeah?"

"I don't mind being shot at."

"Come on."

"Look, I figured there was going to be some rough stuff. This is the CIA we're working for, right? I can handle it."

"You sure?"

"Yes, damn it."

He felt a twinge of guilt. But Greeley was valuable now. Long-term, he'd be a problem, but for the moment it made no sense to get rid of him. Besides, if the agency was willing to ice O'Connell, they wouldn't hesitate to eliminate Greeley. Cutting him loose would be like signing his death certificate.

What difference did it make if they killed him, or if O'Connell did when he was done?

He didn't have to kill him. He could explain the facts of life, cut him in—Greeley was in no position to argue.

But just as O'Connell began feeling almost protective, Greeley started nervously reciting a story about the time he and his wife had been to Paris.

"You have any sunglasses?" O'Connell interrupted.

"Sure." Greeley reached over and, propping up the large, yellow-sided suitcase so he could get into it easily, fished through a twisted jumble of pants and shirts. Finally he found the sunglasses.

"You want to kiss your wife's picture or anything while we got it open?"

Greeley froze, then snapped the luggage closed and stalked away.

O'Connell watched him get into the car. He didn't slam the door; he closed it gently, quietly, with so much dignity that O'Connell couldn't help feeling like an ass.

O'Connell sighed, closed the trunk and walked back around the car. "I'm sorry," he said as he slid into the Fiat. "I was out of line."

Greeley said nothing.

Finally I get him to shut up, O'Connell thought, and I feel guilty.

"Paris has probably changed a lot since you were here last," offered O'Connell after they had gone a few miles without spotting the Peugeot or anyone else.

"Yup."

"How long were you married?"

"Thirty-two years."

"Long time."

"You married?"

"No."

"Think about it?"

"Not really," said O'Connell.

"Why not?"

"Other priorities."

"You ain't gay, are you?"

O'Connell laughed. "What if I were?"

"Just asking," said Greeley. His voice had a serious tone to it, still reserved; he was willing to forgive O'Connell for the crack about his wife, but the ritual had to move along at the proper pace.

"No, I ain't gay."

O'Connell noticed a light blue Ford with what looked like a woman driver pulling from the shoulder onto the entrance ramp behind them as they passed an interchange. He slid the Fiat into the far left lane and picked up speed, giving the Ford as wide a berth as possible.

"What do we do next?" Greeley asked.

"Once we make sure we're not being followed, I'm going to go see someone who can arrange a meeting with a friend of mine in Iran."

"Iran?"

"Very misunderstood country." O'Connell checked his mirrors and changed lanes again.

The Ford was now behind him in the left lane. Though it kept its distance, it was following them.

"I think I've found our friends," he announced. "We'll shake them in Paris. I know just the place."

Just the place was the traffic circle around the Arc de Triomphe, where every driver in the city converged for a monumental fifteen-second game of chicken. O'Connell took his time getting there, flowing along with the city traffic after he left the *autoroute*. Their tail had no problem keeping up, and was two cars back as O'Connell turned off the Boulevard Pereire onto the Avenue de la Grande Armée, the huge Arc dead ahead. The broad boulevard was lined by trees, and the light morning haze added a romantic sheen to the huge monument that commemorated Napoleon's triumphs.

"Now this looks like Paris," said Greeley.

"Hang on," said O'Connell, downshifting as he hit the gas. He plunged ahead into the traffic, pulling the car sharply to the right in the whirl around the monument. Then he cranked back to the left and around another car, now at the vortex, then back to the far edge again, accelerating in a crisscross that brought him to the far side of the Arc near the Champs-Élysées. He caught a glimpse of the Ford gingerly entering the traffic at the other side as he cut in front of a bus.

"Hell—"

"Just hang tight," said O'Connell, flooring the little Fiat and nearly running over the poor slob of a policeman posted at the near end of the circle, ostensibly to direct traffic, but more likely to test his courage. He swung back to the outside, cut off a Renault and escaped the flood of invective by charging down Victor Hugo the wrong way. Ducking quickly up one side street then back across another, he plunged through an intersection and down the roadway, ignoring the lights, traffic and horns.

"If you look out my side of the car you'll see the Eiffel Tower," said O'Connell, but Greeley was too busy holding on to the dashboard to appreciate his humor.

"You're crazy," he said as O'Connell charged down another street, just missing a car coming off an alleyway.

"You should see me in a helicopter."

It took thirty minutes' worth of side streets to get over to the south of Paris where Simon, a transplanted Belgian who took care of much of Renard's European business, worked. O'Connell, once certain he was no longer being followed, settled on a parking space a few blocks from the café where Simon would be.

"Come on," he said to Greeley. "Let's get some coffee."

They got out and began picking their way through the irregular network of streets. O'Connell took no chances. They entered and exited several buildings and doubled back on their trail until he was certain no one was behind them.

It was the first time he had been in Paris in three years, but the large stone buildings, with their off-white facades and occasional awnings, were as familiar as if he'd left yesterday. Simon's café was located halfway down a quiet street in an old residential area. Flanked by a *patisserie* and a used-plumbing shop, it was an improbable branch office for an international arms dealer, but that was the idea. Aside from certain precautions—the shop was checked daily for explosive devices and bugs, and no car could park on the block without being examined by one of Simon's men—there was little to differentiate it from a thousand similar establishments in the city.

Simon didn't own it, but his contributions to the cash flow had put the proprietor's three sons through medical school. He used it as his office year-round, sitting at a sidewalk table one row from the curb in decent weather and inside in bad. He considered himself a connoisseur of legs, and once had bet O'Connell $50,000—actually, the difference in their haggling prices over a shipment of AK-47s bound for Afghanistan—that a better pair wouldn't walk by in five minutes. He was honest enough in such matters to concede when he lost barely a minute later.

"Keep your mouth shut," O'Connell told Greeley. "This guy will kill us if he thinks we're playing games with him."

"They got a bathroom in this place?"

O'Connell was too busy scanning the block and the café to comment on the strength of the old man's bladder. Finally, he was enjoying a piece of luck. Everything was as he remembered—and there was Simon.

O'Connell slid into the chair across from the arms dealer with a smile. "How are you these days?" he asked.

As he said the words, he felt his whole body relax. He was relatively safe here; the arms dealer's bodyguards controlled the block. And he'd done this many times before; it felt natural, good to be back.

Simon's white head popped up from the *Le Monde* crossword. "Mr. O'Connell," he said, as if he had been waiting all morning for him to show up. "I am very well." He nodded at his pair of bodyguards two tables away. "What brings you to Paris? Business or pleasure?"

"Business," replied O'Connell, studying his face. Simon's mustache was trimmed to a thin line above his lip, his full head of hair carefully tossed to appear as if it did not receive any attention. He wore an expensive suit, custom-made in a small shop not far from where they sat. O'Connell remembered that Simon stopped there every other Wednesday to check on the progress of some order or another. Early in their dealings, he had tagged along on one of these visits. Two weeks later, the arms dealer presented him with a suit the tailor had made solely by glancing at him during the visit.

Ironically, he hadn't taken the suit—it was against agency policy to accept gratuities.

The waiter came up. O'Connell asked for two coffees, then pointed Greeley in the direction of the bathroom. One of the bodyguards got up from the table and followed the old man into the back.

"Who is your friend? If I may ask."

"Helping me on a project," said O'Connell. "Something I need your help on."

"Me?" Simon smiled, leaning back as the waiter brought the coffees, including a new cup for him. "But I'm retired."

"You've been retired for twenty years," said O'Connell.

"Yes, but now I'm really retired," said Simon, picking up the small white cup and bringing it to his lips, where he blew on it. O'Connell spooned a sugar cube into his. He wasn't much of a coffee drinker, and French coffee was inevitably bitter.

"You've given up your estate on the Loire?"

Simon smiled. "Why would I do that?"

"If you were really retired," said O'Connell, "you'd spend all your time there."

"I like Paris."

"You like the Loire better."

"Yes," laughed Simon. "And how might I help you?"

"How about two passports for old time's sake?"

"A passport," said Simon, waving his hand. "That is such an easy thing."

"A French one," said O'Connell. "For my friend, too."

"*Je comprends*. And where will you be going?"

"Iran."

"To buy some rugs, no doubt."

"I have to see Renard."

The lip beneath the mustache wrinkled, but Simon said nothing. O'Connell lifted the coffee cup and took a small sip. It was as hot and strong as he expected.

Greeley returned, his feet shuffling slowly. O'Connell ordered a *café grande* for him.

"What are you doing these days?" Simon asked. "We haven't seen you since your unfortunate fall from grace."

"I wouldn't believe everything I heard."

"Oh, we had no doubt that it was a setup," said Simon, a little too smoothly.

"I'm back working on something."

"You're back with the CIA? Now that's interesting."

O'Connell shrugged. It was better to let Simon think he was still connected with the agency; it gave him a little more leverage.

"Can you contact Renard for me?"

Simon shrugged. Favors naturally required some possibility of being repaid, and the Belgian was having trouble seeing the angle. "He does get testy sometimes, when he is bothered by trivial matters."

"Yes. Well," said O'Connell, rising. "Tell him I was asking for him. Come on, Greeley."

The old man looked like he was going to complain that he hadn't had his coffee yet but apparently thought better of it, reluctantly rising and following O'Connell as he walked from the table.

It can't happen, O'Connell thought to himself. The idea that had first entered his mind surreptitiously as a dark joke, the notion that he would offer to steal an atomic bomb and with Renard's help become a very rich man, was just a wild, evil fantasy. The theft couldn't happen without Renard, and he couldn't see Renard without help from Simon. He would have to find some other way to survive.

There was an incredible, inexplicable flood of relief as he stepped away from the table.

"Wait," said Simon. O'Connell stopped at the edge of the street. "Maybe I can arrange something."

He turned around. The block, the world narrowed down to one table, one small little man with a thin mustache who put up his hand and motioned to one of his aides for a telephone.

Sargodha Air Base, Pakistan. 8:30 A.M.

Khan's hand shook when he finally let go of the stick.

He'd shut the engine off and the battered Falcon had wheeled itself to a halt on the runway apron near the hangars, but it felt as if it were still vibrating with flight. The pilot popped the canopy, and for a moment stared silently at the clear sky above. Absentmindedly, he pulled his glove off and began running the fingers of his right hand gently along the controls. He caressed them for awhile, not conscious of the specific items he touched, the identity or purpose of the buttons or knobs. His mind had shut itself off, accepting input only through the hands, registering only sensations of smooth and rough, hot and cold.

For two or three minutes he was lost in this tactile meditation, a newborn trying to make sense of the world immediately around him. Finally he unhooked himself from the seat and clambered out of the plane, still in a daze.

"Major," said the crewman who had come up the ladder to assist him. "Sir?"

Khan handed him his helmet and slipped down past him. On the ground, he bowed toward Mecca and prayed thanksgiving, then began his postflight inspection.

The front of the plane and its wing were fine. The tail was another matter—a good hunk of it had been left behind in India. The engine outlet, which normally stuck out under the rudder like a stubby cigar beneath a Jimmy Durante nose, was a mangled wreath of metal. Both tail planes were chewed-up stubs; the rear ventral fins were completely gone. The rudder itself was intact, though it seemed to be drooping half out of the assembly. Its static dischargers—stubby antennalike pieces of metal that hung off the back—were gone. So was the rear RWR group and part of the top edge of the tail.

What was left of the plane was black. Fat carbon streaks

extended up the fuselage to the wings, sooty marks of the claws that the Falcon had just barely shaken off.

"Are you OK, sir?" asked the crew sergeant, who'd joined the other men staring at the plane in disbelief.

Khan had met the crew this morning, but at the moment couldn't remember a single name. "Yes," he said softly.

"It's a miracle that you brought it in, Major."

The pilot continued around to the front of the plane. Sergeant Dad Ali, his old crew chief, came huffing up. "You're OK," the chief shouted at him, his voice filled with incredulity as well as relief. "Syyid, your plane—"

"Sergeant, are the Mirages all in?"

Ali had to look at the other crew chief, who nodded. "Yes."

"Tark?"

This time, the crew chief shook his head.

He'd seen him go down himself, and yet there was something inside that refused to believe that Tark had screwed up so badly that he'd gotten himself shot down.

Logic should have told him to keep his head on tight. You have to act like a machine, go down the list, not give up.

If logic had failed, luck should have saved him. The same luck, or God's grace, that had saved Khan.

Had Khan followed the wrong strategy? Certainly he was right to insist he was the one to tangle with any Fulcrums they encountered; the results of the dogfight had proven that. What would Colonel Benzair have done?

He would have found some way to prevent Tark's death.

For the Mirage pilots, the flight had gone exceedingly well: their targets had been hit and completely destroyed. Even considering the loss of Tark, the overall mission was a success. Assuming all of Khan's kills were confirmed, the Indians had lost two MiG-29s, and four of the inferior Fishbeds. He had also gained important information about the Fulcrums and their advanced missiles.

In two days of flying, Khan had taken out a dozen planes, his victories limited only by his plane's ability to carry spears to the fray. While most of his kills had come against airplanes and systems Khan considered almost as obsolete as biplanes, he had also acquitted himself well when surprised by the best models in the Indian air force. There was no question that Khan was every bit as good a flier as the drills and tests had shown him to be.

But he'd lost Tark. And the absence of his friend weighed heavily as his small squadron reviewed the mission. Not even his meticulous description of the Fulcrums and their missiles for the intelligence officers could break the depression he felt growing on him. Talking mechanically of how he dodged the missiles, he began ruminating on the fact that he too should have been shot down. There was no way the Falcon should have been able to fly in the condition he'd returned it. No physical way.

One of General Hussain's aides knocked on the door as the session drew to a close and asked him to report to the wing commander "as soon as convenient." Warily, Khan trudged to the small building at the far end of the administrative offices where Hussain's was located.

There were no photos of planes or even the seemingly mandatory poses with members of the general staff on the walls of Ghulan Hussain's office. Nothing interfered with the deep, rich tones of the imported paneling. The desk, the files and the rest of the furniture were all handwrought cherry, and there was no clutter of papers or reports to detract from their highly shined surfaces.

General Hussain, who at five-nine weighed a bit over two hundred pounds, waved the pilot into an overstuffed chair as soon as the secretary let him in. Khan sat and was immediately swallowed by the cushions.

"You've done a tremendous job," said the general.

Khan nodded. He wasn't sure why Hussain had called him here—perhaps to ball him out for losing Tark and the precious Falcon.

"How is your uncle?"

The air marshal's chief of staff, Nur Khan, was the pilot's cousin—technically, his first cousin once removed—but Khan let that pass. Nur was, in age and in relationship, more like an uncle than a cousin.

"Very well, the last time I spoke to him."

"Recently?"

"Not in several weeks, sir."

The general paused before continuing. "You know, of course, that I don't get along very well with the general staff at times," said Hussain. "Nor with the air marshal and his men. Your uncle and I have had our disagreements."

"Yes sir," said the pilot.

"But you and I—there have never been any problems."

"No sir."

"I'm not in favor of this, but there is nothing I can do."

"Nothing you can do about what, sir?"

"The air marshal wants you for a special assignment," said Hussain cautiously.

Khan felt as if someone had yanked his ejector seat on him.

"For what?"

"I didn't think your uncle consulted with you about it. It's not a demotion," added the general. "It definitely won't harm your career."

"But I want to fly," blurted the pilot. "I have to." The worst thing was that he felt his face growing red and tears, actual tears, forming at the corners of his eyes. "I'm the best pilot in the wing, sir," said Khan, holding them back. "You can't ground me, not now. This war—"

"It's not my choice, Major. Believe me, I don't want to. It was my idea to have the Falcons fly deep interception, and I think you did a superb job with those MiG-29s. I have every confidence in you."

"What will happen to my men?"

"We're going to have to fold them back into the main body of Squadron 5. It isn't my decision."

The general rose and began pacing awkwardly behind his desk. Khan felt a tear streak down his left cheek.

How could he cry? He was a professional, a soldier; whatever he was ordered to do, whether he liked it or not, he would do.

He could complain, of course. But cry? Goddamn, why was he crying?

Losing Tark?

They couldn't take his plane away from him. The Indians hadn't been able to. But his own cousin, with a piece of paper—grounding him.

Khan choked a second, then made a supreme effort to get control of himself. "I'm sorry sir."

"You've had a difficult day, son," said Hussain. He stood silently with his hand on Khan's shoulder for a moment, then stepped back. "Do you know how many planes you shot down?"

"We believe it was six, sir," said the pilot. "Four MiG-21s, and two Fulcrums."

"The Fulcrums have advanced missiles, I understand."

Khan was impressed that the general had informed himself about the mission so quickly. "It appears they have medium- or long-range IR homing weapons. I believe they were Russian Alamos."

"And you made your adjustments accordingly. Excellent, excellent flying."

"Thank you, sir."

"Your plane was shot up very badly," said the general. "I examined it myself. It was a miracle that you made it home. The work of God."

"I praise Allah for my return."

Hussain nodded and returned to his seat with a heavy plump. Khan was back in control now, appreciative of the general's tact in letting him recover.

"Perhaps when you report to Islamabad, you will find that there has been a mistake."

"I will go where I am ordered to go, sir," said Khan.

"I'm sure you will, son. The orders say that you are to be in Islamabad tomorrow at noon."

"Would it be possible to fly in the meantime?" Khan offered quickly. "I could—"

"Outside of fitting you into a Mirage slot, I'm not sure I can find a plane for you," said Hussain. "Your old squadron is being ordered south, and I'm afraid I can't send you with them. If you want to fly with Five, I suppose we could arrange something."

It wouldn't make sense to put him in a Mirage. He would be a liability in the unfamiliar plane, replacing someone who had trained for years. Even if Khan were a better pilot in theory, they weren't flying theories anymore.

"I appreciate the offer, sir. It wouldn't make sense to take someone else's slot. It wouldn't be fair."

The general nodded.

"General?"

"Yes?"

"Why take me out now when the Indians are attacking?"

But they both knew the answer to that. How many other families had already made their calculations about the war's likely course? Khan felt disgraced and dishonored. All he could do was stand silently as the general told him a cease-fire was almost certainly going to be declared before the end of the day.

"Perhaps you wish to visit your family or friends," added Hussain. "You have the afternoon and evening. We'll arrange for a small plane to be put at your disposal to make your appointment at Islamabad."

Khan nodded. He would see Hir. Perhaps she could suggest a way of talking his cousin out of this.

There was also the wedding. They would have to put it off until after the fighting stopped.

Khan listened as the general said a few more words of praise. Then the officer reached out and shook his hand, wishing him well. "I'm sure that our paths will cross many times," said Hussain.

Khan left the office feeling considerably more sympathy toward his commander than ever before. Cursing Nur with every step, he walked back to his quarters, his head twisting with every jet engine whining for a takeoff.

Over New Delhi, India. 1 P.M.

Secretary of State John Grasso shifted nervously in the seat, watching through the window as the Indian MiG swung into position next to his Boeing 767. Though assured by both

India and Pakistan that he had free passage, Grasso felt a bit uneasy looking at the warplane, two missiles strapped beneath its right wing. One slip by the escorting pilot and Grasso's next role would be as guest of honor at one of those famous Indian funeral pyres.

"General Chenab is back on the line," said his assistant, Tracy Su-Jan.

Grasso picked up the phone and pressed the yellow button to complete the connection. He had been on the phone practically the whole flight, cajoling, threatening and negotiating with both sides.

The Pakistan army's representative in the cabinet spoke so quickly Grasso had trouble understanding what he said.

"Please, General," said Grasso wearily. "We have a bad connection. Please speak slowly."

This time there was no mistaking his words. The Indians must pull back as part of the cease-fire. And the Kashmir question must be settled by plebiscite. Otherwise, the military could not guarantee to observe the cease-fire for more than forty-eight hours.

Grasso stared at the telephone console, as if the device had suddenly malfunctioned. "General, you know that's impossible. Why in the world would India agree to a plebiscite?"

Chenab responded angrily that the Indians would be ejected if they did not agree. Terrible retribution.

Grasso cut him off.

"Look, General," said the secretary of state. "We're all a little tired at this point. I think that I can get the Indians to agree to a cease-fire, and then to a withdrawal. I may be able to get the UN involved. As for a plebiscite in Kashmir, it's just not going to fly right now. And there's no way I can give them any kind of deadline. This is all a delicate balance," said Grasso, turning to look at Tracy, who was standing in front of him with a folder held tight across her breasts. "If we push too hard, everything will fall apart."

India must be off Pakistani soil by the end of the week, said the general, or it would pay a heavy price.

Grasso held his hand over the receiver. "God, what happened to him?'' he said to his aide. She shrugged. ''General, I understand the gravity of the situation,'' he said, returning to the phone. ''We have to go at this one step at a time. Will you observe a cease-fire?''

Chenab said that was not the issue. Grasso recognized that as a concession and dove for it before the general could say anything else. ''I appreciate your cooperation. We seem to be landing now—I will contact you when I have something new.''

''Tony thinks the Pakistan army is afraid there will be a rebellion,'' said Tracy. ''The Indians have exposed their weaknesses and damaged their prestige. They're looking for some political points.''

''Great,'' said Grasso. ''Just what we need.''

His assistant handed him the folder. ''You wanted a run-down on the Indians you'll be meeting.''

The secretary of state took the folder, his eyes lingering on the inviting curve of Tracy's hip. It was all Grasso could do to keep himself from reaching over and giving her a tap on the behind. He could get away with it—his work area was cordoned off from the rest of the airplane. But a pat would inevitably lead to something else, and there wasn't time before landing.

He imagined her taking off her herringbone jacket and then letting the skirt fall to the ground. She'd step forward, her black half-slip stretching tight. Slowly she'd unbutton her blouse, her breasts aching to be caressed.

''Are you OK, John?''

''Yes, yes, I'm fine,'' said Grasso.

''Who do you want with you at the negotiating session?''

They were supposed to go right into the meeting, straight from the airport. Maybe they could postpone it a bit—to freshen up.

''Well, you, of course,'' answered the secretary of state, struggling to concentrate.

''We are preparing for our final approach,'' interrupted the pilot over the intercom.

Grasso had tried sitting in the desk chair while they were landing once. The sensation of moving backward as the plane dropped from the air made him sick for a week. So he got up, preparing to take his seat in the cabin. Just then the plane banked sharply to begin its landing approach. The sudden shift of momentum sent him flying across the room and into Tracy, and both of them tumbled together into the passageway.

By now his entire staff and the pool reporters traveling with them had buckled up, and so the secretary and his assistant had a full audience as they cartwheeled across the front of the plane. They landed together in a compromising pose at the feet of Bill Schenck, the secretary of state's security officer. Grasso thought he heard a few snickers as Schenck helped him to his feet, but he couldn't spot the offenders as he scowled and took his place in the front row.

Schenck stepped forward to open the door after the jet landed. Grasso, walking up behind him, abruptly stopped when he saw that no stairs had been wheeled out to meet the plane. And they didn't look like they were coming any time soon, either. The airport, a military strip close to the Indian capital, appeared abandoned.

"Careful, John," cautioned Schenck, putting his arm across the doorway.

"Damn," grumbled Grasso, who had no intention of getting any closer to the edge. "Do we have the right airfield? Tracy, go check with the pilot."

The assistant disappeared as the rest of the plane's passengers began stirring.

"How about answering a few questions, since we've got time to kill?" said Kevin Kalm, the CNN correspondent.

Why couldn't a guy like Mike Wallace cover him, Grasso wondered. It'd be better to be grilled by a remorseless investigative reporter than to have to return Kalm's ingratiating smile.

"We know you've been in constant communication with the capitals of both countries," said Kalm. "Do you have an agreement already?"

"No comment," said Grasso.

"Are the Pakistanis issuing new demands?"

Lucky guess?

"No comment."

"Do they want a plebiscite in Kashmir as part of the agreement?"

Grasso wondered if his phone was tapped.

"No comment."

"Does that mean yes or no?"

The distance to the tarmac looked inviting now. Not that Grasso intended to jump—if he could maneuver Kalm to the doorway, perhaps Schenck could elbow him out.

Grasso gave the reporter his best tenured-professor-browbeats-freshman scowl. "I'm not going to comment on anything, Kevin, not even the tie you're wearing."

Titters from the crowd. At least the other reporters shared his opinion of Kalm.

"It's the right airport," said Tracy, returning. "The delegation has been delayed."

"Should I crank out the ladder?" asked Schenck.

It was a great exaggeration to call the shaky plastic contraption a ladder. Still, it beat standing here talking to Kalm, and Grasso had already nodded when Tracy pointed out a cavalcade of cars approaching in the distance.

"Thank you, God," muttered Grasso. "I'll have mother light a candle when I get back."

Government Building, Islamabad. 1:15 P.M.

"Perhaps the cease-fire would be best delayed until the army can launch a counteroffensive," said Nizam, finally seeing a chance to speak as the prime minister paused for a breath. "The army would then demonstrate its vitality. I'm sure a few quick victories would be easy to arrange."

There was a collective gasp as the entire cabinet turned toward General Chenab and saw his face flush. The air-conditioned, secure situation room on the second floor of the ministry building suddenly turned very hot, its dark blue walls reflecting the heat of the army chief of staff's rage as it welled up. The other cabinet members, a collection of mostly timid men, seemed to shrivel instantly; even the prime minister began to tremble. Nizam bit at the inside of her lip, angry herself but trying to remain in control.

She had misplayed it; Chenab thought she was mocking him. Here was the river Chenab's family was named for, mighty in its wrath, rolling up inside his body, swelling his head to three times its size.

"The army does not need a moral victory over the Indians," thundered Chenab. "We have no need for symbolism."

"Some symbols carry a great deal of power," said Nizam coolly. "The army does not look very strong at the moment."

"You forget your position," growled the general. "You are—"

He was going to say "a woman." He meant, "a woman." But instead the words "interior minister" spit from his mouth like sour wine. "These are matters you know nothing about. You owe your position to your ancestors and your party. We don't need your uninformed opinions."

The wise thing for Nizam to do, the calm thing, would have been to sit and listen as the tirade turned to the army's capabilities. She could take it all in, nod, and say finally that this was what she had meant to say. How many times in the past had she exerted her self-control, swallowed her pride and managed to sidestep the torrent, emerging in a better position than when she had started?

But this morning, of all mornings, Nizam was pushed too far. She'd had no sleep the night before. She was anxious that the cease-fire not take place until the army was discredited and nearly destroyed. And she was tired of kowtowing to men who had the intelligence of inbred mongrels.

The princess nearly reminded Chenab that the army had been warned well in advance of the Indian attack, and of the probable southern invasion. She came close to pointing out that the army units that had proven most undependable were those most closely identified with the general staff. Instead, she carefully arranged her papers and slid them into the small portfolio she carried. The princess rose, and with a flick of both wrists, brought her scarf up from her neck and to her head. She slipped a portion across the bottom of her face, turning what was ordinarily a sign of female submission into a defiant slap at the general. Stepping back from the table, she walked toward the door as the prime minister began stuttering that she shouldn't leave.

"I must return to my homeland," said Nizam. "There is much to be done there, and evidently I am not needed here."

Murwan, her aide, hastily followed as she walked out. The guards at the door snapped to attention as her hard, Western-style heels clicked on the smooth tiles. Her bodyguards met her at the end of the blue-tinted hallway, practically leaping as they saw her come, falling in around her. Their boss was angry, they were angry. A male secretary coming up the stairs was pushed to one side as the six men formed a flying wedge for her.

"He misunderstood," ventured Murwan halfway down the long stairway leading to the front lobby.

"Chenab is a dolt," said Nizam calmly. "But in a way he is right. He can speak to me like this because we have no cards to play. We must get some."

"The army eliminated Benazir Bhutto," said Murwan.

"I am not Benazir Bhutto," spat Nizam.

"No. You do not have the legacy of a popular father."

Nizam stopped suddenly on the stairs. She turned and faced her aide. She valued his bravery as well as his honesty, but she hated any parallel between her and the deposed prime minister.

"You will never see a picture of me with a handkerchief to my face, crying about what the army has done," she said.

The bodyguards bristled.

"They wouldn't give you the chance to cry," said Murwan, holding his ground.

Nizam said nothing. She turned back to the steps and continued downward. Her men had already called for her cars; the two black Mercedes pulled up on the sidewalk and met her at the door. She did not notice the extra caution the guards took to make sure no one was lurking outside, nor did she see that two passersby were pushed roughly back as she came out of the building. Nizam saw only the need for action, no matter how desperate.

The start of an idea is generally a subtle thing, but here the beginning was discrete and obvious; it presented itself to Nizam as if one of her ancestors had suddenly materialized and whispered in her ear.

"They could just snatch you off the street," Murwan said as he followed her into the car. "No one would know."

In that moment, she saw how she could cement her position with the Americans, and control the progress of the cease-fire and peace talks at the same time. It would take a bold, nearly reckless stroke, but it was within her grasp.

"I want Zulifar, Fleming, the two Jatoi brothers and the Indian," she said to her aide as the car door was slammed shut, the driver already screeching away. "They will need others to assist them; they can make the choices after I brief them. I want them in three hours."

"The Hindus and Zulifar are in Karachi."

"That's where we're going. They'll meet me at the airport."

"But what about the general and the army—"

Murwan's words trailed off as Nizam leaned forward and tapped the panel of bulletproof glass. "Take us directly to the airport. Alert my plane."

The driver nodded. Murwan watched her a moment, then picked up the secure phone from the recessed panel in front of them.

Near Lahore, Pakistan. 3:30 P.M.

Khan, in his last official act as commander, took it upon himself to notify Tark's father of his death. Jehan Yusuf lived in a small town just outside Lahore; after completing his duty, Khan would drive on and spend the evening with Hir and her family. Commandeering a jeep—it was amazing how much more potent a major's clusters were than a captain's bars—he set out on his 200-mile journey.

Sargodha was far from any ground fighting, and the action there had been limited to a few air attacks, with the largely unsuccessful missile raids on the air base the first morning the most severe. Otherwise, if one ignored the obvious increase in activity at the base, there were few outward signs of war.

Driving south into the heart of the rich Punjab plain, things were different. The Indian army that had invaded across the desert far to the south was now reported turning east. Faisalabad was hundreds of miles from the front, but even as he passed the city in his jeep Khan could sense the tension. Many families had packed their possessions onto automobiles and were heading north. Police officers and militia members manned checkpoints along the highway. A bridge had been partly damaged by a bombing attack, and all the traffic lights he passed were inoperative.

More ominously, a dark pale of smoke hung in the west. The factories and military installations closer to the border were juicy targets for the large Indian air force. Though the PAF was formidable and had acquitted itself well, it could not be everywhere at once.

"Several cities have been shelled, but Lahore has been spared, praise Allah," an old man in a militia uniform told Khan at a checkpoint about ten miles outside Faisalabad. The cities he cited were far away, but the guard spoke of the action as if he had just come from them. Khan had heard the opposite at the base, that there had been no shelling of nonmilitary targets outside Kashmir and the desert areas where the advance was made. But he nodded at the man, glancing at the carbine in his trembling hands. If the Indians did attack here, he wondered, how many shots would he get off before being killed?

"I heard that there was to be a cease-fire," said the pilot.

The old man shrugged as if he didn't care. Even he is doing more for our country than I will be, Khan thought as he drove away.

Lahore was within twenty miles of the border, and as he headed for the suburb where the elder Yusuf lived, Khan braced himself for a scene of confusion. But even after the checkpoints gave way to hastily erected gun emplacements and stockpiles of tank obstacles, the atmosphere was notably calm. There were only a few cars on the road north of the city; most of the sparse traffic was going in Khan's direction, and much of it was military. Looking toward the city as he approached, Khan's eyes were drawn by the white reflected glow of the minarets of Lahore's many mosques. Perhaps these were the real guards of the city.

When he arrived at Tark's home, he was told by a teenager that her father, a painter who specialized in restoring ancient places of worship, was at work at a nearby mosque. Forcing a smile, Khan nodded and left before she sensed why he had come.

He found the elder Yusuf carefully retouching a floral pattern near the mosque's entrance. From the side, he looked almost nothing like Tark, but when the man turned toward him Khan saw clearly his friend in his face. With difficulty, he explained what had happened, saying that although Tark would be listed as missing, he had seen the explosion himself, and there was no doubt that he had died.

And then, most likely because they were in a mosque, Khan added the formulas from the Koran guaranteeing those who fell in battle a special, immediate place in heaven.

Tark's father nodded, then went back to his work. Carefully he applied the orange red paint to the panel, dabbing each stroke with a precision that the original artist would have admired. Khan, who had steeled himself to deliver the terrible news, felt unnerved by the older man's lack of emotional display. He watched him paint for awhile longer, then retreated, walking quickly to his car and heading toward Hir's home.

He was more than halfway to the city when he realized that his fiancée would still be at school when he arrived. He drove on anyway; there was nothing else to do. He was surprised when she greeted him at the door of her house, a large, single-level structure that sprawled on the top of a small hill overlooking about a hundred of her family's acres on the outskirts of the city.

"No school today," Hir announced, a little gloomily. "No school because of the war."

It was all still theoretical to her, something with the vague shape of a rumor. Though so close to India that its soil could be seen from here, ironically Lahore was farther from the war than Sargodha, nestled deep in Pakistan.

Like most Pakistani women, in the city and at work Hir dressed relatively conservatively. The two-piece *salwar kameez* was her de rigueur uniform. Being young, she generally chose colorful patterns, perhaps a bold red, dotted print as tunic with zebra-striped red and white pants, but she had a strong selection of conservative blacks and browns as well. She always had a scarf with her, ready to whip it into use as a covering for her head and face if the circumstances demanded.

At home, however, Hir dressed much differently. This afternoon she was wearing a short red skirt and flowered blouse that revealed the lacy pattern of her camisole. Many young Pakistani women, members of the upper professional and land-owning classes, dressed this way in private. In a sense, they lived a double life, half in the present, half in a world unchanged since the first Portuguese traders arrived on the subcontinent four hundred years earlier.

Khan kissed her quickly on the lips, nervously looking to see if her parents might be nearby. Then he followed her into the living room.

"We've been so worried about you," said Hir, sitting on the couch. Khan went to sit next to her, but she waved him off. "Mother is coming."

It did not matter that they were to be married soon. Unlike Hir's Western-oriented father, Mrs. Ranjha was extremely old-fashioned.

"I've been promoted," said Khan, and suddenly he heard himself telling Hir everything in great detail, starting with the interception of the Indian MiGs yesterday morning, then his promotion and the bombing mission. At some point, Mrs. Ranjha came into the room, but he did not stop to greet her, continuing instead with his narrative. Finally he arrived at the point where General Hussain delivered the news about his reassignment.

"Thank God," said Hir's mother.

The words took him by surprise. "It's a desk job," said

Khan. ''I'm being taken out of the air.''

''Your cousin is wise to get you out of harm's way.''

The pilot felt his face grow red with anger. He controlled it, looking for a way to state his feelings so she could understand.

''It is a disgrace. God reserves his greatest glory for warriors,'' he told her.

''Don't try to determine God's will,'' she shot back. ''You have other responsibilities. You must do as you're told.''

The pilot had never heard her speak so fiercely. Unable to answer politely, he looked to his fiancée. Surely Hir would understand. But her face was ashen, its lovely cheeks stretched back to their bones.

''I thought you would understand why I have to fly.''

''The bombers,'' she said, going back to his story. ''They could easily have hit that school.''

''The attack was very well planned,'' Khan said. ''It was early in the morning, before—Hir, wait!''

His plea was to no avail; he watched helplessly as she ran from the room.

''She will be all right,'' said her mother, coming over and standing by the pilot. ''This war has made us all jumpy.''

''But we were attacked first. And if we do not defend ourselves, we will be crushed.''

''I know that,'' she said sympathetically, placing her hand on his back. It was a small but powerful hand, with a warm and knowledgeable touch.

''I have to report to Islamabad tomorrow. I don't know what will happen after that.''

''I've already notified the mosque that there may be a delay in the wedding. They understand. We must all adapt. Hir will too.''

Paris, en route to Orly Airport. 4 P.M.

''No one's going to believe I'm French,'' Greeley said as he watched O'Connell muscle the Renault through the highway traffic. It was the third car they'd had that day. This one had been supplied by Simon, the Belgian with a Middle Eastern face. He'd also gotten them passports, some other official-looking papers, and airline tickets. ''We're not trying to fool anyone,'' answered O'Connell, ''just give them something to wink at. Keep your mouth shut and let me do the talking.''

''I don't speak French.''

''Neither will they.''

Greeley could feel the jet lag, not to mention the excitement of the past few hours, eating at him. He wanted a drink.

Just then a lady truck driver cut them off and the agent unleashed a stream of vilification in French. His command of the language impressed Greeley as much as his driving skills horrified him. O'Connell pulled the car to the left and then accelerated into a small opening in front of the truck, crossing back again and continuing to speed down the road.

He reminded Greeley of a friend he'd had in the service. On the surface he was cool, but underneath he was a hothead whose aggression came out in his driving. The kid had ended up wrapping a jeep around a tree on Okinawa.

O'Connell's driving abilities were the least of Greeley's worries. He'd realized while he was crouched on the ground in the parking garage just how far in over his head he was.

He never should have let O'Connell think he'd been a real pilot. The way the agent had put it at first, it seemed like more or less a routine job, picking up an old airplane maybe in the middle of the night when no one was looking and flying it out. That Greeley could handle. But obviously things were going to get pretty damn dicey if people were already shooting at them.

He'd have just minutes to get the engines going and get it in the air. Jesus, the engines. You had to watch the temperature at takeoff, especially if they weren't using good gas, which they couldn't, because who made the proper octane anymore? He'd have to over-rev them to get the horses up; they'd be close to overheating on the runway.

His stomach twisting with the sour juice of fear, Greeley turned to the side window and stared at the dull green and brown fields lining the road. He felt a twinge of nostalgia for the farm where he'd grown up. His parents weren't poor, but his decision to go into the service instead of working on the land had been a hardship for them. They'd accepted it bravely, encouraging him to pursue his dream.

Only to be cheated out of it.

He was old, so old. Things didn't work as good as they used to. He had a bit of arthritis in his knee, which tightened up when the weather was damp. Everything else was loose, looser than when he was young. His nerves, for example.

"How come you keep changing lanes?" Greeley asked.

O'Connell shrugged. "Habit, I guess," he said, reaching over and fiddling with the radio, fixing on a pop music station. The music sounded American, though the words were in French.

"You nervous?" Greeley asked.

O'Connell laughed. "Don't worry. Your part's a piece of cake," he said. "You just kick back and enjoy the scenery. Couple of days from now, you'll be buying drinks for the whole bar."

"You sure that was the Russians after us?"

"You owe somebody money?"

"No. But maybe—"

The car took a sudden, sharp plunge to the right, skidding across the traffic and screeching to a stop on the shoulder so fast that the engine stalled.

"You're either with me from here on, or you're out. I'll buy you a ticket at the airport and you're done."

O'Connell, his face barely six inches from Greeley's, spoke so softly it was hard to hear his words over the radio and traffic. But there was no mistaking his meaning.

"I'm with you," said Greeley. "I'm just asking."

O'Connell slid his hand inside his jacket and pulled out his gun; for a second Greeley thought he was going to threaten him with it. Instead, he held it by the barrel and handed it to him. "Stick this in my bag," he said. "We shouldn't need it for awhile. Our baggage will get bribed through but there's no way I'll get on the plane with it."

It was a double-action Browning semiautomatic, big and

black, with a good heft and the clean, metallic smell of fresh oil. Greeley examined it, sliding the clip out and peering up toward the chamber.

"Be careful," said O'Connell as he wheeled the car back onto the highway. "It's loaded."

"I can see that," said Greeley. "Pretty nice little toy." He slipped the clip back into the gun and undid his seat belt to reach into the back.

"Handle guns a lot in the service?" O'Connell asked.

"Always been around guns. I done a lot of huntin' as a boy. We'd get rabbits, woodchucks, things like that. Had a Remington rifle, first gun I ever owned. Was an old center-fire rifle, back from the thirties. Was my uncle's. Center-fire—an old-fashioned kind of gun, the way the ammunition ignites. Was in disrepute when I got it, but my uncle swore by it, and I didn't know center- from rimfire to bonfire, as long as it was mine."

"Uh-huh."

Greeley smiled with the memories, vaguely aware that he'd lost O'Connell's attention. "One time, things were a little slim around the house. It was spring, and we'd put everything into planting or something; I'm not sure. Anyways, my daddy gave me the gun and told me, 'Now James, we're dependin' on you to get us some dinner. Go shoot your mother a nice little ol' Bugs Bunny fer us.' Mind you, I'm thirteen, fourteen, been shooting rabbits and varmints since I was eight. God, I shot so many, I musta controlled the animal population of Columbia County single-handed. But my daddy put it that way—Bugs Bunny. Like the cartoons. Damned if I couldn't get to aimin' when I'd start shakin' and just about blubberin'. Came back empty-handed."

He'd hung his head when his father came to ask how he'd done. It was too late by then to hunt anymore—without a word, his father hopped into the truck, and came back a half hour later with a rabbit, bought from Bill Gedes. He gave it to Greeley, had him go in with it as if he'd shot it. Never told anyone.

"My daddy was my best friend, growing up," said Greeley. "I wish I could be half the man he was."

O'Connell was quiet, no doubt figuring out who to cut off next. Paris was behind them, a mash of lights and looming shadows. The traffic snaked away from the big city, toward rendezvous with wives and children. Off to the right, the sun was heading into the horizon and a collection of low-slung clouds. Although it wouldn't set for awhile, it was already preparing a glorious show of pink and red to close the day.

Means good hunting tomorrow, his father used to say. Made him go out the next day and get that damn rabbit. Never give up, James. Don't let that weak spot in your stomach get the better of you.

"Your father still alive?" Greeley asked O'Connell.

"He and my mother died when I was three," said O'Connell. "Car accident. He was drinking."

"Oh."

"I was raised in a Jesuit orphanage."

"That's too bad."

"It had its positive aspects," said O'Connell, smiling. "For one thing, they taught me how to drive."

Grand Paradise Hotel, New Delhi. 9:30 P.M.

The cold blast of air that hit Grasso when he turned the knob and opened the door to his hotel suite nearly knocked him over. Someone had put the air-conditioning on full and left it running so long the drapes were frosted.

The secretary of state's teeth were chattering before he was halfway into the small foyer that served as an entrance to the five rooms. Already in a foul mood because of the stalled negotiations, Grasso grumbled to himself and went to find his suitcase. But his wife hadn't packed any sweaters—India and Pakistan weren't supposed to be cold this time of year. Shivering, he pulled a blanket from the bed and wrapped it around himself. Then he began hunting through the rooms for the thermostat.

"Where are you, boss?" called Schenck, entering the suite.

"Down here," said Grasso. He was on the floor in the main sitting room, crawling around the radiators.

"Jesus, it's cold in here," said Schenck. "It must be twenty below."

"I'm looking for the damn thermostat."

"It's in the bathroom," said the security chief, turning up the heat. "Needle's off the gauge."

"It figures." Grasso settled into one of the chairs, wrapping the blanket around his chest and tucking the ends under his thighs. "Jesus it's cold. Maybe I ought to change my suite so I can get some work done."

"This floor is the only one we can keep secure," said Schenck. "And you've got the only suite."

Grasso wondered if this might be another tactic by the Indians, who had spent the past eight hours perpetrating various forms of torture on the American secretary of state. First they had added an incredible amount of pepper to the special spiced tea they served at the mini-reception prior to the talks. Then they had packed their delegation with almost fifty people, representing nearly every one of the myriad political parties that held seats in parliament. Each delegate felt obliged to lay out his faction's official position, and Grasso had lost track within the first five minutes of the session.

The Indian prime minister had not attended the negotiations. Grasso wasn't sure whether that meant he was out of power, or displeased with the Americans. Or maybe, Grasso thought sarcastically, he couldn't keep their names straight himself.

"Maybe if we open one of the adjoining rooms and let some of the hot air in," suggested Schenck.

"Anything."

"This goes to Tracy Su-Jan's room," said the hulking Schenck, opening a panel at the sitting room's far end. "I'll leave the key in so you can close it later."

"I can feel the difference already," Grasso said, shedding the blanket and walking to the secure phone system installed near the sofa. It just so happened that he had a perfect view into his secretary's room from there.

"I think Tracy and some of the other folks went down to get some food," said Schenck, noticing Grasso's gaze. "The reception wasn't exactly filling."

"I may have something sent up myself."

"One thing, John. I don't trust the Indian security people. They're from the Third Army command, the ones leading the attack in Pakistan. The word is that they're against a cease-fire."

"I see."

"I called the embassy and they're sending over some marines. They don't have that many to spare, though—there have been some threats of violence."

Grasso nodded.

"It's just that I'm not sure which way the Indians might lean if things got tough," said Schenck. "The employees at the front desk have a pool going on when Ramma Rhabid's faction will take control."

"I think they're behind the curve. If Rhabid hasn't taken over by now, he never will."

"We'll have someone outside the door all night. If the military moves, I can have a helicopter here in four minutes."

The security chief excused himself and left the suite. Grasso picked up the phone and asked the operator to connect him with the White House.

It took almost fifteen minutes for Grasso's old Sons of Italy buddy to come to the phone. The secretary of state, tired from the long day, had begun to drift off to sleep when the president's garrulous voice exploded in his ear.

"John? Are you there?"

"Jack," said Grasso, bolting upright in the chair as if the president had caught him napping at a cabinet meeting.

"What the hell is going on? Where's my cease-fire?"

"The Indians are dragging their feet," said Grasso.

"Kick them in the butts," said D'Amici.

"It's not quite that easy."

"The Chinese ambassador came in this morning," said

the President. "And I didn't like the tenor of his comments."

"That's the translator, Jack. Moran is no good."

"I used Brown."

"Oh."

"The Russians aren't too happy, either. Apparently they're sending some sort of delegation to Beijing tomorrow."

That's all we need, thought Grasso. It would be just his luck for this to lead to a rapprochement between the Russians and the Chinese. His carefully constructed Asian strategy would fall to pieces.

Either that, or it would work so well they'd have a real war on their hands. China would invade India as the last Pakistanis fled to the hills. Russia would take a look at its old treaties with India and decide to drill for some oil in Manchuria.

"Get something together," demanded D'Amici. "And quick. There's a lot more than prestige riding on this."

Grasso hung up the phone, feeling like he had been spanked. He would wave the Chinese flag in front of the Indians, and use it to get them to declare a unilateral cease-fire. The U.S. would guarantee to back the Indians if the Chinese attacked, but only if they stopped their advance now, and planned a withdrawal. Have to grease the skids with trade assistance and credits, but he'd known that coming in.

At least the Pakistanis would favor a cease-fire. Or would they? Thinking back to his telephone conversation on the plane with Chenab, Grasso decided he'd better make sure.

He had his embassy in Islamabad on the line when Tracy came back to her room. She didn't notice that her door was open, and so he had a perfect vantage as she began to undress. Her back to him, she lifted off her sweater and shook her hair back and forth, giving him teasing glimpses of the black camisole she was wearing.

She leaned to one side as she undid her skirt. It slid slowly from her hip, falling to the ground.

"Mr. Secretary?"

"I'm here, Jack," stuttered Grasso. He spoke a little too loudly—Tracy saw him and turned around. She smiled, and wagged a finger at him as if he'd been naughty.

"It's Paul Klein. In Islamabad." His ambassador to Pakistan.

"I'm sorry. Jet lag's getting to me," Grasso said. He looked down at the carpet in an attempt to concentrate.

"What's the situation in Islamabad?"

"Good question," said the ambassador. "Some lunatics in the government are pushing for a counterattack. There was a blowup with one of the ministers this morning—the interior minister stormed out of a cabinet meeting. Apparently she feels an offensive would help the army's political position, though I don't see how."

"She?"

"Princess Ghazzala Nizam, the interior minister."

"She's the separatist, isn't she?"

"That's her. I have no idea what her angle is. She's always been at odds with the army."

Grasso wearily rubbed his forehead. "Chenab complained to me about something this morning. He didn't sound like he *wanted* a cease-fire." He glanced up briefly and saw Tracy's bare leg disappear around a corner.

"I think they'll go for the cease-fire if we can get a solid offer. We may have to sweeten the pot, though."

"Sweeten the pot? How about the fact they won't be overrun?"

"They'll need some sort of salve for their prestige," said the ambassador calmly. "Otherwise the government may fall. If the clerics take over—"

"Spare parts," sputtered Grasso. "We'll replace their losses."

"That's not exactly something they can take back to their people."

Grasso once more turned his attention to his assistant's room, just in time to see the door close. "What do they want?"

"Some sort of promise on Kashmir."

"I'm not even sure I can get the Indians to pull out of

Pakistani territory. Look, lay it out for them—we have to take this step-by-step. We'll give the army whatever support they need, but they have to stop fighting. God, it would be suicidal to continue. What about this Nizam woman—what can we give her?''

"Short of reestablishing her homeland?"

"We're sure as hell not going to do that."

"I didn't suggest we try."

"Get this thing straightened out as best you can, all right? Make sure they'll observe a cease-fire. And see if you can find out what kind of communication Islamabad has had with the Chinese. They're talking in Washington like they might want to jump in."

"That would bring the Russians."

"Exactly."

Grasso leaned down and placed the phone on the receiver. The room had warmed up considerably. Still, that door ought to be open.

"Tracy? I need you to, uh, prepare a cable."

He turned the key in the lock and slipped the door open. His personal assistant was standing there in a jet black silk pajama top. Perfectly tailored to her petite frame, it hugged her hips and made her ample cleavage obvious. The air was filled with the light scent of perfumed powder, tickling his nose.

"Now?" she asked.

"Well," said Grasso, folding his arms around her. "Perhaps it can wait."

She leaned into him as they kissed, her weight a gentle cushion. Grasso's hands slipped downward to cup the cheeks of her fanny. He could tell by the feel which underpants she was wearing—a red nylon bikini, the front worked with a bit of lace. The pace of his heart had quickened; it was a drum pounding between them.

No, that was the knock on the hallway door.

"John?"

"Come back in an hour. I'm going to catch a quick nap."

"Ramma Rhabid wants to see you. He wants to know what our position will be when he takes charge of the government. The parliament's been called into special session tonight for a vote.''

''Son of a bitch,'' said Grasso. ''Son of a bitch.''

Nizam's Compound, North of Karachi. Apx. Midnight.

Nizam eased her body into the water, letting the warmth lap into her muscles. The Turkish bath was her favorite room in the complex, partly because of the water and partly because she could be truly alone here.

This was the only part of her large, sprawling house where the Pakistani princess absolutely followed *purdah,* the custom of separation of men and women that took the veil as its most visible symbol. Nizam disdained the inferiority the custom implied, though she made strategic use of its powerful symbols. The bath (more like a large, heated indoor pool, with electric steam generators on either side) and the wing that surrounded it were called by the women of the Sind a *zenana.* The term was not as loaded to modern ears as a harem, though it had the same essential meaning. No men were allowed here, and in fact few women had ever walked across the smooth wooden floors in the hallway outside to admire the exquisite jade figurines harking from the family's past glory.

Morena Kelso, lying on her back in the water on the`other end of the pool, was an exception. She had been here many, many times. Watching her extend her well-muscled legs in a lazy kick, the princess remembered their first meetings, the delicate dance very much like a courtship.

When the CIA operative first came to Pakistan, she was covered as an embassy official. Assigned to size up and make initial contacts with Pakistanis who might be turned into informants, Morena had singled Nizam out at an embassy party and made broad hints about the American need for different perspectives on events in Pakistan. A few days later, an agent handler—an overweight, bad-breathed man who spoke only English—followed up the overtures with a bald offer to put Nizam on the U.S. payroll.

The princess, onto the game from the beginning, dismissed the handler coldly. Morena made sure to run into her soon afterward, and when Nizam mentioned the overture reacted with practiced shock. This was standard procedure, a *pro forma* attempt to maintain her cover.

Nizam smiled in reply. "Don't play coy with me," she told the young woman. "I know you are CIA."

Morena's response was a carefully raised eyebrow that gave away nothing and yet signaled that she would be willing to deal. From that moment, Nizam knew they would eventually find common ground. A small but important hitch in an arms delivery to Afghan rebels a few weeks later provided the leverage for an arrangement.

The relationship had quickly grown, to their mutual benefit. Nizam became not merely one of the agency's most strategic sources of information, but a key facilitator for many projects too tricky to be undertaken through other channels. In exchange, the agency became a source, at times unwitting, of much of the money she used to build her movement.

Nizam liked Morena, and to the extent that she allowed herself, even thought of her as a surrogate younger sister. But the princess could not afford the vulnerability of friendship, especially with a CIA agent. As hard as she worked to make the relationship appear genuinely personal, she worked just as hard to keep her hidden self distant.

Nizam's business with the CIA had gradually diminished over the past eighteen months. The decline had started with Morena's transfer back to the states, but it was due to much more than that. The princess's information and services were no longer critical, partly because of the changes in the regional political situation, partly because of changes in Pakistan itself. The agency had cozied up to the army and even, rumor had it, to the clerics. Nizam had never had much stock with official U.S. contacts, and she lacked much plausible pretense to work with the U.S. military. But now Morena was here. The agency needed her, and she was prepared to make that need more critical than the Americans had ever imagined.

Nizam gazed across the pool as Morena let her feet sink toward the bottom. Her hair drifted on the surface momentarily and then disappeared as she found the depths. How lithe her body was, thought Nizam. Her own was a collection of soft bulges.

"God this feels good," said Morena, resurfacing. "The flight put a wicked twist in my neck."

"It has been a long time since you were here," said Nizam, taking a few steps before pushing herself into a gentle breaststroke across the pool.

"Too long," said Morena.

"So you need me again." The princess stopped her slow progress across the pool and treaded in the middle, a few feet from the spot where Morena stood, water lapping at her chin.

"We could use your help, yes."

"I seem to have fallen from grace lately."

"Why do you say that?"

"I never see you."

"I'm in D.C. now. You were the one who insisted that there be no new contact."

"We had such a good relationship," answered the princess. "But it isn't just that. You take my information, yes, but once there were operations, different things to be done. Now it seems as if I am like a spare ox, retired from the field."

"Pakistan was the center of the universe when Afghanistan and the Soviet republics were hot," said Morena. "Now they're not."

She is very much in control of herself, Nizam thought, seamlessly slipping from the role of friend to negotiator. But the difference is that she works to get paid, while I work for my birthright.

"I need a helicopter," said Morena. It seemed to Nizam that a slight uneasiness crept into her voice for a brief moment.

"A helicopter?"

"One of your Hueys."

"Oh, I couldn't do that," said Nizam. "They're part of

my guard unit—we are not so far from the fighting that I can spare one."

"There'll be a cease-fire very soon."

"I wouldn't be so sure. The Indians are winning."

Nizam's head was turned away, but she could easily picture the frown that formed on her companion's face.

"They will cooperate. The Indian government is about to fall, and the new government wants peace."

The princess concentrated on her swimming. For a few minutes, the two women paddled in opposite directions, pausing at the far ends of the pool to take long breaths of the moist, warm air that hung so heavy in the room. "What do you need a helicopter for?"

"An operative of ours is stranded near the Chinese border. I have to pick him up."

CIA agents were not always good liars, but they were consistent. Nizam was extremely curious about what Morena's mission might actually be, but it would be fruitless to question her further. "I suppose I could find a helicopter," she said. "But it might take a week."

"That's too long," said Morena. Her breasts bobbed gently in the water.

"Perhaps I could push it along," said Nizam, plunging back into the water and kicking her legs in a powerful scissors that took her across the center of the pool in two strokes. "But finding a pilot may be a difficulty. Our best people are needed, naturally."

"I have a pilot," said Morena. "Someone you may know. Michael O'Connell."

O'Connell? He had been an important CIA operator, facilitating weapons purchases for the Pakistani government as well as some Chinese and Iranian groups. From what she remembered, he'd been kicked out for pocketing money. Why was he coming back?

The princess tucked her upper body under the water and dove downward. The bath was tiled with an exquisite red ceramic dotted with small blue, yellow and violet specks. These small circles seemed to glow as Nizam approached them, catching and magnifying the small amount of light that filtered into the water from the darkened room. She followed the colorful specks to the exact center of the pool, marked by a large bubble of crystalline water, captured and held here as if by magic.

A stranger would not realize until touching the bubble that it was hard, a perfectly polished piece of glass whose luster grew as it was examined. Only then, looking at the bright shadows that lurked inside it, would she realize the glass was not glass at all, but a huge gem. The smaller circles were stones as well, aluminum oxide treated to the most extreme pressures that the earth could exert. Discovered by slaves two thousand years ago, they had been honed and traded, hoarded, displayed, stolen, saved. These jewels were the legacy of Nizam's once-powerful Mogul ancestors, and in her fleeting touch of the center stone their power returned.

She pushed back up to the surface, her lungs hungry for air.

"Wasn't he a thief?" said Nizam, sliding the hair back from her face before starting for the side.

"He has certain abilities that are indispensable."

Nizam, pulling herself slowly from the pool, wondered what those might be. It couldn't be merely to fly a helicopter. Morena took another lap silently, and then she too got out of the water and put on her robe.

"Are you hungry?" the princess asked. "I will have some food prepared."

"That would be nice," said Morena, walking to the couch where a fresh set of clothes was waiting. "And thank you for the helicopter. But I would like to know why you think there won't be a cease-fire."

"I have heard rumors," said the princess. "One is that the Sikhs plan to kidnap your secretary of state."

Morena began laughing. "Oh, Princess."

Nizam felt a genuine twinge come to her cheeks. It was perfect, even if she would have preferred that it had been staged. "You know that I have my sources."

"The Sikhs would never do such a thing."

"I wouldn't be so sure," said Nizam, letting her robe drop as one more hint of annoyance. For a brief moment she felt as if she were a woman of twenty, taut and firm, so perfect was her act.

"You forget what my job is now. I know South Asia as well as you," said Morena, picking up her underwear. "The Sikh party wants peace. It's only a few radicals in the army who want to fight, and even they are in no position to kidnap the secretary. It would ruin them."

Morena's eyes flashed with certainty as well as youth. She had learned much over the years, Nizam thought, but this flaw remained: Her pride confused hard work with hard information.

The princess smiled. She reached over and affectionately tapped Morena on the cheek. "Perhaps you are right. I have only rumors to go on."

THURSDAY, SEPT. 18, 1997

Southeastern Iran. Apx. 6 A.M.

O'Connell walked swiftly down the terminal hallway, heading for the baggage counter. As near as he could tell, they hadn't been followed to Tehran, and they hadn't been followed to this small strip outside Bam in Kermān province.

It was more a dust hole than an airport. Counting police and other officials, there were less than a dozen people in the building. Built by the shah during the early seventies, the terminal had all the attraction of a fifties-style U.S. supermarket. The ceiling was covered with endless rows of fluorescent lights. Only one in four of the bulbs worked, but they were enough to coax a glare from the white-tiled wall. The counters were covered with slick red vinyl and bright white formica; the color scheme reminded O'Connell of the diner where he used to have breakfast.

Every twenty feet or so, a faded tulip appeared on the wall. Called *Laleh* in Farsi, the flower was the symbol for martyrs, an acute reminder of the reign of the Imam: Ayatollah Khomeini. Officially, Khomeini was the past; the present secular government had even made several halfhearted attempts at reestablishing relations with America. But the Islamic Revolution continued to be a force in people's lives, even if the paint was chipped and faded.

There were only two reasons anyone came to this small corner of Iran—the archaeological digs nearby or to do business with Renard. No flights landing here originated from outside the country; unlike Tehran, with its army of black-robed women inquisitors, there were few functionaries. Archaeologists were welcomed because they were working to reveal the greater glory of the Islamic past—and because large fees were required for dig permits. The government did not hassle Renard's visitors, partly because he supplied them with weapons, and partly because their nonchalance was well compensated. But the locals could hold anyone up if the mood struck them.

Speaking Farsi was not like speaking French or German. Even during the years when he was coming in and out of Iran fairly regularly, O'Connell had to think about the words before using them, often stumbling over pronunciation and butchering tenses. He took a breath as he walked down the hallway, marshaling his mind to produce a few coherent sentences of greeting in case they were stopped. He'd used French in Tehran and would try it here, but a coherent stab at Farsi generally made for smoother transitions.

The past forty-eight hours had been an orgy of remembering, waking parts of himself he hadn't used for two years. He'd done relatively well up to now, but he could feel fatigue setting in.

Greeley didn't help things, tugging his arm. "Say—"

"Don't speak English," spat O'Connell from the side of his mouth. "We're French, remember?"

"That guy's gonna open your bag—"

"*Je sais,*" said O'Connell, though he hadn't actually seen it until Greeley pointed it out. "*Monsieur,*" he said loudly to the security man who had grabbed his suitcase, "*voici mes papiers.*"

The man was momentarily distracted by the passport O'Connell waved in his face. He was short, and his dull green paramilitary uniform bulged at the stomach. He looked more Latino than Persian; stick a cigar in his mouth and he could pass for a member of Fidel Castro's entourage.

O'Connell gave him another few lines of French, saying he had only just arrived after a terrible flight. When the man's expression didn't change, O'Connell tried Farsi, repeating a condensed version of the spiel. He stumbled at first, but as he continued he caught the rhythm, and even managed to rouse a smile at his denunciation of the pilot.

More importantly, O'Connell took out the letter from the Iranian embassy that Simon had forged for him and gave it to the official as he spoke. Inside the envelope was fifty dollars, American.

The man read and returned the letter, palming the bill as carefully as a practiced magician and waving them through. It had cost five hundred to get past customs in Tehran. This was a bargain.

Their next stop was the restroom, where the supermarket motif found its greatest expression. The dull pink walls did their best to contain the glare of a triple bank of fluorescents while the large red and white floor tiles highlighted an assortment of stains. The porcelain accoutrements were a uniform gray, and lined both sides of the room without the benefit of barriers or other concessions to privacy. Greeley settled onto one of the toadstools and began huffing and puffing.

"Something I ate doesn't agree with me."

"I told you not to eat in Algiers," O'Connell said. A bilious odor began filling the lavatory.

"First you tell me not to drink, now you don't want me to eat. I think you hung around those Jesuits too long."

As O'Connell washed his hands he considered slipping the gun out of the suitcase and into his belt, but decided not to. They were likely to be frisked once they got to Renard's, and the arms dealer might interpret the Browning as a sign of ill will.

"I'm going to wait outside," he told Greeley. "Don't talk to anyone."

Halfway out the door, O'Connell was grabbed by the arm

and yanked into the hallway. The man he had bribed stood a short distance away as two younger Iranians spun him around and pushed him face-first against the wall.

The sudden jerking of his body made him bite his tongue. It hurt like hell, but at least it kept him from saying anything in English, which he might have done without thinking. To his surprise, the frisking was expert and almost gentle. Taking his bag, the men herded him toward an office at the end of the hall, where they pushed him into a chair placed in the exact middle of the room.

The walls seemed to have received only one coat of paint since they were erected, and that was a thin white that had yellowed and did little to cover the tape and nail marks.

At least they weren't covered with blood spatterings, O'Connell thought grimly. His two escorts took up positions on either side of him. They were in their early twenties at most, considerably taller and more athletic than the man giving the orders. In contrast to his uniform, they wore bulky gray *kurtas* over gray Western chinos.

"What is your real name?"

O'Connell tried to read the man's face before responding. Was he a suspicious policeman or just a greedy one? Either way, it was too dangerous to change his story.

"*Je m'appelle Jacques Lazare,*" said O'Connell, giving the name on the passport and documents. "*Je suis français.*"

"What is your real name?" repeated the official in English.

"*Je m'appelle Jacques Lazare.*"

The man on his left swatted O'Connell's ear with his forearm.

"What is your name?" There was a hint of boredom in the official's voice, the sign of a professional seeking to induce despair.

"*Je parle un peu d'anglais,*" said O'Connell.

Another swat, this one hard enough to send him halfway out of the chair.

O'Connell calculated that he could take one of the younger men, but not both at the same time.

"What is your real name?"

"Jacques Lazare. I am here for digs."

The man in the green fatigues scowled. "My belief is you are CIA," he said.

O'Connell gave him a puzzled look. They'd say that to anyone. One of the young men said something in Farsi too fast to decipher. He guessed it was about Greeley, though, because when the official nodded the man left the room.

None of the men seemed to be armed. Still, a gun might be as close as the desk drawer.

"Who are you?" he asked. It was a challenge to speak English with a Parisian accent.

"We are the police," said the official. "And we are the ones with questions."

"Your name is Ahmed?" said O'Connell, guessing from the conversation.

The man told him he was too smart to be a tourist.

"I have been to Iran many times," he responded in Farsi. "I know many people in the government."

"Why does an American come to Iran?"

"Je suis français."

The kid gave him another swat. O'Connell let it push him out of the chair. He rolled groaning on the floor.

"Get up," said the official. The younger man grabbed his arm. As he pulled, O'Connell managed to get his feet under him and sprang into the young man, catching him off guard and kneeing him in the groin as they fell against the wall. O'Connell brought his left arm up against the man's nose in a sharp motion that crushed the cartilage into his sinuses. Blood poured down the kid's face as he slipped to the floor.

O'Connell had his arm around Ahmed's neck before he had a chance to open the door. He yanked hard and the Iranian's chest began quaking for air. His fingers pried at the sleeve of O'Connell's leather jacket, but a kidney punch took the fight out of him. O'Connell put him out with a chop to the back of the neck.

The door began opening before he could retrieve his gun from the bag. O'Connell jumped behind the door as Greeley came through, then flung himself into the Iranian behind him, riding him to the floor.

This kid was tougher than he'd expected, and O'Connell couldn't keep his arms pinned even though he had his face mashed into the floor. As he pressed his knee into the Iranian's side, O'Connell realized he had overestimated his own strength. His opponent began pushing himself upward despite O'Connell's blows until Greeley flattened him with a well-aimed kick to the face.

O'Connell lay on top of the man a moment, catching his breath. "I guess I didn't give him enough money," he said when he finally stood.

O'Connell retrieved his gun from the bag and put it inside his waistband. He threw three more fifties to the ground. "Let's go find a car."

There was only one person in the hallway, and he looked to be about eighty years old. O'Connell kept his hand on his gun as he passed, just in case.

Three men were standing in the roadway in front of the building, leaning on a battered yellow cab. All three spotted the greenbacks O'Connell had folded into his fist; all three quickly offered their services and eternal gratitude as the agent looked over the cab, midsize Toyota and Land-Rover parked behind it. When he pointed to the tan-colored Land-Rover, its driver gave him the smile of someone who'd just won the lottery.

He wore it until halfway down the access road to the highway, when O'Connell told him where they were going.

"I do not no understand," said the man in English that was a little too stumbling to be believed.

"Of course you do," responded O'Connell. "All of the drivers here are on my friend's payroll."

The driver considered this for a moment. "One generally knows when a ride is needed."

"Monsieur Renard knows we're coming."

"It's a long drive," said the man.

"It's not that long," said O'Connell. "And you'll be paid well." He let two twenties flutter down to the front seat. The driver reached over and took them.

"I have been this way once or twice," said the man.

What the driver had said was true; Renard rarely left his guests to make their own arrangements. That and the airport reception committee worried O'Connell. These were manifestations of indifference, as opposed to malice: If Renard wanted to kill him, the agent knew, he would have sent someone much more efficient than government-issue thugs.

But it was too late to be guided by caution signs.

"That was a good kick you gave that guy back there," O'Connell told Greeley after the driver had settled onto the main road.

"You looked like you were having some trouble."

"Maybe I'm getting old."

Greeley laughed, and they settled back into their seats and watched the desert pass. The road was well maintained; their heads hit the roof of the vehicle only occasionally as the driver sped toward his destination.

"That's a pretty mountain up there," said Greeley, leaning over the front seat to look up ahead.

"Oh yes," said the driver. "It is the nicest mountain in all of Iran, perhaps in all the Middle East. I have seen mountains in Jordan and other places, but these ones have something special."

"Where did you learn to speak English?"

"Oh, it's nothing," said the driver. "I worked in Saudi Arabia and there I learned."

O'Connell doubted that, and not just because Saudi Arabia wasn't exactly known for its English classes. This guy smelled a little like SAVAK—the Iranian intelligence agency that had been abolished by Khomeini after he came to power. Renard had a number of former SAVAK people working for him. He also had extensive contacts among the Revolutionary Guards: where everyone else saw two sides to every coin, the Frenchman saw three hundred and sixty degrees of exploitation.

"You like Saudi Arabia?" Greeley asked.

"The money was very good," said the driver. "But I missed my family."

"I know how that goes."

Forty-five minutes later, just after they had started to climb into the mountains Greeley had admired, the driver braked to a stop. A bright red Toyota pickup blocked the road ahead. Two men clad in plain khaki uniforms but with no visible weapons approached the Rover, one on each side.

"What do you want?" said the first to the driver.

"I'm an old friend," said O'Connell from the backseat.

The man looked them over and then said something to the fellow on the other side of the car. They were Palestinians. O'Connell's brain did the necessary computations and spit out, "Monsieur Renard is expecting us," in Arabic. Then he sat back in the seat and told the driver to go on.

The driver glanced at the guard, then worked the shift lever gently. The two security men did nothing.

They took the sharp switchback up the foothill slowly. There was a camouflaged outpost directly across from the turn; with Renard's access to weapons, not even a tank could get past unless he wanted it to.

The Rover proceeded up to another turn, past a checkpoint where more guards—these ones with machine guns showing—sprawled on the hood of a second pickup. Continuing to climb, the driver geared through another sharp curve and suddenly they were in a lush, hillside oasis. An innocuous wrought-iron fence flanked each side of the road, punctuated at regular intervals by brick pillars. The air was filled with the sound of birds.

Renard had created the woods and stocked them with exotic birds and animals. On one of his earliest trips, O'Connell had been invited along on a tiger hunt, complete with PLO officers as native bearers. He'd heard stories that the arms dealer's recreational safaris had included human prey. While he doubted this was true, Renard would have thought it so useful to have such rumors circulating that he might have started them himself.

The driver slowed and pulled the Land-Rover through a short tunnel. The hard-packed dirt changed to gravel as they passed into a large courtyard. Two more pickups were parked here, along with a pair of Toyota Land Cruisers; tucked into the far corner was a British armored car, a World

War II relic that Renard occasionally started up and drove around his domain as a joke for visitors.

The real tanks were kept in a guarded bunker around the corner.

"Jesus, look at this place," said Greeley.

"Yeah, peaceful, isn't it?" said O'Connell, stretching his legs as he got out of the car. The courtyard was surrounded by a tiled wall, light blue stones tracing a delicate, flowing pattern along the edges. No guards were visible here, but O'Connell knew that they were being watched through a video camera in the shrubbery to his right; another camera at the far end caught them from a different angle, and still a third would track as they walked up the path through the garden.

The driver left the motor running as he retrieved their suitcases from the trunk. There was no question of asking him to stick around; Renard would either have one of his own people drive them out, or they wouldn't be leaving. Ever.

"Here," said O'Connell, shoving two fifties into the driver's breast pocket.

"God be with you," he said.

"Yeah, let's hope so," answered O'Connell, picking up his bag and leading Greeley toward the mansion's entrance.

"Would you look at this?" said Greeley as they stepped into the shrub-lined formal garden. Its lawn and flowers, watered by an extensive underground network of sprinklers and porous aquifer rocks, rivaled the formal Renaissance gardens of Europe. According to Renard, it was modeled on a particularly decadent example in northern Italy. An army of engineers and landscape experts had been employed to construct the elaborate underpinnings for the garden and the microclimate essential for the plants' growth.

"Are those peacocks?" Greeley asked, pointing at a pair of preening birds. As if on cue, one turned and fanned its tail.

"They're hell on the plants," said O'Connell, repeating one of the lines Renard used when he gave tours.

The two Americans continued to the far end of the garden,

descending a small set of stairs and walking through a corridor formed by tall shrubs. The large flagstone here had come from upstate New York—there was something symbolic in that, but O'Connell couldn't remember what it was. Two steps down the stairway, a turn—they were examined by another suite of cameras mounted in the brush—and the palace appeared before them.

That was the only thing you could call it. To O'Connell, it seemed a miniature version of the Taj Mahal, though the only thing its design had in common with the great Mogul monument in northern India was the large bulb dome and two smaller companions set back from the central arch that beckoned the eye. From this angle the building appeared to be a series of rounded walls cascading upward to the grand hall, a Persian palace influenced by the castles of southern France. While it looked as if it had been here for hundreds of years, it was almost brand new when O'Connell took his first tour of the grounds ten years before, while still in the army.

Greeley practically dropped his suitcase, involuntarily whistling at the grandeur. Even O'Connell couldn't help but be impressed.

Their admiration was cut short by the appearance of two guards, dressed in plain white trousers and shirts. Tall and muscular, they set the luggage aside and patted down the visitors without ceremony or result—the agent had returned his Browning to the bag a few miles back.

The preliminaries completed, the visitors were escorted inside, through hallways lined by finely polished marble and rich inlaid floors. O'Connell felt the old rush of adrenaline returning. He worked it with his fingers, running them as a pianist might, keeping the energy where he could see it.

They were left in a room just off the main corridor. A large table was cluttered with food—various cheeses, fruit, three different kinds of pâté and a small roast beef. A cluster of liquor and wine bottles were off to one side.

"What happens now?" Greeley asked.

"We wait," said O'Connell. "It shouldn't be long."

"Can we eat this stuff?"

"I doubt he'd poison us before he knew what we wanted," said O'Connell sarcastically. He watched as Greeley turned toward the booze. For a moment, he thought his companion was going to pour himself a drink, and considered what to do. A binge would ruin them.

"Oh Lord, am I a sinner," said Greeley, pulling his hand back.

O'Connell was overwhelmed by a sudden rush of inappropriate nostalgia. Father Fran had used the same expression countless times, mostly when he caught himself starting to mouth a curse.

"I'm not going to drink, don't worry," said Greeley, moving away from the table. "I promised."

O'Connell nodded and sank into the Italian leather couch, trying to banish the ghosts of his conscience and self-doubt. But the argument that had begun simmering in his brain as soon as he shook Simon's hand at the café exploded now, practically shaking his body with its violence.

No matter what the agency was trying to do to him—and no matter how much money the arms dealer would promise—he could never justify letting Renard get near the weapons. Too many people would be put at risk. He just couldn't be responsible for that.

But what else could he do? Stockman and the CIA were after him. He had no protection against them; he couldn't even hope to safely sneak back to Washington and spill his guts before a Senate committee.

What if he went openly? If there was so much attention they couldn't hit him?

How? Fly back to Paris and call a press conference? Who'd believe him?

Fly back to Paris in the Golden Bear and call a press conference. Spill his guts before the international media—they'd have to believe him if he had the plane with him.

Never make Paris.

Russia, then. Much safer, too. If all else failed, the Russians would want to know about the plane.

It was a dangerous gambit. Even though he'd ducked his pursuers, Stockman probably had a team in Pakistan. And if O'Connell pulled it off, Renard was bound to realize he'd been double-crossed.

But could he live with himself if Renard got hold of a bomb? Even if he were rich?

O'Connell folded his arms tightly across his chest. He could do this. He had to.

Sargodha Air Base, Pakistan. 6 A.M.

Disappointed with his fiancée, Khan left her house without having dinner and returned to his base. He made excellent time; his uniform meant he was one of the few people who could ignore the curfew. Intending to get an early start the next day, he did his best to escape the activity and tension at Sargodha and get to bed. But it was no good; he lay awake for hours, listening as planes came and went.

Khan's imagination flooded with jets in different formations, dodging missiles, blowing up and magically reconstituting themselves. Sometimes he was in the cockpit, punching the weapons up; sometimes he was a disembodied consciousness floating over the scene, taking it all in, powerless to alter it. When he finally fell asleep, his mind began replaying the morning's mission. Two angels from the Koran flew with the planes, and both stayed with him as they went against the Hindus. "Go to Tark," he shouted to them. "He needs you." But the angels refused.

He woke just as his wingmate's plane exploded. In the distance, antiair was going off, and the muffled explosions felt like part of his dream.

"It's not my fault," the pilot told the empty room. "I did my best."

Either the words were magic or fatigue finally overwhelmed him; Khan slumped down to his pillow and fell asleep. He awoke two hours later, not much better rested. The clock, at least, had put him out of his misery: it was 5 A.M., an acceptable hour for rising. He stood and did his stretching exercises, said his prayer and went to the cafeteria.

He had it largely to himself. Despite the constant rumors

of an impending cease-fire, the war continued with a vengeance. The Pakistan army had begun a counterattack in Kashmir during the night, and most of the base's planes had been thrown into the fight.

Munching a thick piece of *chapatti* bread with his morning tea, Khan listened as two intelligence officers debated how successful the assault would be. At best, said one of the men, a dark Pathan who had somehow procured a chicken for breakfast, the attack would confuse the Indians for a few hours. The other man, sipping slowly from a large cup of black coffee, maintained that the Indians had over-extended themselves, and would be pushed back to Delhi if they weren't saved by a cease-fire.

No doubt these men had important jobs, but for Khan their conversation demonstrated the utter futility of working behind the lines. He got up, pocketed a sweet roll and went to roust the Mushshak pilot who was to take him to Islamabad. The man was already waiting for him. Reassigned to northern patrol duties, he viewed his stop at the capital not merely as a welcome detour but as an honor—Major Khan's recent exploits were already well known.

The pilot's name was Lieutenant Umar but everyone referred to him as Um, he assured Khan. A solemn, slimly-built young man, his thin beard and small, slanted eyes made Khan think he might have some Chinese blood in him. He knew of the hero's reassignment, and after pushing his light observation plane into the air, began commiserating. He, too, wished to fight, though he was being exiled to a base in the Northwest Frontier Province where his main duty would be guarding against invading mountain goats. Um longed to trade in his observation plane for a Mirage, or if luck were really with him, an F-16.

Khan listened sympathetically. Even if he hadn't mentioned that he came from Karachi, Um spoke Urdu with an accent that gave him away as a *Mahaju*—a descendant of the Muslims who had crossed over from India at the time of the Partition. The fact that he flew the single-engined propeller plane was likely due to his lack of political and family connections, not his piloting abilities. Many of the

Mahaju still thought of themselves as refugees; as a group, they had not been able to integrate themselves sufficiently into Pakistan's power structures to claim the elite positions that Khan's family took for granted.

"There is always the possibility that we will encounter a MiG, Major," said the pilot as he angled his plane on a direct route to the capital. "Yesterday I was on my way back from spotting for an artillery unit near Jhelum. Two MiG-21s passed right over my head—apparently I was too slow for them." Um gave him a bashful smile, hinting that modesty kept him from ascribing his escape to anything more than luck. "By the time they turned around to find me I was hidden in the hills."

"The MiGs can be deadly," said Khan.

"I don't worry so much about MiGs, to be honest," answered Um. "My problem is ground fire. Even our own people shoot at me, before they realize who I am. A lucky shot could take down this plane."

"An unlucky shot."

"Lucky or unlucky, it all depends on your perspective."

Khan soon found himself describing his near-fatal encounter yesterday. By all rights, Khan admitted, he should not have returned.

Both men fell silent. The lieutenant concentrated on his flying; Khan became absorbed with the view. Similar to a Cessna or other small spotter plane, the single-engine, propeller-driven Mushshak (the word meant "efficient" in Urdu) had a bulbous canopy jutting forward from its high overhead wing. In an odd way, it reminded Khan of the F-16, as if the fighter's bubble top had been welded in front of the lighter plane's wing. In any event, the design was perfect for an observation plane, giving the pilot and his passenger a wide-ranging view over the patchwork of irrigated fields and scrubby hills. They were flying toward an ancient salt range, and in the growing light the odd formations of rock looked like a collection of grotesque gargoyles, mustering to defend Pakistan.

"It's too bad," said the lieutenant as Khan stared toward the dark shadows. "There will be a cease-fire soon and everything will return to normal. I won't have a chance to become an ace like you.''

The sentiment was merely an echo of his own feelings, but it shocked Khan. Here they were, hoping that the fight would go on, so they could win personal glory.

''Here, Major, take these binoculars,'' said the pilot, reaching over with a pair of high-powered glasses. Inevitably, Khan's eyes drifted back toward the mountains where the counterattack had been launched, now starting to fill with the light blue fingers of early dawn. But instead of seeing planes, Khan spotted the large hulk of a bird ducking across them. It was an optical trick—the bird was not near the mountains, or he never would have been able to spot it. Still, Khan watched in fascination as the animal worked its wings with slow grace, stroking the air with a gentle push as if he didn't want to disturb it more than necessary.

''That must be the largest eagle I've ever seen,'' he told Um. As he spoke, he remembered the bird on the runway yesterday. It had been years since he noticed eagles. Now they were all around him.

''The glasses make everything seem larger. Just think what an Indian AA battery looks like.''

Yes, thought Khan. I wouldn't have your job for the world. He followed the bird for a half minute more before it faded into the background of the distant mountains.

Islamabad's white government buildings were still yellowish stalks in the morning light when the Mushshak pilot landed. Khan had no difficulty finding an air force jeep and driver when he announced his destination, and was soon speeding through the broad streets of the nation's capital. The familiar closeness of the bazaars and the crowded roadways that were regular features of other Pakistani cities were unknown here. Even if the hour had been later and civilian activity not curtailed by the war, the city would have seemed almost empty to him.

Dark green trucks were parked at several corners, but he saw no soldiers on the streets until they approached Constitutional Avenue, where the presidency and parliamentary buildings were located. The driver turned into Shakaparian

Park, the large expanse of space near the center of the city dominated by Rawal Lake. His cousin's headquarters was in a brand new building at the far end. It was more like a piece of abstract art than a building, a huge slope of concrete narrowing into a triangular peak that seemed ready to leap into the air. It had been praised variously as an echo of past Mogul glories (the slashing motion suggested a horseman's charge, claimed one admirer) and a harbinger of Pakistan's future jet fighters. But its main purpose was to top a well-fortified bomb shelter which extended thirty stories below and could survive even a direct hit by the largest bombs in the American and Russian inventories.

The bunker was the air force's command center. Even in peacetime it was a busy place. Now it swarmed with people, bees rushing to keep the PAF fighting. Walking into the building was like swallowing amphetamines. Khan's heart began to gallop. He watched impatiently as his bags were x-rayed. Finally he was cleared through a metal detector and handed back his papers. Waving off a guide, Khan made his way to the elevator.

His cousin had two offices. The one above ground in the triangle was largely ceremonial; even during peacetime he rarely spent time there. Khan descended to the first sub-basement, where he had to run another security gamut—this one even more strenuous, with his service number punched into a computer and the clerks eyeing him suspiciously until his identity was confirmed. The area where he stood was the nexus point for the hallways to the bunker elevators and maintenance areas. Barely a thousand square feet, there were perhaps fifty fully armed men and several large attack dogs standing guard around it.

Khan's clearance finally granted, he was directed to a set of elevators down a hallway to the left. These connected this portion of the building with the underground complex. Except for an elaborate emergency tunnel, the elevators were the only way to get below.

Smart weapons and nuclear bombs had effected quite a revolution in bunker technology, not to mention decor. While the word *bunker* conjures images of sandbagged trenches and dim caverns cut into the side of a mountain, the Pakistani air force command center was more like a modern office complex and shopping mall plunged beneath several thousand tons of concrete, steel and dirt. Large gardens sat in the center of each level. These bio-rechargers complemented the more conventional (if finicky) air- and water-exchange machinery. Special banks of lights approximated external conditions, though the shift from night to day was somewhat more abrupt than the architects had planned.

Khan's elevator stopped about a hundred feet down and he had to walk several hundred feet laterally to get into a second car and continue to his destination. After a short ride, this one also reached the end of its shaft, and Khan stepped across a series of air locks into a third to complete his journey. The offsets were just one of the precautions against a well-programmed missile that might try to worm its way into the command center's heart.

Armed guards checked Khan's credentials again when he exited the elevator. The energy he had felt upstairs had begun to dissipate; this was good, he thought, for it was best to deal with his cousin calmly. Nur was motivated by logic, and Khan intended to lay out a grand speech for him. Weighted with facts about why he should remain in the air, it would be an eloquent appeal to his cousin's noblest principles.

"Well, well, a war hero who carries his own bags," said the general, suddenly clapping him on the back as he walked along the corridor. "I will have to remember this when I am interviewed about you."

"Why are you taking me off the line?" Khan responded, his preparation forgotten.

Nur merely smiled and hugged the major, who found himself trembling with anger and frustration. "Come inside, come inside," he said, opening his office door.

"Why are you putting me behind a desk?"

The general leaned to one side in front of the doorway, looking at him. Once he'd been as slim as Khan; now his stomach hung off him almost as if he were pregnant. The pilot was looking with new, embittered eyes on the man he'd always regarded as a hero and role model.

Nur straightened and filled the hallway with laughter.

"Who would be so stupid as to put Pakistan's best pilot behind a desk?"

"Why else am I here?"

"Come on," said the general, taking the young man by the shoulder. "Let me get my briefcase, and then we can go."

"Go where?"

"To Kamra," said the general.

Nur uttered the city's name as if it were a magic spell. Headquarters for the Pakistan Aeronautical Complex, it was at Kamra that Khan's Falcon had been upgraded.

"I don't want to be a test pilot," said Khan, but his cousin ignored him. Following along silently, he mentally rehashed his arguments as they took the long journey back to the surface, then rode in a limo out to the airport, where a Dassault-Breguet transport waited for them. He planned an all-out assault once they were in the air, this time with a more studied demeanor. But Khan didn't get a chance to speak. After a few derogatory comments about the army and the fact that they had lost the war before it began, Nur became silent, gazing out the window. Ordinarily, the general was anything but a brooder. Khan sensed that it would be useless to say anything now, and so added his own silence to his cousin's.

Had Nur already given up on the war? Was he thinking of cutting a deal with a new government set up by an occupying army? Khan could not conceive of life under the Hindus, or worse, their Sikh slaves. As the plane touched down and then rolled along the runway, his brain frothed. He was afraid to speak. One word might release a torrent of denunciation.

Khan did not wish to disobey the family, but surely he could not stand for this. Walking the few steps to the door, the pilot felt as if everything he had ever believed had been proven wrong by mathematical formula. Squares had five sides instead of four; triangles were circular.

His cousin was not a hero.

The flight attendant popped the hatch and Khan followed Nur out onto the tarmac. He looked at his feet, breathing slowly, concentrating so hard on controlling his emotions that he did not see the huge airplane sitting directly across from the Dassault-Breguet.

"What do you think of your new plane?"

Khan looked up. There was an angel before him, a large, magnificent black angel with broad wings and a massive sword.

It was more accurate to call it an angel than a plane, for it was like no other jet Khan had seen. The closest any came was the American F-22, which the Pakistani pilot had observed only from a distance. This craft was large, nearly twice the size of his Falcon, with a similarly bulbous canopy. Two huge engine bulges began where the fuselage disappeared, molded directly into the wing, a diamond-shaped wedge whose leading and trailing edges were adjustable flaps. There was no tail fin—instead, the rear wings angled up at approximately forty-five degrees, again with variable attack and trailing surfaces. The plane's surface was a dull, seemingly porous black, made of an exotic polymer that was more like finely tufted hair than solid metal.

"It is unbelievably light," said a man in a gray suit who sidled up next to the pilot as he admired the jet. "At first, we were worried because as the size increased there was the potential for shortening the range. But we have made many breakthroughs."

"Sardar headed the development team," said Nur, clapping his hand on his cousin's back. "I would say he did a remarkable job."

"Does it fly?" asked Khan.

The general and the engineer laughed, as did a third man, a foreigner, who walked forward from a group of officers and mechanics on the far side of the plane.

"They say it can fly sideways," Nur told Khan.

"A slight exaggeration," said the foreigner, a Frenchman. He was very short, and it took three steps for him to accomplish what the others would have done in one or two. But it soon became obvious that he was a pilot, and a very good one: As the general went to greet the other men, the foreigner delivered a brief but thorough lecture on the plane's flight characteristics. It was all fly-by-wire, with a comprehensive computer-assist system more advanced than the Falcon's. The plane started out more aerodynamically stable than the F-16 through a wider range of speeds, and the combination of the positive controls and its native flying characteristics made it capable of amazing maneuvers under all regimes. From sub- to trans-sonic to Mach 3 and perhaps Mach 4, it was more a dream of flight than an airplane.

"Imagine a Fulcrum married to an F-22," said the Frenchman, whose name was Louis Denoux, "and you begin to understand the capabilities. The reactions of the controls can be so precise they will surprise you."

A contract pilot brought into the country secretly, Denoux had begun flying tests four months before. The new plane could turn tighter than the Falcon, he said, at both low and high speeds, thanks to the basic design, infinitely adjustable flaps and thrust vectoring. The aircraft's flight computers would decide how specifically to help accomplish the maneuver—varying the flaps through a turn, for example, adjusting the thrust, or both. This would be transparent to the pilot—all he would have to know was how tight he wanted to turn. As far as he was concerned, he did the same thing no matter whether he was subsonic or cranking it out beyond Mach 2.

But that was hardly the plane's major accomplishment. Its stealthy characteristics reduced it to the size of an insect until very close range. The power plant (a purloined and heavily modified Pratt & Whitney variable-cycle engine) would let the jet cruise around Mach 1.6, with fuel efficiency twice that of the already vastly improved F-16. Top speed was still undetermined; they had been riding out over Mach 3, but had not rigged it specifically for speed.

"The controls are similar to your Falcon," continued the Frenchman. "With more computer capacity, of course. You will feel comfortable immediately. But you'll want to be careful with the indicators, especially at low altitude. The plane rides so smoothly you may not be able to tell that you've let the speed bleed off—the feel is different, lighter than anything you've flown.''

Khan nodded. Already he was imagining what it would be like to fly.

"We call it the Snow Leopard," said Nur. "And it is beyond anything the Indians have. Still worried about being a test pilot?''

Khan's face turned red. How easily he'd been bought off. "I would rather be defending my country."

"You will be," snapped the general. "We had planned to turn the plane over to Colonel Benzair in a few months," he added in a more gentle voice, "but circumstances have forced us to change our timetable. I understand, however, that I am getting the best interceptor pilot in the country. Even if I thought some of the reports were made to flatter me, your record over the past few days has shown that it is true. You better get busy," the general added, nodding toward Denoux. "You will be flying a mission tomorrow night."

Southeastern Iran. 11 A.M.

Though the furniture was more than comfortable, Greeley found it impossible to sit and so paced the length of the large room, contemplating the sleek marble walls and wondering when they were going to get going. Every so often he tried to start a conversation, but O'Connell was more absorbed than ever.

He hadn't exactly been a laughing hyena when they'd first met, but his companion looked positively morose now, sitting on the couch, arms folded. Greeley, on the other hand, was feeling more and more energetic. Overpowering the Iranian thug at the airport had been unexpectedly reassuring. He even had flashes of his old confidence, anticipating the B-50.

Fate had a way of balancing everything out. The less you

thought about it, the easier it was. That was the only way to survive.

Three hours passed like that, O'Connell slouched on the couch, Greeley orbiting the food and booze but not touching any of it. Finally a white-suited man with close-cropped hair and a slight limp arrived to take them to their audience with Renard. O'Connell rose from the couch and Greeley followed along dutifully. "I want to talk to him alone," O'Connell told him.

"Sure," said Greeley, continuing behind him.

O'Connell shook his head. "All right. Just keep your mouth shut."

The attendant led them a short distance down the hallway. Here the floor was covered with a thick carpet decorated with vivid blue waves on a white field. It looked so magnificent Greeley felt awkward stepping on it, as if he were walking on a painting. An ornate iron gate stood at the end of the corridor; the attendant pushed it aside and they entered a large atrium filled with exotic trees and small, well-cared-for shrubs. Small birds flitted through the warm, almost humid air, filling the room with their songs.

The atrium, about the size of a baseball infield, had a brook coursing through three-quarters of it, and as their guide led them over a small footbridge, Greeley noticed a school of fish treading water just under its shadow.

"They're piranha," said O'Connell.

The wisecrack heightened Greeley's curiosity, and he stooped down to get a closer look.

"Come on, if you're coming," growled O'Connell, and Greeley rose and hustled down the slate pathway between the trees to catch up to the two men, leaving the room through another iron-gated portal.

This passage was darker than the others. Lined with wood, its long beams ran in the direction they were walking, thick ribs of polished red.

"It's hand-carved cedar," O'Connell said as Greeley caught up. "Don't get overly impressed, or Renard will spend hours telling us about it."

Greeley felt like telling him to lighten up, but held his

179

tongue as they reached the end of the hallway and took a sharp right turn into a small antechamber where a pair of guards snapped their weapons across their chests. That was probably more for show than anything else, Greeley realized, but the Uzis, equipped with large magazines and wooden butts, made him quicken his pace.

O'Connell ignored the men. Like their guide, he stopped next to the doorway and leaned against the wall to remove his shoes. Greeley hesitated, remembering that the heel of one of his socks had a hole in it. His fear of being left behind overcame his embarrassment, however, and he yanked his shoes off, making the hole bigger, and followed O'Connell inside.

"I'd heard you were dead," rang out a voice.

"Wishful thinking," responded O'Connell.

The room was somber. Ornately carved wood lined all four walls, panel after panel repeating a pattern of rounded triangles from top to bottom. The only light came from a large window on the left. A long, narrow rectangle that pinched into an oval at the top, it was filled with a pale blue glass that softened the strong rays of the sun.

"Who is your friend?" asked the room's lone inhabitant, sitting on one of the pillows on a short platform at the far end of the otherwise empty space.

"A pilot," answered O'Connell.

"I thought you did your own flying."

"I only fly helicopters. This is my fixed-wing man."

"Oh yes," said Renard, eyeing Greeley. The attendant had retreated to the doorway. "So nice to meet you."

Greeley nodded and took Renard's hand. The Frenchman's grip was wet and loose, soft as a girl's. His long ponytail bobbed up and down as they shook. Though he looked to be in his fifties, he had a full head of hair. His face was smooth, unconcerned. His voice bordered on effeminate. Wearing dark pants and a black button-down shirt with a woven, patterned front, he appeared pudgy and relatively tall, though he was sitting down. He looked more like a rock star gone to seed than the vicious arms dealer O'Connell had warned him of.

"An adventure with the Iranians at the airport, I understand," Renard said, turning his attention back to O'Connell.

"Was that your doing?"

Renard laughed, pointing his finger at the agent. "If I had arranged a reception, would you be here to join me? No, I just didn't have the time to notify my friends and I decided, well, so what if I don't?"

O'Connell frowned. The arms dealer flicked his hair and turned to Greeley, surprising him by using his name. "Do you like my little house, Mr. Greeley?"

"It's really somethin'."

"Yes, it is, isn't it? Why don't you two sit down and tell me whether you've come to do more than admire it?"

Greeley folded his right foot—the one with the hole in the sock—under himself slowly, his knees stiff from the plane. He was lucky. If the weather had been more humid, his arthritis would have locked the joints solid by now.

"I'm looking for transportation to Pakistan," said O'Connell.

"Pakistan? There's a war there."

"The thing I like about you, Renard, is that you state the obvious with such flair."

"Still the same, cynical Mr. O'Connell. The CIA did not completely succeed in breaking you, then?"

"Why would they try to break me?"

"We hear strange things in the Middle East. We hear rumors of your death. We also hear that you gave away many secrets under the pressures of their torture."

"They wouldn't need me if they decided to screw you."

"I'm sure they wouldn't. Nor would they have to torture you, I imagine."

"I'm on my way to Pakistan, Renard, and wondered if you could arrange some transportation."

"I'm hardly a travel agent."

"It might be worth your while to help me into the country. And out."

"Out?"

"I need the airport at Jindaran put at my disposal. Or another one."

O'Connell's tone changed abruptly, his words dancing together in a way that made them impossible for Greeley to understand. For a moment, he felt as he did at the onset of a fever, his brain swimming with a virus. Then he realized O'Connell and Renard had begun speaking French.

The arms dealer's ponytail did a little jig as he tilted his head back and listened. He occasionally punctuated O'Connell's comments with a short *"oui,"* but mostly he listened.

"I assume you do not speak French, Mr. Greeley," he said finally.

Greeley shook his head.

"Does it make you nervous to know that your partner is keeping secrets from you?"

He shrugged. It didn't make him feel comfortable, at all, but at the moment there wasn't much he could do about it.

"Would you like some lunch? You've had such a long journey, and this will be boring for you."

After an almost indiscernible nod from O'Connell, Greeley struggled to his feet. Forgetting his shoes by the door, he followed the white-suited attendant back through the atrium to a dining room in another part of the complex. Here he was met by a young woman in a diaphanous gown that looked a lot like the nightie Olissa had worn when she was in the mood.

"We can make anything you desire," the woman offered as he sat down. The invitation seemed to extend to more than the menu. All Greeley could think of was the hole in his sock. "Perhaps you would like to start with some wine?"

"Wine would be fine," he managed.

"There is roast rabbit today. Perhaps with some kasha."

"Sounds great," said Greeley, hoping they were still talking about food.

"Very good," said the young woman, bowing and leaving the room. She returned quickly, carrying a crystal decanter filled with dark red wine and a clear, finely chiseled goblet. She put the glass down and poured the wine. Greeley's nostrils exploded with the smell of ripened, carefully fermented grapes. As he reached out his hand toward the glass, it began to tremble.

Don't do it, James, he told himself.

One little sip.

You won't take one little sip because there's a whole bottle here. And a lot more—this place is just pure temptation.

O'Connell might cut him out. Might even just leave him here, strand him in the middle of southern Iran.

But one glass. He wouldn't begrudge him that. Even if he did, where was he going to get another pilot now?

What would Olissa say?

Olissa would let him drink. She'd let him drink so many times before.

"You know what?" said Greeley, looking up at the young woman as she finished pouring the wine. "I think maybe I'm not as thirsty as I thought. I think, like, could you take the wine away?"

"Would you prefer a white wine, perhaps a—"

"Just water," he said quickly. "That's really all I'd like to drink."

Nizam's Compound, Northeast of Karachi. 11:15 A.M.

Morena gave her tea a deliberate swirl and then dropped the spoon next to the plate, staring at the liquid before picking it up and sipping. A few yards from the veranda, a purple thrush sailed into a small tree next to the courtyard's pond and began singing.

Such a pleasant prison, the CIA deputy desk chief thought. Morena wasn't exactly being held here against her will, but it was obvious that the princess wanted to keep an eye on her while she attended to her own schemes. Clearly Nizam saw the renewed CIA contact as a potential for leverage, but Morena was not sure how. While her ultimate aim was obvious—she'd often confessed that the restoration of her homeland had been her single-minded goal since she was a child—her immediate plans were not as easy to decipher.

The United States would never support an independent

homeland in Pakistan; there were enough problems in South Asia as it was. Eventually, there would be a serious conflict between the princess and the Pakistani military—one of the reasons the agency had steadily reduced its contacts with her.

Morena felt fairly confident that Nizam did not know about Golden Bear, and she wanted to keep it that way. She would make contact with O'Connell on her own this afternoon or evening, size up the situation, and use the princess's help as sparingly as possible. There was one complication, however. Before coming here, Morena had tried to contact Westlake without success. She was worried about that—he ought to have been waiting for her call.

A short, brown-robed man stood a respectful distance away, watching as she finished her tea. The man—he'd told her to call him George—had been outside her door when she awoke. Princess Nizam, he'd informed her, was busy this morning, and wished him to see to her every need. Morena did not like the way he raised his eyebrow when he said that, but the man apparently had meant nothing beyond arranging for breakfast.

"George," she said, deciding she had waited long enough. "Do you think you could arrange a telephone?"

The pale-skinned man took two steps toward the table. "A telephone, Miss?"

"Yes. I'd like to call the embassy in Islamabad."

"I'm afraid this would be impossible, Miss."

"Why?"

"There are no communications to the capital."

"Just get me a phone."

The man shrugged but did not move. Morena stood up and began walking toward the administrative offices, the parachutelike legs of the Pakistani *salwar* she had borrowed from the princess billowing as she walked, drag chutes slowing her progress. George followed behind her silently.

She was halfway across the white-bricked porch when she was met by Murwan, Nizam's number one aide, who appeared from one of the small offices opening onto the passageway.

"There you are," he said, as if he had spent half the morning looking for her. "And did we have a pleasant breakfast?"

Morena had never liked Murwan. Like most Pakistani men, he treated women with barely disguised disdain. "It was fine," she said as she continued toward the door that led into the communications suite.

"May I ask where we're going?"

"To make a phone call."

"Oh. To Mr. O'Connell?"

"To the embassy."

"The embassy?"

This seemed to puzzle him greatly, as if he couldn't tell which embassy she was speaking of.

"The princess mentioned that there had been rumors about the secretary of state being kidnapped," said Morena. "I doubt they're true."

The cheeks beneath Murwan's white whiskers flashed crimson for a second.

"That is a foolish rumor," he said.

"I realize that."

"It's my fault," said the aide abruptly. He was less than a half foot from her, and suddenly gripped her arm, as if he needed it to balance himself. A thin perfume of tobacco wafted from his mouth with his words. "I heard it from someone in the ministry, and thought I should tell her. There is no basis to it, of course."

"Of course," said Morena. She looked at his ill-fitting Western-style suit, the baggy polyester pants cinched at the waist with a belt two sizes too big. His dark blue shirt, buttoned at the collar, clashed with the brown jacket. In the United States he could have been mistaken for a homeless man. "The embassy will enjoy the laugh."

She shook off his grip and continued into the office. An undernourished young man with large green eyes beneath bushy eyebrows sat in front of a large console. He wore a telephone headset around his neck.

"Get me the American embassy in Islamabad."

The kid shook his head. "Only military calls are allowed."

Morena gave him a who-are-you-trying-to-bullshit squint. The operator turned to Murwan, and they exchanged a few words in Urdu.

"A private line," said Morena, though she knew the conversation would be tapped.

"He will try," shrugged Murwan. "But it is a lot of trouble to go through for a rumor."

"Where is the princess this morning?" Morena asked, taking a stiff-backed chair across from the console.

"She had meetings with representatives of the party," said Murwan, who remained standing. "And then she reviews the militia. It is leaving for Sadiqabad, east of Karachi."

"I thought it wasn't allowed outside of the bounds of the old tribal area."

Murwan shrugged. "The army is no longer particular about who saves its neck."

The militia had always been a major point of contention with the army. But now it was being shifted to an important defensive position just to the south of the point where Indian troops had burst across the desert into Pakistan. Things must truly be desperate.

Renard's Palace, Southeastern Iran. Shortly before Noon.

"I can provide you with a car and driver to Pakistan," said Renard, shifting on the cushion to reach the wine his servant had just brought. "And better credentials. Honestly, who would think you were French?"

O'Connell focused his gaze on one of the satin pillows. He was remembering how to deal with Renard, how to affect the stolid demeanor of a jaded agent just doing his job.

"Are you sure you wouldn't like some of this?" asked his host, holding out the elaborately etched crystal glass. "Les Genevrières-dessus is one of the best wines of Meursault. White burgundies are so underrated.''

''No thanks.''

''I'm surprised the Muslims like you so much,'' laughed the arms dealer. ''Ordinarily, they don't want to be out-Islamed.'' He refilled his glass. ''At some point you will tell me what this is about, I suppose.''

''A very big payoff,'' said O'Connell.

Renard curled his head to the side and closed one eye, playing the clown. ''There are always big payoffs.''

''This one is special.''

''You know me, Michael. I like to deal in specifics,'' said Renard, straightening and sipping his wine.

O'Connell shrugged. Reluctance was an important part of the act.

''You shouldn't feel as if you are playing from a strong position,'' said Renard. ''I owe you nothing. And as far as the CIA is concerned—''

''Who says I'm working for the agency?''

''You wouldn't have me think that you're going to Pakistan on a sight-seeing trip, would you? My contacts told me practically your whole mission.''

''What did they tell you?''

''That's not important,'' said Renard, his ponytail shaking. O'Connell had caught him in a lie. ''What is important is what I will get in exchange for not killing you now.''

The agent laughed. He'd remembered Renard as being smoother than this. But at least the arms dealer hadn't heard that the agency had decided to dust him. That gave him more maneuvering room, and kept Renard wary of him—a necessary prerequisite for staying alive.

''I wouldn't be so self-assured, if I were you,'' said Renard. ''Perhaps I will turn you over to the Iranian authorities. I'm sure the men at the airport would like the opportunity of interrogating you.''

O'Connell decided he had played Renard's impatience far enough. ''The Pakistanis have nuclear weapons,'' he told him. ''I'm going to steal one.''

The Frenchman frowned. ''Everyone knows there are no

devices in Pakistan. They were destroyed several years ago.''

"Trust me.''

"This does not sound like you, Michael.'' Renard studied him, then gave him an impish smile. He had a small dimple in each jowl, as if a hole had been drilled into the flesh. "Perhaps this is a plan to trap me,'' he said.

"By whom?''

"The CIA does not like me.''

"If the CIA wanted to get you, they'd have the Israelis do it.''

Renard shifted uncomfortably. His fear of the Mossad had not diminished. "I have a very good bomb shelter.''

"If this is too much for you to handle, Renard, just say so. I didn't realize you'd lost your balls.''

"But you haven't lost a bit of your sharp wit.'' Renard's snarl was comforting. It was a sign the agent was getting to him. "What makes you think the CIA will let you get away with this?''

"They won't know about it. They haven't exactly had time for an inventory, and so they'll have to take my word when I tell them I'm giving them everything.''

Renard looked doubtful.

"There are real devices,'' said O'Connell. "I know it for a fact.''

"How do you get paid?''

"You put the money in an account. I trust you, Renard.''

"Now I know it is a trap, or a joke.''

"You have no exposure at all. You help me get into Pakistan, and take care of the delivery when I get out. You sell the weapon and we split the proceeds, fifty-fifty.''

"How will you get out of Pakistan?''

"That's my problem.''

"You need no help inside Pakistan? Not even weapons?''

"Everything is already arranged,'' he lied. It wouldn't be safe to use Blossom. Despite several hours of brooding, he had yet to settle on a new plan. He could hook up with some former *mujihadeen* gunrunners who had worked with him before; transportation to the base could be arranged and they would have more firepower than he'd ever need. On the other hand, it might be easier and simpler, if more brazen, to present himself to the Energy Ministry, claiming the CIA had planted some beaconing devices on the planes. They'd take him there themselves.

There was an undeniable thrill to walking out on the rope without a net, making it up as you went. As long as you didn't go too far, or panic.

"Such a confident man," said Renard, refilling his glass. "Who would ever suspect that you are dead?"

With great difficulty, O'Connell managed a smile. "How's that?"

"Two Pakistanis are being held for your murder in Paris. Simon tells me that there have been several news reports. I had heard a week ago that they were suddenly interested in finding you. Inquiries were even made in Iran, believe it or not."

O'Connell remembered the incident in the parking lot outside McDonald's, connected it to Paris. But why?

He knew they had nukes, that's why.

It wasn't Stockman or the agency at all.

Shit.

Shit, shit, shit.

"You needn't feign ignorance with me, Michael. I assume the news of your death was for Pakistan's benefit. You have another way of dealing with your CIA friends?"

"Yes."

"There will be a lot of risk if you stop here." The deep timbre in Renard's voice was reserved for the end game. O'Connell had made a very big, very dangerous mistake, but now he had to play through. "It is a problem for you as well as me. Even in Iran, there are CIA spies. And no doubt there will be some sort of American gizmo tracking you."

O'Connell regrouped behind his best plasterboard face. "I'll worry about the agency and the Paks," he said. "All you have to do is sell the weapon."

"Yes, that is easy for you to say."

"If it's too much work—"

"Ten million," said Renard hastily. "That is what I can get."

"It's worth three times as much."

"It's priceless," agreed Renard, "but ten million is the most we can hope for."

"Put five million into one of your Israeli accounts before I leave," said O'Connell. "If there is more, we can settle up later."

"That will make the Mossad suspicious."

O'Connell shrugged. "It is difficult to tell where the Mossad sits in any transaction."

Renard eyed him doubtfully, but O'Connell knew he would agree. For one thing, five million was a ridiculously small cut, a bargain that Renard couldn't pass up. And he would now conclude that the Israelis were somehow involved; he could figure on them as buyers of last resort.

The rest was settled quickly. An airstrip where fuel and the account number would be waiting. A rough timetable.

Renard, showing uncharacteristic magnanimity, offered him ten thousand dollars, cash, to help with incidentals.

O'Connell declined.

"Naturally, if you attempt to retrieve the money from the account prematurely, things will not go well," said the arms dealer.

"Of course not."

"And you trust me?"

"You're a man of your word, Renard," said O'Connell. "Besides, I have friends."

The arms dealer nodded solemnly.

The driver, a noncommunicative, generic muscle man, met the Americans in the courtyard. A black Toyota Land Cruiser, its surface freshly polished and gleaming in the afternoon sun, stood with its back hatch and doors open.

O'Connell, beginning to feel the effects of the long journey, propped his jacket against the window as a pillow. The jostling of the vehicle, and Greeley's chatter about the sights, made it difficult to drift off, but within a few miles his brain started to slide toward the familiar restlessness that often preceded sleep, tossing up images and problems as his concentration lagged.

The dead American thermostat salesman lying on the cold cement floor of the parking garage. It would have taken some doing to have him mistaken for O'Connell. Only the agency could have pulled off that bit of misinformation—most likely, as Renard had suggested, to mislead the Pakistanis. They'd feel safe with him out of the way.

Or perhaps it had been done to make *him* feel safe.

Should he trust Stockman or not?

Renard had just offered him five million dollars for a bomb; maybe he should trust that. In fact, from what he knew of Renard, he was better off trusting him than Stockman.

No way he could figure this out with Greeley always talking in his ear.

"Greeley, I'm not listening, all right? I'm trying to think."

"You don't have to be a jerk. I just asked what kind of helicopter it was."

"What helicopter?"

"The one over there," said Greeley, pointing out the side window. "I asked you about it twice."

They were passing a small clump of cement block buildings at the foot of the mountains, perhaps a former oil site or maybe a listening post, though the equipment needed for either venture was nowhere to be seen. Right in the middle was a concrete pad and a Bell Jet Ranger.

It took a few seconds for his brain to tell his mouth to tell the driver to turn off the road.

Renard's man glanced toward the back without slowing, and O'Connell's stomach tightened immediately, fearing he'd miscalculated once again.

Instantly, he had the move figured out—grab the guy's neck with his right hand, yank him back, give a quick left-handed roundhouse. Don't overestimate your strength this time, he told himself. Put everything into it right away.

If the guy was smart, he'd hit the gas. O'Connell could brace his knee into the seat to hold himself steady. Then he'd slip his left hand behind the son of a bitch's neck and break it.

"Pull over," he said in a low grunt.

"What are you saying?" asked the driver in Arabic.

Maybe the guy really couldn't speak English.

"Go back to those buildings," responded O'Connell in Arabic. "I want to look at that helicopter."

The driver complied with O'Connell's directions, spinning the Toyota around and driving up right next to the helicopter. Except for the color, the gray Bell Jet Ranger III was a spitting image of the last helicopter O'Connell had owned. Deluxe model—full controls on both sides. It seemed in reasonably good condition, and had only recently been flown—a half hour before at the most, O'Connell guessed as he leaned in gingerly and felt the warm seat cushion.

So where was the pilot? Or anyone else, for that matter?

O'Connell glanced toward the squat masonry building opposite the chopper, fifty or so yards away across the faded but smooth patch of cement. The building, the largest here, had a forlorn cast to it, the gray blocks battered by years of sharp winds. A thick wooden door covered the entrance, and smoke slipped from a chimney at the rear. The other buildings looked like abandoned pillboxes, leftover from a war—there were no doors or windows on any of them.

No vehicles anywhere, just the helicopter. It almost certainly belonged to smugglers. Probably dealing in archaeological artifacts pilfered from the local sites, though southern Iran was convenient for many things.

O'Connell didn't bother making a catalog as he hopped into the chopper. They wouldn't get very far if there was no fuel. But worst-case scenario, he could go back and borrow some from Renard. It'd be a hell of a lot faster than driving.

"Get our bags," he said to Greeley, reaching down to the battery switch and clicking the instruments to life. Hell, they'd topped her off for him. No time for a full preflight check—O'Connell jabbed at the idle cutoff switches, knocked the fuel boost on, held the mixture rich two seconds. Going on three and he had it back, reached for the ignition, engaged the engines, the clutch a little puzzled about being woken up so soon. He revved the RPMs, the needle sliding past 1,400, 1,500 before the rotors started beating the air with a heavy, sluggish womp.

O'Connell jostled himself into the seat, played with the throttle, got the feel. The blades cranked steadily now, and the helicopter strained to keep itself on the ground.

The noise of the motor brought two men running from the little building. O'Connell, who'd been watching the door, leaned on the throttle collective and then pulled it upward, increasing the rotors' angle of attack and pushing the helicopter forward. The men were yelling something—not all that politely. O'Connell pulled up farther on the collective, increasing the engine and rotor speed, and held his left rudder pedal down (the increasing RPM hiked the torque, which heightened the helicopter's natural tendency to kick its tail out to the right; the pedal controls adjusted the tail rotor to compensate). The helicopter sped forward and he buzzed the two men, then spun around and headed back to the far end of the runway where Greeley was running with the bags.

O'Connell turned around in time to see a third man run from the building carrying a Kalashnikov rifle. He was fiddling with it, trying to get a clip in. In a few seconds, he'd open up on full automatic. O'Connell left Greeley on the ground and charged back toward the building.

The gunman, still having trouble with his weapon, was too close to the building to hit with the skis. The best O'Connell could do was rear back like a bronco, sending a gust of wind and dirt toward the man, hoping to blind him. It didn't work, at least not very well—as he headed back for Greeley, crouched at the end of the pad, O'Connell heard the distinctive ping of small-arms fire hitting the underside of the fuselage. He plopped alongside him and leaned over to get the door as Greeley jumped in headfirst.

"The bags," O'Connell screamed at him.

Greeley's only answer was a muffled curse. O'Connell cursed as well, then yanked the throttle and pitched the helicopter ahead. The Bell's nose ducked forward as if nervous about the gunfire, then jumped uneasily into the sky as O'Connell pushed it hard to his left.

The Iranian with the Kalashnikov had burnt his clip and was putting in another when O'Connell skipped the chopper out of its quick U-turn. This time he gave it everything he had, zooming in on the men as if he were flying the gunship he'd cut his teeth on in the army.

The gunman had made the mistake of getting too far from the building, and O'Connell went after him full bore. He missed spearing him, but the rifle went flying from his hands as he hit the ground. Meanwhile, one of the other two had taken out a pistol and was shooting wildly; O'Connell pitched down the helicopter back and sent him sprawling for cover.

"What the hell are we doing?" groaned Greeley, who'd barely managed to get himself upright in the seat.

"You made such a goddamn fuss about your suitcase in Paris, and now you just want to leave it here?"

"Shit."

O'Connell buzzed the Iranians again. They gave up trying to retrieve the gun and dove into the small building, hugging the ground as the chopper skimmed in, just barely missing the last of them. He was aware of a thousand things as he kicked back toward the bags—the oil pressure gauge, nice and healthy, the Land Cruiser beating a retreat in the distance, the lightly clouded sky.

"Get out and get the bags," he said to Greeley as he dropped down next to them. Greeley looked at O'Connell like he was looking at the devil, but he hopped out of the cabin, pitched the bags in and then slid himself back into the seat. The Allison 250-C20J engine beat the twin blades into a frenzy as O'Connell took the Jet Ranger up, its rate of climb topping at a perfect spec 1,280 FPM. A hundred feet off the ground he looped back, getting his bearings as he looked at the compass and found the road toward Pakistan.

"Well at least you finally found something to smile about," said Greeley.

War Breaker

A Hospital in Northeastern India. Noon.

After Gen. Arjun Singh passed out, his head floated in an ocean of constantly changing temperature. One moment the commander of India's Third Army Group felt like he'd been dropped into a lava stream, the next into an arctic pool. He had a vague sensation of being lifted onto a stretcher, and then flying through the air—medivacked to a field hospital. The sensation was repeated an hour later, as he was taken to a hospital in India. He knew he was being moved though he could not see around him; the knowledge was planted in his brain by some force he couldn't detect.

The general had been injured as a young man in the war to liberate Bangladesh. It was a light wound, comparatively; a piece of shrapnel lodged in his chest. It had been a painful ordeal nonetheless. Even under sedation, he'd felt the sickening suck of his skin around the wound, braced himself as each wave of nausea shook his stomach. He knew he wasn't going to die, but he was sure he had found a strong equivalent of the poetic descriptions of hell.

His feeling now was strangely peaceful. Physical pain was gone; in fact, all physical sensation had disappeared—he existed as a disembodied mind, hovering between his body and the spirit world. He had a vague awareness of having been operated on, and now being in a hospital room, but otherwise his universe was a blank white cloud that surrounded and supported him.

For many hours the general stared at this cloud, without anything happening. And then with no warning, with no thunder in the distance or lightning, without a catastrophe or a change in his mental or physical state, the mythical figure of Shiva appeared directly in front of him.

The god's bright sword flashed in an arc over his head, waved by one of his two left hands. The other left arm was held straight across his chest, in the stylized pose of a dance. A serpent curled around one of his right arms; the other held a cup. Shiva's red-bronze skin shone brighter than even the sword; he wore only a loincloth, and his muscles rippled with enormous power.

The representation of the god was a common one, seen not only in old Hindu art and texts but in the popular movies that filled the dull afternoons and evenings of so many of the country's youths. Arjun was a Sikh, but even if he had been a devout believer in the Hindu pantheon, he would not have confused this product of his imagination with anything approaching the god it was supposed to represent. Nevertheless, he viewed it with awe, amazed that his mind could conjure up such a vivid image.

The figure brought his sword down to his side with a swoop, attaching it to his belt by sliding it through a thin piece of string that magically held itself open. The snake slithered around the god's back and curled over his thigh as two of the god's four arms disappeared.

The general expected that the figure itself would disappear next, and felt himself actually wishing that it wouldn't. He wanted the apparition to remain in front of him a little longer, at least until he could remember what childhood movie or story had given birth to it.

"You do not believe in me," said the ghost. Its rich voice reminded Arjun of his second-in-command, Brigadier General Shastri. How strangely the mind worked—it could not have picked a character more opposite the poet-soldier.

"Of course not," Arjun replied, speaking as if he had been called on in religious class to answer a question. "You are a caricature of the primal forces that shape the world."

There was a swirling noise, and the figure disappeared, consumed in a flame.

"I have always liked the Sikhs, despite their intransigence," boomed Shiva, unseen. "They know the value of war. Hindus do not. Muslims pretend to, but the Sikhs are bathed in blood from birth."

"We fight to restore justice," said Arjun, defending himself as well as his religion. "We have been persecuted since the days of the Fifth Guru. We have been tortured, driven from our land—of course we fight."

Shiva appeared again. There was a sword in each of his four arms. He propelled the blades around with dazzling speed, whirling the air with such force that they seemed to slash at Arjun's face. He began to feel faint.

"No wonder the Hindus do not trust you," said Shiva. "You are a particularly brave and stubborn example of your race. How many times have they reminded you that it was Sikhs who murdered Gandhi?"

"Many times."

"Mankind will never change," said the god of his imagination. "You fight because you need to flirt with destruction—it's the only way you can emulate the gods."

"We fight for justice," replied the general weakly.

"Vanity is everything to you, Arjun Singh. You have all the amenities of your office. You worry about your status. You are monstrously ambitious—you intend to restore the Sikh homeland, don't you?"

"Yes."

"So you can lead it?"

"No."

Arjun felt himself slipping into a funneling hole, a drain at the center of the bed.

"It's all the same to me," laughed the god. "You act for me, whether you acknowledge it or not. Your reasons are not important. You are doomed to seek your own destruction, and sooner or later, you will succeed."

"We do not seek destruction," whispered the general.

As soon as he had spoken, he was pulled upward, yanked from the bed. Shiva disappeared. There was buzzing in the general's ears, the same sound of the dead that had greeted him at the door of the trailer when he went for his men.

Vaguely, he saw the form of a nurse standing over him, felt his body again, briefly, felt something warm slipping into his arm.

Grand Paradise Hotel, New Delhi. 12:25 P.M.

For the first time in nearly twelve hours, the American secretary of state felt relaxed enough to slide back in his chair and loosen his tie. The seat was an ultramodern model, designed to look as uncomfortable as it felt, but Grasso was too tired to mind. He watched as the last of the Indian delegation filed from the stark white conference room, noticing for the first time that the only decoration on the walls was a stainless steel band that ran just under the ceiling and probably symbolized some Hindu god.

Everything in the country stood for some god or another; Grasso wondered how they kept track.

Tracy waved her hand in front of his face, just in time to keep his eyes from glazing over. "What's top priority?"

"Go over to the embassy and get the cables out," he told her. "Then join us at the airport."

She nodded. There was no need to give more direction; Tracy was twice as bright and three times as efficient as she was beautiful.

And she was beautiful. Grasso had a sudden urge to stand up and take her in his arms. The movie *Casablanca* flashed through his mind, and he saw himself as Bogart, momentarily overcome by passion, grasping his woman and bending her backward in a long kiss.

The vision evaporated as his undersecretary for Asian affairs, Tony Jordan, asked if he wanted him to go to Pakistan as well.

"I need you to stay here and baby-sit these guys," Grasso said, smiling at Tracy to dismiss her and then reluctantly turning to Jordan. "Keep on top of the new prime minister. We need this cease-fire to take hold."

"George Habib is still over at army headquarters."

"Let him stay there. He's done great so far."

"As long as they don't start asking him when he's going to deliver on all his promises."

Grasso nodded. He'd need to get the department of defense to sign off on a laundry list of arms and parts sales, including tank engines, but he could worry about that later. The president had said to get it done, whatever it took. That meant supporting the new government that had formed overnight, and it meant promising arms deals ostensibly aimed at "internal security." Not to mention the agricultural agreements. Peace was never cheap.

"What are you going to tell the media?" Jordan asked

Grasso as they got up to leave the room.

"The whole shot," replied Grasso, mentally outlining his spiel. "India has agreed to an immediate unilateral cease-fire. Positions will be frozen, no shooting unless fired on. We're working on plans for a withdrawal."

"Peace in our time."

"Yeah, as long as the Pakistanis go for it," said Grasso. Jordan looked doubtful. "They better," the secretary added. "The Indians are kicking their butts."

"The Indian general who led the southern campaign was injured yesterday, and he's in a hospital. George says that helped cool off the army brass. They halted their advance."

"Whatever it takes," muttered Grasso, walking from the room. He was already preparing for the Pakistanis. This press statement would be the first step—give Islamabad a little love kiss.

Schenck met him outside the elevator, and they got in together. Grasso felt as close to Schenck as to anyone in his entourage; closer. Schenck had run the international security department at IBM before coming to State, and made his mark with Grasso early: On their first trip together, he broke into the laundry of a Moscow hotel to retrieve the secretary's formal dinner jacket after the jerks had closed without returning it in time for dinner.

"So how many points am I going to have to give you for the Giants this week?" Grasso asked.

"Oh, I don't know. Washington looked a little slow last week."

"Too many big guys," Grasso kidded. "You get over two hundred and eighty pounds and you can't take the heat."

"I don't think the Indians are doing a particularly good job," said the security director abruptly. "Just about anyone can walk in off the street here. I have two of my guys watching the entrance, but there's so much going on it'll be impossible to control if things get queer."

"We're done here, Bill. Don't worry about it."

"Pakistan's going to be worse."

"Relax. We're the good guys."

"That's what has me worried," said Schenck as the elevator car slowed to a stop. He stepped in front of the secretary, shielding him as the door opened. He scanned the lobby and then stepped out.

The reception area was a long rectangle divided into three sections by columns, plants and a few pieces of furniture. Though the hotel was as busy as it had been in years, the room seemed almost empty because of its huge size. The far corner, however, was filled with floodlights, camera equipment and the assorted paraphernalia of the international media. The TV shots of his press conference would make the place look tight and crowded.

The reporters, alerted to the secretary's arrival by the sight of his assistant, began buzzing. Two of Schenck's men slipped up and flanked Grasso as he walked toward the cordoned-off press area; the security director melted into the background to make sure the car was ready.

"There's a rumor that there's been a breakthrough," said CNN's Kevin Kalm, snaking in front of the secretary as he walked to the podium.

"Yeah, yeah," said Grasso, momentarily forgetting he was supposed to be playing the gracious statesman. You need CNN, Grasso reminded himself. They'll be watching in Pakistan. And D.C. After this trip, you can talk to Ted Turner himself.

"Are you going to make a statement?"

"Now why would I do that?" said the secretary. "This is only a press conference."

Kalm seemed to take him literally. Grasso slipped past him and continued the last few steps to the dais.

The wooden podium was extremely high; even standing on his tiptoes, he could barely see over the top. No way he was going to let that image go to Islamabad, let alone Washington. Grasso stepped to one side and cleared his throat, thanking the reporters for coming.

There was a mad scramble to relocate the microphones. Grasso felt one of his security men grip his left arm firmly as the reporters rushed forward. The man either didn't know his own strength or misjudged Grasso's—the secretary's biceps felt as if they had been slipped into a vice. He winced, then grinned stoically.

"I have a short statement," he said. "And then I'll take questions. The Indian government today at twelve-thirty P.M. local time declared a unilateral cease-fire. All Indian units on Pakistani soil have halted their advances, and will fire only if fired upon. I see a broad opportunity for peace and a basis of, uh, mutual understanding between India and Pakistan. I'm on my way now to Islamabad to continue talks."

"Is a withdrawal likely?" asked a woman reporter from Reuters about midway back in the pack.

"We'll see," said Grasso. "But I would emphasize that I'm optimistic."

"Do you think the Pakistanis will really stop fighting while the Indians are on their soil?" asked Kalm.

"I hope so," said Grasso. "We view this as the first step of the process toward a lasting peace."

"Do you think this could turn into a nuclear confrontation?"

Grasso squinted at Kalm.

"How?"

"Well, uh, Professor—"

It was that professor crap that drove him up the wall. "Maybe you haven't done your homework," said Grasso, drawing appreciative snickers from the crowd. "The disarmament treaty that both countries signed remains in force and is being observed. I can assure you of that. There are no nuclear weapons on the subcontinent. And let me just mention that it was the Pakistanis who led the way in reaching a treaty in that area. The Pakistanis have a long history as peacemakers."

Now the snickers were for him, but Grasso didn't care—that was for Islamabad, and the press people could go to hell. All of them.

"OK, thank you," said Grasso, turning away. "We've got to go now." He had to push a bit, then the two security men helped clear a path. His stride widened as he walked toward the lobby entrance. He gave himself a good grade on his performance—some points in Islamabad and a put-down of Kalm. Not bad for a two-minute statement of the obvious.

There was a bad moment then, a terrible moment halfway to the door. Schenck's men had fallen a half step behind, one speaking into his two-way radio, the other still scanning the clump of press people. Grasso was anxious to get to the airport, and his jacket flapped open as he hurried along, his belly a fat, white-shirted target.

An Indian darted in from the side and lunged toward him, his hand streaking up with something dark in it.

There was a flash and another flash; Grasso felt the blood rush from his head.

The rest happened in slow motion: The man closer, his hand up, level with Grasso's chest. A huge arm appeared, the branch of a tree, slamming into the Indian's side. Grasso felt himself going down, pulled down. There was screaming.

"Get him out of here," Schenck shouted, grabbing the diminutive assailant to his chest in a loveless embrace.

Grasso felt himself hauled to his feet and then he was running, sandwiched between two large torsos. There were people with guns everywhere.

It was impossible to breathe. His side was caving in, his ribs collapsing. His lungs screamed as the damp air hit him just outside the hotel door.

Like so many men who had spent their youths reading books instead of playing football, the secretary of state had a catastrophic view of pain—if it hurt more than a bruise, he thought he was going to die. As he was hustled out of the Indian government building and then literally thrown headfirst into the rear compartment of his Lincoln, he assumed that he would look down and find a gaping red hole in his stomach. Grasso lay face down on the seat, his feet sprawled on the floor as the car screeched away from the curb. They'd gone a full block before he finally rolled to one side and looked down at the brown leather covering the seat. Seeing no blood, he slid over, kneeling toward the back seat as if he were praying, and looked at his jacket.

Intact. His shirt was still white, except for the small spot from the coffee he'd spilled earlier. He'd had the air knocked out of him, that was all.

Grasso climbed upright into the seat. They were in the heart of the city, the limo driver doing his best to speed along the crowded boulevard.

"I'm OK," said Grasso, knocking on the bulletproof glass separating them. "I'm OK. Take me to the airport."

The driver nodded and the secretary of state slipped back, regaining his composure. He had a pocket radiophone that tied him directly to his security team. He took out the device, about the size of a wallet, and flipped it open.

"Schenck, what the hell's going on?"

There was no answer.

"Bill? Are you all right?"

Moyers, one of the men who had thrown him into the car, responded.

"Bill's with the Indians, Mr. Secretary."

"What happened?"

"Looks like it was a misunderstanding. Guy had a camera in his hand—just wanted to take a close-up."

"Shit."

"Sorry if we hurt you, sir."

"No problem. I'm fine," said Grasso, leaning back into the seat. "You guys did your jobs. Good work."

"Thank you, sir."

"Make sure Jordan gets the full story to the press. That I'm fine. We don't want any rumors screwing us up in Pakistan. Tell Schenck to wrap things up as quickly as possible. Have him call me. I want him on the plane, if he can make it."

Grasso dropped the phone on the seat next to him, leaving it open. He sat for a second, looking outside to get an idea of where he was, then took the cellular handset from its cradle in the seat panel. Dialing the embassy, he got the ambassador's assistant on the line.

"Melissa, has Howard come back yet?"

The aide sounded surprised. "The ambassador called from the meeting and said he was on his way, Mr. Grasso. We have a secure line to Islamabad waiting for him."

"Good."

"We heard there was an incident at the hotel. There was a report that you were shot."

"What was it Mark Twain said?" chuckled the secretary, amazed at how fast the news had traveled. This was going to become state department folklore; might as well start putting the right spin on it. "Why don't you get out a bulletin that I'm still alive and kicking?"

"Right away."

"Have the ambassador call me as soon as he's gotten off with Islamabad. I'm on my way to the airport."

"Yes, sir. I'm glad you're OK, Mr. Grasso."

"Well, so am I," he laughed. The secretary hung up the phone and looked out the car window. They were making better time now, out on the highway to the airport.

He'd call D.C. from the plane. The president would want to know what was going on.

The incident would help him in Islamabad. There was a macho culture there, and they'd appreciate how he hadn't been fazed by it all. He'd tell them they'd have to observe the cease-fire. Forever, damn it. No conditions.

Kashmir had been simmering for over fifty years, and the problem wasn't going to be solved overnight. Things were too mixed up with religion and politics to be settled easily. India would withdraw to its pre-attack boundaries. He already had an off-the-record agreement that they would.

But if he didn't solve Kashmir, they'd be fighting for three or four more generations. What if he proposed a formula for a semiautonomous state, under UN supervision?

Grasso let his mind wander, considering the possibilities of a settlement. But cut loose, his imagination returned to the chaotic scene in the hotel lobby, the man looming out in front of him.

He'd thought he was going to die. It was a dark, empty sensation, centered in his stomach. He tried to bring his attention back to the Kashmir problem, but his brain wouldn't cooperate. Through some trick of psychological association, the scare at the hotel had tossed up an incident with a neighbor's dog when he was five.

He had gone to return something for his mother, had just rung the bell, when a brown Great Dane mix with black paws appeared from nowhere, bounding up to him. The dog was merely being playful, but he panicked and found himself backed against the fence with hard paws pressing against his chest. The dog was barking, Grasso screaming. The neighbor came running, but too slowly. The worst thing about the whole incident was that he'd wet his pants, a fact he didn't even realize until he was in the doctor's office, being checked over to see if the animal had broken any skin.

Forty-three years later and that remained one of the major defining moments in his life. He still flinched when he heard a dog bark.

There was a bump in the front of the car. It felt as if the driver had run off the road; he was struggling with the wheel. There was another bump, a hissing sound.

The tires had been shot out. The car was sliding sideways on the road. Grasso felt his stomach begin to hurt again as he grabbed the radiophone. "Somebody's after us, for real this time," he said as the car skidded to a stop. "We're on the road to the airport, being attacked."

There was no answer. Grasso was just reaching for the cellular phone when two men with AK-47s appeared at the driver's side window. Two huge trucks blocked off the road, one in front, one behind. A man with some sort of grenade launcher pointed the weapon at the windshield.

Grasso leaned forward and tapped on the window. "We'll have to go with them," he said to the driver. He spoke softly, his mouth suddenly dry and his voice cracking.

Kamra Proving Grounds, Pakistan. 4:30 P.M.

Khan squirmed in the seat as he edged the throttle into take-off position and the Leopard began the run. The new g-suit he was wearing squeaked and cracked every time he moved. The material was thicker than he was used to, and more annoying, one more thing stealing a precious piece of his attention.

205

Nice big fat runway running up between his legs. The Leopard's seat had the same thirty-degree tilt, and his hands were in the same position as if he were in the F-16. Khan lifted his eyes toward the horizon as the plane began to accelerate, looking at the spot he was flying to.

Ride a little mushy. This was a bigger plane beneath him, more steel girded to his loins. Check that—more carbon-resin fibers and alloys. He was sitting higher, moving a little faster than he had expected.

A good, stiff headwind buffeted the plane and he sliced into it, coming up easy, a kite grabbing a puff of wind. The F-16 seemed to pop off the runway; the Leopard glided. Khan held the thick black control stick as if gripping a baby's hand, and let the plane gather momentum at its own pace.

What a contrast to the first time he had flown an F-16. He'd yanked nervously on the stick, not used to having it on his right side. His pull was way too hard. The Falcon had been his first "electric jet," where the controls relied on electronics instead of pure muscular pressure. It was a little like driving a car with power brakes for the first time. The nose shot up and the plane threatened to stall. The engine saved him, its hearty thrust grabbing him by the collar as he recovered.

Khan heard his breath quicken as his new mount passed the last beacons marking the runway area. A tiny little button on the left elbow panel—so small his gloved finger nearly fell off it—worked the landing gear. After he pressed it, the flight computer ran a quick check to make sure it was an appropriate time to fold up, then cranked the wheels through the slipstream, sealing itself up tightly. (Khan could direct the computer to override by hitting two buttons on the far left of his dash, below the master armament panel.) Though similar to the Falcon's overhauled cockpit, there were a lot of new things to assimilate here, including the increased role of the flight computer.

For all he had accomplished, he was an amateur in this cockpit, dropped back to square one in the unfamiliar plane. Every time he was given a new assignment, the old feelings of flight school returned, excitement mixed with a healthy dose of apprehension. The quickened pulse and shallow breath might last only a little while—he'd been pushing the Falcon before the end of the first flight—but there was no denying they were here now. The man at the stick of the Snow Leopard, the PAF's top war ace, was just another pilot qualifying, hoping against hope he wouldn't wash out.

The flight plan called for a straight, steady climb from the runway, nothing taxing, and a rendezvous with Denoux. The French test pilot was waiting in a chase plane at 10,000 feet due east. The Leopard was lined up perfectly; all Khan had to do was sit tight and get comfy.

He worked his eyes around the controls. The layout was familiar, though even such old standards as the altimeter had been given a special dose of "new and improved." Its face was tinted yellow at the moment, the color changing every ten thousand feet.

"Looking good, Major," said Denoux, slipping alongside Khan in his bright red Chenyang F-6, an old Chinese-built plane that was probably older than its pilot.

Khan flicked the talk button on—same position as the Falcon's, on the left side of the throttle. "Feels fine."

"Let's start with your orbits," said the Frenchman. "Take her up gently."

Khan slipped into an easy bank to the north and continued to gain altitude, his left hand moving the throttle tepidly as his right eased into the direction of the turn, carefully feeling his way. The engines were a soft hum in the back of his head. There was a lot of power here. He'd probably never go this slowly again immediately after a takeoff; Khan could tell the plane wanted to go faster.

"Take a few turns and climb to thirty thousand," Denoux told him. "I'll meet you up there."

Khan acknowledged. The squeaks from the g-suit became louder as he worked through the series of rising spirals, his body shifting to move the plane. He pushed his shoulders back in the seat, as if he were pressing back into the wings themselves. Ideally, there was no separation between pilot and plane; the fuselage was a second skin, an extension of your legs and arms. The instruments were part of your brain.

The moment he'd finished his preflight prayer and locked down the canopy, the details delivered during his four-hour briefing had flown out of his head. Now they were coming back, tiptoeing in. The plane could be put into different flight modes with a switch to the right of the stick: high-altitude cruise, low-altitude cruise, in tercept, dogfight 1 and 2. The thin red switch governed software that gave the computer different sets of expectations. These were actually overrides; the flight computer constructed a mission-specific profile based on the data that was fed in prior to takeoff. The more generic modes could be selected from the dash where the override was located; the blue switch to take over the multimode display and bring up the menu was across from his left index finger.

He took the turns in a thirty-degree bank, like a hawk spiraling on a thermal to get to altitude. The plane eased through the air like a glider and not a 65,000-pound mass of shaped polymers, plastic and metal. These were standard turns, nothing like the high-g yanks the Leopard was designed for. On those turns the airframe would literally plow and skip through the sky, pulling 8 or 10 g's as easily as a car turning a corner.

The new plane could manage fully decoupled turns, an extremely valuable asset in a dogfight. The ability meant the Snow Leopard could turn without having to bank; flipping someone off its tail should be child's play.

The massive rudders—larger than the F-16's wings and accounting for a third of the plane's empty weight—were barely moving now. The thrust-vectoring nozzles, designed to give a hand at high speeds when the control surfaces were less efficient, slumbered at the back of the bird, resting until needed.

Khan came through the first suite of maneuvers and realized his stomach had settled down. The plane was starting to feel familiar. He swept his eyes down through the cockpit again, glancing over the grid of the right CRT, pausing on the dull green radar warning screen (blank, temporarily inactive), across the three dials—vertical speed, altimeter, airspeed. He looked at his left hand, resting easy on the throttle, his right thumb curled around to the switch that worked the FLIR and IRST settings.

"How does it feel?" Denoux asked as Khan finished the turns and met him at exactly 30,000 feet.

"Like a dream," said the pilot. "How does that thing feel after this?"

"Like I've given up a Ferrari for a motor scooter," laughed the Frenchman. "But I do like these old MiGs," he added, referring to the fact that the Chinese plane was essentially a Russian MiG-19 with a few extra bolts and washers. "You can really feel what you're doing."

Their controller cleared them for Echo Range, a swath of restricted airspace to the north of the factory where Khan would have room to stretch his legs. He put the Leopard into a real climb, accelerating to Mach .9 and hitting 50,000 feet before banking sharply to his left and entering the area. His flight suit squawked like hell but he ignored it, enjoying the ride as the nose tilted up beneath his feet. It had a lighter touch than the Falcon, and he felt like he was a bit farther forward.

Level again, Khan put his head down and worked the right multi-use display through a check of the flight systems, making sure everything was operating satisfactorily. There were several options—the simplest had the computer do the work itself, merely alerting the pilot to problems. But Khan took a more conservative approach, working through the full flight list, a color-coded display of how the plane's systems were functioning. The computer gave its own assessment in a column at the far right—row after row of the word OPTIMUM flashed in green as he went through the list. The Leopard was patting itself on the back.

Checks complete, the pilot clicked his talk button. "I'm going to punch it," he told his chase.

"I'm watching," replied Denoux.

The throttle seemed to stick. Khan resisted the urge to push it harder, stayed with gradual, gentle pressure. He kept his eyes straight ahead. The speed scale on the left side of the HUD pegged at 525.

Malfunction?

No, here it was—he felt the speed increasing before it registered on the screen. He glanced down at the speedo, screwing around as he passed through the sound barrier.

He only got it to Mach 1.15 before it was time to take his turn. That speed was impressive in some planes, even in a stock F-16, but in the Leopard it was timid. The plane's engines were designed to cruise out around Mach 1.6; they could accelerate to two or more times that much. The variable-cycle power plants were chameleons, changing from turbofans to turbojets as the speed increased. At the lower speeds, the turbofans pushed through the expanding gas like an ordinary jet engine, albeit much more efficiently. As the speeds picked up and the combustion temperatures increased, the fans were bypassed and the air ignited directly—a ramjet. Both technologies had existed since the beginnings of jet flight; the trick, perfected by the Americans from whom the Pakistanis had purloined the engines, was combining them. Matched to the computer-controlled airframe, the power plants gave the plane hypercruise capabilities matched only by the American F-22, one of the prime inspirations behind the Pakistani design.

Khan put it a bit more to the test on his second leg, hitting Mach 1.5. As he started the third run, he clumsily knocked his elbow against the side panel below the throttle, whacking his funny bone and sending a sharp tingle from his pinky to his neck. Reacting to the pain, he accidentally jabbed the throttle, punching it off its position and then back in a half of a half second. The plane's computer-guided controls responded abruptly by almost completely stopping and then revving the engine. The result was an instantaneous, flat drop that surprised the pilot, but otherwise left him in full control. The product of the complicated vortices generated by the plane's control surfaces and speed, it was a characteristic that would be handy in a dogfight.

The discovery of one of the plane's quirks didn't quite compensate for his awkwardness, however.

"Problem?" asked Denoux.

"Just getting used to the flight suit," said Khan.

"You'll be grateful for it when it keeps your heart inside your chest at 10 g's."

Khan took this turn faster than the others, serious now, accelerating through and then into the run. He was doing Mach 1.6, 1.7 and it felt good. He didn't bother to slow to take the turn at the far end. Tight and hot, the pilot leaned to his left. The wing slammed around and he was flying in the other direction and, incredibly, still doing 1.5. Not even the Falcon felt this easy in the air.

"Now you're getting the hang of it," said the Frenchman from his chase plane.

Two turns later and Rocket Khan agreed. He knew it because he'd stopped comparing the Leopard to the F-16. This was something better, a second body for him, his plane. Truly his plane.

An hour into the flight, as relaxed as he had ever been in an aircraft, Khan brought the Snow Leopard to 40,000 feet and began a series of slow-speed, high-g maneuvers, some hard rock 'n' rollin' to get an idea of how precisely he could fly it. He tucked his shoulder down and did a quarter roll into a turning maneuver that changed the Leopard's direction by ninety degrees. The move required him to fly upside down for a short period of time. He did it easily and started looking for something that would strain the aircraft a bit more, put himself to the test.

The Cobra maneuver. As soon as the idea presented itself, he knew he would try it.

The classic Cobra was perfected by Russian pilots. Properly executed, it seems to run the jet backward in the air for a short period of time. As it begins, the pilot is flying relatively slow. He drops the plane's power even lower and then suddenly jerks back on the stick. The jet gallops upward, rearing like a pony that's come to the end of a cliff. A good Cobra gets the nose back past 90 degrees—here's where it's pointing backward—perhaps as far as 120 or 130 degrees. Forward airspeed drops rapidly—naturally, because now the wings are acting like drag chutes. Ideally, the plane walks on its hind legs across the sky, neither climbing nor (more likely) stalling and plunging over. At some point, hopefully before flameout, the pilot eases the rearing snake's head back to the front, kicks the engine in the pants and flies onward, a few pounds of sweat lighter. A perfect Cobra does not lose or gain altitude, and pushes forward airspeed close to zero for half a blink.

Khan had first seen the maneuver done in the United States by a marine F/A-18 pilot during one of the Red Flag exercises. The American pilot, who demonstrated the maneuver for his eager Pakistani friend, had modified it slightly, taking it a little faster and quite a bit higher—he had seen a MiG-29 bounce through a runway after an engine flameout while practicing one, and figured the extra room gave him a margin of safety.

It also gave him room for his own special addition—he stood the plane on its rear end and pulled back even harder, letting the Hornet literally fall out from under him in a tumble loop. The attack jet seemed to touch its nose to its tail in the maneuver. It was the closest thing to a running somersault Khan had ever seen in an airplane.

Unfortunately, Khan wasn't the only one who saw it. Pulling such acrobatics in a specially designed and reinforced stunt plane was tricky enough; doing them in a fighter just off the flight line during the warm-ups for an international exhibition was a little like showing up for the Indy 500 in a stock Honda Civic and mooning the judges on the first lap.

And winning the race.

Not ten minutes after the American landed—before he could collect on the beers Khan and his friends promised—a red-faced U.S. Air Force colonel collared the pilot and brought him in. Rumor had it that he had been transferred to either a drill team or an outfit in charge of dry-cleaning flight suits.

The Leopard was smooth at 10,000 feet, and the pilot ran the computer through its checks once more. This was a subtle plane that took out the bumps for you. That meant it was more difficult to feel a problem. He walked his head through the cockpit again, his eyes focusing on each element in the display, absorbing each dial and readout. He wanted everything burnt into his brain.

He'd do the Cobra up here, with plenty of margin for error. And no somersault.

The HUD indicated he was set for normal flight mode. He clicked the mode over to dogfight 1—close encounters of the high-g kind—and took his eyes through one last, meticulous tour of the instruments. He was doing 515 miles an hour. The light tan engine monitor on the lower half of the left side of the dash had two words in red letters lit brightly across the middle, POSITIVE and OPTIMUM. Though in theory referring to the status of the ram engage and the oxygen-added fuel burn, respectively, Khan read them as a message from the computer—go for it.

He eased the throttle off, dropping his indicated speed to a lazy 350 knots or approximately 400 miles an hour. He had a perfect day, clear and bright, unlimited sky, miles of empty space around him. Reflections from his helmet danced across the glass, wispy clouds of light. Khan checked his position on the range, then glanced over at Denoux, whose red chase plane was banking a few thousand feet below, off about a quarter of a mile.

Ready, he told himself, and he pushed the Leopard through a turn, straightened for a few hundred yards. With his speed hovering down at 230 knots, he pulled back suddenly on the stick. The rear end of the jet skidded back under him. He was riding a wheelie, and there was a jump. Engine still humming. Denoux was saying something but he didn't hear what. The angle of attack indicator turned red, flashing now, he had 90, 100, 110 degrees.

Be careful; this is a big plane, bigger than any others you've flown. Careful, just hold . . . until he was bumping, bumping backward 135 degrees. Too far and you lose it. One-thirty-seven, too far you're too far Khan.

The same feeling he had felt, winged by the Fulcrum's missile.

Too far and he brought it back and he was flying too slow. Way too slow, but somehow still moving forward. The engine hadn't stalled and he had perfect control.

He was level, flying perfect and picking up speed. He had plenty of sky.

"What the hell are you doing up there, Major?" said Denoux, an angry red bee crossing above the Leopard. "That's not an acrobatic plane you're flying."

"It's a hell of a plane," replied Khan.

He had never tried the maneuver in the Falcon. He'd been too scared. This was a much different plane. And he was a different pilot now.

"If you crash, you better go down with it," said the Frenchman. "The general will strap you to an exhaust if something happens to the plane before your mission."

Karachi. 5:15 P.M.

From the air it looked like a scene from an epic movie, as if the whole thing were staged.

A flood of people surged down Airport Road and the highway from Hyderabad, past the fancy Western-style restaurants and toward the heart of the city. A few automobiles and buses were caught in the crowd, tiny islands in a thick stream. The line of refugees stretched back toward the desert for miles, bracketed by two huge funnels of black smoke rising in the distance. Ahead, the mass of people snaked toward the city, blurring into the haze of smoke that surrounded Karachi like a puffed-out bit of dirty cellophane wrapping.

O'Connell saw why the airport hadn't answered his calls as the hulking wreck of the control tower came into view. The hangar area was a confused tangle of burned-out planes, with less order than a stadium parking lot after the Super Bowl let out. A forlorn 727, its nose broken, sat at the far end of the pockmarked runway.

If the Pakistani forces couldn't protect one of the country's most important commercial centers, O'Connell thought, how long would it be before they were completely overrun? The Golden Bears might already be on the way.

Given the choked highway leading back to the city, it was

senseless to land at the airport. O'Connell took a turn to the south and headed toward Clifton Beach, a posh resort and exclusive residential area on the southwestern side of the city. Like everywhere else in the world, it had gotten a bit gaudy in recent years. A huge roller coaster that had been only a sketch plan when he was last in the country now jutted into the sea, its rails claiming to be the highest and scariest in the Islamic world. A clown face loomed toward the sea from the girders, sticking its tongue out at gray dots of ships well offshore.

They were Indian ships, O'Connell realized as he flew over the empty park and aimed the helicopter northward along the coast. Their Harriers and missiles had probably been responsible for the destruction, though from here they seemed as peaceful as fishing boats.

The whole way down he hadn't been challenged. He wondered how long that bit of luck would hold.

The cranes of the containerport behind the West Wharf loomed ahead, obstructed by dark pillars of smoke. Though it had looked from the distance as if the entire city were in ruins, the only fires were in the commercial port. He turned and flew over Karachi proper, passing the mangrove swamps that lay inland from the shore. The treetops and reeds fluttered passively; a few birds, alarmed by the noise of his engine, took to the air.

The Masjid-e-Tuba Race Course and its open infield was within easy walking distance of the city's main hotels. O'Connell at first thought he would land there, but as he skimmed in above the board Sunset Boulevard he found that the field had been turned into a refugee camp. Tents and hastily erected lean-tos crowded deep into the bleacher area; even if O'Connell had wanted to brave the chaos, there was not a square inch open to him. It was the same at Ahmad Ali Park, a short distance away. Half the people of southern Pakistan seemed to have come to Karachi, swelling its already considerable population.

More ominous than the refugees were the men patrolling the hotel roofs, pointing M-16s in his direction as he hovered nearby. O'Connell edged the helicopter a bit higher and circled back westward from the park. He wanted to stash the Jet Ranger in a place where he could retrieve it later. Even with its limited range and crew capacity, it might come in handy. The beaches, which had been largely deserted, seemed the best bet.

O'Connell glanced at his passenger. Greeley had stopped his monologues as they approached Karachi. He was staring down at the city in awe. "Don't go catatonic on me," O'Connell told him. "We're gonna land soon."

"Where?"

"I'm not sure yet. We're supposed to meet somebody at a hotel in the city. I want to put the helicopter down someplace we can get it later."

Greeley nodded, continuing to stare out the windows as O'Connell came out over Kiamari, where the piers ran into the sea to form a sheltered harbor area. There were a number of soldiers patrolling the beach to his left, but to his right the shoreline looked empty.

The port area to the north would be packed with soldiers and whatever remained of the local coastal patrol, not to mention firefighting equipment. But O'Connell didn't intend to go that far. He tucked in over the railroad tracks, flying below the long billow of black smoke that extended almost two miles south along the shore. It slowly wended its way south toward the amusement area, intent on smacking the clown face for its impertinence.

Up ahead there was a highway bridge that made it possible for autos to cross the train tracks toward the water. A wide bridge, it spanned two roughly parallel track sections, with lots of space on either side.

A made-to-order helicopter garage, O'Connell decided. He could put it in on the far side. It'd be a tight fit—the chopper was only a bit over nine feet high, but the space below the bridge couldn't be more than fifteen. But that would make it harder to steal.

Better check first, though.

"What the hell are you doing?" asked Greeley as O'Connell headed the Bell over the tracks and under the overpass. It seemed to be about the same height as the section where he intended on parking.

"Just making sure I got enough clearance."

"What if you don't?" Greeley asked, but by then they'd squeezed underneath and come out on the other side.

O'Connell brought the helicopter back alongside the bridge, hovering as he examined the area under the highway. It would have been easier to park near the tracks, but he had to assume the trains were still running. A chain-link fence blocked off the most promising spot; O'Connell hovered for a moment, considering whether he could angle the helicopter enough to squash the fence without hitting its top on the underside of the roadway.

The aircraft kicked up a lot of dust and dirt. The Jet Ranger was a good helicopter, but it was not as adept at maneuvering into tight spots as a newer model would be. Now if he had one of those fancy no-rear-rotor models from McDonnell-Douglas, this would be a breeze.

He'd wanted to lease one when he opened his helicopter business, but it would only have sunk him into bankruptcy quicker.

"You ain't thinking of landing it under there, are you?" asked Greeley. "Even if you fit, you'll suck all that dirt and stuff into the turbine."

The pinch in the old man's voice decided it. O'Connell edged the chopper's nose up and glided in, a perfect landing that left the front half of the aircraft sitting on the quashed fence. He misjudged his distance from the pillar—if there were three feet of clearance there he was lucky—but he was in without any damage. Getting out would be tricky—backing up was probably out of the question, and pulling straight through meant getting past another fence. But that was a problem for later.

"They have a word for people like you," said Greeley.

"Yeah?"

"Asshole."

O'Connell started laughing uncontrollably, even as Greeley's face grew indignant.

"It's not funny."

He couldn't stop laughing. All the tension in his body

rushed out of his chest, a balloon losing its air.

"I don't see what the hell you're laughing at."

"Your damn eyes almost popped out of your head," O'Connell said between gasps for air. "You looked like Buckwheat."

Greeley flung open the helicopter door indignantly and jumped onto the flattened fence as the rotors wound down. He tripped and tumbled to the ground. Tears started flowing from O'Connell's eyes.

"I don't need your help, honkie," said Greeley when he came around to help him.

"Honkie?" O'Connell's laughter stoked up again. "Honkie? Hell, Greeley, nobody's used that word in twenty years."

"Whitebread. Whalebone."

"Whalebone?" laughed O'Connell. "Whalebone?" Greeley glared at him and rose to his knees. "You all right?"

"Leave me the hell alone," he said, storming off up the railroad tracks.

O'Connell hoisted the bags from the chopper. He paused to check the Browning, wedged into the inside pocket of his leather jacket, then began walking down the tracks. The spasm of laughter had loosened the knots in his back and sides, and O'Connell felt almost relaxed.

"You ought to wait up," he yelled to Greeley, who was about fifty yards in front of him. "I got your suitcase."

Greeley ignored him. He wasn't a fast walker, and even with the bags O'Connell drew to within twenty yards in a half minute.

"I didn't mean to insult you," said O'Connell.

Greeley stopped, but didn't turn around.

"I didn't mean anything. I'm not racist or anything."

Whatever Greeley thought of O'Connell's denial, he remained stock-still, his head tilted up toward the highway.

"Here, I got your bag and everything," said O'Connell, finally catching up and dropping it down. "You all right?"

O'Connell didn't hear the reply, if any, because he finally realized what Greeley was staring at—a large group of men were clambering down the embankment toward them.

As automatic as a machine, O'Connell pulled off his jacket and folded it around his arm. He felt the tightness return to his muscles as he slipped the gun up under the coat, ready to shoot. He tapped Greeley lightly in the arm and told him to follow along.

''Do what I do,'' said O'Connell, starting forward as if the crowd were not there.

They were civilians, and appeared unarmed. Having materialized from nowhere, they quickly multiplied. O'Connell estimated that there were more than fifty, and though they didn't look necessarily hostile, he made it a point to fix his gaze on a point far away.

''Hello,'' said one of the men in English as they drew near.

The spell of silence broken, a babble of languages began beseeching them to take them to safety in the north. The pleas were interspersed with praise of the U.S. and various European countries, as if the foreigners could be flattered into doing the impossible.

O'Connell continued to ignore them, pressing forward as the men swarmed around him. There were a hundred people here, maybe two hundred.

Something in Greeley's face must have told them he was the easier mark, and they slipped past O'Connell to surround the old man as he walked. Their tone became increasingly plaintive. They were desperate to leave the country. Several began crying and wailing, pulling pictures out and shoving crumpled rupees at Greeley.

His pace, slow to begin with, became a crawl; finally they overwhelmed him and he stood surrounded by the mob.

''Come on,'' said O'Connell gruffly, fighting his way back through the crowd to his companion. He tugged his arm and Greeley began moving again.

They got only a few yards before they were stopped by a man who launched himself at their knees. The others fell down in front, beseeching them, saying they were desperate to save their families.

''Out of the way,'' shouted O'Connell, angrily pulling the

man off his legs. "Out of the way."

The man rolled back hastily, and O'Connell took several steps forward before realizing that Greeley hadn't moved. He cursed and waded back into the crowd, grabbing him again.

"What do they want?" Greeley asked.

"They're Hindu," O'Connell explained as they pushed forward. "They're afraid the Muslims will go on a rampage. They say they'll be killed if we don't help them."

"God."

"Yeah, well, it's not our problem right now, you know?"

"Can't we do something?"

"Don't be so fucking American, Greeley. Sooner or later one of those army people down the beach is going to get curious about all the fuss." O'Connell pushed him forward. "If we don't get moving, we're gonna cause a massacre—and we're going to be in the middle of it."

They waded a few more yards, but it was no use. Even more people had appeared—women and children now, whole families blocking their way. O'Connell cursed. The Browning felt like a hard rock in his hand. It might scare them if he pulled it out. Then again, it might push them into a frenzy.

He and Greeley pushed forward another step, only to have the mob press even closer. "Out of the way, move out of the way," O'Connell repeated, shouldering people aside and alternating his commands between English and Urdu. He wrapped his left arm around Greeley's right. "As soon as there's an opening," he told him, "run with me. We'll try for the road."

The embankment to the highway was ten yards away, at most. Given the number of people here, it might as well have been in the Himalayas.

O'Connell looked for a potential path, some smaller bodies to knock aside. He'd shoot into the air twice, whip around and push his companion up the hill. They'd leave the bags here; maybe that would satisfy the mob.

O'Connell reached over and pulled his jacket off his hand, exposing the Browning. Just as he began waving the gun over his head, there was a burst of submachine-gun fire behind him. O'Connell's first instinct was to duck down, and he brought Greeley with him.

The crowd was transfixed, like animals caught by the sudden sweep of headlights. It took two more long bursts before they fell back, and another before they were sufficiently panicked to stampede toward the water.

By then, O'Connell had realized they weren't being fired at. The shots were coming from three soldiers standing at the top of the embankment, their rifles pointed into the air.

Were the soldiers going to help them, or kill them?

"Let me do the talking," O'Connell said to Greeley, starting up the hill. Two soldiers came down toward them; the others scanned the crowd.

He had a good cover story, courtesy of Renard—documentation saying they were reporters for CNN, with personal letters from General Chenab and some more obscure figures in the information ministry. As long as the army is still disciplined, O'Connell thought, these guys will respect Chenab. The letters are like gold.

But in a few steps he realized that the men, who were now reaching out their hands to help, weren't Pakistani soldiers. They had uniforms, all right, but the insignias were all wrong.

He felt a slight tremor in his knees but he strode through it, managed to point to Greeley. The men directed their attention to the older man, helping him up the incline as O'Connell went ahead.

Another few seconds to think what to do.

His gun was obvious and they would have shot him if they considered him hostile.

O'Connell looked back toward Greeley as he sidestepped his way the final few feet up the embankment. He had to seem like he was in total control, like he ought to be here, then figure out who the hell these guys were.

"Michael."

If he would have expected any voice, this one would have been the last.

"Michael," she repeated, and O'Connell, just reaching

the roadway, turned to see Morena Kelso standing in front of the door to a long black Buick, a polished refugee from the sixties. It had official Pakistan government flags flying from all four corners. "Come on," she said. "Hurry."

He walked toward her in disbelief. "What are you doing here?" he asked. His voice had a tremble in it.

"I'll explain in the car," she said, waving her hand at the men to take his bag into one of the pickup trucks that were escorting her. She reached out and took his hand, patting the Browning. "Put this away and get in."

The Oval Office, Washington, D.C. 9:15 A.M.

Carl Stockman, the CIA's deputy director of operations, squirmed in his seat. The president of the United States was taking a call at his desk a few feet away, barking into the receiver at some congressman who'd had the misfortune of returning a call just as the private briefing on the secretary of state's kidnapping was about to get under way.

"I don't care who's on the committee," said President D'Amici. "You're the chairman. I made a campaign promise and I intend on keeping it, damn it."

Even though D'Amici's ire was legendary, the DDO had never been this close to it. The two other men in the room—Walter Jablow, director of the CIA, and National Security Director Henry Morse—stared at the carpet as the president chewed out the committee chairman. Stockman, however, found it impossible to take his eyes off D'Amici. The deep ridges and heavy lines that packed his forehead spoke of experience. His cheekbones, tinged with red, added emotion to intellectual eyes. His mouth—that said you didn't want to cross him.

The storm quickly ran its course. "Listen, Daniel," said D'Amici, softening his tone, "let's take another shot at this. I'm going to send Andrew over this afternoon. You tell him what it will take. But I want a bill." The president finally looked up from the desk, giving them a signal that he would soon be with them. "Well of course I trust him, he's my son,'' said D'Amici, laughing into the phone. ''Hell, I trust you, too. Well sure. This is important.''

D'Amici hung up the phone and scribbled a note on a pad. Stockman fingered the black binding of his portfolio nervously. He had all of the cables from India regarding the kidnapping in it, but he didn't bother opening it; there wasn't anything useful there.

''What I want to know is why the hell, with all the resources of the CIA, we can't even determine which faction in the goddamned country took him,'' said the president, still jotting.

''It's a difficult country, Jack,'' said Morse.

''I don't want excuses. We're not talking about some tourist here—this is the goddamn secretary of state.''

''His own security team—'' offered Morse, but the NSC head didn't get very far.

''The hell with that. This isn't a security council meeting, Henry; I want results, not bullshit.''

''We've narrowed the likely kidnapping suspects to three groups,'' said Stockman. ''All three are extremist Sikh—''

D'Amici put up his hand. ''Didn't I see something that gave me the idea the CIA heard something was up?'' The president flipped through a brown briefing log that contained summaries of a week's worth of communications from south Asian stations.

''There's an alert from one of my people, reporting a rumor,'' said Stockman uncomfortably.

''Are you following that up?''

''The agent is temporarily out of contact,'' explained Stockman, glancing at Jablow. His boss sat at the end of the sofa, white-faced and silent. ''She was in Pakistan at the time and had picked up a rumor second- or third-hand.''

''Pakistan?'' said D'Amici.

''It was probably just nonsense, Jack,'' said Morse. ''Those sorts of things are started all the time. You'd be amazed at the stories you hear.''

''Why wasn't it checked out?''

''It was put out as an alert,'' said Stockman. ''But frankly, not even the agent thought it had any validity.''

D'Amici's frown grew deeper. The furrows in his head seemed to have burrowed another inch into his skull. "What does he think of it now?"

"She, sir. The agent is a woman."

D'Amici grunted, waiting for an answer to his question.

"I sent her in on a fact-finding mission. She has no set agenda and her presence was strictly need-to-know, which didn't include the Islamabad office," he said hurriedly, hoping he wouldn't have to explain. "Even I don't know specifically where she is at any given moment. As soon as she checks in, we'll find out whether it might be a lead or not."

The press of events over the last twenty-four hours had taxed even the Snowman's legendary cool. Westlake had missed his appointed call-in, and the DDO's discreet inquiries had turned up nothing. He suspected the very worst, especially since two Pakistani intelligence intercepts had referred to a "Kahuta matter." The intercepts had been culled by a computer from telephone transmissions and were devoid of meaningful context, but they were enough for Stockman to appoint a working group to research the matter more thoroughly. Kahuta was the base the team had penetrated two weeks before, looking for the Golden Bears.

O'Connell, meanwhile, had narrowly escaped an assassination attempt in Paris. Fortunately, Stockman's people had been on top of that one—not only did they help the Paris police catch the Pakistani agents, but they succeeded in making it look as if O'Connell had been killed. The ruse had fooled the Pakistani intelligence services; Stockman had a copy of their "mission accomplished" wire on his desk upstairs.

The real victim had been a talented CIA agent named William Bozzone, part of a shadow team that had staked out the airport. The DDO had put off calling the man's wife until after this meeting was over.

As much as he hated that task, it was the least of Stockman's worries. In all the confusion, O'Connell had lost his agency shadows. Even without the Pakistanis watching for him, it was not going to be easy for him to get into the country and make it to his rendezvous point with Blossom.

Stockman wasn't even sure Morena had arranged a meeting.

Could O'Connell pull the whole thing off, even with Morena and Blossom's help?

The DDO wasn't even sure he could keep the operation secret anymore. Not only would he have to concoct a story to explain O'Connell's appearance—and faked death—in Paris, but he'd already had to tell the Islamabad office that Westlake and Smith were in country, so its agents could help look for them. It wouldn't take a genius to realize he had something under way. Link that with O'Connell, and any Senate committee staffer worth his government salary would be able to piece things together.

Especially if the bombs were used. Time was running out.

The DDO held his breath, waiting to be quizzed by the president or the NSC head on Morena's mission. A CIA insider would realize that it was unusual for an agent to be sent on a private mission by the DDO. And he had practically identified who it was by saying it was a woman.

"I still think our best bet is to work through the Indian government," said Morse. "Even though they're slow."

"The Indians are conducting an intensive search, and we're working with them," said Jablow, finding his voice for the first time in the meeting. "We're in constant communication."

Everyone in the room glanced reflexively at the black box Stockman carried with him. It was his "football," a communications set that enabled him to keep in touch with the agency's operational center. It also connected with his private, emergency line. The DDO half expected the three small LEDs on the top of the box to light. With his luck, it would be his wife—she sometimes found that the private line was the only way to reach him at work, and had called once or twice to remind him to pick up milk on his way home.

"When you find him," asked the president, "will you be able to get him out?"

Stockman met the full force of D'Amici's glare head on. "It would be easy for me to say yes, sir. But until we have some sort of information—"

"Get the information. This is a friend of mine, for Christ's sake. I sent him there. I'm responsible.''

There'd been no ransom, no message. The secretary's car had been found deserted, his driver killed. The textbook said the secretary was dead.

"We have Delta Force scrambled," said Morse, shifting uncomfortably in his seat. "And air force units in Saudi and the Emirates are on full alert."

The president put his fingers on the bridge of his nose and then propped his elbows on his desk, taking in the situation. The traces of anger disappeared and his face became softer, more understanding. He looked like a father contemplating a son's poor report card, not the most powerful man in the world worrying about his country's impotence.

In that brief moment, the DDO imagined what it would be like to tell the president, flat out, that Pakistan had nuclear weapons and a way to deliver them.

And how do you know that?

We were involved, sir. Not me personally, but I found out about it when I took over as DDO two and a half years ago. It was Director Woolsley—I don't know precisely what he had in mind, sir, but obviously he had something up his sleeve. Maybe he thought this would be a hedge against the Indians, maybe he was running some sort of operation against the Chinese. Woolsley was one of the old-timers sir, as bad as Casey ever was; I haven't figured out half the things he was up to.

Don't blame your troubles on the dead. What is the situation now?

I did my best to deal with it.

To cover it up, you mean.

I have a man on his way to undo it. The Pakistanis built the bombs themselves. They held back material and assembled them surreptitiously. It wouldn't be a problem, because we're still watching their F-16s and their Mirages, but you see sir, where we really went wrong was, we helped them build three airplanes to drop them. Old propeller planes. Used to be U.S. bombers, thirty, maybe forty years ago. Only problem is you can't see them on radar.

Maybe the director thought they'd be used for conven-

tional bombs. Maybe he didn't think they had the nuclear material. I don't know what to believe, sir.

We were keeping tabs on the planes—I did that on my authority, sir; I didn't think it was necessary to bother you with any of this, as long as we had it under control. But we lost them somehow. I had a team go after them, and they came up empty.

Those people are dead, or at least I think they're dead. We have one more shot. I have a man on his way to the planes' base. A very good man. Actually, he's the man who came up with the idea for them, or at least made it happen.

It would take me a year to explain why I didn't tell you about this at the very beginning. I didn't even tell Director Jablow. Under the circumstances, sir, I thought it best to keep it contained. No, sir, I wouldn't try and rationalize my actions. Nor what the agency did. You see, we were different then. If you think we're bad now—and I admit, we have our problems—we were worse. Even more, unaccountable. Crazy. A few overzealous people trying to conduct their own diplomacy. And other things.

I'm working to fix that. We've made progress.

Stockman closed his eyes. The president would fry him. "Well, do you?"

Stockman looked up at D'Amici before realizing the question had come from Morse.

"Do you think he's alive?"

"We should be prepared for any contingency," answered the DDO.

Karachi Grand Hotel, Karachi. 6:45 P.M.

Morena kicked off her shoes and slumped into the high-backed chair next to the dresser. Reaching over the side, she retrieved her pocketbook and took out the pack of Camel filters she'd bought at the airport when she left D.C.

She rarely smoked; the first taste of nicotine now as she lit the cigarette sent a wave of energy through her body. She took a long drag and held it in. The coarse air scratching her lungs felt strangely pleasant.

They'd been driving down into Karachi when she'd seen the helicopter skimming in low toward the beaches; she'd made a wild guess that it was O'Connell and had her driver head in that direction.

Maybe more than just guessed. She'd known somehow. By intuition. Or some connection in their souls.

She was still wearing the Pakistani clothes Nizam had lent her. They were drab and bulky, good cover in the city but a nuisance now. She got up and pulled the light green *chunni* from around her neck, wadding the scarf in her hand before dropping it to the floor. Then she took off the long shirt, let it flutter from her shoulders. The baggy trousers collapsed around her ankles, and as she took a step toward the bureau Morena felt as if she'd undone leg chains. Balancing the cigarette on the edge of the bureau, she reached into her overnight bag and took out a pair of khaki pants, along with an oversized blue oxford shirt.

She'd buttoned the shirt halfway up when she saw herself in the mirror, plain-looking, almost middle-aged. I should have brought the camisole, she thought to herself, remembering her decision while packing.

Why? To make him want her again?

Morena put the cigarette back in her mouth for another puff, then pulled off her shirt and bra, tossing them on the bed. She had only one other choice, a flowing red skirt with a thin, almost sheer white blouse. Once she'd changed, she stood before the mirror and pulled her hair loose around her shoulders, primping the curls. Her reflection fretted back uneasily, breasts round and nipples clearly visible beneath the shirt.

What did she want? For things to be as they were? Their situations were so different now.

My God, she told herself, he broke more than the law. He helped these people circumvent the treaties. Now they had nuclear weapons again. How could he live with himself?

And yet the attraction was there, burning. Morena took a last puff on the cigarette, then crushed it out in an ashtray on the desktop. She took off the blouse, replaced it with the oxford. The reflection of the gaudy gold wallpaper behind her made it difficult to judge how much makeup to apply to her face. The subtle rouge softened her face. How ironic— she spent so much of her time looking hard and untouchable.

So much was confused, beyond her feelings for O'Connell. Should she leave the agency when this was over? What would her father have done?

Once more she turned her attention to her hair, tucking the dark brown curls behind her ears. More subdued. He used to love playing with her hair, caressing it, winding his fingers through it.

So much to figure out.

Karachi Grand Hotel, Karachi. 7 P.M.

"If I'd known you were going to be involved, I would have walked right out of his office." O'Connell looked at the floor, escaping the velvet gaze of her green eyes.

"I had nothing to do with the assignment."

"You're the deputy on the desk."

"You know this didn't go through the desk. This is Stockman's project."

Morena got up from the bed where she'd been sitting and walked toward him. There was suppressed anger in her voice; O'Connell guessed that she had only recently found out about Golden Bear, and didn't like it.

"I don't know who belongs to what," he said. "I've been away for two years."

She pulled the hassock over and sat down on it. The air around him seemed to moisten, the light scent of perfume mixing with the still lighter aroma of tension. O'Connell leaned on the arm of his chair, a Louis XIV reproduction that was the highlight of the room's jumbled decor. Morena perched on the end of the hassock, no more than two feet away, her elbows on her knees and her chin in her hands. The top two buttons on her blouse were undone.

There was only one light on in the room, a small lamp on a large highboy behind Morena. Most of its illumination was absorbed by the dark blue fabric of the walls and the strange mix of furniture considered late-swank in Karachi. There were two television sets, one on the low bureau where it could be seen from the bed, another in the corner on a table to O'Connell's right. The ability to place two TVs in every room had undoubtedly earned the hotel a five-scimitar rating from the local Baedeker.

"Michael, I don't blame you for being angry with me. They showed me evidence and I believed what Carl said; I had no reason not to."

"No reason?"

"I'm the one who should be angry," she answered, but her voice was quiet, shading toward submissive. "You never said anything to me."

"Get off it, Morena."

"You shouldn't have helped them, not for this."

"I was told to, goddamn it." O'Connell stood up and took a step, but there was nowhere to go without brushing past her. He leaned back against the wall with his arms folded.

"But you should have known better. You knew they could be used for nuclear weapons. Didn't you suspect the Pakistanis would try to get around the treaty?"

He remained silent.

"Did you tell anybody? The desk? The director?"

"Did you help frame me?" he asked harshly, seeking to escape.

"You know I wouldn't do that, Michael."

Green, soft eyes that held him there, paralyzed him.

"We have a job to do," she said. As she rose he could see the outline of her nipple against the shirt. "I haven't been able to get in touch with Westlake. We have to go ahead without him."

"We?"

"Chéri, pourquoi es-tu si difficile?"

Her voice was like the beginning of a spell.

"Ne parlez pas Français," said O'Connell. "Don't speak French to me."

"Mais tu toujours—"

"Not anymore."

But it was too late. Her hand reached out and touched his cheek. Her perfume flooded his head and he had no more defenses. They embraced.

On their own, his hands slowly worked their way up her back, sinking in, absorbing each muscle. Her neck was warm and soft. He unbuttoned her shirt and slid it down her shoulders to the floor.

His awareness of the rest of the room slipped away. She stepped back and carefully removed her skirt, then undid his pants, tugging at the belt gently. It felt like a fall, sliding into her, diving down, falling back, back to silence and peace, away from where he was now.

Karachi Grand Hotel, Karachi. 7:15 P.M.

Greeley made his way down from his room and out to the terrace in front of the hotel, where he'd seen a few guests gathered for drinks earlier. They were gone now, and the small lounge area looked deserted. He sat anyway. He wanted—he needed—a drink.

He'd promised he wouldn't drink, but the scene on the beach and the reality of the war voided all promises. It wasn't like he was going to get drunk; just a glass or two of Scotch to take his mind off things.

O'Connell had said drinking was prohibited in Pakistan because it was a Muslim country, but the woman who had rescued them at the beach explained that the prohibition did not apply to foreigners. She hadn't noticed O'Connell's frown as she led them to the hotel desk, telling them to take rooms on the sixth floor near hers.

She'd already had an effect on O'Connell. Greeley sensed there was a history there—he didn't imagine they were poring over a map at the moment.

Greeley sat at the table for several minutes before a waiter appeared. The tall, dignified fellow seemed a bit nervous, perhaps because he was dealing with an American. He bent over the table and offered an indecipherable greeting. The man was speaking English, but understanding it through his accent and tortured syntax was not easy.

"Could I get something to drink?" Greeley asked.

"Drink?" said the waiter, adding some other words Greeley couldn't make out.

"Yes. Do you have Scotch?"

"Scotch."

"Yes."

The waiter said something else, a question. Did he have alcohol?

"Alcohol, yes," said Greeley. He'd heard of near beer, but nonalcoholic Scotch? But maybe it made sense; some people would like the flavor, but wouldn't go for the alcohol if they were Muslims. "Scotch," he repeated.

They nodded at each other a few times, and finally the waiter moved away. Relieved, Greeley took a deep breath and scanned the street.

A curfew was in force. Every few minutes, a patrol car or a jeep passed nearby. It was hard to see into the street from here, but the guns mounted on the backs of the jeeps were ominous, prominent shadows.

Were it not for the war, the city would look very much like an American one. Change the signs, and Greeley could be sitting in some part of Manhattan. As he'd seen from the air coming in, there were as many large buildings in Karachi as there were in a Western city. A few were exotic looking—most notably a large tower that looked like a rolled-up waffle iron. But mostly it seemed familiar.

He'd been to Bangkok briefly while he was in the service, and recalled it as the one city he'd stayed in that had no point of comparison to the U.S. The architecture, the people, the combination of singing and clucking that was their language. Dirt roads and bicycle carts. Taxis—what were they called? Rickshas. No, that was Japan.

Olissa loved to hear his stories about the places he had traveled while he was in the service. He was always sorry that he'd met her toward the end of his military career, when he was in the States. The time they had been to Paris, their one big splash, she had really enjoyed it.

How am I going to fly this plane, Greeley thought to himself, trying to keep his mind from focusing on her. Landing would be the toughest. He'd done that only twice. There was a long checklist, a couple of pages. The turbochargers. Don't turn them off while you're descending. No kidding. You're thinking of the wrong plane, James; that was the airline trainer.

God, he had to remember this absolutely correctly—there wasn't going to be a second chance. Think clearly—he'd sat there a million times, with nothing else to do but listen. Turret locked. Hydraulic valve at normal. Your wheels locked? Yes, yes. Speed, speed—what was the speed?

One-fifty? One-fifty knots, which was 172.5 mph, then come down for the approach, depending on the weight; come down to 110, was it? He had to remember precisely—didn't Jackie tell him again and again it was absolutely critical?

How fast had he been going the times he landed? Hell, those were perfect landings.

Greeley was closing his eyes feeling for the stall speed when the waiter came with his drink, a large tumbler-sized glass filled with an amber liquid that smelled like decent Scotch. He grinned at the man sheepishly, and reached into his pocket before realizing he had no Pakistani money.

"Can you put it on my tab?" he asked.

The man didn't understand him.

"My room," said Greeley, retrieving the key from his pocket. That the man understood, writing down the number on a pad before returning inside. Greeley picked up the glass and toasted his missing partner.

"Guess I won't be seeing you for awhile, huh? Some top secret business to take care of?"

O'Connell was a cool son of a bitch in action. He'd kept Greeley moving when the crowd threatened, and he'd been ready to use the gun to get them out of there.

Guilt stopped him just as he was about to take a sip. He'd gotten this far without drinking. And now because nobody was sitting and watching him he was going to what, get drunk? When he might have to fly in a few hours?

Their faces, all around him. Grown men crying. Their

arms thin, emaciated. Faces of the dead.

Olissa.

Greeley placed the glass down on the table and studied his hands. They were the worn hands of an old man. Somehow they had made their way to Pakistan, trying to fulfill a dream he'd had more than forty years before.

Forty years ago, he could have flown the plane. He was qualified; he should have had the chance. Thirty years ago, still in the air force, he'd finally mustered the courage to make a formal request, ask to go back and get his wings. Bust him back to lieutenant, he offered; he'd start again.

Too old, they told him. You're a good officer, James Walter Greeley, but you're too old. It's in the regs. Besides, we need navigators. Don't you understand? It's not because you're black . . .

The smell of Scotch from the glass was overwhelming. Greeley pushed it to the middle of the table and once more began working the controls of an imaginary B-50, pulling the flaps down, juicing the engines. He punched his arms and legs through the routine, stabbing the air.

About midway down the runway he realized he was being watched, and looked up into the faces of two police officers, who were standing silently in front of his table.

"Hi," he said sheepishly. "What can I do for you?"

The men said something to each other that was completely incomprehensible. Then the taller one asked in English, with a British accent, to see his alcohol permit.

"My passport?"

"Your permit, sir," answered the man.

"I don't understand."

"You need a permit to drink alcohol. Where is it?"

"I don't have a permit. I'm an American."

"Where is your passport?"

"Upstairs."

More words he didn't understand. Greeley stood up. "I'll just go get it and be right back," he said.

"Stay, sir," said the taller officer.

"I didn't even drink it. Smell my breath."

The officers looked at each other doubtfully. OK, if he

saw somebody talking to himself and acting like he was flying an airplane, he'd think he'd been drinking too.

"Look, you can come up with me," the pilot said to them. "My passport is in my room."

"How did you come to Karachi?"

Well now, Greeley had to admit that was a good question. O'Connell had told him they were to say they were American journalists, and so he did, adding that they were in the country to show the world how great a job Pakistan was doing in the war.

The police officers weren't impressed.

"I swear I didn't have anything to drink," said Greeley. "Not even a sip. I'm kind of on the wagon," he added confidentially. "See? It's still all the way up."

Nervously, Greeley reached down for the glass to show them. The shorter policeman knocked it out of his hand with a quick, violent slap.

"What the hell," said Greeley angrily.

"You will come with us," said the taller policeman.

"Baloney."

"You will come with us," he repeated, placing his hand on his holster. His companion already had his revolver out.

FRIDAY,
SEPT. 19, 1997

Karachi. 6:25 A.M.

His name was an incantation on her lips, a magic spell summoning him from the dark dungeon where he'd been exiled. It caressed his ear, lifting him upward with the gentle pull of a kiss, bathing him in a honey-perfumed air.

"Michael," she said, and he opened one eye to see Morena standing across the room, buttoning her shirt.

He was lying on a bed in Karachi, back in Pakistan, sent on what amounted to a suicide mission by people who had screwed him once, and might be planning to screw him again. The people who were supposed to help him were missing, possibly dead. The Pakistanis had a price on his head. He was counting on an old man to help him steal a plane he had last seen two years ago. And he'd made an arrangement with an arms dealer that would make him an international pariah.

"Michael," she repeated, "you have to get up. Your friend has been arrested."

He could smell the faint fragrance of her perfume as she

reached down and shook him. He groaned and rolled over in the bed, turning onto his side and pushing his feet onto the floor. He sat there, still disoriented.

"He was drinking without a liquor license, right out on the sidewalk," she scolded. "Where did you dig him up?"

"Greeley?"

"They put him in jail. I've already contacted Nizam; she's working on his release."

"Maybe we ought to just leave him there," said O'Connell. His eyes still weren't quite focusing. He had gone so long without sleep that his brief taste of it was a debilitating drug.

Morena had her hands on her hips, frowning at him. Black curls of hair spiraled down the sides of her pale face. The room was ablaze with lights.

"Come on," she said. "I'll meet you downstairs in five minutes."

Morena was waiting impatiently when he stepped out of the elevator. His shoes squeaked loudly on the slick tile until he reached the red carpet in front of the desk. The clerk was huddled in his chair against the back wall and remained snoozing as they passed. The Buick with its government tags was parked next to the sidewalk.

"Now that you're awake, there's something else," Morena told him as the driver put the car in gear. "The secretary of state has been kidnapped."

"What?"

"It happened sometime yesterday. The news reports were sketchy. He was in New Delhi, and had just gotten an agreement for a cease-fire from the Indians."

"The Indians took him?"

"I don't know," said Morena, sitting back in the seat. She glanced toward the front of the car before continuing. "The Sikhs wanted to disrupt the peace process," she said. "But the cease-fire seems to be holding anyway."

A note in her voice hinted that she wanted to add something else, but couldn't in front of the driver. They were separated by a piece of glass, but O'Connell wouldn't have trusted that either.

The city streets were peaceful and empty, yesterday's chaos shoved into the back alleys and hidden by the darkness. The lack of activity itself was a clue to the crisis; ordinarily it would never be this quiet in Karachi, not even on an early holiday morning.

Morena placed her hand on his thigh. "Someone from the prison called the hotel, probably looking to see how much they could shake us down for. He's been there all night."

Their destination was a detention facility halfway out of town. Set just behind the old ruins of a British fort, the prison's slick concrete walls seemed two hundred years old, even though they had only recently been erected. If the architects' intent had been to fill incoming prisoners with a sense of dread, they surely had succeeded; even O'Connell felt a shudder as they passed the guardhouse.

The sergeant who greeted them at the front desk burped loudly when Morena asked where Greeley was.

"You pig."

"Easy, Morena," said O'Connell, touching her shoulder. "*C'est sa manière de demander* a bribe."

"That's his problem."

"Here," said O'Connell, intending to provide an incentive for improving the sergeant's manners. But as he reached into his pocket Morena put her hands on the desk and leaned forward until barely three inches separated her face from the guard's.

"Listen to me. I'll have the interior minister on the phone in ten seconds if you don't do what I say."

The man grunted, then glanced toward O'Connell, who was holding a hundred-dollar bill in his hand. As the sergeant leaned forward to take the money, Morena grabbed it.

"Let's go," she said, holding the bill between her fingers and folding her arms. The sergeant showed them an enormous frown and muttered something inaudible, but got up meekly from his desk and led them down the corridor.

The stench of mildew and sweat grew stronger the farther they went. Every hundred yards and at the top and bottom of every staircase there were barrier checkpoints made of bulletproof glass and metal. Lethargic guards manned each one, not bothering to feign alertness as they slid their doors open. The first man they passed had a small outbreak of acne covering his left cheek; the skin disease grew progressively worse at each post until finally, at the base of the third flight of stairs, they found a man whose face was constructed entirely of pus.

Morena walked impatiently a step or two behind their portly guide, the hundred-dollar bill folded tightly in one fist. In O'Connell's experience, Pakistani men tended to stare openly at Western women, but Morena's scowl cowed each of the men they encountered as effectively as a pistol pressed against their cheekbones.

The corridors were all the same, long and gray, fabricated from polished concrete and lit by bare bulbs. Cells were marked by steel doors with small window slits. There were no numbers; O'Connell wondered if there were even records showing who was kept where.

The Pakistani criminal justice system could be harsh, but was generally considered fair and by certain standards humane. O'Connell realized that this was a special place, most likely reserved for political prisoners and other unusual cases. Moving past another checkpoint, he worried about what would happen if Morena's faith in Nizam or her authority was unfounded; they could easily be on their way to their own cells.

Through yet another checkpoint, O'Connell heard a cat mewing at the far end of the hallway. It was a soft, gentle sound, in great contrast to the sharp clicks of the heels on the cement as they walked. The animal must be calling for its breakfast.

It was only when they stopped in front of a door three-fourths of the way down that he realized the cry came not from a cat but a human, its song not of hunger but of pain. His anger at Greeley evaporated; for the first time he worried about what had been done to him.

The sergeant worked a key into the lock and then nodded down to the checkpoint, where the guard pushed an electronic device that buzzed the door open.

''About time,'' said Greeley, looking up from a wooden

bench anchored to the opposite wall.

"Are you all right?" Morena asked.

"I'm fine."

"They didn't hit you," she said, turning and glaring at the sergeant. It didn't sound like a question.

"Nah. They don't speak English too good, though."

"You need an alcohol permit to drink in Pakistan," Morena told him as they left the cell.

"Now you tell me."

"I told you not to drink in Pakistan," said O'Connell.

"I didn't drink. Honest," said Greeley, who huffed a bit to keep up with them. "I didn't have a sip."

The keeper's pace was considerably faster now that his mission had been accomplished. Morena continued to clutch the bribe money in her hand as they briskly retraced their steps back toward the front door.

O'Connell stopped Greeley as they passed the last checkpoint. "You sure you're OK?"

Greeley gave him a funny look. "What happened to you?"

"What do you mean?"

"Shit, you're civil all of a sudden."

"Screw you," said O'Connell. He continued into the administrative area just in time to see the guard stretch his hand out to Morena for the bribe. O'Connell watched as she unfolded the bill from her hand and held it in front of her chest. Slowly, to the Pakistani's amazement, she ripped it up, letting the pieces flutter to his desk.

The man began shouting in Urdu that she was crazy. Morena merely turned and walked out of the building, leaving O'Connell and Greeley to catch up.

A Hospital in Northern India. 7:45 A.M.

They were saying something about an operation. His leg. Was he going to lose his leg?

Gen. Arjun Singh, whose Indian troops had smashed through the weakly defended Pakistani frontier and practically split the enemy country in half, lay helpless in his hospital bed. His mind fluttered between fever-ridden consciousness and befuddled dreams. There were doctors in the room, trying to tell him something, trying perhaps to ask his opinion.

No, he told them. I would rather die than live as a cripple. Bury me in Lahore, when it is liberated.

They couldn't hear him. Arjun tried lifting himself, shouting, and they still didn't seem to hear.

A red hand pushed against his chest, setting him back on the bed. A fiery face loomed over his. Shiva.

"Why worry about your leg?" the god laughed. "You'll get a new one in your next life. Perhaps you'll have several."

"You again," said Arjun, struggling. The god's hand was gentle, despite his horrific appearance. It pushed him back as a nurse might. "I don't believe in reincarnation. There is only one God."

"Why argue about nuances?" said Shiva. "You can't deny my existence when I stand before you."

"My fever creates you."

"You are worried about how you will lead with only one leg. What kind of image will a general set if he must hobble in front of his men?"

"No," said Arjun, but it was true. "I do not believe in you. You are only something from a movie I saw years ago, when I was young."

"I've been around much longer than that," said Shiva. The apparition poked Arjun's foot playfully. "Tell me—should I have you reincarnated as a foot soldier?"

"There will be no fighting in the next generation," said the general. "Once we have accomplished our goals, there will be no need for soldiers."

Laughter filled the room.

"A Sikh who believes in peace," said Shiva, sitting on the edge of the bed. "It is a difficult concept to fathom, even for a god."

"My army will recapture our sacred lands, and we will once more be free."

"And the Muslims will not fight back?"

"They will be destroyed."

"Every one of them?" Shiva's face, grim and taut, loomed above his. "How many men have you sent to their deaths, General Arjun Singh? How big is the pile of limbs from the men you have left as cripples? How loud are the wails of the orphans you have made?"

"I fight for justice."

The god stepped back from his bed, folding his arms. At least he had only two today.

"You have fought for revenge and for honor, for the sheer sake of destruction, but you have never fought for justice. Wars are not fought for justice—it is too paltry an aim."

"Why are you tormenting me?" Arjun asked, tears forming in his eyes.

"Tormenting you? I'm simply talking to you. Surely you did not expect Brahma or Vishnu—they create and preserve. I destroy. I am *your* god."

"I believe in the one true God."

"You have always been surrounded by Hindus, and have been unsure what to believe. The only faith you truly know is destruction—my faith. That is why you make war."

"No," said the general. "I believe in justice."

"You're going to lose your leg," Shiva laughed. "It will join the others on the cremation pile you created in your pride, in your envy of the gods. And then you will lose your life."

The room was spinning. There was a hum in Arjun's ears, spirits surrounding him, touching him. They were the hands of all the men he'd sent to their deaths, crying for revenge.

"Eventually you will succeed," predicted Shiva. "The world will end in a fiery explosion of hate and fury. That will be your justice."

En route to Nizam's Compound. 9:30 A.M.

"You know, I think my brother-in-law used to have a car like this, somewhere around the early sixties or so. Wasn't in this good a shape, though." Greeley turned and looked into the back. Morena and O'Connell were sitting glumly, each right next to a door. Both looked morose, as if they'd been the ones sitting in jail for the past six hours.

"We almost there?" he asked the driver. The man nodded solemnly. Greeley sighed and settled back to watch out the window. They had been going uphill almost since leaving the police station; now they rounded through a valley and began another steep climb. Just as they did, the ruins of an old building came into view directly on their right.

It was a castle, or something like a castle. Three huge remnants commanded the hillside. The closest pair each had parts of two walls nearly intact. Ornamental glazes ran in horizontal bands across the red-brown brick walls at different heights. The decoration was intricate and subtly different on each structure. Triangles and loops laced through the facades in light yellow, blue, black and red. The corners were marked by round columns, tapering as they reached upward. Sections of what had been second and third stories remained, set back from the outside walls and angled; the tops appeared to have been octagons, though they were in such poor shape that it was impossible to tell. Huge archways marked the entrance to both buildings, but time and thieves had chipped away the blocks, and now only the suggestion of curves remained.

There was more left of the third building, set further back from the others behind a level plain occupied by a single tree. This structure had been considerably larger and a substantial portion of its central dome roof remained, the white bricks still shining with the early sun. The facade was constructed of blue, white and yellow tiles, all ornately patterned; there were archways in the side walls and one huge one at what must have been the main entranceway. The corner columns were intact, and seemed to give the building a strong set of arms and shoulders.

"That is the palace of the Nizams," said the driver. "The princess's ancestors ruled this countryside since the Moguls came to Pakistan. It is an ancient family."

Greeley watched the rays of the sun pick through the

bricks as they passed. Several large birds perched on one of the walls, ugly dark birds. One flapped its wings angrily as if the foreigner's gaze disturbed him.

"They say it is haunted," said the driver. "No one will go there because of the vultures."

"Nizam would shoot anyone who trespassed," added Morena from the back.

The Buick came to a complete stop a few yards down the road. Two militiamen appeared from the side of the road and glanced at the driver, then turned and pushed away a large rock and some shrubbery to reveal a roadway on their right. It was not a rock at all, Greeley realized as they passed, but a dummy made of plastic.

Though the road was dirt, the driver went faster here than he had on the highway, and Greeley gripped the side of the door nervously. He had just opened his mouth to complain when the car began braking. They entered a short, narrow pass in the hills; on the other side there was an iron gate manned by four more soldiers. The gates opened, and the driver once more stepped on the gas, proceeding down a long road and passing a small military installation along the way. To one side was a set of barracks, nestled in a hollow beside a large grassy field. A helipad and a group of maintenance sheds sat across the road. A cluster of microwave towers looked down from the hillside.

After everything else he'd seen, the building that served as the princess's headquarters was a letdown. A low-slung concrete affair that sat at the end of the boxed canyon, it looked more like a bomb shelter than the majestic palace he had expected. Actually, the facade was made of polished granite, not cement, but otherwise the building's designer had let function, not fashion, guide him. The walls could take direct hits from large howitzer shells and remain intact. The stubby square pillars that marked off the small veranda at the entrance were spaced close enough together to prevent any vehicle wider than a motorcycle from driving up the steps and into the courtyard beyond. Even the decorative touches on the grounds were austere—the only marking of Nizam's ancestral heritage was a small obelisk in the center of the driveway loop in front of the house. The black stone gleamed like glass. Narrowing sharply at the top, it might be a spear stuck handle-first into the ground by a giant, a warning against would-be invaders.

The prison dampness had aggravated Greeley's knee. It had tightened during the long car ride, and he almost tripped getting out of the car.

"What the hell are you doing?" O'Connell asked as Greeley placed his hands above his head and began a deep knee bend.

"Yoga," said Greeley, lowering himself and breathing slowly. "It's for my arthritis. A lot of people think yoga is for sissies, but basically it's just stretching." He returned to the top position and repeated the movement. "My wife got me into it. Best thing going for the joints."

O'Connell shook his head and took a step toward the house. Morena grabbed him.

"The princess knew the secretary of state was going to be kidnapped," she said in a low voice when he turned back to her. "I don't know how she got the information, but I don't like it."

"Jesus, Morena." O'Connell glanced at the porch, where the driver had joined two militiamen and was looking back at them with curiosity. "Why the hell didn't you tell me?"

"When? In the car? The hotel was probably bugged, too. Don't worry about it—let's just thank her and get the hell out of here."

The three Americans passed silently through the portico into the courtyard. Though it looked like one building, the complex was actually a series of linked structures around a large central garden (called a *mazdan* in Urdu). The large L at the back and to the right of the courtyard contained the princess's administrative offices; on the left a squarish rectangle formed her private living quarters. These three sides were joined by a veranda, marked by round colonnades. Pink granite covered the walls, making them appear softer than those outside, though they were every bit as protective.

A few steps into the garden they were met by an older man who singled Greeley out and said in rapid English that he apologized on behalf of all Pakistan country and hoped everything had become OK.

"Our customs are different, Mr. Greeley," said the man. "We have much bureaucracy, and then there is also strictures of our Koran. You must do as Romans in Rome," he added, wagging his finger.

"I didn't even take a sip, I swear—"

Morena cut them off abruptly. "Tell the princess we are here, Murwan."

"She already knows," he said. The light froth evaporated from his voice; his English, too, improved. "She will meet you shortly. Here—" Murwan gestured to two men waiting behind him. "You are to wait in the guest house."

The room they were shown to was considerably less impressive than the reception area in Renard's palace, but this one too featured a large table laden with food. Greeley walked to it immediately, marveling at the different dishes, none of which was recognizable.

"I assume—" started O'Connell, but Morena stopped him, pointing to the ceiling. The agent nodded, and they stood together in silence, frowning.

"This is great," said Greeley, examining a dish of spicy beef. "What's it called?"

"Nihari," said Morena.

"It smells good," he said, filling a plate.

"It's brain and tongue," said O'Connell.

Greeley returned the meat to the bowl and pointed to another dish. "This?"

"Tandoori," said Morena. "Chicken."

"They cook it underground," said O'Connell.

"This looks like potatoes."

"They are," answered Morena. *"Alu-puri,* a bit spicy. It's good, though."

Greeley hesitated, thinking of the Algerian food and its aftereffects.

"That white stuff is yogurt," said O'Connell.

A week ago, Greeley would have looked at yogurt as an adventure; now it was comfort food compared to the rest of the spread. He was debating whether to trust his head or his nose when Nizam entered the room, accompanied by Murwan and the two men who had shown them here. The princess had an arresting air despite an almost dowdy physical appearance and what seemed to Greeley garishly colored clothes—a long purple shirt over baggy green pants, with a huge yellow sash draped across her shoulder. Her black hair was pulled back into a tight bun, and she wore no jewelry except a plain green ring. Greeley guessed she was in her early forties.

"Mr. O'Connell, how nice to see you again." She turned quickly to Greeley and extended her hand. "I am Princess Ghazzala Nizam."

Greeley hesitated for a moment, wondering if he was supposed to curtsey, or maybe kiss her hand. He decided finally to shake it.

"I must apologize for our police," she said, taking his hand with a concerned smile. "They are too enthusiastic. It is because of the war."

The princess continued to hold Greeley's hand as she spoke, which made him uncomfortable. But he didn't think he could just yank it away. She had a firm grip, though her fingers were soft. Olissa's were always cracked from dishwater.

"What brings you to our country? Especially at such a time. We have a cease-fire, but there is no telling how long it will last. The Indians are animals."

"We're here to report on the situation," said O'Connell.

"Really, Mr. O'Connell?" The princess, still holding Greeley's hand, turned toward the agent. Her English had a pronounced British accent. "I had understood that you were here to help rescue an agent near the China border."

"I had to tell her," Morena said. "It's all right."

Greeley knew—or at least, thought he knew—that there was no agent near China. Nevertheless, the act Morena and O'Connell put on with glances and frowns was pretty convincing.

"I was frankly surprised to learn that you had made it to Karachi, Mr. O'Connell," continued Nizam. "A friend assured me that you had been killed in Paris."

"What?" said Morena.

"Obviously they were too optimistic," said O'Connell.

"Yes." The princess pulled Greeley along with her gently as she took a step toward them. He was standing right next to her now, looking down at her head as she spoke. Her hair was thin and brittle, like fine strands of steel wool. "I understand our intelligence service was to blame. Naturally, I haven't alerted them to their error," she added pointedly. "But why would they want to kill you?"

O'Connell shrugged.

"You must excuse my ignorance; my sources with some areas of the intelligence service are not what they should be. It is the military's fault. They do not trust me."

"Why's that, I wonder."

"Perhaps their animosity toward you is related to the problem with your friends, Misters Westlake and Smith," said the princess. "I understand they had shown some interest in a facility at Kahuta that is under the jurisdiction of the Institute for Nuclear Science. Why would that be?"

O'Connell shrugged. "I've been out of the loop for a long time."

"It's a shame that they were killed," the princess said. Greeley tried to remain emotionless. "Do you think they were tortured first?"

"You'd have a better idea of that than me."

"Does the CIA think my country has nuclear weapons?"

"Anything's possible."

"Perhaps I would not know of them," said Nizam.

"Perhaps."

"Princess, we only came here to thank you," said Morena. "Now we'll be on our way."

"You're leaving?"

Finally Nizam released Greeley, walking to Morena. The younger woman's body tensed ever so slightly. Greeley recognized the expression on her face as one his daughter-in-law occasionally used when they were playing poker, and she was wondering whether to raise or fold.

"You're leaving without even eating?" Nizam took her hand now. It was as if she were Morena's mother, complaining that she never visited. "Aren't you hungry?"

"We've had breakfast already," she lied.

"I wish you would stay."

"Why?" asked O'Connell.

"It's just that I may be able to help you. I have information about your secretary of state." Nizam's voice plunged a full octave. "We believe we have discovered where the Sikhs are holding him in northern India. If you wish, I will help you rescue him."

Kamra Proving Grounds, Pakistan. 10:12 A.M.

All Thursday afternoon and well into the night, they had Khan fly the Leopard. As soon as he would land, the maintenance crews ran to the plane; he would be barely out of the cockpit when preparations began to refuel it. By the last flight he felt as if he had run three marathons back-to-back; his feet scraped hard along the tarmac as he walked to the inquisitors waiting to review his efforts. But the intensive familiarization had its desired effect. He couldn't know every little nook and cranny of the plane, but he was at ease in it. His body had adjusted its motor memory to the controls. There was no more geek factor.

That night, Khan slept deeper than he had in months, perhaps even years. It was as if someone had piled dirt on him; the blankets felt so heavy when his alarm sounded that he just let it ring and ring, until it gave up and shut itself off. When he next opened his eyes it was after ten.

If he didn't hurry, he'd be late for his 10:30 meeting with his cousin.

The pilot mustered his strength and literally rolled out of bed, nearly tripping onto the floor but managing to catch his balance in a dance that took him to the bathroom and the shower. He was still heavily fatigued—he didn't realize until after he had withstood the cold blast of water from the faucet head that he hadn't removed his underwear.

"I can tell you haven't had breakfast," said Nur when Khan reported to his office, a commandeered conference room in a building right next to the Leopard's hangar. "As a matter of fact, I'm not sure you've woken up yet."

"I'm awake, sir."

Nur laughed and, rising from his desk, slapped him on the back. "Come on, son, let's go get you something to eat."

All of Kamra was a highly secret and very secure facility; the Leopard project was an island fortress within the island fortress. The development team had separate, quarantined quarters, as well as their own mess and recreation areas. Nothing elaborate—the cafeteria where they went for breakfast served everyone involved in the project and yet was barely bigger than a good-sized kitchen.

At this hour, they had it to themselves. The civilian chef, seeing the general walk in, greeted him warmly and promised to bring *khagina,* a spicy version of scrambled eggs, over for him and his guest as soon as it was prepared.

"And coffee for my young cousin," added the general.

Even before he sat the pilot's nose filled with the pleasant odor of garlic and onions placed on a hot skillet. He hadn't eaten since breakfast yesterday, and his digestive juices started rumbling in anticipation of food.

"These are like no other eggs in the country," said Nur. "The cook once owned a restaurant in Karachi."

The breakfast set down in front of Khan was immense. Besides the *khagina,* there were sweetbreads, *alu-puri* and deviled kidneys—considered a delicacy and a treat, though Khan couldn't stomach the thought of eating them and gave them directly to the general.

Nur ate with as much relish as Khan. They were silent, concentrating on the food. Finally, his plate almost cleared, the pilot remembered his arrival yesterday, and how he'd been convinced his cousin was going to sell out to the Indians. Now he was ashamed.

"I owe you an apology," he said. "Yesterday I thought, well, I didn't know what was going on."

"You were angry that I was taking you from the fight," said Nur. He waved to the attendant, who came to clear the table. "Do you know who this is?" Nur asked the airman.

"This is Major Syyid Khan. They call him the Rocket."

The attendant, barely old enough to shave, nodded respectfully as he took their plates.

"He has shot down a dozen enemy airplanes in less than two days of action."

"You're exaggerating, General," said Khan, turning red.

Duly impressed, the skinny youth dropped his tray on the floor as he turned from the table. Chuckling, Nur suggested Khan accompany him on a walk.

But the general's cheery mood dissipated outside. Khan realized his exuberance had been a front; he must be thinking of the details of the mission and how to present them.

A cease-fire had been declared yesterday; even so, Khan expected to fly, perhaps on a reconnaissance mission over the border. The Leopard could be outfitted with task-specific belly packs; while originally intended for different types of air-to-air weapons, one of the briefing officers yesterday had said that a reconnaissance package was among those ready in the hangar.

Even in a plane as advanced as the Leopard, there was bound to be danger. He would be in hostile territory miles from his base and on his own. But Khan felt confident, proud of his plane and sure of his abilities. He wanted to reassure his cousin, but Nur's grim demeanor kept him quiet. He was afraid of seeming too much of a braggart.

They were halfway down the runway before the general spoke, and then his question surprised the pilot.

"And how is Hir Ranjha?"

"She is fine," said Khan. He had not had much time to think about his finacée in the last twenty-four hours.

The general stood with his hands on his hips, surveying the vast complex. His voice, when he continued, had the tone of a command. "You are to be married next week."

"With the war, the arrangements have been postponed."

"Yes," said the general. He continued to scan the Aeronautical Complex, studying the area where PAF Mirages were refurbished. Perhaps he was remembering his early days here. "Hir Ranjha will be an excellent addition to the family."

Jim DeFelice

"I don't think she cares for this war," said Khan. "She doesn't understand why we must fight. She cried when I told her about our bombing mission."

For the first time since they had come outside, the general turned and looked directly at him. His face was mournful and his voice soft when he spoke.

"These are terrible things we must do, even driven by necessity. It is for survival, but that barely redeems us. I, too, have my doubts." The general put his arm around Khan's shoulder and slowly began walking again. "I told you to be ready for a mission tonight. You are to fly deep into India, rendezvous with a tanker in the Bay of Bengal, and fly back. Along the way you will be dropping small rockets—they are not bombs but special electronic devices that will confuse radars for a brief period when activated. They are crucial for another mission."

"Another mission?"

"With luck, it will never be flown," said the general. "More likely, it will go off tomorrow or the next day. If so, you will have a small role in it, besides this." Khan nodded as the general continued. "The Leopard was not designed as an attack jet, but it is the only plane that can accomplish our task. The devices will be loaded into a special weapons dispenser and the computer sufficiently prepared so that even an interceptor pilot will have an easy time."

The general smiled briefly. It had often been a joking rivalry between them—Nur had trained primarily as an attack pilot, while Khan relished the role of interception and dogfighting.

"I'm flying even with the cease-fire?"

"The cease-fire. Yes. The Indians have kidnapped the American secretary of state, and it is doubtful they will sit still for peace. There is logic to our actions."

Khan looked at him expectantly, but Nur did not explain further. Instead, the general placed both hands on his shoulders and looked at him gravely.

"You cannot be captured," he said. "There will be no parachute in your plane tonight."

Nizam's Compound. 10:40 A.M.

O'Connell squeezed Morena's arm as the last of the princess's aides left the room. "What's her angle?"

Morena nuzzled into him, as if she were going to give him a kiss. "Let's go outside," she whispered.

They left Greeley hovering over the food. Morena led her old lover through the portico to the front of the compound. When she reached the driveway, she turned and hugged him. "They'll have cameras watching us," she said. "But they can't hear."

Her body was warm and heavy in his hands, and it took effort for him to concentrate. While his instincts warned him away from Nizam, he also knew he should be just as wary of Morena.

It was impossible though. He'd never been on his guard with her, and something inside kept pushing him toward her.

"Does she really know where he is?"

"It's possible," said Morena. "She has plenty of contacts, despite her complaining."

"Why tell us?"

"She's looking for leverage."

"So why not just give us his location and let us be the ones to die trying?"

"She wants more leverage than that."

"Yeah." O'Connell glanced back toward the house. If there were surveillance cameras watching them as Morena suspected, he couldn't spot them. "Does she know about Golden Bear?"

Morena, continuing the diversion for whoever was watching, pushed up and kissed him. It was a sure way to guarantee they'd pay attention, O'Connell thought, but he couldn't stop his lips.

"I got the feeling she didn't know everything," said Morena as they parted. "I think she knows part of the story, or maybe only suspects it. How much would the military tell her about the bombs?"

"Not even that many people in the military know. In theory, she'd be the last one to be told."

Morena's green eyes were narrow with the full light, thin round bands around the jet black pearls. "If she knew, she'd want it for herself. She'd come right out and try and make a deal."

"Maybe she doesn't know where it is."

"Then she'd propose some sort of swap—we help her get the weapons and she helps us find the secretary of state. She must be maneuvering inside the government; that's why she wants to help us get the secretary back. She thinks the U.S. will be so grateful that we'll back her. Having the weapons on top of that would give her unlimited bargaining power."

O'Connell thought grimly about what the princess would do with the planes and their weapons. But was she any more dangerous than the people who had them now? How much could he extract from her without letting her in on Golden Bear? He would have to be wary of her men.

They might not need her. Assuming he could get back and get the helicopter in Karachi. In theory, he and Morena and Greeley could go on to the base alone.

Unless the Paks had changed their plans. One good thing—if they had interrogated Westlake and Smith before killing them, they'd know that the CIA had no idea where the planes were. With that information, and figuring that O'Connell was out of the way, they'd feel safe enough to avoid doing anything, like suddenly sending troops to a semi-abandoned mountain airstrip, that would arouse suspicion.

"We have to go and get the secretary," said Morena. "Even if it may be a trap."

"We?"

"I need you to help me."

"The planes are more important, Morena."

"Tell me where they are and I'll tell Carl. He can have the base bombed."

"It's not that easy, Morena. They'd scramble the bombers once anything came near. Besides, I got screwed once; I'm not getting screwed again. As long as I'm the only one who knows, the agency can't stick another knife in my back."

Her eyes looked as if they'd been stolen from a cat. "Why don't you trust me?"

"Why should I?"

"Michael, so many people are going to die. Don't you care about that?"

"What's that got to do with anything?"

She pressed her lips together. "First we get the secretary of state."

"I'm not coming."

"Yes, you will, it's an order." She turned to go back into the house.

"Screw you, Morena. Morena—"

He still loved her. It was the only reason he was acquiescing.

That and he didn't know what else he could do.

Nizam's Compound. 11 A.M.

"Now we'll see how good a pilot Mr. O'Connell is," said the princess as she passed the two guards at the entrance to her office. "Tell Sar that I expect the helicopter to be here no later than one P.M."

"I believe it is too risky to let them travel all the way to India," said Murwan, trying to keep pace as the princess entered her office suite. She worked in the same wing as her private quarters. Most of her staff were across the compound; there was only a female secretary here, and Murwan practically knocked her over as he pulled out the wooden chair across from the princess's desk.

"But that is the beauty of my plan—there must be risk involved," answered Nizam, who made up for Murwan's arrogance by motioning her secretary to her. "If it were too easy they would think that I arranged it."

"They think that now."

"They may suspect it, but that will not affect their decision to go. They are obliged to. Morena knows that I will not give her the information unless she does things my way. They will rescue him, and that will erase whatever doubts they have, at least long enough for us to maneuver within the government. And if in the meantime we get the details on this nuclear project they are after, so much the better. No doubt it is a wild goose chase, as you suggested, but it intrigues me. It would be just like Fazal and his mongrel Chenab to circumvent the UN treaty. Manny,'' she said, calling her secretary by her pet name, ''please make a connection to General Chenab's office. I would like to speak to the general as soon as possible.''

The assistant bowed and Nizam noticed that she gave Murwan a wide berth as she left the room. Manzzoor was a slender girl, pretty and intelligent but subdued even by traditional Muslim standards. Though her employer had taken it as a project to toughen her, she'd made little progress.

''You're not telling the general of this.''

''Just that we are working with the CIA. I will make it seem as if it is their idea.''

''That is foolish. It will provoke them further,'' said Murwan sharply. ''If you push the army too far they will crush you. With the cease-fire—''

''Who are you talking to, Murwan? To me? I do not like your tone of voice. You may disagree with me, but you will show the respect my family deserves.''

''I am trying to show you reality, Princess. Your support is not so great that the army will hesitate to move against you if they feel threatened.''

''You will address me as I deserve to be addressed.'' The princess felt her cheeks flush. ''What is wrong with you, Murwan? Have you forgotten your place?''

The aide grasped his hands together, squeezing the fingers white. It was several seconds before he could manage an answer.

Nizam, too, had difficulty controlling herself. Murwan had often disagreed with her, but there was a bitterness in his voice that she could not account for, a tone she had not heard from him before.

''I know my place quite well, Princess,'' he said, barely moving his mouth as he spoke. ''If you wish to dismiss me from your service, you may.''

"Don't talk nonsense."

Murwan bowed his head. "By your leave."

"You may go," she said firmly.

After he left, she noticed her right hand trembling. She pushed back her large desk chair and sat, placing her arm on the desktop. It did not stop moving until she pressed down hard against the edge of the polished mahogany.

Murwan's family had served the Nizams for hundreds of years. The princess believed that the minor branches of their families had intermarried during the days of Mogul rule, further solidifying the connections. Even if his tone had been intemperate, she knew he had spoken only from genuine concern. Among her many advisers, underlings and retainers, Murwan alone had the courage to consistently speak his mind. That was why she valued him so much.

Had she overreached?

Her current position depended on a collection of intrigues, promises, blackmail arrangements and open bribes. The web was difficult to hold together. If she were removed from the equation, either by being jailed or assassinated, the party would flounder. No one else could provide the focus for the movement, nor would they have the same motivation. Without an obvious heir—she had vague hopes for an eight-year-old nephew currently studying in England—the slim chance of independence would forever pass.

But to hesitate with the opportunity so close would be just as fatal. Perhaps never again would the central government and the military both be in such a weak position.

If her people didn't support her as Murwan implied, wouldn't the army have moved against her years before? Surely, they would never have let her movement get this far.

The princess felt a tremor return to her right hand. She slammed it against the desk. She would tell Chenab flatly that she was working with the CIA. The implication that the U.S. was behind her would hold the army at bay long enough for her to prepare her next move.

While she'd been wrong about the effect of the kidnapping on the cease-fire, the war was far from concluded and the army's hold on things remained precarious at best. No one expected the cease-fire to last. They were still rushing everything they could find to reinforce the front. She had even sent her own militia units into the desert to help, reserving only a token contingent for her own defense.

"Manny, have you gotten General Chenab yet?" she called into the other office, neglecting the intercom.

"His office says he is at the front," answered her secretary on the speaker.

"Nonsense," said Nizam. "Chenab would stay as far away from the battlefield as possible. Tell them to have us put through. Be polite though; tell them it is an urgent piece of information that I feel he should have for his benefit."

"Yes, Princess."

She would start by apologizing for her outburst at the cabinet meeting, and end by promising to give the army as much credit as possible. It was best to be diplomatic.

Northwestern India. Apx. 5 P.M.

The kidnappers had been relatively gentle as they wrapped his face in gauze to blindfold him, but all the jostling stretched the tape around his cheekbones and made it itch like hell. For several hours now, riding along in the backseat of what seemed to be a late-model van, the secretary of state had wanted to scratch at the edges, but couldn't. His hands were bound together with a chain that was attached to another at his feet; there was no way for Grasso to get them higher than mid-chest.

A separate bandage, sodden with spit and sweat, gagged his mouth. This was fairly loose; Grasso figured that if he really tried he could work it free, though there seemed little point in doing so. He'd still be blindfolded and manacled, with no chance to escape.

He thought about escape because he wondered if it were his duty to try. He remembered *The Bridge Over the River Kwai* and a half dozen other movies, wondering how close to his situation they might actually be.

Early in the administration they'd discussed what to do in

the case of an abduction. He hadn't taken it very seriously; no high-ranking U.S. government official had ever been kidnapped. It was just another of those interminable meetings clogging up a day better devoted to something else.

Now he wished he could remember even the rudimentary outlines of what was said. Perhaps he should try and puzzle out who his captors were and where he was being taken. See if he could catch some clue about where he was.

Unlikely. Even if he were more familiar with India, he'd seen so little since being taken from the car that he might as well be in Arizona. While he'd always had a good sense of direction, Grasso was learning that a blindfold and fear easily overpowered an internal compass.

The secretary of state shifted his legs gingerly on the bench. The empty space next to him was like the air above the edge of a cliff. He felt he might plunge into an endless pit if he moved too much.

He'd fallen there already, fallen yesterday, when he got out of the limo. He'd told his driver to get out too, said to remain calm, that they wanted them alive.

A moment later, the man glanced at him over the roof of the black Lincoln, his hands in the air, waiting. His look was tinged with reproach as well as doubt.

Grasso had wanted to say something to encourage him. He felt it was his duty to speak, but the words hid from him. All he could do was force a smile.

He was pushed down to the ground. There was a helicopter above, landing. The wind kicked up. He was dragged off the roadway.

Grasso heard two shots, tiny and unimpressive, not what they ought to be. Death should come with a roar, not with a thin, tinny sound so slight it could be easily missed.

They threw Grasso headfirst into the helicopter and the engine kicked into high gear. He tried to glimpse out the aircraft as they lifted off, but couldn't manage it; someone was already pulling a hood down over his head.

But he didn't need to see. He knew they'd killed his driver. A little more than a day later, and he couldn't even remember the man's name. The driver wasn't part of the traveling security team; he'd come from the embassy. Even so, Grasso ought to remember it, at least his first name.

Around the world, they'd be burning code books and shredding paper. There was a crisis team, some sort of work group. They would proceed under the assumption he was dead.

The van slowed considerably, then turned off the highway onto a rough road. After a short distance, it pulled onto a soft shoulder and stopped.

The door on his right opened. "You will get out now," said a voice from outside. He felt hands reach for him.

Stepping from the van, Grasso stumbled. He couldn't get his arms up to break his fall and scraped his face. Dust and dirt choked his nose and he began coughing.

Two strong hands lifted him back up. An unintelligible conversation ensued as he was brought to his feet. The hands reached around from behind him to loosen the gag, slipping the cotton bandage down. Then they took a cloth and gently wiped the corners of his mouth. They were large hands, powerful but gentle. They reminded him of his father's. A finger poked under the tape in front of his ear, then slowly worked its way around his cheekbone to his nose.

When the blindfold was finally removed, he opened his eyes slowly, afraid that the sudden glare of light would blind him. At first he could see only a white haze; gradually he was able to discern the shapes of trees in the distance. He was standing before a dry, arid plain, with the sun dodging between clouds to his right. It must be late afternoon.

Silently, the man behind him knelt and put a key into the leg chains, removing them. He undid the manacle binding his arms and legs together; only the chain between his hands remained. Grasso wondered if they were going to kill him.

Perhaps that was why they had undone the blindfold. No need to hide from a dead man.

But no. Two of his captors appeared before him, kerchiefs thrown around their faces. What did you call these coverings the Indians wore? Like a shawl only narrow and long, useful for many things. Women wore a version over their heads, to use as veils.

The men turned and began walking, and Grasso felt a nudge from behind, indicating he should follow. This man, too, the one with the soft hands, had his face covered.

If they had firearms, they weren't obvious. In the distance he saw a Jeep Cherokee; they were heading for it.

Yesterday they had changed vehicles several times and driven for hours, well into the night. Finally they'd stopped and he was brought, still hooded, into a private house. He spent the night in a windowless room, shackled to the bed, occasionally dozing off, only to awaken with nightmares of his driver's death.

Like the dog.

If he survived, he'd have a new set of nightmares.

What the hell were those cloths called? Salwar something? No, that was a tunic women wore.

Grasso glanced to his left and saw the highway they had turned off. The traffic was light but relatively steady, with cars passing every ten or twenty seconds. At most, the paved macadam roadway was a hundred yards away.

The two men in front were nearly at the Cherokee. There were maybe twenty yards between him and them.

Grasso stopped. The man with the soft hands came up behind him.

"Why are you stopping?"

"I have to, have to relieve myself," he managed.

The man patted him on the shoulder and moved a respectful distance away as Grasso, his back to the highway, undid his fly.

You could make it. It would take them a few seconds to react. If you shouted and put your hands in the air, someone on the road would stop.

Even if he were hit by a car, it would be better than being gunned down by his captors. It would be a moral victory, cheating them.

The man with the soft hands looked back. Grasso continued to go through the motions, and the man, apparently satisfied and suitably modest, went on.

Run now. He's twenty yards away. You can make it.

They would have guns in the car. It was unlikely he'd escape alive.

Was it his duty to try? Or to kill himself, so he couldn't be used for whatever purposes they had in mind?

He was the secretary of state of the United States of America, the most powerful country in the world, one of its most important officials. His responsibilities were not personal responsibilities, but responsibilities of a nation, of the world.

The Cherokee started up. Grasso saw himself starting across the field, running for the highway, shouting. The car would pursue him, but he would make it to the highway, flailing his arms. A gun would be fired.

"OK?"

Grasso looked up at the masked man with the soft hands sitting in the backseat of the Cherokee, which had driven over to him. Nodding, he got into the car.

CIA Headquarters. 8:10 A.M.

Stockman looked at the phone an instant before it rang, as if he had a premonition.

He'd been at the CIA building for nearly three hours already. In meetings all night Thursday, he hadn't left for home until nearly 2 A.M. Once there, he didn't even bother going upstairs to the bedroom; he knew it'd be impossible to sleep. The DDO made himself coffee and looked at a test pattern on the TV for awhile before writing a note to his wife and coming back to the office.

He'd hoped for news, good or bad, but there was nothing, either on Golden Bear or the kidnapping. At least he could openly fret about the kidnapping. He had assistants checking constantly with the Indian police, their investigators, their army. Everyone said it looked like the secretary had been "beamed" away, like a character on "Star Trek."

There had been arrests, of course. Hundreds of them. Every Sikh, every separatist group within a hundred miles of the capital was under suspicion. But there had also been a major blunder. Grasso's security team had apprehended a man involved in a disturbance just prior to the snatch. At the time, the incident appeared to be a case of jumpy nerves. The man had been turned over to the police for routine questioning at the hotel. In the confusion, he'd been released.

Stockman glanced at his phone, picked it up midring.

"This is an unsecure line," she said. "Blossom has offered to help get him back."

"Where?" Even though she'd caught him by surprise, he knew Morena could only be talking about one person.

"Won't say. Blossom is playing an angle."

"Tell me where you are and I'll send people."

"Can't. A mission has been planned."

"What?"

"It's useless to push. It's Blossom's way or no way."

The DDO picked up a pencil from his desk and began sketching lines on a yellow pad. He rarely took notes while on the phone; instead, he drew boxes and circles and arrows, unconsciously working out the flow of his emotions.

"We'll have to go south." She must still be in Pakistan. He had to assume the phone line was tapped. He couldn't press her for information. Already she'd probably said too much.

"I need O'Connell," she was saying.

"No. He has his own store to watch."

"I absolutely need him."

"Get someone else."

"I can't."

"Get someone else."

"Impossible."

Presented with a hypothetical, a CIA analysis team yesterday had speculated that the Pakistanis would use nuclear weapons if a cease-fire breakdown appeared likely. A satellite report earlier this morning showed Indian troop movements along the Kashmir front. There was a host of intercepted communications indicating the Pakistani army was on the move, obviously fearing a new attack.

"There's got to be another way," Stockman told Morena.

"I can't get another pilot. He's already been over the plan

and he's familiarizing himself with the helicopter right now.''

Morena knew the mission, and she knew Blossom. She'd already made all the calculations, from a much better vantage point than he had. But if he let her take O'Connell, he'd lose his last chance of getting the plane and the bombs. Surely she knew that.

Maybe there was no chance. If Westlake and Smith were dead, what made him think the Pakistanis wouldn't get O'Connell next? Maybe they'd smoked out the Paris hoax, and this was a diversion, a way to kill O'Connell and Morena without directing suspicion to the nuclear problem.

He should have pushed O'Connell for the location of the base when he had him sitting in the office.

But he hadn't wanted to go to the air force for an air strike then, and he still didn't. That would mean exposing the agency, and himself, publicly. He'd been relieved when O'Connell didn't tell him.

''Carl?''

An unsecure line, probably monitored by half a dozen countries. They'd said way too much.

''Do it,'' he told her, and hung up the phone.

In the few minutes of conversation, Stockman's pencil had filled half the page. He'd pressed so hard he'd dug through the top few sheets of the pad.

The DDO rose and slowly began pacing the room. Shaking his head, cursing himself, he paused to look down at the bookcase next to his door. The case itself was like the other units lining the room: government-issue simulated walnut, three shelves high. But there wasn't a single agency report or policy book in this unit, not even a stray copy of *Foreign Affairs*. These were Stockman's personal books, talismans of what he believed was important.

As a young man at Yale, he had known the world through books. He'd been amazed when the CIA recruited him; up until then, he'd always considered himself an intellectual, an introvert. They'd given him another way of looking at things. They'd made him a man of action, turned his insides out.

He'd done well. But part of him remained the skinny kid in the library, hunched over a desk for hours, reading Marcus Aurelius. *Huck Finn.* Chaucer. *The Taming of the Shrew.*

He laughed to himself, imagining Morena as Kate and himself as Petruchio. He had been a boorish clod, trying to seduce her; to her credit she'd never given in.

Plato, a few books on Vietnam. Neil Sheehan's *A Bright Shining Lie.*

It hadn't been his mistake. Good God, what had the director been thinking of when he authorized the plane? A weapon that was nearly impossible, maybe wholly impossible, to track. Woolsley had to know there would be nukes, no matter what the estimates said. And had to know that sooner or later, the Pakistanis would want to use the weapons he'd helped them get.

Perhaps the last president had authorized it himself. Like many other presidents, he'd sometimes used the director and the agency to run backstairs foreign relations.

It wasn't Stockman's fault. His only mistake had been not making it right immediately.

Calling O'Connell back had been a last grasp at keeping it quiet. Now three agents were dead, and the odds were stacked so heavily against O'Connell that even if Stockman had ordered Morena not to use him to retrieve the secretary, he didn't have a chance at getting to the planes.

Maybe no one did. But if he just sat and waited now millions of people would die.

The DDO walked slowly back to the desk and picked up his phone. "Get me the president," he told the operator.

Nizam's Compound. 3 P.M.

The princess obviously had excellent connections with the French. Not only was the Aérospatiale Super Panther II O'Connell was sitting in a hot piece of equipment, but the specially fitted glass vision-enhancement frame on the windshield was an expensive and almost impossible-to-purchase gadget.

O'Connell knew because he'd tried to get one himself for the Pakistan Air Force. A product of typically creative French engineering, the panel was the display end of an advanced Viviane night-seeing system allegedly not for export under any circumstances. It eliminated the need for clumsy night goggles, turning the lower two-thirds of the windshield into an infrared projection screen.

O'Connell wasn't up on the latest U.S. infrared technology, but he suspected this was still close to state-of-the-art. The images were as clear as if he were looking through a pair of field glasses. The magnification could be changed instantly, items tagged and followed by the computer. Best of all, the glass painted things in pastel blues and yellows, a pleasant change from the vomit green of most infrared setups. But of course the French would be color-coordinated.

The canvas the crew had attached to the outside of the windshield was a poor training aid, straining with the wash from the rotor and constantly threatening to fly away. But it was the best they could manage on short notice.

O'Connell turned the radar off, wanting to simulate as much of the mission as possible; if they were going to sneak in, it would have to be left off except in emergencies. Even using the ground-hazard module might tip off the Indians. He pitched forward, relying solely on the infrared to direct him across the hilly countryside he was using for practice.

Like everything else on the attack version of the sophisticated new French chopper, the avionics and control systems were first class. The settings for the radar and the infrared system could be switched on the cyclic control stick between his legs, which looked like a Y-shaped zucchini. The hands-on-stick arrangement put all of the important gear literally at his fingertips, but the layout was unfamiliar and a bitch to get used to. The first time he flipped the infrared on he'd nearly kicked the Panther over. He still wasn't comfortable with the grip, and didn't know if he'd have it completely mastered in the few hours he had left before he would leave with four of Nizam's men to make a run at rescuing the secretary of state.

The canvas flapped at the windshield. The HUD tried to

adjust to the streaks of light that snuck in beneath the errant cloth, alternately lightening and darkening the display. It was distracting, but even with the washed-out streaks the display was readable.

The infrared unit, working off a pear-shaped pod atop the cockpit, had a range measured in miles, not yards. Or kilometers, as the French insisted. Two klicks to the hillside— the HUD, tied into the flight computer, threw up a warning of insufficient clearance approaching.

"One-eighty," barked O'Connell a second before he let the chopper's tail slide behind him, jerking and shaking into a hard but efficient turn.

Took a second to steady it. Bird responded much better than what he'd been flying lately, but it still wasn't an Apache.

Apache might have dumped him on that, though. This chopper had a forgiving margin of error.

O'Connell adjusted his torque and spun back to the right, watching his direction and heading change on the CRT display in the middle of the cockpit. The multi-use display was as zoomy as the infrared system, with brilliant colors and instantaneous response as modes were changed.

Though the cabin was considerably bigger, the Super Panther was lighter and a bit shorter overall than the military versions of the Huey he'd cut his teeth on as a young trainee. Its overall shape reminded him of a Sikorski S-76, a helicopter he'd flown once or twice. The Aérospatiale had armor plating and several other niceties designed to increase survivability, as the salesmen liked to say, but the extensive use of composites held the weight down and helped give the chopper a loaded range close to 750 miles. The fenestral tail assembly, a funky set of stabilizers framing a relatively small rotor fan molded into the fuselage, made the electronic rudder controls highly responsive—almost too responsive for the unfamiliar pilot.

"Shit," said Greeley, as O'Connell once more overcorrected with a heavy jerk. "You're gonna drop us before we even get going."

"Jesus, Greeley, why don't you relax?" O'Connell eased

the throttle upward with his left hand, increasing power as he settled into a hover. (Though it may seem counterintuitive, it can actually take a bit more power to hover than to move ahead slowly in a helicopter. The throttle and rudders must be worked together to create a kind of midair equilibrium as the craft is steadied. Because of the pressures working on the helicopter, it is generally more difficult for a pilot to hover than to fly straight ahead.) Because this was originally intended as an all-European model, the rotors on the French helicopter spun clockwise, opposite of the way they turned on an American bird. That made all of the rudder moves exactly the opposite of what O'Connell was used to. "You got the computer figured out or what?"

The old man gave a disparaging grunt. O'Connell could have handled the navigational system himself, but if he didn't give Greeley something to do he'd talk his ear off the whole flight.

Leaving him behind was out of the question—not only would he be likely to tell the princess everything he knew, but O'Connell intended on taking off for the Golden Bear base as soon as Morena and the secretary of state were out of the helicopter. He'd have to find at least one place to refuel along the way, but that was a minor problem.

"I know which of these stupid buttons to push," answered Greeley. "This is considered navigating?"

"You'd rather stick your head out and spot stars?"

"You youngsters could learn a thing or two by paying attention to the basics instead of relying on gizmos to do everything."

"If you're too good to be a navigator, Greeley, maybe you ought to take the stick."

"No thanks. I ain't flyin' nothin' that doesn't have wings."

"We got wings," joked O'Connell, pushing the helicopter forward again. Nizam's helipad was just over the next line of hills. He'd try a few more maneuvers and then take it in.

"You're calling those stubby things wings? Christ, I've got whiskers bigger than them."

The stubs were actually weapons pylons. The left side was

fitted with a 20-mm cannon pod. The right would get a packet of rockets for the mission.

One thing he'd say for Nizam, she didn't fool around. No wonder she didn't get along with the military—her gear was better.

So were her men. He knew the leader of her commando team, a half-British, half-tribesman named D. B. Fleming. They'd worked on several projects together in the past, and O'Connell thought it wouldn't be too difficult to convince him to come along on a second mission.

Assuming they made it through the first.

"I'm surprised this damn TV doesn't get dizzy with all the circles we're makin'," said Greeley. He flipped the dashboard mapping unit from bird's-eye view to 3-D projection, which modeled the terrain in front of them. The on-board computer's storehouse of maps was supposedly complete for Pakistan and most of northern India, though O'Connell realized from his experience with American systems that no computerized map could be counted on as 100 percent accurate. Generally what they were wrong about concerned the most critical part of the mission.

"I'll tell you somethin'," said Greeley, playing with the screen, "if we had this gear in the B-50, we wouldn't have used it. The plane would have rebelled. I'd've set it to watch Uncle Miltie and relied on the map."

"This *is* a map."

"Ah," said Greeley, waving his hand. "A map's something you unfold. A map's got detail. Where's the detail on this?"

"There's more detail than you could ever get with a paper map. Increase the magnification. Christ, look at that—it shows you the goddamn hills and everything."

"It's not the same."

"I'll bet your navigator would've liked it."

"I doubt it."

O'Connell slowed the Panther down and took another turn to his right, then lined up to go back home. He was about as used to the equipment as he was going to get.

"See, a real navigator, not one of your computer kids who

plays with Nintendo and thinks it's navigating, a real navigator, he's like an old-time sailor,'' continued Greeley. O'Connell had been with him long enough to know when a dissertation was coming, but there was no way of ducking this one. "An explorer. See, because he uses his imagination to fill in the blanks and cross the ocean. Like a Christopher Columbus. Magellan. We're talking airplanes and boats here, but it's the same thing.''

"You're talking out your ass, Greeley. I bet if you asked any navigator you flew with, he'd have loved to have this equipment.''

"No way. You don't understand navigators.''

"You'd prefer to fly without instruments?''

There was a loud snap and then the sound of a machine gun ripping at the front of the cockpit. Bright waves of light punched into O'Connell's eyes and the helicopter pitched downward, to the left.

There was a buzz in the back of his head he hadn't felt in ages. He was choking back nausea.

"Hang on,'' he screamed to Greeley.

A machine gun pounded the front of the helicopter. Goddamn. There was something wrong with the rotor.

You cannot blame God for your misfortune, Mr. O'Connell. When we put ourselves in situations that are unkind to us, it is not His fault.

O'Connell gripped the stick, shaking like a jackhammer. He was cringing, ducking the bullets that must be blowing straight through the cockpit but were somehow missing him.

It wasn't a machine gun—the canvas had torn loose. The chain was beating against the chopper's roof. How they still had rotor blades was beyond him.

The infrared display couldn't adjust quickly enough to the explosions of light as the tarp smashed against the windshield again and again. His own eyes were blinded, and the sick swell of his stomach extended up his throat, out to his arms, to his legs, paralyzing everything.

Bumping like hell. You're going down.

"You got the pad on your left, a hundred meters,'' said Greeley, his voice tense but even-toned. He'd punched up the 3-D model and was bent over the display. "You got twenty meters altitude."

O'Connell fumbled, found the switch for the landing gear. The bucking increased. He was standing on the pedals, hard, trying to keep the chopper under control.

"Watch the tree on the left," said Greeley, practically falling out of the helicopter as he leaned out the door to get a glimpse of the landing area.

The canvas beat furiously. Dirt and dust all over. O'Connell cut the engine and they did a plop-skid onto the edge of the landing pad.

When he finally undid his belt straps, O'Connell put his hand on Greeley's arm.

"Thanks."

"I still think maps are better," said the old man calmly.

The rotors' relatively high head and the Super Panther's "survivability features" had kept the blades from shearing off, even though they'd received a severe pounding. Two pins out, two pins in—the maintenance crew had a complete set of spares on in less than a half hour.

The night-sight housing had been dinked and the equipment needed to be recalibrated. There were also several major gashes in the roof metal directly aft of the overhead windshields. Otherwise, damage was minimal. While even a few canvas fragments sucked through the engine could have been disastrous, a quick examination showed the power plants were clean. Some of the cloth and one of the eyelets had found their way into the cold-air duct system used to reduce the exhaust's infrared signature, but aside from chipping and charring, no harm had been done.

O'Connell was subdued as he watched the crew repair the helicopter. He had come close to losing it. Once more Greeley, of all people, had saved his butt.

"Are you sure you're not hungry, Michael?" Morena startled him but he said nothing as she slipped her arm around his shoulder. "Are you all right?"

He could still taste the stomach juices in his mouth and had no desire for food. "I'm fine."

"I had an idea," she said. "Maybe once we get the course coordinates we should stop somewhere and call Stockman."

"Fleming would realize what was up. Besides, who knows how long it would take for Stockman to get somebody there," he said. "You think it's a setup?"

"I don't think it's a trap," she said, mulling it over. "It's too elaborate."

"Yeah, but I wonder if maybe the princess knows where the secretary of state is because she snatched him herself."

"Then why not just stage the rescue without us?"

"More convincing."

"Maybe." Morena squeezed his arm and then went to the helicopter, looking inside the crew compartment. One of the mechanics was working on the weapons pod, but most of the prep work was done. "There enough room for all of us?"

"Sleeps ten."

She leaned in, continuing her inspection. O'Connell found himself staring at the round curve of the perfectly tailored khaki trousers.

"You like being deputy on the desk?"

Morena turned around quickly, a hint of anger in her green eyes. "What brought that up?"

"Nothing, really."

"I haven't slept my way to the top," she said.

He wanted to ask why she assumed that was what he was thinking. Instead, he made a wisecrack. "You're not at the top yet."

O'Connell grabbed her hand as she brought it up to slap him. He could feel its strength, the power in her whole body.

Why had he said that? He certainly wasn't jealous.

Resentful? She hadn't done anything to help him. Instead, she cut him off. It was worse than she'd been in a position of power, or some power.

No, the real thing was that he still loved her, and she didn't seem to love him back, not really. She could use it as a weapon, as something to manipulate—she'd staged the kissing scene for the guards. He couldn't do that. His feelings were real. Inexplicably real and beyond his control.

"Let go of my hand, Michael." He let go. She slapped him so hard his face stung. "Don't ever imply that again."

Her cheeks were fuller than he remembered, signs of age maybe, though her face remained young. He put his arms around her. She let him pull her close to him. Her eyes remained open as they kissed, hard green eyes.

"Why did you do that?" she asked.

"Why did I kiss you?"

"Yes."

"I wanted to."

She looked into his face for a long moment and then slipped away. He watched as she walked down the roadway back toward the compound, watched until he couldn't see her anymore.

"Ready to fuel up, sir," said a crewman. O'Connell moved out of the way as the men pulled the gas truck over to the Panther, running the line to fuel her up.

Twenty minutes later, a small pickup rounded the bend and made its way over to the helipad. Greeley was sitting with the soldiers in the back, munching on something as he got out.

"I brought some bread," he said, holding up a bag. "Thought you might be hungry."

"No thanks."

"Good stuff," said Greeley. "Got some weird lamb thing, too. This Pakistani food is really pretty good, once you forget what it is." He turned back toward the truck and shouted for them to retrieve his thermos. "Filled with coffee," he told O'Connell confidentially. "The stuff they make here'll keep us awake for a month."

"And have you pissing the whole way."

"Don't worry—I'll just keep the door open."

O'Connell got in the Panther and began fussing with his gear, readying the preflight check. The commandos, outfitted in austere battle dress, mustered on the tarmac outside the helicopter, waiting as the princess's black Buick rounded the turn and headed for the helipad. The sun was setting behind the hills; there was a faint glint off the windshield as the car bounced to a halt.

Morena got out first and walked toward them briskly, a gun hanging from one shoulder and a bulging knapsack over the other. She'd changed into a black T-shirt and dungarees.

The role of access agent is genteel, at least on the surface. Much of the work is done at parties, where the agent smoothes and schmoozes. Morena had been perfect for it, her chosen weapons well-cut dresses and watered-down wine coolers. Her outfit and demeanor now were 180 degrees in the other direction; set chin and blackened face, dark clothes and a brown kerchief tied tightly around her head.

"What kind of gun is that?" asked Greeley, sounding as if he wanted one for himself.

"A Ruger Mini," said Morena, climbing aboard. "It's a machine gun."

"Like an Uzi?"

"Something like that." She let the pack down with a heavy thud and sat on the bench immediately behind the navigator. "Here's the sketch of the base," she said, opening the knapsack. Besides the maps, there were a dozen large clips in the bag. "It's basically the same drawing we saw this afternoon. And here are the course coordinates."

O'Connell looked the map over. The route had been planned carefully, with elaborate twists through the terrain. Even if Nizam had set this up as a charade, it would be wise to keep to her script. O'Connell handed the sheet with the waymarks for the INS to Greeley, so he could enter them into the computer.

Their path lay over the Rann of Kutch at the western tip of India. It was a barren, bizarre landscape, half salt marsh, half desert. Thinly populated, its geography was irregular enough to make low-level radar surveillance problematic—though it also meant flying close to the ground could be tricky. He would proceed out of the Kutch into the foothills of the Aravalli Mountains. Their target, an abandoned British airfield dating from the 1920s, was marked in red. Fleming and O'Connell had worked out a plan for the assault hours before. They would circle in from the north, dropping two men armed with mortars to provide a diversion. These men would draw fire from one of the two gun emplacements

Nizam's intelligence reported at the base. Meanwhile, O'Connell would hustle to a spot not far from a small building where the secretary of state was believed to be held, dropping the rest of the assault team. Taking off again, he would either circle and attempt to draw attention away from the team, or provide covering fire if a frontal attack on the building was necessary. They would use different colored flares to communicate; a radio system was unnecessary and might prove a liability.

Nizam's information had the kidnappers' main defenses oriented toward the east and south—the direction the Indian authorities would most likely come from. The key to the operation was launching the diversion at the east end of the field quickly. The whole thing would then unfold like a misdirection play in football, the defense diving for the fullback while the halfback took the ball off-tackle.

O'Connell, the quarterback, studied the sketch of the base, trying to visualize what lay ahead.

"Here's the refuel," said Morena, tracing the red line that marked their route home on the larger map. This line was much more direct, a straight flight over the desert. The theory was that Indian defenses would be geared toward someone coming in, not out of the country. And Pakistani defenses, as the Indians had sufficiently demonstrated, were weak.

"This is at the very end of our range," said O'Connell. He estimated that he'd have flown nearly 700 miles by the time they reached the small blue circle, which was still inside India. If they got into too much of a pissing match at the airfield, they'd find themselves walking home.

"It's the best they could do. They took a big risk getting that far into India as it was."

O'Connell frowned.

"There's a school building here, and they've parked two trucks there," Morena continued. "Will the refueling take long?"

O'Connell shrugged. "It may."

"You are ready, Mr. O'Connell?"

"Yeah, I'm ready, Princess," he said, turning to the cockpit door. Nizam stood there, having finished speaking to her men. She had dressed for the occasion, wearing a brightly embroidered blue tunic and an array of jewels. A large red pendant encased in an elaborate gold setting hung around her chest; he guessed it was some insignia of her family.

"Good luck," she said. The bracelets on her arm jingled as she extended it. "You will take care of my helicopter?"

O'Connell shook her hand warily. "I hope your information is as good as your equipment."

"They are both the best I can provide. Good luck to you, too, Mr. Greeley."

She turned in a swirl and walked back to her car.

Greeley continued studiously entering the course information into the flight computer, tapping at the keypad as if he were throwing darts. He paused after each number, checking not once but twice against the sheet.

"God, Greeley, we'll be here all night."

"You want me to get this in right, or what?"

"Look, you can check it on the map," said O'Connell, reaching over and hitting the program's map display mode. "You were the one who was so hot on paper maps."

"Who's doing this, me or you?"

"I'm just trying to make it go faster."

"The pilot has certain duties, and the navigator has certain duties. You don't hear me telling you how to fly."

"You will though."

Greeley pulled the sheet away and continued entering the numbers. Morena, supervising the stowing of gear in the back, suppressed a laugh. O'Connell, annoyed, got out of the helicopter to stretch his legs.

"We are almost ready to leave, Mr. O'Connell," said Fleming. The commandos were gathered in a small, silent bunch a few yards from the Super Panther. The agent checked his watch.

"Five minutes?"

Fleming nodded. He wore the light-skinned face of a northwestern tribesman, weathered so he looked well past his forties, though O'Connell knew he was only in his late twenties. He'd begun his career by working with Afghan guerrillas when he was twelve.

"We'll have to catch up on old times," said O'Connell.

"Yes, I have had many adventures since we last met."

"I have something else that will interest you. We'll discuss it on the way home."

Fleming nodded solemnly and O'Connell returned to the helicopter. Greeley had managed to get all the numbers entered into the computer and was now playing with the map displays, zooming in on different legs of the trip.

"I didn't say I didn't like computers," Greeley said, anticipating him. "Just that I wouldn't rely on them one hundred percent. I got the paper right here if I need it."

"Morena, you ready back there?"

Before she could answer the air filled with a piercing wail; the men outside immediately dropped to their knees.

"What the hell is that?" said Greeley.

"It's the evening call to prayers over their loudspeakers," said O'Connell. "We're going with Allah."

Kamra. Shortly after 7 P.M.

Khan heard the call to prayers as he lowered the canopy. He was already breathing hard, and tugged on his seat restraints as if to catch himself. He was going to be gone a long time—he had to pace himself.

The Snow Leopard's engines rocked the plane gently as he started to mouth the words of his takeoff invocation.

"Tower to Leopard one. Mission is go. Proceed to runway three-six-two."

Khan finished his prayer and acknowledged. Then he unzipped the pocket on his right leg and retrieved a small pillbox. He didn't like bennies and rarely used them. But this was a special case.

They weren't the only pills with him on this flight. He had a cyanide capsule taped on the top of his left-hand glove.

A Muslim soldier who is killed in battle is considered in *shaeed,* a special state of blessedness. He is forgiven all his sins and lives forever.

277

Khan swallowed quickly, as if his parents were watching. The amphetamines slipped easily down his throat, leaving only a faint plastic taste in his mouth. He placed the small red pillbox back in his pocket. It had been a gift from his mother.

Another few breaths, a visual check of the cockpit. Mask on and everything set, set. Stop checking, Khan, and get in the air.

The pilot looked over the side and spotted one of the ground crew watching him expectantly. He made a show of the thumbs up. A big, confident show as the jet eased forward, the plane's wheels exploring each crack in the pavement, sending a slight tingle up the aluminum leg struts and straight into Khan's spine.

''Tower, I am proceeding,'' he said. Those were going to be his last words for a long, long time.

The plane was impatient to get going. It came off the concrete a full hundred feet sooner than Khan thought it would. He felt a slight push in his seat as the wheels cranked up, the plane trimmed for quick acceleration. He was climbing and bang, through the sound barrier. Running now.

By the time he made his first turn, a forty-five-degree cut to the south toward the Indian border, the Leopard was in supercruise at Mach 1.4, flying at 40,000 feet. The pilot glanced at his throttle handle as he switched the Leopard and its computer into ''plane'' mode, the automatic cruise that kept it on the preprogrammed course unless he decided otherwise. He adjusted his helmet and put his eyes out into the fading blue sky, watching night slip in. The thin, curved mirror at the right edge of the wide-panel HUD set danced with flickering red streaks, a last twinkle of available light bidding him good hunting.

Twenty minutes later a little nudge on the HUD monitoring his small belly tank told him it was almost empty. Unlike the cylindrical containers fitted to most planes, the Leopard's tank looked like a flattened triangle whose shape imitated the plane's lower surface. It was made of metal, however, not the honeycombed composites of the Leopard's hull. And though the exterior was painted with a retinyl Schiff base salt—a radar absorbent material first used by the Americans on the SR-71 spy plane—the tank increased the Leopard's radar profile at 200 miles from that of an insect to a large bird. Given Khan's mission, the difference was enormous.

Besides, it had served its purpose. Khan prepared to eject the now useless $25,000 piece of equipment, pushing the Leopard into a steep descent. Though he was flying over a sparsely populated area, the tank could conceivably destroy someone's house. While he had the option of just dropping it, he did not relish the possibility of killing someone with his garbage. He was going to drop down and make sure he had a good, clear path before he let go.

Hir's distress at the bombing mission to India still nettled him. As a soldier, part of him wanted to dismiss her concerns out of hand. There were many risks in war. No matter how carefully the line between civilians and fighters was drawn, inevitably it was crossed over. As long as they had taken steps to minimize the danger to civilians, they had done their duty. The Koran exonerated him; these people were infidels, not worth consideration in a fight to preserve the faith.

And yet, he could not completely ignore his fiancée's tears. What if they *had* hit schoolchildren? What if it had been Hir's students, or worse, Hir, in danger? Would he have accepted the mission as easily?

Ten thousand feet. The backup altimeter's pale yellow dissolved into a pure white, noting the altitude drop. Khan eased off on the stick and moved his thumb over to the radar button, clicked it on. The LPI (low probability of intercept) radar sounded a gentle but annoying ping in his earphones every thirty seconds to remind him it was activated; though difficult to detect, it was nonetheless the most obvious emission from the plane and the computer had been preset to remind him when it was on. The pilot reached to the panel next to the right multi-use display and hit the ground-scan preset; the screen gave him a view of the approaching terrain.

He was still flying faster than sound. Khan held the throttle steady, letting his speed slow as the increased air resistance took its bite. The terrain was clear if a bit uneven in front and beneath him. With his pinky he pulled the safety guard off the tank disengage and then punched off the gas can, tossing it away. Immediately he disengaged the radar, pulled upwards and watched the HUD measure the increases in his speed and altitude. At fifty miles to the border he was back at 50,000 feet and Mach 1.4.

Unlike his previous mission, where the planes had avoided the Indian defenses as much as possible, Khan's flight plan called for him to fly straight through active radar areas. It is a common misconception that a stealth airplane is completely invisible to radar. But even the stealthiest plane will show up on a radar screen if it is parked next to the antenna. The question is how close to the antenna the plane can get before being noticed. Stealth techniques reduce that distance; a B-2 bomber, for example, cannot be picked up on most ground radars until it comes within eight miles of the radar site.

The lower detection distance dramatically reduces the reaction time for air defenses. More importantly, the reduced distance can allow a stealthy plane to see the radar well before there is any chance of being detected. It can then choose to employ appropriate countermeasures, or more likely, duck the defenses altogether.

In effect, the Leopard reduced the Indian's radar coverage to tiny clouds immediately in front of the antennae. Under optimum circumstances, Khan could get inside five miles of a source before being detected. Given his operating speed, the way radar operators were trained and their equipment constructed and programmed, his appearance on a screen at that point would probably be dismissed as an aberration. By the time the operator had reached for the squelch, the Pakistani plane would be gone.

The Leopard did not have to rely on preflight intelligence to help it locate ground radar; wire-thin probes extending from the nose, wingtips and tail surfaces constantly fished for microwaves, feeding an IMP (indication of microwave propagation) unit designed to profile the enemy radar coverage. The system was many times more effective than the detection devices on the Falcon. There, the pilot had to react almost immediately when an enemy radar was detected. Here, he could have a cup of tea before deciding whether to turn, accelerate or simply yawn.

No, not yawn; anything but yawn. The pep pills hadn't kicked in yet, and Khan found himself becoming mesmerized by the faint yellow glow of the horizon bar that underlined the enhanced image projection portion of the HUD. He shook his head violently from side to side, knocked his knees up and down against the bottom of the padded dash a few times, trying to stir his blood circulation.

The left multi-use screen that was keyed into the radar detection system suddenly glowed yellow, and Khan no longer had any trouble focusing his attention. The pilot punched the threat-modeling keys and saw his course plotted against a blob representing the probable radar coverage. The source was calculated to be north nearly fifty miles; he was moving away from it and had a good margin of error.

Fifteen minutes later the margin narrowed considerably. Khan was just dropping through the clouds en route to his first target when the radar detector turned yellow again, then quickly changed from yellow to pink. (Yellow was close, pink was a danger zone. Red meant he'd been detected, and he better get the hell out of there or smile for the camera.) He was within twenty-five miles of an active site, and flying straight for it.

The pilot pushed his nose down, dropping to 500 feet and the relative safety of the ground haze. The g's pushing against his chest felt like old friends, and now he noticed a tingle in his head and arms. The pills were starting to work.

Khan told himself to stay calm as he prepared to activate the radar, which he needed to do to launch his rocket cargo. It would have been much safer to use a ground-directed version of infrared in such a situation. Ironically, such a unit had not been included in the Leopard because no ground-attack missions had been envisioned when it was designed. Khan's targeting was being handled by a jerry-rigged addition to the flight computer's tape that allowed it to use its dogfight 2 program space as an attack map. The computer tied the radar and the INS together to locate the proper launch envelope and cue the pilot to fire. Given Khan's lack of experience as an attack pilot, it was an excellent setup, but it had its drawbacks. He had to fly along a set course to launch. There was also a possibility, though slight, that the radar would be detected.

But Khan had no time to worry about possibilities. The radar began blipping its "I'm on" message in his ear and the program flashed a series of blue dots on the top quarter of his HUD, telling him his altitude was considerably lower than planned.

As long as he held his course, he would intersect with the proper envelope before it was time to launch. Raising his head was too dangerous now.

Another problem. The FLIR lit up with a large gray ghost. It looked like an airliner, four very white engines, fifteen miles off. Its radar flickered toward him, long thin fingers groping in the night.

Even a jetliner might luck into a radar read if it were close enough. Or if it were an AWACS plane, with a flight of MiG-29s right behind.

But the Leopard hadn't detected the massive radar beams such a plane would put out. Even though this was the first real test of its systems, everything else had worked perfectly until now; there was no reason not to trust it.

The battle-tested avionics in the Falcon had occasionally messed up, hadn't they?

Khan pushed his eyes away from his glove and its cyanide capsule, back to the HUD, where a small red triangle began to glow in the middle of the screen. He took his left hand off the throttle briefly to punch a small button on the armament panel below the flight computer center; the button opened his weapons bay and armed one of the rockets.

The airliner, or whatever it was, passed directly overhead as he concentrated on the targeting triangle. Only his eyes mattered now. His body responded unconsciously, moving the plane as they directed, the triangle turning purple and now black.

There was a whoosh as he squeezed the trigger on the

stick. A small missile carrying the radar-jamming device floated out of its pod. There was an almost inaudible crackle as the missile fired its solid-propellant engine and sailed down to its target, preparing to impale itself in a wheat field about five miles from the massive radar that had turned Khan's warning screen pink.

He took a sharp turn to the left and then back to the right. The airliner was gone, and though his radar detection gear still showed that he was in a dangerous area, he was rapidly moving away from the defenses.

Exactly ninety seconds after firing his first missile, Khan put the Leopard into a sharp forty-five-degree turn to the southeast. His HUD immediately gave him a triangle and he prepared to fire again. Once more his radar detection gear turned pink; he was well within ten miles of the source but flying in what the experts would call a slot of anomalous propagation several hundred feet off the ground, where reflections from the earth's surface blinded the gear from even the bulkiest plane. The ride got bumpy as the triangle changed color—even the ultrahigh-tech Leopard couldn't completely overcome the basic problems of gust response. Downdrafts poked at the jet like a shower of pebbles, and this approach to target was considerably more difficult than the other, even though it was only ten miles due south.

The triangle went purple and then back to red. Khan cursed, saw from the altimeter indicator on the HUD that he was too high, poked his nose down and squeezed as the shooting cue appeared.

Quickly he flipped the radar off, rolled his flying mode back to dogfight 1, normal interceptor mode. Two breaths and the detector cleared; another breath and he was climbing, accelerating back to Mach speed. He slipped the computer to plane mode, letting it take the stick as he tried to relax, his ears ringing with Benzedrine.

Northern India. 10:30 P.M.

''There is also a story which I do not necessarily believe,'' said Fleming, who was leaning forward between O'Connell and Greeley. "But I will tell it to you because it speaks of the powerful legends of the Jam people."

Fleming's preface was unnecessary; he'd been telling them stories no one would necessarily believe for the better part of two hours now, practically since O'Connell had slipped the helicopter over the gray shadows of marshland that marked the dividing line between India and Pakistan.

Threading his way through the southern Aravalli hills, O'Connell considered asking him to be quiet, but he wanted to stay on the friendliest possible terms with Fleming. He would have to broach the idea for the second mission as they returned from India with the secretary. He'd let Morena and the secretary off, then head for another base to refuel before Nizam could give Fleming any new orders.

The princess might alert the military. But more likely, she'd be content to have helped rescue the secretary of state. She'd have the leverage she wanted. Morena would be a hero. And he'd get the plane and the bombs.

And Renard's money. Why was that still tempting him?

Long odds against making it to the plane. But fate was pushing him on; he couldn't change the direction of things.

"The fort had withstood two assaults," continued Fleming. "They were bloody charges by mounted horsemen, but the fort was stout and the defenders skilled. At the end of the day, the English had done so well they concluded it was safe to sleep. One trooper woke in the middle of the night, just in time to look out in the moonlight and see an army of leopards marching toward the fort. The spirits of the fallen horsemen, you see, had come back to avenge their deaths."

"That's it," said Greeley, watching the equipment intently even as he listened to Fleming. He pointed to the small yellow blob on the infrared about ten miles ahead. "That's the power plant."

O'Connell nodded.

"We got fifty miles from the turn," said Greeley, who had done a quietly flawless job tracking their position on the mission. He seemed to be a born navigator.

"That trooper was my grandfather, the sole survivor,"

said Fleming, hastily wrapping up his tale. "But I'll save the rest for the ride home." He slipped back to prepare his men. Morena, who'd been sitting so quietly behind Greeley that O'Connell feared she'd fallen asleep, leaned forward. "You OK?" she asked. "You look like you're getting tired."

"I'm fine."

"Here, have some of this coffee," said Greeley, picking up his thermos. "This stuff'd wake the dead."

"More likely burn a hole through my stomach," said O'Connell. But he held out his hand for a cup anyway.

Morena patted his shoulder. For a moment he thought she would lean forward and kiss him. He wanted her to, but she moved to the back to get ready with the others.

"I never met anyone would talk so much," said Greeley. "I thought he'd never shut up."

"You're complaining about somebody talking too much?"

"You got to turn up ahead there," said Greeley. "My stories are true, at least."

"I got it," answered O'Connell. He took a quick sip from the coffee—he could feel the caffeine jolt as soon as the warm liquid touched his lips—and gave the cup back to Greeley so his hands were free to maneuver the chopper.

The yellow lump had grown larger and brighter, breaking itself into its component parts—two large buildings housing power turbines and three or four smaller structures. O'Connell slowed the aircraft almost to hover as he searched for the valley that was supposed to be less than a mile from the plant. Finally he spotted the gorge, which opened onto a vast plain. Their target lay straight down the pipe.

"One more sip," said O'Connell. He held the cup for a moment in front of his face, letting the steam warm his nose. He gulped a full mouthful of liquid before handing the container back. Then he flattened the helicopter down, trying to keep his back and the cooled thermal signature of the exhaust as low as possible.

The twin Turbomeca engines powering the Panther had an appetite for acceleration, and within two minutes of taking the turn O'Connell was running fifty feet over the ground at just under 200 miles an hour.

"There ought to be a road next to us somewhere," said Greeley, "but I can't see much out there."

"You're not checking the stars?"

Greeley laughed.

"Don't worry about it," said O'Connell. The computer said they were right on course. He had the night screen on far scan. A vague yellow haze marked the horizon. The world directly in front of them was empty.

The adrenaline started pumping inside. It'd been a long time since he'd done something like this. He loved it.

It was his fatal flaw, the reason he was so impulsive. It was the reason he became a helicopter pilot, and then a CIA agent, when he could have done something honest with his life. The Jesuits had suggested a career as an international lawyer—"that language facility, Michael, a gift from God."

They were smart enough never to suggest he become a priest.

"That's got to be it," said Greeley, pointing at the small clump of yellow growing at the bottom of the screen. The computer gave it a distance of forty-five miles, then began counting down, telling him how much longer he had to relax.

If the Indian army were behind the operation and not the fanatical Sikhs Nizam claimed, there would be all sorts of defenses waiting for them. Divisions of men, tanks, MiGs, radar and more night-seeing equipment than a troop of owls could muster.

They'd be waltzing into Little Big Horn. And probably screwing any chance anyone had of rescuing the secretary of state.

Hell, Grasso would already be dead if the army took him. They'd kill him and blame it on radicals. Nizam's information might simply be part of their cover.

At least in that case the base would probably be empty.

If it were a setup, the whole thing would be over without a shot fired, in and out.

Always doubts. Too many possibilities, blocking his way.

He had to ignore them. Time for action. Everything else was beyond his control. Fate had taken him here; all he could do was play through.

"There comes a time to accept on faith what you would otherwise doubt."

"What?" asked Greeley.

"I'm just talking to myself."

"Sounded like a prayer."

"Just something one of my teachers used to say," explained O'Connell.

By the time he eased off on his power and began slowing, the airfield was less than ten miles away. He was barely at treetop level, grateful there were very few trees to measure it by. A cluster of buildings lay dead ahead, the most prominent a tower at the eastern end of the complex—as Nizam had predicted.

"We got three miles," announced Greeley. There was a sudden rush of air into the helicopter as Morena slid the back door open. A pair of commandos crouched by the doorway, the helicopter engines suddenly very loud despite the French engineers' efforts at dampening the noise.

"Uh-oh," said Greeley. "Something's moving down there."

O'Connell ignored him—too late now—and continued in toward the spot just behind a hangar on the north side of the field where he was to drop the first team. A flare suddenly ignited overhead and the air in front of them began popping with firecrackers tossed into the wind.

Bullets. So much for a setup.

"Go," shouted the pilot as he held the helicopter three feet off the ground. The craft rocked; two men jumped out.

Small arms fire, nothing close.

Morena leaned out the door as O'Connell pulled the helicopter around toward the second drop site. She fired a flare point-blank at the tower in an attempt to momentarily blind the defenders. Burnt powder stung O'Connell's nose. The scent was strong, as if the helicopter had caught fire.

"You're going there, you're going there," said Greeley, pointing the way.

Two rockets exploded on the northern end of the airfield, about a hundred yards from the spot they'd just left—the diversion. The sky turned brilliant red as something on the ground exploded in flames.

O'Connell goosed the engines, shoving gas into them as fast as he could. The screen in front of him was a parade of yellow- and blue-tinted shadows, the French gear adjusting and counteradjusting to the different light and heat sources in front of them. He searched desperately for the second drop point, hoping that no one on the ground had the sense or luck to hit them head-on with a flare.

"There, there," Greeley shouted. The cockpit was a mash of noise and crosscurrents, wind washing in from the door. O'Connell caught a glimpse of Morena leaning against her restraint belt, dabs of light exploding from her shoulder. She was shooting her little machine gun, moll-style.

"Watch the fence!"

O'Connell saw it at the last moment and nudged the chopper up without breaking stride, gliding down as Greeley shouted to land. They were less than twenty yards from the small, two-story wooden building where the secretary was supposed to be.

Morena lept from the door, the first one out.

Like so many other pictures of her, it burned itself onto a back corner of his brain, burrowed into his subconscious as he whisked the control stick back and pulled out. He loosened his foot on the pedal and the helicopter circled around, running back toward the tower where the first team was trying to draw all the attention.

They hadn't taken fire at the second drop. Good sign.

As they approached the northern edge of the airfield, the tower flashed orange. O'Connell kept coming, his finger poised over the weapons trigger on the control stick. The gun was locked to fire in line with the cockpit; they'd dispensed with the elaborate targeting system, which would have required more practice than he had time for.

He half expected a tank to appear behind one of the buildings. When it didn't, O'Connell began to think that maybe Nizam's intelligence had been correct, and maybe this was all going to go the way they planned.

The runway ended a few yards away to the right. There were some shadows there and then two bright yellow balls coming at them.

"Gun emplacement," said Greeley, but O'Connell had already figured that out. He pushed the chopper forward and pressed the button on the left hook of his handgrip. Tracers poured from the helicopter toward the sandbags. He raised his chin and the bullets danced into the emplacement.

For a second he was back in the army, flying an Apache. There was an exercise he used to do where he tipped the helicopter to the left, then swung in a backwards seesawing arc as the weapons officer peppered the target. He worked through the maneuver now, his feet leaning under the dash, the machine coming up with him. There was a touch of vertigo, the blood in his head not quite keeping up with the rest of his body. It felt familiar, vaguely comforting.

"Whoa," said Greeley. "This is like a goddamn amusement ride."

"I need you to keep lookin' out."

"Yeah, I'm trying."

There was no more gunfire from the emplacement. In fact the resistance seemed to have ended completely; the flares were dying overhead and the tower continued to burn. O'Connell edged forward cautiously, crossing the runway toward the two small buildings standing across from the tower. As he flew, he clicked the knob that switched the gun control from the cannon to the rockets. The HUD recorded the change as he lined up to target the building.

"Hold on," he warned Greeley, and then pressed the button, three rockets flinging forward in unison. The chopper stuttered. One rocket missed; the other two hit home with a dull thud, as if the structure were a sandpile. O'Connell wondered if the weapons had malfunctioned.

"Bunch of people on the ground over there," said Greeley, pointing to the very end of the runway behind them. "Here we go again."

O'Connell swung around as yet another flare passed overhead and the men began filling the air with automatic rifle fire. They were either lousy shots or the armor plating worked very well; he didn't feel a thing.

He was spinning around to shoot at the men when he saw the muzzle flash. The sky around him barked.

Heavy stuff, a 12.7-mm antiaircraft shell he guessed, though it wasn't exactly a good place to get out and grab a sample.

"There it is," said Greeley, pointing across the field. The gun was set behind a low block wall maybe twenty feet beyond the very edge of the runway. Ignoring the men below who had just fired at them, he dipped to his right and let off two bursts of rockets, neither with much effect, then tried to hustle away. The flight out of the battery's field of fire was agonizingly long; two explosions rocked them even as they reached the edge of a small drop that provided some protection.

The helicopter hadn't been hit, but it did seem to be groaning. O'Connell checked his instruments calmly. Oil pressure and hydraulics were still nice and high. The gas was shading down past a quarter of a tank, but they were all right.

For now. That gun wasn't going to miss all night.

"There's the signal," said Greeley, pointing to the red flare that arced overhead.

It was as if Morena had read his mind. The helicopter roared with acceleration as O'Connell popped back over the hill, making a beeline for the back of the building. Morena, either impatient or not sure they'd seen her signal, let off another flare. Her team had set the building on fire with incendiary grenades, and it burst into flame as the helicopter approached, throwing long shadows across the flare-illuminated field.

Greeley hopped past him to get to the door as O'Connell nosed the chopper in.

"Down a bit more," he shouted. O'Connell, holding the control stick gingerly, hovered just off the ground as the squad jumped in. There was a series of crashes and thuds behind him. One of the soldiers let loose with a burst of his rifle out the door.

"Go," said Morena, her voice a screech. "Get out of here!"

He obeyed automatically, jerking his body to the left. The machine followed, rolling away from the landing zone and back in the direction they had come. This was a mistake; it kept them in full sight of whoever was firing at them. Muzzle flashes filled O'Connell's peripheral vision. He pushed his turn wider, farther from the enemy position.

To get to the first team he had to pass the 12.7 again. If he continued his arc across he'd be an easy target.

He was yelling before he realized he'd made a decision. "Hang on."

O'Connell pushed the Super Panther II directly for the big gun, full speed, whipping in as a misdirected shell flew past.

"Shoot that flare to tell them we're coming. Greeley, get up here and help me spot."

The green tint of the signal flare shot from the back of the helicopter. O'Connell searched the ground ahead vainly for the men.

"Greeley!"

The antiair crew recovered and lobbed a shell toward them. It exploded far to the right. A second was closer.

Greeley fell into his seat with a grunt as O'Connell pulled the helicopter to the left, thinking he'd gone too far. A purple splash ahead told him he hadn't—the team had lit a ground flare.

But that gave the enemy something to focus on. His path was lit by small arms tracers and he couldn't tell what the hell was going on.

Two big booms overhead from the 12.7 as he hunkered down, a bare foot or so off the ground.

"Closer," shouted Fleming, practically throwing himself forward. "We're going to have to get out."

"Screw it," said O'Connell. He pushed the stick sharply to left and yanked on the collective; the helicopter jumped away.

"Hell," said Greeley, leaning toward the back. "You can't leave them. Morena's down there."

"Damn it, who told her to get out?"

O'Connell backed out several thousand yards from the airstrip. Thanks to a rising hump of land, he was out of the big gun's line of sight.

The firing stopped, but all hell would break loose once he went back in. They knew where he was going now.

O'Connell felt a gentle touch on his shoulder and turned to find an unshaven face staring at him. It belonged to the secretary of state.

"Thanks for rescuing me."

"You all right?"

"I think so."

"I'm Michael O'Connell. This is James Greeley. We're gonna duck back in there, so keep your head down."

The secretary stuck his hand over and shook Greeley's, then clasped the pilot's. It was a small hand, almost feminine. The man didn't seem scared. If anything, his soft voice seemed to be trying to reassure O'Connell.

The pilot started the helicopter forward again. Hopefully, Morena had reached their team and he'd only have to make one stop. He had most of his rockets left. They'd been ineffective up to this point, but hope springs eternal, especially when prodded by desperation.

O'Connell wheeled and pointed his nose up, heading back toward the drop point. As they approached, a fresh purple flare lit up about fifty yards away. Fixing the flare as a reference point, he circled to the left with his cannon blazing, then switched over to the rockets. Three salvos of rockets leapt from the helicopter toward the gun emplacement and surrounding field.

A fourth round. A fifth. By the time he clicked into an empty canister he was already sliding backwards. He spun the helicopter to its right, still sixty yards from the LZ.

Greeley had his head out the window. "There," he shouted, pointing to the right.

Morena was silhouetted in the failing purple light, waving the little Ruger machine pistol at the exploding yellow flowers across the field as if she were watering a garden. O'Connell twisted the throttle to accelerate. The Aérospatiale took a step forward and began choking, as if someone had hit it in the chest.

Or put a bullet into one of its engines.

For the second time in less than a week, O'Connell said a prayer. This one wasn't fancy or very long, nor was it one the Jesuits would have especially approved of.

"God, don't fuck up now."

Whether it was his praying or his pounding the motor controls, the chopper kicked forward with a lurch. O'Connell's head roared with noise, explosions, the rasping whine of the blades. Someone in the back fired toward the Indians.

The helicopter groaned as people jumped out, then in, rolling, thumping. Cartridge gas everywhere.

"Go!" Morena was screaming. "Go, go!"

But it wasn't until Greeley tapped him that he spun the chopper to the northwest and gave it everything he had, running as fast as possible from the huge, shaking thuds of the 12.7.

Washington, D.C. 2 P.M.

The U.S. intelligence agencies share a Washington, D.C. headquarters in a nondescript brick building a few blocks from the White House. Officially the office of the director of intelligence agencies—a post traditionally held by the head of the CIA—it includes several administrative sections for the National Foreign Intelligence Board as well as the CIA, DIA, NSA and INR, the state department's intelligence agency. It also holds safe rooms for secure meetings.

Stockman was sitting in one now, tie off, calmly trying to explain the difficulty of the Pakistan situation to two air force generals and underlings who had been hastily assembled to draw up an interception plan. Part of him felt contempt for the men, who were having trouble comprehending what he was telling them. Another part felt almost indescribable relief at finally letting it all out.

There was no question that his career was over, that the end of this crisis would leave his life irrevocably changed, but he felt oddly at ease with it all. The president's reaction, businesslike and grave, had been many times calmer than he had hoped for.

"Honestly, Stockman, I wasn't even sure how a B-50 was configured," said Curtis, seated to the left of him. A two-star general, he was a problem solver for the Pentagon and an expert on tactical air. "I had to have one of my aides look it up. It was based on the B-29, you know."

A few of the other men laughed. "God, that'll have the radar signature of Mount Rushmore," said one.

"I've been trying to explain that," said the DDO. "The planes have a radar masking system that makes them look exactly like a civilian airliner the Indians use. They have a way of intercepting signals, retransmitting them and altering the aircraft's signature so they can make it look like a single-engined plane, or any of several different aircraft. The system is very sophisticated," he added, leaning forward for emphasis.

"The Pakistanis?" said Curtis. "I just don't believe they're capable of that."

"The Pakistanis have already developed a hybrid F-16," answered Mark Chafetz, a colonel who wore an intelligence insignia. He spoke with a crisp assurance. "Their technical capabilities are very advanced. They have several projects under wraps at their aircraft rebuild factory in Kamra. Was this one of them?"

"This was done at a different facility," said Stockman, glad that he had finally found someone who knew where Pakistan was. "All different people. But top, top-notch."

"I have some familiarity with the PAF," said Chafetz, whose short, compact body could have belonged to a fighter pilot. "The pilots are well trained and they've done remarkable things with hand-me-downs. This is all absolutely possible," he added, addressing the rest of the air force delegation. He turned back to Stockman. "Do you know precisely what they've done?"

"I don't have a spec sheet, if that's what you mean. There's really only one person in the agency anymore with detailed information."

"Get him."

"He's in Pakistan, trying to stop it." That was as much as Stockman was going to tell them about O'Connell. "Besides the radar, there was work done on the rest of the plane. The heat signature has been reduced."

"That's irrelevant," said Dalton, who was Chafetz's boss. "You're going to have to get pretty damn close to use infrared anyway. If this thing is supposed to look like a civilian plane, or even just another military plane, we ought to assume it works, and go from there."

"Set up one of the bomb bays in the plane to carry Sparrows and you could kiss anything that gets close enough to ID it good-bye," said Chafetz.

"Shit, I know what they're doing," blurted a tall, red-haired major in the back. "They supplement the waveforms."

Everyone looked at him. His face turned nearly as red as his hair.

"What's the possibility of defeating it?" Curtis asked him.

"Well, you'd have to understand the mechanics of it first. Now does it amplify waves that already exist, or create its own?" He glanced at Stockman, who hadn't a clue what he was talking about. "We could probably figure it out. If I had a team from—"

Stockman cut him off. "By the time we do that, half the continent will be in ashes."

"We need a better idea of where the base is," said Curtis.

"I've had two teams going over the country with microscopes," said Stockman. "We know it was planned for the area near Gilgit, but we haven't been able to find even a carport out of place."

"I have an idea," said Chafetz. "Even if they used thermal masking, the engines would still be making a lot of noise."

"They'd probably try to muffle them somehow," said Dalton.

"But there'd still be four of them. We could adapt a Rivet Porcupine flight."

"That's a very hot area for an RC-135," said Dalton. The electronics surveillance aircraft, which were based on the Boeing 707, carried a wide array of sophisticated spy equipment, but they were slow, defenseless airplanes. They survived by standing off hostile territory. "Especially if the Pakistanis are as good as you say they are. Besides, the equipment would have to be tuned to the proper frequency."

"We could adapt it," said the major who had interrupted before. "We could borrow the programming from drug interception flights, maybe two tweaks, that's all. Out comes the cruise missile detector cartridge, in goes what we're looking for." He mimicked the motion, as if the procedure were as easy as slipping a new cassette into a tape deck.

"Do we want this interception over Pakistan or India?" Curtis asked.

"It would be better over Pakistan."

The general shook his head. "Maybe with three tracks, one over each ocean, and something over Afghan, assuming the Russians don't blow a gasket."

"There are only two Porcupines in Greece," said Dalton. "I'm not even sure both could be gotten down there in time."

"This has the highest priority," said Stockman. "This has absolute preference over everything."

"Our lives would be considerably easier if you could give us an idea of where we'd find them," said Dalton, a bit of the viper in his voice.

"If I knew that, general," replied the DDO testily, "I wouldn't need you. My best information is that it's near Gilgit, but they could be anywhere. We have total satellite coverage and we still can't locate them."

"We can cover the western flight with F-22s out of the U.A.E.," said Curtis, referring to the United Arab Emirates. "But I think you're going to need the Navy off the other coast."

"It'd be best to involve the Indians," said Chafetz. "They have MiG-29s capable of reaching just about anywhere in Pakistan, and they'd be highly motivated."

"The president is considering that option," said Stockman.

Prior to this meeting, the DDO had finished a session with two SAC representatives—three B-2 bombers on Diego Garcia were circling in the Indian Ocean, standing by for a bombing raid. He'd doubled the number of people trying to find the base, and told them everything he knew, but he didn't expect a breakthrough.

O'Connell had obviously been mistaken. His information was two years old, after all. Still, if Morena called back—when Morena called back—he'd tell her to put a goddamned gun to the bastard's head and get the site location. He should have done that in the first place. But he should have done so many things.

Stockman had practically forgotten the two agents in the press of the last few hours. The rest of the kidnapping crisis group was dubious about Blossom's rescue operation. To a man, they'd dismissed it as a wild goose chase.

"You may have no other choice but to tell the Indians," said Chafetz after Stockman had finished briefing the officers on the bombing plan. "If those planes split up, it'll be nearly impossible to locate and shoot down each one of them with our resources alone."

Approaching Calcutta. 11:45 P.M.

It was routine now, slipping into a nice pink tunnel and waiting for the targeting cue to change color. Several times Khan's FLIR gear picked up planes in his vicinity, including two MiGs south of Allahabad, but the Leopard was truly invisible, or seemed to be, and all he had to do was sit tight and hit his buttons. The bennies had calmed a bit, their tingle reduced to a feathery lightness at the very top of his forehead. He was wide awake.

The triangle went black and he punched, pulled straight into a climb and veered north, giving the massive glow of India's biggest, poorest city a good berth.

The launch point for the rocket was almost exactly 1,500

miles from the runway at Kamra, and the Leopard was running low on fuel. Straight-line at high altitude, the 2,400 kilometers would have been an easy jaunt for the fuel-efficient jet, but the mission's maneuvers had upped his gas expenditure considerably. Khan had enough to last the 200 miles or so to the tanker rendezvous, but just barely.

The second leg of the mission would be shorter, with drops near Hyderabad and Bombay before scooting over the border to a landing at Thano-Mikhi. It ought to take an hour less than the trip in.

For Khan, used to three- or four-hour patrols in the Falcon, this was a real endurance test. While the drugs helped keep him awake, they couldn't erase the cramps and aches. It didn't take a weight lifter to fly a jet with electronic controls, but the pilot's body was undergoing many of the same stresses a marathon runner experienced. The success of the mission depended on his physical reserves as much as his mental acuity. He rallied them now, stretching and twisting, pressing his shoulders back into his seat as the Leopard accelerated upward through a cloud bank and some rough weather. The huge city to his right threw eerie reflections into the clouds, tinting them with a pale, animating light. Lightning flashed in the distance, and Khan felt as if he were passing from one world to the other, hiding himself among God's angels, avoiding the demons of the earth. Breaking through the top of the clouds was like plunging into a dark nectar, the stars twinkling before him.

He was off-course slightly, heading too far into Bangladesh. There was nothing to worry about—the former East Pakistan had no air defenses to speak of. Khan examined his left heads-down display, set on radar detection, then turned to the right CRT, where his position was smartly marked out on a color-coded map. Bangladesh was a light tan; the ocean a cheerful blue—cheerful because it reminded Khan of a Western-style dress his fiancée wore.

He'd had more than four hours now to contemplate the nature of his mission. The rockets must be the final pegs in a plan to open a wide door in the defenses around each city. He was obviously laying the groundwork for a revenge raid, a strike against civilians as retribution for Indian attacks. Unless that attack were purely symbolic—and the PAF did not deal in symbols—it would almost certainly have to be nuclear.

But Khan had difficulty accepting the only logical conclusion about the nature of his mission. Pakistan had destroyed its atomic weapons when the disarmament treaty had been signed several years ago. The only planes he knew of that could be modified to drop the bombs, attack-configured F-16s, were monitored by the U.N. and U.S. Even if some way around that were found, most of his drops were outside the F-16's most optimistic combat range.

But look at the airplane Kamra had made for him. Who was to say that it couldn't put together a bomber?

The young major momentarily ignored the computer's cue to return to his course, staring into the empty sky before him. His duty was clear, but his eyes blurred the red markers and lights on the HUD into a vast fire, consuming millions upon millions of people.

And if the Indians had weapons as well? If they too had been able to deceive the UN, and the Americans?

"Oh ye who believe," Khan said aloud to the empty cockpit, mouthing the full version of his pilot's prayer to steel himself. "Shall I guide you to a gainful trade which will save you from painful punishment? Believe in Allah and his Apostle and carry on jihad in the path of All with all your possession and your persons. That is better for you. If ye have knowledge, He will forgive your sins, and will place you in the Gardens beneath which the streams flow, and in fine houses in the Garden of Eden: that is the great gain."

The pilot yanked the plane sharply to the south, a ninety-five-degree decoupled turn that grabbed nearly 7 g's and slammed them hard into the side of his chest. For some reason it felt good, his blood pumping hard as he recovered, his lungs gasping for the sweet, clean oxygen pumping up through the tube that snaked across his chest.

He began descending from 50,000 to 30,000 feet, checking the dedicated fuel gauge to the right of his knee as he did so. The preflight calculations had been optimistic; he was already on reserve, and in fact the needle on the old-fashioned backup was crowding empty.

Which, unfortunately, agreed with the HUD display nudge. It gave its first yellow flash. Five more minutes and it would turn red. Ten minutes beyond that he'd be swimming.

Khan's milk cow was a refurbished Boeing 707, outfitted in essentially the same style as an American KC-135 and flying the colors of a Malaysian cargo company. Operating out of Burma under a secret agreement with Pakistan, the plane ought to be no more than five minutes ahead, according to the flight computer and its preprogrammed way markers.

Too little margin for error. A bank of clouds loomed ahead, dulling the effectiveness of his FLIR. Even though it was considerably better than the one inhabiting the Falcon, it wasn't omniscient, and still had difficulty working through clouds. Reluctantly, Khan activated his radar, sending its powerful beams out ahead of him. He couldn't afford to fumble for the tanker.

He no sooner flipped the switch than the HUD outlined his target, tail to him forty-five miles almost directly due south, running a track straight down the 89th meridian. Khan had to slip a little lower; at 19,700 feet, he should have been beneath the Boeing, not above, but he didn't want to break radio silence to find out why the plane was so much lower than planned. The entire exchange was to be carried out in complete radio silence, if possible.

The scope clicked out several other targets in the vicinity, too far for IDs. But now the radar detector put in its two cents and the computer flashed a warning—NATO-style I-band radars approaching.

Even more definitive—Ferranti Blue Fox. The signals belonged to Harrier jump jets of the Indian navy.

The radar profiling screen molded a pair of yellow bubbles growing in intensity. The threat identifier was like having a copilot and tactician along; the computer's graphic layout showed him the enemy's vulnerabilities and would have made an attack child's play. But there wasn't enough gas, and he had no missiles; go after these jokers with his cannon and he'd end up in the water before he got off a shot.

Break off from the refueling to avoid them and the same thing would happen.

Khan glanced at the cyanide capsule taped to his glove, then watched the tube as the Harriers came on, their beams growing more intense and the CRT shaping a pink area he was headed straight for. The sky cleared—he went back to the FLIR, got everybody on the screen, then dialed his radio around to the Indian frequencies, listening for a challenge.

They were after the tanker. They apparently hadn't targeted it yet, but his milk truck was dead meat if their trigger fingers got restless.

The Boeing's running lights came into view just as the jump jets hailed the lumbering plane, asking it to identify itself. They were still fifteen miles off.

He had four, now three, straight in. The boom was out and the refueling guide lights on, waiting.

They were well within the Indians' missile range. Impulsively, Rocket Khan flipped his radio mike on.

"Hey, ya'll, you're gonna have to stand in line if ya want a drink."

A Texan would have had his ears fumigated after that assault on the American fighter jock's twang of choice, but neither Indian pilot was a linguist. Khan's jabber—coming from a plane they hadn't spotted—surprised the hell out of them.

Or at least Khan hoped it did as he keyed the flight computer for manual refuel. The computer took care of some of the standard book-keeping—popping on and then dimming his fuselage, wing and tail-lights, pushing hot air across the canopy bubble to prevent icing. Khan, meanwhile, studied the two rows of director lights set like jewels in the tanker's Buddha belly. Easing his speed back, he pinched his neck up, a kid stretching at a fountain for a drink.

He hadn't had a chance to practice a refuel at Kamra. But like the F-16, the refueling slot was directly behind the pilot, and lining up was merely a matter of following the directions provided on the light strips—the left side told him whether to go up or down, and the right whether to move forward or back. But his hand was unsteady. The boomer in the rear of the tanker took two swipes with his stick but failed to find the funnel-like fixture sucking at the air behind Khan's head like a pair of thirsty lips.

The red light began to flash. "Fuel tanks are empty," said the audible computer warning.

Stop whining you pessimist, he thought, hoping they'd been extremely cautious when writing the fuel warning program. He nudged the Leopard a bit more to left, using the Boeing's yellow centerline stripe as reference. The tanker stumbled with turbulence and Khan just barely saved himself from a knock on the head.

"Identify yourself," said the Indians. They were closing, one above, one below.

Khan willed the tanker still and lined up again. The nozzle hit, slipped off, hit, slipped off, hit and swooshed with a connection. The Leopard swallowed gratefully.

"Identify yourself or we will shoot you down," said one of the Indian Harriers as he swung around the Boeing's wing.

If he *did* somehow convince them they'd stumbled onto an American spy plane, would they turn around and go back to their carrier? Or would they shoot him down anyway? He was in international airspace, but somehow that didn't seem likely to affect their decision.

"This here is Colonel Tom Wright, USAF," said Khan, appropriating the name of the only pilot who'd had a better score than he did at the Nevada dogfight competition. "You guys coming back over China with me?"

If either of these men had ever been to the U.S., Khan was dead. Fortunately, his unmarked black airplane looked a lot more American than his accent sounded.

"Captain, we request to know the nature of your mission," said one of the Indians.

"I ain't a captain," said Khan, wondering if he should sound angry or amused. American pilots were generally easygoing, even when they were being superior. "I'm a lowly major. And I can't give you boys any info." Info was definitely the right word. "You supposed to be here? I thought I had this there gas station alone."

"What is your unit?" demanded the Indian pilot.

"Call Washington if you need more info," said Khan.

"What are you flying?" asked the other pilot.

"Don't get excited," Khan shot back. "I don't want you to start spitting on my wings."

Drool, not spit. But it was too late to correct it.

The pilots either didn't hear or didn't notice the flub. His computer helped his radio work out the frequency to eavesdrop as they radioed their carrier for instructions, giving their controller an enticing description of the "black-painted plane" that had not appeared on their radar screens. He didn't like that, but at least they bought his bogus accent—they were calling him an American CIA special.

Khan checked the fuel—halfway there. He could break refuel now and take them out. But if the tanker got caught in the cross fire, he wouldn't have enough gas to finish his mission.

The carrier began radioing instructions—two more planes were being scrambled to assist. They were to force the American to an Indian air base. Or terminate his flight. Khan wondered if the tanker pilot was hearing all this.

"You are to return with us," said the lead Indian pilot. "Your tanker, too."

"I'm in international airspace, turkey head," said Khan. He didn't know if it was an epithet or not, but it sounded like it ought to be one.

"Major, we insist."

One on each wing. How to get behind them without taking so much time that they could launch missiles?

The flat fall he'd discovered by accident when he'd whacked his elbow on his first flight. Put him behind and below instantaneously.

Only 80 percent full. That wasn't enough.

"Major, you are to break off your refuel now."

"I'm coming," said Khan. "But I have a slight problem."

"We don't care about your problem," said the Harrier pilot as the planes changed their positions. One moved directly behind him; the other climbed over the tanker's wing, sitting next to the Boeing's cockpit.

Khan had to give the tanker pilot credit. He held the old Boeing straight and true, pouring juice down the Leopard's throat, even with the Harriers making faces at him.

Hitting the electronic countermeasures would fuzz their radars and maybe confuse them momentarily. It was thin, but any advantage was useful. But to make it work, Khan had to hit the ECM and bump the throttle at the same time. He stretched his fingers out toward the dash—couldn't do it.

Here was a flaw in Kamra's brilliant ergonomic design. It would be a bad time to take his hand off the stick, but that was the only way to do it. In theory, the computer could hold the plane steady.

The fuel indicator was still clicking away, counting the juice like a greedy accountant. Ninety percent capacity; that was going to have to be enough.

Get the ECMs and then the flares, just in case they launch right away.

"You have ten seconds—" began the Indian.

Khan's right hand flew across the cockpit. An electronic shock wave erupted from the Leopard's fuzz-buster. There was a loud snap as the plane stuttered in the air, dropping a hundred feet. The white underbelly of a Harrier shot overhead, a frog who'd had his lily pad yanked out from under him.

Khan barely got his hand back on the stick when he opened up with the cannon. He was so close he could see his first bullets sail across the Harrier's wing. The spray moved from right to left, at least one round crunching into the fuselage as the plane dove sharply to starboard.

Khan turned to grab the tail of the other Harrier, which had begun to accelerate away. The Indian pilot tried to start a scissor but he was way overmatched. The stealth fighter was in textbook kill position as its cannon began melting the top of the enemy plane. Bursts of red and white sparks ate at the jump jet, disintegrating the intricately painted camouflage and then the carefully milled metal, erasing huge swaths of the plane as if they were wrong equations on a blackboard.

As Khan followed the jet downward, the left wing snapped away. An instant later the cockpit exploded; the Harrier pilot had ejected.

The man had seen the Leopard. If he lived, his information would be invaluable to the Indians. Khan swept into a wide turn. Should he shoot at the falling pilot?

A parachute blossomed in the upper portion of the HUD in front of him. The small ball below the chute jerked upward and then it too unfolded, legs and arms spreading out in the shape of a cross. It was an easy shot, a fat orange starfish.

If logic had been involved, Khan could have explained his decision to leave the man alone. The carrier had already been alerted, and his uncle had specifically stated that completing his mission took precedence over secrecy. Making sure the man was dead would have taken at least one more pass and consumed fuel he ought to conserve. Besides, the other plane, though hit, had escaped.

But logic had nothing to do with it. There was an inexplicable difference between shooting the man's airplane down and going after the man himself. Khan broke off.

As he banked away, trying to find his course on the right-hand video screen, the sky lit with a tremendous explosion.

The 707.

A voice inside him screamed in anger. Instincts and the plane took over. The radar went to rapid-search, looking for the Harrier he had first fired at, but obviously not damaged critically. The bogey was cued up, running south, 500 feet above the waves, getting away. The Leopard leaped to pursue, an agile cat chasing down a scared, considerably slower rabbit. If he'd had any sort of air-attack missile in his belly bay at this range, the Harrier would be dead. Khan counted off the distance aloud—five miles, four, three. The Harrier pilot saw him and made a cut to the east.

Two more bogies in the distance. Khan glanced at the CRT on his left, which outlined their radar profiles in yellow. Didn't have him yet.

He angled the Leopard to follow the escaping Harrier, lined up an attack in his head. Two miles; the Indian was big and bright in his screen. He jinked again to the south, gaining a precious half mile. Another jink, and Khan guessed he would save some acceleration for a dive just as the Leopard came on, trying to twist back toward his friends.

I can cut him off. I can cut the bastard off. And kill him.

Two miles again. Another jink to the east, farther away from Khan's course.

"What the hell am I doing?" he shouted at the stars, catching himself, pulling the Leopard up and over, twisting back toward India and his mission. "What the hell am I doing?"

General Arjun's Hospital Room. Five Minutes to Midnight.

For hours he floated on water, alone in the world. The sky, if it was a sky, was purer than anything he had ever imagined, let alone seen.

Arjun knew that in reality he was lying on a hospital bed or perhaps an operating table, his life ebbing from him. But temporal reality had no meaning anymore.

Something had happened to him in the past few hours that he couldn't explain. He had forgotten everything, dissolved into something akin to pure emotion, a joy almost, that had no relationship to words.

He had passed from one country of the mind to another. And so when Shiva appeared again, a dark cloud hovering above him, his loose clothes shimmering with the sinister heat of destruction and chaos, Arjun spoke confidently. He greeted the Hindu god of war as if he had been waiting an entire lifetime for him to appear.

"You have given up," said Shiva immediately. "It's about time."

"I haven't given up," said Arjun.

"You recognize that I am real," said the god.

"You are a way of perceiving."

"You are ready to renounce your religion?"

"No, I have only now come to know it," said the Sikh. "Now I believe fully. My belief before was imperfect."

"It is a sad folly, mankind," said the god. "Always going in circles, from life to death, death to life. And with what goal? Destruction. Why? Because it is the only way mortals can aspire to become gods. Well, you will soon succeed— the Indian nation is about to be consumed in fire. And then there will be retaliation."

"No," said Arjun. "That will not happen."

Shiva laughed. "Well this is an interesting development!" he roared. "A Sikh who has become an optimist, and one who trusts the Muslims!"

"They are the same as us, at their core."

"You are going to tell me next that you do not hate them."

"I don't."

"Ha! The Pakistanis have nuclear weapons. Your own intelligence experts made such a guess."

"The experts said they didn't."

"They admitted the possibility, however slight. The weapons will be used, and you will be forced to retaliate with your biological plague. You know the plan well."

"I helped prepare it."

"You renounce it now?"

"It is a doomsday dream, but it will not be executed. I did not understand before, but my eyes have been opened. I thought once that it was possible to liberate my people by seizing land; I see now that little will be gained by force and destruction. And just as I realize that, I know that the Pakistanis will not use their weapons. Man will not destroy himself; the true God will not let that happen."

"You contradict *me?*" In that moment Shiva grew mon-

307

strously large, filling the sky before him and flashing a flaming sword in both hands.

"I don't fear you, Shiva," said Arjun. "Nor do I envy you. I only pity you, and what you represent."

The god flailed his arms in a frenzy. The air became intensely hot; Arjun felt as if he had been set on fire.

"Mankind is doomed to destroy itself; your war is proof of that. Your whole race is proof of that. The Muslims and the Sikhs, the Hindus and the Christians—you will fall upon yourselves again and again."

"I have been as responsible as anyone for the war," said Arjun. "I now realize my error. If I can make such a journey, millions of others shall. The final outcome will be peace."

There was a furious wail, and what had been a peaceful ocean was now a howling typhoon. Shiva's hands were lightning bolts, hurling in every direction. Arjun lay calmly, observing it all as scientifically as possible, wondering if he had died.

"I believe in the one God, Invisible," he said firmly, and then began praying, uttering words he had not mouthed since childhood.

There was a loud explosion and a rush of fire followed by blackness. Shiva was gone, and Arjun felt himself being pulled downward. Pain returned suddenly, intense, searing pain. A figure in white loomed over him, whether a doctor or an angel, perhaps a devil, he couldn't tell.

Northern India. 11:58 P.M.

Greeley watched O'Connell glance at his watch and then back at the fuel gauge. "I don't know, Greeley," he told him.

"We're talking thirty seconds away. I figure you have two more minutes' worth of fuel, give or take ninety seconds."

"You're a real comfort."

O'Connell, his hands and face purple from the reflected hue of the instruments, moved the controls with a robotlike precision so unlike the easy motions he'd used earlier that Greeley knew he didn't expect to make it. He'd heard once that helicopters never took hard landings when their engines died, that running out of fuel meant a slow, gentle hover to the ground. He wasn't eager to be disabused of that notion.

The secretary of state, a short, tired-looking man, huddled just behind the pilot's seat, looking at the fancy cockpit systems with great interest. Greeley belonged to a generation that still held government officials, most of them anyway, in awe. There was something special about a man like Grasso; he might be small of stature but he had scaled heights Greeley could only imagine.

And Greeley had rescued him! What an incredible turn his life had taken in three days. If only Olissa were here to see it.

His kids would get a kick out of it. The grandkids—he'd have years' worth of stories. Assuming he made it.

Jesus, of course they were going to come out of this alive. Come on, James, you're going to pull it off; look how far you've come already.

"Greeley, you sure you read that damn thing right?"

"There," he said, practically shouting as he spotted a dim green light floating in the air a hundred yards ahead. O'Connell steadied the helicopter as they approached the telephone pole where the battery-powered signal light was mounted. There was a building to the left; the school yard they were to land in was just beyond.

"I'd get it down as quickly as possible," Greeley said.

"No shit, Sherlock. I was thinking I'd sit up here until the tank was bone-dry."

Morena mustered the soldiers. As O'Connell touched down, she slid the door open and the squad jumped out, clutching their weapons anxiously.

The power cut, the night-vision gear and everything else in the cockpit abruptly died. Greeley was startled by the total darkness, and it took a half minute before his eyes could even adjust enough to see the pencil-thin light beams splaying across the lot as the commandos looked for the parked fuel trucks.

"Wait, Mr. Secretary," said O'Connell, grabbing Grasso's arm as he moved toward the door. The helicopter was empty except for them. "How were you being guarded when we rescued you?"

"What do you mean?"

"I mean, was anyone with you?"

"They locked me in the room and left me."

"You weren't tied up?"

"They took everything off. They were pretty easy on me, all things considered."

"What are you getting at?" Greeley asked.

"I'm not sure," said O'Connell. "There were a hell of a lot of bullets fired at us, but none of them hit."

"How do you know?"

"Get off your butt and check," the pilot snapped. But then he added, a little softer, "I know what bullets hitting a helicopter feel like. I thought it was just the plating, but the more I thought about it—look across to the front of the nose when I flick the light on." O'Connell illuminated the small search beam atop the rotor. "What do you figure the odds are of not one bullet hitting us?"

Greeley hesitated. Maybe they'd just been lucky.

"Besides, I had the distinct impression our missiles were duds." O'Connell turned back to Grasso, who was kneeling on the floor and leaning toward them. "Did you see the people who captured you?"

"A couple of times I had glimpses," said Grasso apologetically. "I don't think I could identify them."

"Did they have beards?"

"No."

"Sikhs always have beards," said O'Connell, still holding onto the secretary's arm. "I'm pretty sure we've been set up. I don't know what the deal is, but I want you to stay close to me when we get into Pakistan. Assuming we didn't land in the wrong place here."

"What do the Sikhs have to do with it?" Grasso asked.

"The person who told us where you were made it sound like the Sikhs had kidnapped you."

"Maybe they shaved their beards to confuse me."

"Maybe," said O'Connell. "Or maybe it was someone on the Pakistani side who wanted to prolong the conflict so the military would be discredited and the government would fail. Someone like Nizam."

"Nizam?"

"The CIA informant who put this together. Blossom is her code name."

"You're not talking about the Pakistani interior minister, are you?"

"Yes, I am."

"She's on the agency payroll?"

"Yes, sir."

"You've got to be fucking kidding me."

"Sssh," said O'Connell.

"Who the hell is responsible for that? I'll kill him. Princess Ghazzala Nizam is a separatist—what are we doing dealing with her?"

"She arranged this mission. This is her helicopter."

"Oh, Jesus."

A dark figure suddenly appeared in front of the cockpit. The three of them froze before realizing it was Morena.

"We found the trucks," she told O'Connell, leaning into the open window. "But there aren't any keys and we can't find a pump. Fleming is trying to hot-wire them. If that doesn't work, we'll have to roll the barrels over here."

"I want to talk to you," O'Connell told her. He turned back to Greeley, shoving the pistol into his gut. "Take this," he said, then jumped from the helicopter.

Greeley felt a twinge of responsibility for Grasso, huddled behind the seat, not unlike the feeling he got looking in on his kids when they were young.

"They know what they're doing," he said, trying to sound reassuring.

"I'm sure they do."

"Want some coffee?" asked Greeley, retrieving the thermos. "It's still hot. Real strong, though."

Greeley had just begun pouring the coffee when he was startled by a knock on the window next to him. It was O'Connell.

"There's something coming down the road. If I yell, get out of the helicopter. Get the secretary."

"I'm right here."

"Quiet," said O'Connell, ducking down.

Greeley sat frozen as a pair of headlights traced the wall of the building not far from them, then started in a diagonal line across the school yard. The secretary of state crawled forward, flattening himself between the seats as if staying low would keep the chopper from being seen. Greeley looked into his bloodshot eyes as the lights came toward them. "We'll be OK, baby," he said.

As soon as the words were out of his mouth he felt a horrible embarrassment.

Grasso patted his leg. "I know we will," he said mildly as the lights passed, miraculously missing the helicopter. There was an amused upswing to his voice as he added, "And call me John."

North of Bombay. 4:30 A.M. (Saturday).

When the last rocket slipped from the Leopard's belly, Khan's body deflated like a punctured balloon. He accelerated promptly and climbed toward the heavens, not caring that he was flying straight through a danger area marked out by the radar detector. He was done now, the most difficult and frustrating mission of his life complete. He had only to get home, and he could do that with his eyes closed. His scope cleared as he walked through a turn signaled by the INS, lining his plane up for a Pakistani runway approximately five hundred miles away. He switched the flight computer into auto and watched the Leopard find the preprogrammed coordinates.

As they reached 45,000 feet, the detection equipment picked up the weak pulse of a pair of Doppler radars a hundred miles to the east; he knew even before the threat identifier made its automated calculations that the radars belonged to a pair of MiG-29s. He would have loved to tangle with them, but he had neither the fuel nor the missiles, and meekly pushed his throttle to increase his speed, running away from any possible danger. The MiGs passed blithely by.

Too bad he didn't have another little green pill, or perhaps some of Hir's special spiced tea. His concentration was steadily sinking despite the different tricks he tried to stay awake. His black flight boots were hundred-pound magnets draining the energy from his body.

Khan liked especially to fall asleep in Hir's lap, her hand gently rubbing his temples, brushing the hair from his face. They had spent a pleasant evening on the veranda of her father's home not two weeks ago, talking of the future. She would continue to teach after they were married. She felt as if she made an important difference in the children's lives, helping them toward the future. Khan, thinking himself very Western, nodded in agreement.

He dozed off as she spoke, his nose tickled by the gentle scent of her perfume, a gift he'd brought from America. The sun, a bright yellow blur, hugged the horizon. It was so strong he could see it past his closed eyelids.

Khan realized with a start that he was staring at the yellow fuel caution light. He banged the controls awkwardly as he took over from the computer and rechecked his position—he was still in India, just over the Kathiawar Peninsula and dipping deeply into his reserve fuel.

He eased the throttle back, trying to cut his fuel consumption. The Leopard's engines groaned, upset at being deprived.

No matter how pessimistic the fuel settings were, it was going to be close. He was still over 150 miles from the airstrip. And more problems. Doppler radars again, long distance, but heading toward the border.

Even so, he had to let his altitude continue to drop; he needed a good glide effect if he was going to make the strip without running dry. The spinner went from light tan to orange as he dropped to 30,000 feet.

It would be dawn soon. Soft red fingers slipped over his shoulder, helping him keep a steady course. According to the computer, the MiGs hadn't seen him yet. Even so, they were flying almost a perfect intercept. There was no way of knowing whether these were the same planes he'd spotted before, but Khan hoped they were; it would make it more likely that they'd reached the end of their range and patrol.

His black box suddenly lost their radars. Had they turned off? Or did they know he was out here?

They might have caught a whiff and gone to their FLIR setups. They were fifty miles away, and no infrared should have been good enough to catch him at that distance, but there was no way to be sure.

Their angle would make them difficult for his own sensors to find. He might not know they were after him until they launched. Then it would be too late. He had flares and chaff, but no fuel to maneuver.

How simple it would be if his tanks were full. He could choose from a number of different strategies. Spin back and take them head on, macho them out like an American jock would. Or play it more subtly, sneaking in close and then popping up behind them. Or a better use of the plane—wait above them, exploiting the Leopard's high-altitude capabilities and its giddyap. He'd love to fight them in this plane. Avenge Tark, avenge the tanker.

The red fuel light turned his thoughts from revenge to survival. Khan leaned forward in his seat against the restraints, trying to strain every ounce of momentum into the plane as it slid toward the border.

A big whack from an Indian ground radar being turned on. The warning screen flashed pink.

He crossed the border with his eyes glued to the left CRT screen, waiting to hit his ECM when it went red. But his detection gear lost the radar, then found another—ground unit, Pakistani-type. Khan touched the switch that poured out the PAF identifier signal, then activated his radar. He clicked the unit from navigation to far-scan mode. No interceptors. Nothing anywhere but flat, dry land and a waiting air strip.

He would be out of gas any second now. But there were the runway lights, dead ahead. He had just about enough momentum to make it from here if he went dry.

Khan opened up his radio. While generally it was a point of pride not to admit that you had, say, a hundred pounds of fuel (and only two or three minutes' worth of flying time) left in the tanks, he was so low now that pride was beside the point. "I have a fuel caution," he told the tower matter-of-factly. He received direct, priority clearance—too bad that wasn't enough to satisfy the audible computer warning ringing in his ears.

Khan depressed the tiny round button that told the computer to lower his wheels. They would steal airspeed but he thought he could make it now, knew he would make it now. He caught the sunrise out of the corner of his eye. It was a huge, red sun—he turned for a glimpse, and the far-off rays seemed to warm his face.

A black flutter caught his attention and he quickly looked back at the runway. There were birds everywhere—huge black bodies, vast missiles that could take him down as surely as any cannon. Birds were an unlikely but very real hazard to pilots, even in high-tech fighter jets. One could completely destroy an engine; Khan had even heard of a bird smashing through a canopy and knocking a pilot fatally unconscious.

The Leopard was completely surrounded. There wasn't even room for evasive action. They were all around him, above and below, on both sides, hundreds and hundreds of birds that had appeared from nowhere. All he could do was continue in, hold onto the controls.

They stayed with him all the way, flying in slow motion, moving their wings strenuously up and down. He was in slow motion too; the birds and the plane kept exactly the same pace. Through some trick of the atmosphere and dust he saw the individual rays of sunlight filter through the formation, brilliant golden fingers guiding each bird's black wing. He was part of the flock, fluttering gently, touching down unharmed, mission complete.

SATURDAY, SEPT. 20, 1997

Nizam's Compound. 5:25 A.M.

There was a click and a stutter of static on the phone line, and then something she had never heard over the direct microwave connection to her Islamabad office—a busy signal. In that second Nizam realized that the army had decided to move against her. Her heart plunged straight to hell, burning in fire and acid, streaking down a pit that had no bottom.

There was an explosion outside and the busy signal was replaced by a shriek, the brief wail of a ghost denied proper burial, then a blankness that meant the microwave tower had been blown up. She rose from her chair and screamed curses as two PAF F-7s streaked over the compound. Standing at the glass door overlooking the courtyard, Nizam yelled at the sky, as if that might keep the army and its mutinous forces at bay.

There was shooting, a lot of it, in front of the house. The princess opened her top desk drawer and took out the Walther P88 fifteen-round 9-mm automatic. She checked the clip and flicked the safety off, holding it in her left hand as she ran from the office into the adjacent den. The guard normally posted at the end of the hallway was gone. Nizam slowed her pace to a swift walk, preserving her dignity as she entered the garden. The sound of gunfire was drowned out by the roar of a helicopter that appeared over the north corner of the house. Nizam ducked back inside the doorway just as a barrage of bullets began peppering the granite face of the building. It was a short spray; the helicopter came under fire and fluttered away, the wash from its rotors pelting her with dirt and small rocks from the garden.

The aircraft gone, she ran across the courtyard toward the offices. Twice she almost lost her balance and slipped; even the carpeted floor of the short corridor leading to the communications room seemed slippery as she hurried inside.

One of her assistants was there, frantically working the radio. "They have us surrounded," said the young man, whose name was Jimale—literally, "tomorrow." He was shaking. "I can't reach Islamabad. I have tried army headquarters as well. I am now trying the American embassy."

A half dozen of her staff, all women, huddled in the corner of the office. They had the eyes of frightened animals, caught in the corner of a barn as fire licked at the doorway.

"The Americans won't help," Nizam told the telecommunications operator. "And I imagine the rest of the government is under siege as well."

"The other men have taken positions outside," said Jimale. He was a good boy, the son of a family that had been close to her father. "Perhaps I should join them."

"Stay a moment," said Nizam, touching his shoulder as he rose. "Monitor the radio."

"Yes, Princess," he said, sitting. There was a trace of relief on his face, perhaps because he thought he had been spared death for a few minutes longer, perhaps simply because he was happy to be given a task.

"Where's Murwan?" she asked. He shook his head, and her heart fell again.

The ground shook with two fresh explosions as another pair of jets raced over the house. The whoosh of a Stinger rocket and then a muffled explosion followed.

Nizam started out of the office to go to Murwan's room, then stopped. She would not find him there, and it was senseless to waste time contemplating the mistakes of the past.

Yet another bomb shook the building's walls and floor. The princess nearly stumbled before steadying herself against the inner doorway of the communications room.

Two of the secretaries in the corner began openly weeping. "Cover your faces," Nizam shouted harshly. Immediately she regretted it. "I am sorry," said the princess, walking to them. "You must be brave now." She touched each young woman gently on the cheek. "It is time to be brave."

Her people couldn't hold out for long. Even if they'd had enough warning to take their defensive positions, her soldiers would eventually be overrun. She had sent much of her equipment and two brigades that would normally be headquartered here to the front; now she saw why her troops had been so vigorously solicited.

Nizam had known many of the people defending her since childhood. All had ties to the old kingdom. Some believed their ancestors had ridden with Genghis Khan. Generation after generation had allied themselves with her family, surviving all attacks, opposing the British and then the resurgent Hindus and finally, the Pakistani government itself. They would fight to the death to protect her.

That would be senseless. Clearly the army would win. If she surrendered, her people would no doubt be pardoned—they were more valuable in the Pakistani army than in graveyards. All the women would be let go—the generals were interested in the princess, not the small fish that swam around her.

"Make me a flag to surrender," she told Jimale. "It makes no sense to fight on."

His face whitened and then grew puffy, tears welling in his eyes. "I will never do that for you, Your Highness," he said. "I cannot bear the thought." A teardrop slid down the side of his cheek. Nizam touched it with the tip of her scarf, and a flood suddenly appeared. She pressed the handkerchief into his hand.

"I intend to surrender," she said. "I do not want anyone dying for me."

"I have need of a weapon," said Jimale, his voice firmer than ever before.

Nizam wavered for a moment, then handed him her pistol. "You girls, come with me," she said to the huddle of women. The princess turned away and walked from the room quickly, knowing they would follow. She was at the far end of the hallway, near the front of the building, when she heard the shot from the room.

Today was a day for the old ghosts to return. The sound brought her back to a time when she was fourteen. Her father had taken her hunting, up into the mountains in the northern reaches of the country. They were tracking monkeys, using pistols instead of rifles to increase the sport. She had gone hunting many times before, but using a handgun changed everything for her, bringing killing so much closer. The sound of her gun startled her when she fired. Her bullet passed through the lemur's head, a perfect shot.

It was one of the few times she had ever cried in her father's presence. It was different than other hunting, she tried to explain. Her father insisted it wasn't, insisted and despaired that he had no male heirs, that this girl would always be a poor substitute.

He walked with her now, the halls filled with his tobacco smoke. The firing outside had stopped, both sides waiting for the final assault. She could hear trucks and perhaps armored vehicles coming up from the valley. Leaving the women crouching on the porch, she walked to the front veranda and stepped boldly out the doorway.

One of her male clerks knelt next to the obelisk at the front of the compound. He was holding an M-16 awkwardly in his hands. The princess strode across the white pebble patio to the monument. "Do you know how to use that?" she demanded.

"Of course," he said, frowning, but his voice was high-pitched despite his efforts. He was fifteen or sixteen, a thin rail of a boy, and this was almost certainly the first time he'd held a weapon.

"Give it to me," she said, reaching out her hand.

He stood. He had a lot of growing to do, but already he was as tall as she was.

"Well?"

He gave up the gun reluctantly.

"Give me your undershirt," she said.

The young man, embarrassed, looked around. Several militiamen held positions further down the driveway; they nodded slowly and he pulled his light blue dress shirt off, fumbling with the buttons. Then he pulled the white undershirt off in a rush.

Nizam touched his face. "Remember this day," she said gently, and then took the shirt, draping it on the barrel of the rifle and walking slowly, steadily, fully erect, down the driveway.

Approaching the Kirthar Mountains, Southeastern Pakistan. 5:35 A.M.

At times like this, O'Connell wished he smoked. Not that he wasn't juiced up enough already—his heart was beating so loudly he could feel it plainly over the throb of the rotor. But smoking would give him something else to do with his hands—there were only so many times he could fiddle with the knobs.

It had taken an eternity to refuel the helicopter, fumbling with siphon hoses. Coming across India wasn't a problem, and they had slipped into Pakistan without challenge. But nearing Karachi O'Connell had been warned off by a PAF combat air patrol, advising him he was approaching a no-fly zone. An unwelcome pause followed the information that he was flying for the interior minister; by the time the jet pilots directed him to "proceed immediately and surrender" at a PAF air base, O'Connell had the helicopter hunkered into the hills, heading for a small airfield he knew Nizam used deep in the Kirthar mountains.

The fighters lost him in the ground clutter, but that hardly eased O'Connell's fears. They hadn't sounded exactly friendly, and Fleming hadn't taken it very well, either.

"That looks like it," said Greeley, who leaned toward him as he pointed, though the base was on the far right. "What are we going to do?" he whispered.

An extremely good question. He needed to get on the ground to find out what the hell was going on, but landing in the wrong place might be fatal. He had a bit over a quarter of a tank of gas, but that wasn't going to keep him in the air indefinitely.

Your problems, Michael?

Lack of knowledge. Nizam obviously set up the rescue, which meant she'd probably done the snatch. Was she working with the military, or did the military catch wind of the operation and decide to cut in? Was it just a coincidence that he'd been challenged? Surely the military wouldn't want to screw with the secretary of state.

Additional problems?

Fleming seems upset, and he has a notoriously short temper.

Options?

Land at this airport and refuel. Try and find out what's going on.

Then?

Go to the U.S. embassy in Islamabad.

And the Golden Bear?

I don't have enough range to make it.

You're just going to leave it there, let all those people die?

It's not my responsibility.

Why did you sign up in the first place, then?

What else was I supposed to do?

You've been in tighter spots. The base is undefended; you can walk right in. If you need more incentive, there's always Renard's five million dollars.

A military helicopter might draw some attention.

All those people, Michael. Millions will die.

It's not my fault.

"Michael, what are we going to do?" Greeley hissed again. "You better make up your mind where we're goin'."

"We're going to land. You got my gun handy?"

"Uh-huh."

"Mr. Secretary," said the pilot loudly. "How you doin' back there?"

"OK," said Grasso, moving up toward the front.

"Say Morena, you want to come here for a second? I want to make sure this is the right place," said O'Connell. Fleming came with her. "The airfield is straight up ahead," he said, adding quickly in pidgin French, "*Sois prêt. Dans la merde.*" Roughly: Be ready; we're in the shit.

"*Pourquoi?*"

O'Connell glanced back at Fleming, as if just realizing that he was there. "I'm going to put down at the far end of the field," he said, adding, "*Prends ta brindille*"—have your twig ready. The word for gun—*canon*—was too obvious.

"What did you say?" It was Fleming.

"I'm telling her I'm not sure what we're going to find there," said O'Connell.

"They're trying to reach us," said Greeley, poking O'Connell on the shoulder as if on cue. But he hadn't invented the distraction—a controller was asking them where they were going.

"That's a pretty good question, isn't it?" O'Connell said to Greeley, clicking on his mike. "*Salaam aleikum,*" he told the controller, using the standard Muslim greeting and continuing with a short sentence in Urdu announcing literally that he "wanted to be landing now." He was screwing up his tenses and he knew it—he switched to English, retrieving the cover story Renard had supplied to announce he was with CNN. An Australian reporter, mate.

"Who the hell's gonna think we're Australian?" prompted Greeley.

"You can do better?"

"Geez, you shoulda stuck with French."

The controller, meanwhile, said that they did not have

clearance and could not land. The airport had been ordered closed by the army.

"Thanks, sport," said O'Connell cheerfully. He killed the radio as the controller began asking for details of his flight.

The airstrip lay at the top of a plateau a few hundred yards away, unlit but clearly visible in the early morning light. Two rows of dark brown Quonset huts marked the near edge of the installation. Hangar buildings and a squat tower lay between them, dark shadows.

"Couple of two-engined transports parked next to the strip," said Greeley. "But I can't see anything on the runway. Doesn't look like anybody's awake yet."

O'Connell brought the chopper in toward the huts, trying to get an idea of what might be going on. He didn't necessarily have to land here; he had enough fuel to fly for another hour. But to where?

"Truck on the road," said Greeley. "Shit—"

A bullet ricocheted off the thick side windshield as O'Connell hit the gas. Now *these* guys weren't firing blanks—the bullet took a good chunk out of the supposedly bulletproof glass.

A squad of men poured out of the truck as O'Connell pulled away. "Fleming, what the hell is going on down there?" he shouted.

"This is a CIA trap, you bastard," said the Pakistani.

"Bullshit," said O'Connell, but his effort at logical argument was dampened by the cold chop of Fleming's M-16 slamming into his neck. The helicopter responded to the involuntary jerk of his body, whipping sharply to the left, out of control. There was a flash and a loud boom beside him. Greeley fired twice more as the rear compartment exploded with the rapid burst of Morena's Mini-14.

If the Aérospatiale had had its wheels out, they would have scraped through the shingles of the small hut in their path. As it was, O'Connell barely wrestled the helicopter level when he came under fire once again. The chopper started fluttering; shutting out the commotion that continued around him O'Connell whirled the bird around, killing the safety on the cannon and squeezing the trigger even before the HUD cued the weapon ready. His first shots tore up the macadam. O'Connell's forefinger tightened as he pushed the faltering engine with his left hand for all the power it had left, his path now smashing the bullets straight through the truck.

Morena, meanwhile, opened the rear door and emptied an M-16 magazine as O'Connell banked the helicopter around, back toward the airstrip.

"Oh my God," said Greeley as the truck exploded in a fireball. The chopper shuddered with the shock wave. From the corner of his eye O'Connell saw two men engulfed in flames leaping from the back of the truck.

There was no doubt this time that the bullets that had been fired were real; he was rapidly losing oil pressure.

"What's the situation back there?" he yelled.

"We're OK," Morena shouted in his ear. "One of those planes is Nizam's. She keeps it gassed up."

"Where's Grasso?"

"I'm right here." He leaned forward, an M-16 in his hands. "You OK?"

"Yeah," said O'Connell. "We're going down, though."

The gear stuttered out as O'Connell managed to get the helicopter into a rough autorotation, the engine dead. He glided over a hangar building, aiming to come down beside the two-engined Fokker F-27 marked out with official insignias. Behind him, Morena pushed the bodies of the dead commandos over, looking for ammo. The helicopter stunk of death.

O'Connell had his headset and restraints off and was ready to leap out as they touched down. "Let's go, Greeley," he said. "It's your turn now."

"Wait. Listen to this—"

Greeley took off his headphones and held one side to O'Connell's ear. A civilian radio broadcast was announcing that the military had taken over the country, arresting defeatist elements in the government. The Indians were being given an ultimatum: If they were not completely withdrawn from Pakistani soil by noon, a terrible counterattack would be launched.

"What is it?" demanded Grasso.

"There's been a coup," said O'Connell. "My bet is the princess was one of the people they moved against. Let's get the hell out of here."

Morena was on the tarmac already, smacking her fist on Greeley's window, telling them to hurry. Her face was flushed, dark red, as if a devil had taken over her body.

The broadcast's threat could mean only one thing— Golden Bear. Nizam's plane would get them to the base, but there was no way of knowing what they would find there, or even if they'd make it in time.

The best thing to do was take this plane and get the hell out of the country. He'd rescued the secretary of state, for Christ's sake—that ought to be worth something.

Millions of people would die . . .

O'Connell found himself at the edge of a tornado, running toward the plane. Morena, the secretary and Greeley were a few yards ahead of him, heading for the plane's open door.

He had almost reached it when he realized he was going to the Golden Bear base. He turned back to the helicopter for the assault team's weapons.

The dark interior felt like a tomb. Blood covered the floor, and the air was still heavy with the gases expelled from the cartridges that had killed Nizam's men. Fleming sat upright against the far wall, surprise pasted on his lifeless face.

O'Connell picked up an M-16, then saw a bazooka-style Chinese weapon and its ammo pack stowed at the far end of the compartment. He wrestled with the straps, still holding the rifle in one hand, as if the commandos might come back to life. The ammo case was so heavy he had to drag it past the bodies, clutching the launcher in one hand and the rifle in the other. He lowered it out gingerly, but then had to drag it across the concrete.

O'Connell had just reached the Fokker's rear stairway when a burst of rifle fire caught him from behind, knocking him flat to the ground. Two bullets tore through his right arm, which dangled momentarily and then crashed to the ground, heavy with pain. He managed to turn and somehow position the M-16 to fire, raking the field behind him.

With great difficulty, he stood and fired again, burning the clip. He reeled backward, into Morena's arms.

"You've killed them, come on," she said. Her voice was soft again, but her eyes belonged to a demon.

"Get this into the plane," said O'Connell, tugging at the ammo pack. He dropped his rifle and managed to throw the bazooka through the open door.

"We've got a problem," she said, but she didn't explain as she grabbed at the pack to hoist it aboard. She was strong but it was too heavy for her to lift without him helping. It took supreme concentration, a flailing effort from his wounded arm, and when the metal knapsack fell into the plane he felt a rush of dizziness seize him by the temples. As he crawled into the Fokker, pain clamped down on his forehead, his eyes shut in agony.

He opened them into the death gaze of a young Pakistani soldier sprawled on the cabin floor, pistol in his hand.

"Come on, come on," said Morena. "You've got to fly this thing."

"What do you mean?" groaned O'Connell. "Let Greeley."

"He can't."

The thought of the old man he'd gradually befriended being killed wrenched O'Connell harder than the bullets had. Weighted with sadness as well as pain he made his way into the cockpit, where the secretary of state was leaning from the copilot's seat into the middle of the console—helping Greeley, who was setting up the controls.

"Greeley!"

"Which one of these goddamn switches turns on the engine?"

"You're alive?"

"Come on, which one starts the damn engines?"

"How the hell do I know?" A rush of indignation momentarily restored his strength. "You're the pilot."

"I never said I was a pilot."

"Here," said Grasso, pushing a switch. The propellers spun but the plane didn't start.

"There's the fuel," said Greeley, stabbing the buttons

near the starter and opening the fuel lines. The cockpit gear was labeled in German.

"What the hell do you mean you're not a pilot?"

The plane bumped forward as both engines roared to life. Greeley had already loosened the brakes; the Fokker moved out toward the runway on its own.

"I never said I was a pilot. You asked if I could fly a B-50. I can."

"What the hell are you talking about?"

"I was a navigator in a B-50. Your records were wrong." Greeley struggled with the wheel, trying to get the plane to turn. The Fokker didn't seem too sure about what it wanted to do, skidding and sliding as Greeley played with the throttles, trying to smooth the engines. "The air force screwed me out of my slot because I was black."

"What do you mean, the air force screwed you?" said O'Connell.

"My brother owns a Beechcraft," said Grasso. "Maybe I can help."

But Greeley was too busy to hear. He pulled his wing flaps down into takeoff position and got the plane to stutter to a half stop on the end of the runway by standing on the brakes.

"Get this thing moving," yelled Morena from the back. "We've got company."

"Let me see this," said O'Connell. "You got to put the throttle full." He reached for it, then yelped with pain.

"Sit back," commanded Greeley, pushing him roughly with his arm. "Too many people telling me what to do. I can handle it if you all just sit back."

O'Connell fell into the flight engineer's seat directly behind the pilot. The plane started moving again as Greeley let up on the brakes and goosed the engines. They swerved across the runway, onto the apron. The pop of small arms fire began outside, followed by the now familiar staccato of Morena's Mini.

"Just push the throttle open all the way and pull back," said O'Connell. He knew the rudiments of flying. He could get them up; it was in his memory somewhere.

"Yeah, yeah, I know that part," said Greeley. The plane began bumping forward, picking up speed.

"Pull up, pull up or you'll hit the truck," shouted Grasso. "Pull up!"

For the first time in his life, O'Connell's memory failed him. He tried to lean forward, gripping Greeley's seat. "Set the flaps," he advised uselessly as the plane stumbled into the air. It shook like all hell, its airspeed dangerously low. They were taking shots in the fuselage.

"Does something say 'landing gear?' O'Connell, which one of these goddamn switches is for the gear?"

He scanned the console near the center hump. His head shot through with pain as he extended his arm. Greeley caught the cue and pulled the gear in. The plane lifted a bit, steadied itself.

"OK, OK," said Greeley. "I got it."

"Set a course due north. We're looking for a really huge river," said O'Connell, slipping back into his chair.

"Where are we going?" asked Grasso.

"We have another mission," O'Connell grunted. He looked up and Morena's eyes appeared, soft now, the wildness back in its hiding place deep within her soul.

"It hurts like a son-of-a-bitch," he told her.

Thano-Mikhi Airstrip, Pakistan. 5:45 A.M.

Even more than sleep, Khan wanted to take a bath. A really long bath that would soak through his skin and waterlog his bones.

Members of the Kamra development team had flown into the small, desert-steppe air base the night before to act as his ground crew. He turned the Leopard over to them, spent thirty seconds looking for the missing intelligence officer who was supposed to debrief him, then decided he had other priorities.

Thano-Mikhi was a tiny outpost, so insignificant that Khan had never even been here before. Four ancient F-86 Sabres—the same type the United States had used in the

Korean War—sat in the middle of the paved hangar area. As far as Khan could tell, they were the only jets besides the Leopard here. The Sabres, gleaming in the morning sun, had their tops up and seemed to be waiting for their pilots, Sidewinders on their wingtips and drop tanks strapped next to their bellies.

He shuddered at the prospect of flying one of them against even the oldest Indian MiG. The F-86s had been mothballed before Khan ever joined the air force, but obviously no one was checking birth certificates right now.

Khan figured he would pop his head into the administrative building to see if someone could show him the way to a tub. His skin was already opening its pores in anticipation as he entered the corrugated steel building.

"Major Khan, I was just coming to collect you," boomed a voice halfway down the hall.

The pilot's eyes took a second to adjust to the dim inside light. A three-star army general walked toward him, a broad, fake smile on his face.

"I am General Dara," said the man. "I have orders for your next mission."

"Sir?"

"The Snow Leopard has been placed under my personal command for Operation Disposer. You will follow my orders until it is complete."

Follow the orders of an army general?

"I am a member of the governing committee," continued the general, noticing Khan's apprehension. "There has been a change in the government; Commander Fazal is now the head of state. I do not think it necessary to show you my credentials, but if you wish—" Dara reached into his breast pocket and retrieved a letter, holding it out to Khan as if their ranks were reversed.

Khan read quickly. Addressed to all military personnel, the letter stated that certain steps were being taken to facilitate the successful conclusion of the conflict with India. It was signed by three people—General Fazal, the head of the military and the de facto head of the country; General Chenab, his personal representative to the cabinet; and Dara.

"I trust you will follow my orders now without delay," said the general. "Your plane is being refueled now."

"Where is my cousin?"

"Your cousin has other duties to attend to," said the general. "Do not worry about Nur," added Dara quickly, seeing Khan's shocked reaction. "He is fine. Things are unsettled at the moment. We have a job to do, and it must be carried out quickly."

"Am I going back into India?"

"No," said Dara. "You are to provide combat air patrol for three very special planes. Your cousin told you there was a second part to your mission, did he not?"

Khan nodded.

"I will arrange to have him contact you when this phase is done," said Dara, slipping his arm around the young man's shoulder and leading him outside. "He will be very proud that you have done so well. He is busy at the moment—you know your cousin, always in the thick of things."

Khan tried to remember if Dara's name had ever figured into any of Nur's diatribes. For once he regretted not paying more attention to his cousin's political preoccupations.

Had his cousin been sacked, or worse? Or was what the general saying essentially true? Nur had a great many concerns, helping to run the entire air force; he might not be able to spare time for his cousin, no matter how important the mission.

"Is something wrong, son?"

"I'm very tired sir," said Khan, squinting in the sunlight. "I could use a good rest. And a bath."

"I'm afraid there's no time for that," said the general, nodding to two MPs who met them outside the door. They were dressed in full combat gear, their rifles at the ready. "These men will take you to some breakfast. Perhaps a shower can be arranged." He looked at his watch. "You must be in the air no later than eight A.M. In the meantime, security is of the utmost. Talk to no one. If someone accosts you in any manner, these men will kill him."

The general's sober eyes dismissed any possibility that he was joking.

"Am I a prisoner?"

The general smiled indulgently. "You are a very important person, Major Khan. You are a war hero and the only Pakistani who can fly the Snow Leopard. In a few hours, you will be flying the most crucial mission of your life. In the meantime, nothing must interfere with your success. Have faith, Major," added Dara. "Remember the scripture."

Khan looked at him blankly.

"A great army is gathering against us," recited the general. "For us, God is enough, and He is the best Disposer of affairs."

Over Central Pakistan. 6:15 A.M.

Gradually, O'Connell's eyes regained their focus. He'd been hit by two bullets, both in his shoulder. Morena wedged cloth over them, taping bandages tightly over his back to stop the bleeding. When the color returned to his face, she took the shirt she'd been using to brush his head and rubbed it against her own neck, as if its sticky dampness might somehow refresh her.

"Michael, where are we going?"

"It's near Gilgit," he replied, his voice low but steady. "It looks like a junkyard."

"We can't just go in there without support."

"The plan was for minimal defenses. Anything else would have made it easy to detect," said O'Connell, trying to find a position on the stiff vinyl engineer's chair that might be comfortable. Every so often the plane bucked a little, and his face flashed with pain. "If we surprise them, we can be gone before they know what's happening."

"How do we get away?"

"Greeley, here," groaned O'Connell as he tapped the pilot's seat next to him, "is going to fly us."

"Oh great."

Greeley looked over at her with a stony imperiousness. "We're in the air now, aren't we?"

She shook her head. "We can't risk the secretary."

"Risk me for what?"

"The Paks have nukes," said O'Connell. "And they have three planes to deliver them. We're going to the base to stop them."

"We can have the base bombed," said Morena. She could feel her cheeks flush as she stared into O'Connell's eyes. I'm in charge here, she told herself. I'm the one with the responsibility. My first duty is to return the secretary of state, alive. All we have to do is tell them where the bombs are. This is my call, and I'm making it.

And yet she didn't seem capable of overruling him.

"Michael, this won't work. Let's have the base bombed."

"It's too late," said O'Connell. "Their broadcast means they're ready to go. Even if the U.S. had bombers nearby, they'd launch as soon as they were detected. This at least is one of their planes, and civilian. We can get through."

"We can have fighters shoot them down."

"Once they're in the air they're invisible. That's the whole point."

"Are you telling me the Pakistanis have nuclear weapons?" Grasso leaned toward them. His face was almost pure white, its skin so taut his jaw and cheekbones looked as if they would burst through his face. But his voice had a deep, authoritative tone. Beside him, Greeley looked as if he'd just been punched in the stomach.

"Yes, sir," said O'Connell. "They've converted three old bombers to carry the weapons."

"How do you know this?"

"The agency helped build the planes. I helped."

"You helped?"

"The planes, not the bombs. I was under orders."

"Jesus Christ."

"The base isn't guarded," O'Connell told Grasso. "Not the strip itself. If we land on the runway where the planes are, all we'll have to deal with are a few mechanics. By the time the security troops get there, we'll be in the plane. I know the layout.''

''You know what the layout was two years ago,'' said Morena, trying to regain control of the conversation. ''They may have changed it since then.''

''Those old planes would be sitting ducks against a fighter,'' said Greeley. His voice was steady, though a trace of shock remained on his face.

''They're outfitted with high-tech gear that masks their radar signature to make them look harmless,'' said O'Connell. ''They pretend to be something else—they can dial in a dozen or more different planes. To the Indians, the B-50 will look like one of their own transports. Once they're close, they'll use something to confuse the ground radars. Considering they only need a minute or two, it's not that difficult. They may have had spies plant jamming devices, or run conventional bombing missions somehow, I'm not sure. But the planes work. You have to get up very close to see what they really are. That's why we have to stop them.''

O'Connell's righteousness angered her. ''If you were so committed to stopping them, why didn't you tell Stockman where they were?''

''I told you. He didn't want to know. Besides, I did—they're near Gilgit. It's not like there's a hell of a lot up there. The analysts see them every day. They're right out in the open.''

He was acting now as if he were truth and justice personified, and she knew that was baloney. At a minimum, she wanted him to admit he'd been wrong. And yet she wanted to help him; she had to.

''If there's a way we can stop those bombs,'' said Grasso, ''we have to try.''

Morena turned to him. ''Mr. Secretary—''

''No, this is more important,'' said Grasso. ''Much more important.''

White House Situation Room, EOB. 9 P.M., EST.

The room quieted immediately as the president, accompanied by his son and two secret service agents, strode quickly from the doorway to his seat at the large round table. The room, located in the basement of the Executive Office Building, had only recently been refurbished. Outfitted to serve as the central command headquarters of the U.S. government, it had an impressive array of the newest gadgetry. Each place at the circular table held two small cathode-ray tubes. With the help of a hard-wired panel of controls and a miniature keyboard, the display could be tied into a wide variety of commands, including NSOC and NOIWON, the highly secure national intelligence networks.

As the president sat down, he turned to the national security director and said in a sharp voice, "Let's go." Morse directed everyone's attention to the computer screens, telling them to switch into channel three, where two lists of top-ranking Pakistani military officers appeared on the screen—those believed behind the coup, and those likely to oppose it. The gist of Morse's comments—Stockman had seen a contingency assessment a week ago that was behind much of the director's thinking—was that the top army officers did not command respect outside their ranks. If the civilian government acted quickly to bring in major families not connected with them, the coup would collapse.

The DDO only half listened, turning instead to watch the president, who seemed to be taking the measure of each of his assembled aides. D'Amici spent a few moments sizing up each man (there were only two women, both low-ranking assistants). Without exception, they seemed not to notice the president's gaze. D'Amici made some mental calculation before moving on to the next person in the circle. He would nod slightly, as if adding their thoughts to the total in his head.

The president worked his way around the table counterclockwise as Morse briefly turned the floor over to a State Department analyst who had just spoken with the ambassador in Islamabad. The DDO glanced briefly at his video display, which now flashed an order of battle in two columns, again dividing the Pakistan military establishment into rebels and loyalists. It was safer to keep his eyes here, to avoid the president's. But for some reason that he couldn't explain even to himself, he looked up just as D'Amici came to him.

The reproach he expected was not there. Nor was there a glimpse of betrayal or even hurt. The president's eyes were easily held; in a moment he nodded as he had with the others, and turned to the next man, one of the air force generals who had prepared the interception plan.

Had he been given a reprieve? Stockman felt an uncontrollable rush of childish joy. Perhaps he would not have to resign; perhaps some lesser penance could be arranged. When the discussion changed from the coup to the atomic weapons and it was his turn to detail the interception plan (which the president had already approved), the words practically tripped out of his mouth.

"As you can see from the map on display channel two, our patrols are now on station to cover the southern and central territory of the country; the last component should arrive within the hour. Our problem is limited fighter coverage." The DDO pushed a button on his keyboard, which superimposed two circles showing the farthest reaches of the fighter patrols the air force had placed on standby. "The far northern mountains around Gilgit cannot be reached comfortably in our present configuration. We have some options," said Stockman, his voice slipping more and more into its familiar rote. He could be giving his yearly introductory address to new farmhands, not presenting the most important—and possibly the last—National Security Council briefing of his life.

There were three recommendations for further action. One was that one of the B-2 squadrons on standby be ordered to proceed into Pakistan and bomb the most likely targets before they could be confirmed as Golden Bear sites. The second was that the Indians be informed of Golden Bear's existence and offered help in locating it, essentially tying them into the American effort. The third called for the fighters to shift their orbits well inside Pakistani territory, which would involve moving tankers and their accompanying escorts as well. The options were not mutually exclusive; in fact, Stockman expected all to be in play.

Nodding at his air force companions, the DDO stood back and waited for the barrage of questions not only about the operation but about the Pakistani bomb program. Though word of the weapons had begun making its way through the government the moment he'd called the president, this was the first time the person responsible was actually available to give the details.

He wasn't responsible. He had inherited the project. He had, in fact, tried to stop it. He had done, was doing, the right thing. He didn't deserve to be punished, not severely.

He'd forgiven O'Connell for his involvement; he, too, should be forgiven.

Instead of the onslaught Stockman expected, there was silence. The only question came from the president himself, and it caught him off guard.

"What about the secretary of state?"

"I honestly don't know, sir," he replied. He hadn't bothered checking the last update from New Delhi, realizing that if there were any real news he would have been telephoned directly. "I—the operation should have been launched last night, but I haven't, uh, been able to get a report yet. Bill Guyton is keeping tabs on that, and he hasn't had anything to report."

"I don't want that lost sight of," said the president, who then turned to Morse. "That still has a high priority."

Stockman nodded. The president didn't seem angry, just adamant that his friend be rescued.

By now, he was almost certainly dead. Morena had probably been sent on a wild goose chase.

"What's your recommendation?"

"That we adopt all three options. With the coup, there's a good possibility that the planes will be put into action. If we bring the Indians in right away, we may be able to prevent retaliation—assuming we can down the plane or catch it on the ground."

"It may just give them an excuse to use whatever chemical and biological weapons they have stockpiled," suggested the secretary of defense, Robert Stone.

"We may provoke the Pakistanis further," said one of the

State Department representatives.

"I have already assured the Pakistani prime minister that we will work to preserve his government," said D'Amici. He put his hand up, cutting off any debate. "All of our resources are to be devoted to preserving the elected government."

"What if the coup leaders are in charge of the nuclear project?" asked the secretary of defense.

"I'm assuming they are," said D'Amici. "The prime minister knew nothing about it when we spoke."

Stockman realized that the president shared his assessment of the coup—its plans included launching the doomsday attack. If that were correct, the planes might already be on their way.

"As far as the Indians are concerned," continued D'Amici, "I'm willing to take a gamble. I know Ramma Rhabid, the new prime minister. His son studied in America with Andrew." The president turned to his own son, who served as his personal assistant, standing behind him. "He's a man of deep convictions, and he believes in peace. I see little alternative."

"Can he hold the rest of the country with him?" Stone asked.

"If he couldn't, there wouldn't have been a cease-fire," said Morse. "Nor, I think, would it have lasted."

"It's definitely a risk," agreed the president. "But at this point it's a risk we have to take. It's a way of demonstrating our goodwill to the Indians. If they retaliate, not only will both countries be destroyed, but there is a good possibility that China will use the raid as a pretext for military action. I assume you are aware of the satellite intelligence detailing their troop movements."

The discussion continued for several minutes, with some questions about Indian capabilities, and debate about what the Chinese and Russians were really up to. There were a few pointed remarks about what other programs the Pakistanis and Indians might have hidden. Stockman's boss deflected them. The DDO had never really cared for Walter Jablow, but he had to admit that the head of the agency was staunchly though subtly defending the institution and his people, Stockman especially. Jablow had taken Stockman's confession well; his only comment was, "Let's get it fixed."

As the meeting rushed toward its conclusion, the DDO found his thoughts centering on the president. Certainly in the context of the agency's history, Stockman's sins had been minor. He had striven to take care of the mess; his error was not alerting the president to it when the new administration took over. In fact, that could now be seen as a definite asset; the president could truthfully tell the Indians (and Congress, if it came to that) that he had known nothing about it.

Perhaps Stockman wouldn't have to resign. Perhaps he could accept another assignment, outside the agency, exile to a trade commission or something, and begin working his way back from there. Perhaps he could even stay in place—look at how Gates had rehabilitated his reputation after Iran.

There were countless other examples. Stockman rose at the end of the meeting, filled with new hope—and determined to find out—to prove—that his optimism was justified. When he had called the president, he had offered his resignation; D'Amici hadn't said anything. Now he would humbly offer it again. He sensed that the president would scold him severely but tell him, at least temporarily, to stay put. Stockman was too critical to the present plans to just leave.

Any reprieve, no matter how temporary, would be a sign that he might eventually return to grace. And he would make the most of that chance. He was so grateful. The fact that the president had let him lead the solution teams was a sign that he still valued him, even trusted him. No matter the penance, the DDO would perform it.

"Mr. President," Stockman said as D'Amici rose to leave. "Sir?"

D'Amici motioned with his finger to wait, then turned to give his son some instructions. The rest of the room emptied quickly through the other doors; with the exception of the Secret Service bodyguards, the president and the DDO were alone when Andrew left.

Stockman felt his heart pound rapidly in his chest. He could remember only one other time when he was this physically nervous. It was in Saigon; a Red agent had been holding a pistol three inches from his chest.

He got out of that, too.

"Sir, I wanted to say that my résumé, my resignation I mean—" his heart pounded so hard his throat shook. "My resignation will be on your desk in the morning."

"I expect it there before you leave tonight," said the president, turning and leaving Stockman alone in the darkened room.

Northeast of Gilgit. 8:45 A.M.

At first, Greeley kept his eyes dead ahead, straight on where he was aiming, tilting the wings as he came around the mountainside. His hands were locked on the wheel so tightly that the veins in his forearms stood out.

As O'Connell described it, the complex where they were to land consisted of two sections with separate facilities and runways. Side by side but separated by marsh and a mine field, the bases looked like a pair of junkyards, and in fact had been. The portion that would be on their left as they approached had a concrete runway and housed an assortment of inoperable wrecks, as well as the small contingent of men assigned to the project. They would call the tower, act like they were landing there, then veer off and head for the other strip, a packed dirt runway that O'Connell predicted would be flanked with even older and more disheveled planes.

"Let's get this show going," said O'Connell as they cleared the mountain and the outlines of the first runway came into view in the distance. He reached over from behind and took Greeley's headset. Wincing as he leaned to tune the radio, he cleared his throat and then harangued the controller in Urdu as if they were having problems. O'Connell then switched to English—speaking in what he apparently hoped might pass, over the radio at least, as a very excited Pakistani accent. O'Connell said he was from the Ministry of Energy, repeating the name Munir Ahmed Khan several times.

Greeley pulled the plane's right wing up higher and shot a glance at his ultimate destination. A few wrecks lay scattered in weeds on the sides, most so discombobulated it was difficult to tell that they had ever been airplanes. An old corrugated steel hangar sat at the far end, with some black shadows in front. A glint of sunlight reflected off the top of the hulks, a golden glint.

Three glints. The planes were at the end of the runway.

O'Connell saw them too. "Son of a bitch," he said. "They're ready to go."

Greeley eased the Fokker through a thirty-degree turn, moving his feet carefully and holding the wheel more gingerly now. Just as O'Connell had said, there was a long concrete strip on his left, lined by weatherworn buildings. And a pair of spent Starfighters on the grass. Jesus, he hadn't seen those babies in years.

"They stuck to the plan so far," said O'Connell. He leaned over the secretary of state, putting his head practically on the windshield. "We can do this."

"What are they saying?" asked Grasso.

"They're asking embarrassing questions," answered O'Connell. He steadied himself in the aisle and began talking into the microphone excitedly, switching between languages—he might be inventing new ones, for all Greeley knew—saying there had been a fire in one of the engines.

"Make a pass at the main airfield," O'Connell told him, "then loop around and land on the other. Get us as close to the planes as you can. Morena and I will come out shooting—when things quiet down, you and the secretary run like hell for the closest bomber."

O'Connell threw down the headset and disappeared in the back with Morena.

"You OK?" asked Grasso.

"I can get it in." Greeley knew he didn't sound as confident as he intended.

"All you have to do is just hold us steady," said the secretary of state reassuringly.

340

"Let me make sure I know where I am." Greeley pulled the plane to the right. His hands were too heavy on the controls—the Fokker banked so sharply that for a second he thought he'd lost control. But the plane was very forgiving, and he nudged it back, easing off the throttle.

No way he was going to get this down right. There were so many things to remember—what did he do with the flaps? God, and he thought he could fly a B-50?

"Just make a nice easy turn and head in straight for the runway," said Grasso. "Then do another circle and land. I'll get the wheels out and watch your speed for you."

Greeley complied silently.

"There's a bit of a wind from the west," said Grasso as Greeley lined up for the fake approach. "There's a flag fluttering down there."

Greeley felt his stomach curdling as he brought the plane in. When Grasso lowered the landing gear he thought he'd made a fatal error, drag slamming him and the wheel starting to shake. But his reflexes were solid; he throttled and had his airspeed back up before the stall warning could sound. He focused on the small patch of concrete yawing in his window, realizing he was too high for a landing but that was OK, because he was just faking it, pushing his body to the left and then back to the right, taking the plane with it, turning.

"You're too high if you come in like this."

"I know," snapped Greeley. But he was already into his approach; no time to do it again. Dead quiet where he was going, two or three people working on the beautiful old planes at the other end. Longer wings, they'd done something to the wings. The engines looked weird too. Not to mention the paint job.

"You have to slow way down."

Greeley's hands trembled. There was no turning back.

Too fast, too fast. Stop, stop.

He pushed his eyes into the dirt and the plane followed, bumping, coughing, wheezing, the plane unsteady, very unsteady, the wind picking up unexpectedly and he couldn't compensate.

Jesus Christ, hold it. This is your only chance, don't blow it.

A tumult of colors in slow motion, a spinning jumble of shapes that hit against each other, realigning the universe.

But no sound. A second of weightlessness, then a hard thump and pain.

His head bloated by the onrush of blood, O'Connell momentarily forgot where he was. The plane had come in too fast and then braked unevenly, pirouetting in a wild dance down the fortuitously wide runway. The starboard landing gear collapsed, a blessing in a way, since it helped slow the plane and paradoxically made its path straighter. As they came to a stop, O'Connell shook off the dizziness and undid his restraints, wobbling a little but grabbing hold of Morena, who was already struggling with the door.

"Wait a second. Let me get my head clear." He knelt on the floor, his shoulder throbbing. Morena said nothing. "You two all right?" he called to the front.

"Yeah," answered Grasso. "We're about twenty yards to the closest plane. I don't see anyone yet."

"Wait for us to clear the way," yelled O'Connell. Morena looked down at him expectantly. "Give me your gun and you work the rocket," he told her. "I can't hold it." He took the Mini-14 from her with his left hand, then turned and looked out a window on the other side. "Let's do this— you open the door and wave, like people are hurt—I'll jump them from the other side."

"How?"

"I'm going this way," said O'Connell. He held his breath, kicked open the emergency door and found himself rolling in the dirt, his shoulder pounding. He could hear shouting, Morena's door popping open.

She was yelling as he pulled himself around the back of the plane, crouching low. Sirens were sounding. They'd send a rescue crew and vehicles from the other half of the base, send everything they had, but it would take a couple of minutes, driving the long road around.

O'Connell had convinced them that safety lay in the ability to fool the Indians—and everyone else. It was the Purloined Letter defense: Make things as innocuous as possible, no big installation, no easily detectable defensive measures. It had worked, too—the CIA had spent millions in satellite reconnaissance without being able to figure out where the base was. But the Pakistanis hadn't counted on being attacked by the person who'd given them the idea. They were vulnerable now, ridiculously vulnerable—only two soldiers were among the half-dozen men running toward the Fokker.

O'Connell let them get practically to the plane before opening up, taking them from the rear first, killing the two soldiers and knocking the rest of the men down. The clip was empty in a matter of seconds.

"All right, all right," Morena was shouting. "Come on, come on."

He threw the Ruger down and ran to one of the soldiers, grabbing his rifle and wedging it into the crook of his left arm. More people started firing from across the way—there were more here than he thought. A truck emerged from behind one of the buildings.

There was a loud hiss behind him, followed by a sound like a bottle rocket, then an explosion. The truck erupted in flames.

"Take out the two airplanes on the end," O'Connell yelled to Morena. The blast of the rocket launcher had knocked her back against the plane and she struggled to regain her firing position. Grasso and Greeley emerged from the front, both of them carrying automatic rifles. "Get in the plane," shouted O'Connell, waving them toward the nearest B-50.

Another whoosh. A tremendous explosion—the plane farthest away exploded.

No, it was a fuel truck next to the plane. Flames erupted up a gas line, then the plane itself ignited, debris blowing into the B-50 next to it.

O'Connell opened his mouth and realized it was full of dirt. He was lying on his back, knocked off his feet by the shock wave from the explosion. There was gunfire in the bomber nearest him. The two others were on fire.

"Morena, Morena," he called to the sky. "Get going. Go."

He felt something tugging him, saw her face.

"I'm not leaving you," she said.

"I'm not staying."

He was on his feet, running to the plane, clutching the M-16 in his left arm. If he still had a right arm, he couldn't feel it—his whole side was numb, a block of wood he dragged along.

Out of the corner of his eye he saw figures running toward them. He wheeled and let off a burst. It hit harmlessly into the dirt, but it sent the men scrambling.

Crouching, he took better aim.

A loud rumble ignited behind him. For a second he thought the last B-50 had caught fire, that he would die here.

But it was just the engines catching.

More soldiers. O'Connell started firing blindly, ignoring Morena's shouts to get in the plane.

The moment he popped his head up into the cockpit, Greeley wanted to cry. And it wasn't remorse for the three men sprawled in the crew compartment where Grasso had shot them.

As originally built, the B-50 cockpit was a mass of levers and dials, the latest in 1940s technology. Essentially a B-29 on steroids, the plane was a far cry from the dial-a-ride, computer-assisted sleds that now rule the skies. The "greenhouse"—the entire front end was glass, giving the plane unrivaled visibility—could feel cramped, but most crews grew to like the togetherness as well as the view. That was how Greeley had learned to fly. Sitting behind the pilot, he had absorbed each pull of the lever, each maneuver, down to the shifting of weight as the pilot strained to pull the big plane into a turn. It would take him only a second to remember how those sticks worked.

But as he climbed into the cabin, his nostalgia was replaced with panic. There were no more sticks and long levers; the controls had been thoroughly modernized. Even the normally wide-open passage between the pilot's and copilot's seats that led to the bombardier's station up front was filled by a half-height panel of video displays.

Grasso, his rifle still clutched in his hands, stood to one side as Greeley stepped over the dead Pakistani crew and fell into the plush pilot's seat feeling old and ancient. He might just as well be in the cockpit of the space shuttle.

"Oh God, Olissa," he said softly. "Oh God."

Not only were the wings outside black, they'd been lengthened considerably. And instead of the four-bladed supercharged prop engines, there were four slimmer but even longer turbo jobs with five thin variable-pitch propellers mounted in front of an identical, counterrotating set. Rocket boosters were attached outboard. This was as different from the plane he'd flown in as the Fokker was.

"What's wrong?" asked Grasso, climbing into the copilot's seat.

"They've changed everything around," Greeley said. "There's supposed to be levers here, not these little knobs. And look at this goddamned TV set."

"You flew the other plane," said Grasso.

Greeley looked at the unintelligible ranks of controls. He'd been stupid to think he could fly it. He should have told O'Connell everything. He should have laughed at him, showed him out the trailer door. It was a crazy man's decision to go along, a suicide wish that was about to come true.

A lunatic's chance at living out a dead dream.

"You've got to get the engines going," said Grasso.

"I don't even know how to do that."

Grasso pointed at a series of buttons. A small tape below them read IGNITION. "Look. Everything's in English."

Greeley rubbed his face with his hand, wiping some of the sweat away. On a hot night, when things between them were good, Olissa would come into the kitchen and rub his face with a fresh dish towel. And then she would kiss his neck, slowly begin rubbing his broad back.

It was obvious enough. There was a wheel for the controls. These could only be the throttles. So it went a little higher and faster. None of that would matter, really, once he got it off the ground.

He had to get off the ground. He could feel the heat from the burning plane warming his side.

There was a sudden burst of rifle fire below, right under the cockpit. Greeley's hand jumped to the buttons, hitting them in succession. There was a slow thump on his left, another on his right, then a shudder—he found the throttle and the shudder revved into a dance.

Flaps, Greeley. Find your foils. Turret locked? Hell, there is no turret anymore, or at least no switch. You've done this a hundred times. You were meant to do this. They robbed you of your chance; don't blow it now. He held the brakes with his feet.

"Tell O'Connell to pull the chocks," shouted Greeley.

"What?"

"There ought to be blocks under the wheels, holding us— we got to slide them out."

Grasso disappeared. Greeley thought he heard more firing outside, but couldn't be sure—the engines drowned out everything. The vibrations hugged him like an old friend, hugged him like Olissa might.

Adjust the throttle. You got a problem in that number three, not too smooth—probably running rich. It's out of line with the others—remember that when you fly. Memorize that difference.

Tail flap back and forth. Everything works. Path clear in front; you'll just clear the Fokker if you hold it straight.

These controls are easier than that plane you just flew. Practically an airliner. The stabilizer and trim are marked, for cryin' out loud—there's takeoff position. Like flying a textbook.

There were two sets of three toggle switches marked ROCKET ASSIST. Maybe it needed the rockets to help takeoff, even though the runway was pretty long. Must weigh a lot more. Would using them make things more difficult, or easier?

A humvee appeared at the far end of the runway, tearing toward them.

"Let's go, let's go," shouted Greeley, turning around. Grasso was clambering back into the cockpit, Morena behind him.

"There's a hundred of them. Jeeps, trucks, everything coming at us," said the secretary of state, out of breath. "There's nothing holding the wheels."

"Go, go!" O'Connell shouted from the back. "Get us out of here!"

Greeley turned back to the controls. A dozen .30-caliber machine gun bullets laced the front end of the fuselage, a few slicing straight through the cockpit. But Greeley had already plunged the ganged throttle forward, felt the roll, felt it like old times, like he'd dreamed. He closed his eyes, then opened them—the humvee seemed like it was trying to block them off. Greeley put his fingers on the rocket toggles and let them rip.

The whole world was sound. Shaking, shaking, shaking.

Pull back, James. Pull back and let it go.

He saw it in his mind, the plane stuttering with the sudden force, off a bit because he'd fired the rockets in the wrong sequence, stumbling toward the humvee, dust and fumes and hope all over the place.

The right wheel of the plane caught the canvas top of the rear part of the truck. That was no more than a minor annoyance to the remade Superfortress, eager to be in the air again. It sliced upward as a diver would slip into the water, making a graceful, reverse plunge into the blue sky, its broad wings withstanding the extra thrust, happy for it, overjoyed.

Greeley eased back, perfect, perfect, a born pilot.

"I made it, Olissa," he said aloud. "I finally made it."

Over Northern Pakistan. 8:55 A.M.

Khan shifted uneasily in the Leopard's seat. For the first time since he'd been introduced to the plane it felt claustrophobic. There was more room here than in any other fighter he'd ever flown; still he felt hemmed in, jammed under the front dash and squeezed by the side consoles. Even his helmet was tighter on his head, his ears ringing with the hollow whisper of the plane's engines.

There were eight American Amraam missiles in the Leopard's belly. The ground crew had treated them gingerly when they loaded them into the bay, and the colonel who appeared after Khan's meeting with the general said they'd cost many times their weight in gold on the black market. They were the only air-to-air weapons of their kind in Pakistan.

He had flown to a set of coordinates near Gilgit, a mountainous area in the far north of Pakistan. About fifteen minutes ahead of schedule, he was supposed to meet a trio of planes calling themselves Golden Bears 1, 2 and 3. He would fly with them to the Indian border.

After that? Dara said they would be on their own once they crossed over; he could go home and sleep.

He wished he could sleep now. More importantly, he wished he could talk to Nur to find out what was going on.

Khan scanned the horizon, then checked the heads-down display on his left keeping track of the radar as he orbited around his meeting point. Unlike last night, this mission called for him to use it to detect approaching fighters and engage them, not slink away.

It was clear. He'd picked up a small civilian airliner briefly about fifteen miles to the northeast; that had been the sole aircraft he'd even come near since taking off. All Pakistani flights had apparently been grounded, and the Indians were still observing the cease-fire. The only thing in the air was a large storm front coming down out of Afghanistan.

Dara hadn't given him any details about the planes he was to meet, not even what type they were. "They'll know who you are," said the general just before takeoff, adding cryptically, "trust only your eyes. They'll be painted black and gold."

They could only be bombers. Apocalyptic bombers.

Khan got a bogey cue over his headset as his radar smacked onto four targets—almost 150 miles away to the south, charging hard but flying below a thousand feet. His radar sorted through the ground clutter, filtering the interference and trying to identify the contacts and their heading. The flight computer was in high gear, trying to justify the millions that had been spent in its construction. Its small gallium chips were like a team of AWACS operators, sifting through the disparate signals, preparing to feed the pilot a streamlined set of information and suggestions.

But they couldn't lock on the approaching jets from this distance. Khan knew instinctively they must be Indian interceptors and turned to meet them. His heart began racing and his chest swelled to take in as much oxygen as possible. His brain demanded a rich, red flow of blood, ravenous for it; every cell in his body wanted the cool, sweet air filling his mouth and nose, anxious to hold off the effects of fatigue one more time.

Khan switched off the mapping function on the right CRT and had the computer put the radar threat detector there, leaving the Leopard's own radar scan displayed on the left.

Blank, then yellow.

Something big was poking its fingers toward him, fortunately from far away. The source was airborne—and, according to the threat identifier interpreting the signals, American.

American? The computer program spit up ''Lisa'' as the code name for the radar type, a version Khan was not familiar with. He guessed that he was looking at some sort of early warning or perhaps spy-plane radar, flying just outside Pakistani territory. His ship was too slinky for it at this range, slipping through its net like a minnow dodging a tuna trawler.

Meanwhile, the low-flying planes he'd detected held their course. As their distance closed, the Leopard's black box worked its magic. His assumption had been right—these were MiG-29s, four contacts close together and coming in very hot. He pictured a fighting wing formation, saw the Indian invaders sweeping in to shoot down his Golden Bears.

Khan slipped his stick to the right ever so gently and came to a bearing head-on toward them, their distance now approximately 175 kilometers, or just about 110 miles, and narrowing rapidly. He was still invisible to the Indians, and would remain so for two to three minutes, even as they closed, so long as they remained on passive detection.

The Amraams in his belly were the most potent weapons Khan had ever carried. True fire-and-forget missiles, they were equipped with their own radar and guidance systems, had a top speed over Mach 4 and a reliable range close to sixty miles. But he had never practiced with them; the pilot did not like the fact that everything he knew about the weapons came from a spec sheet.

The HUD targeting system snapped in and four small, triangular ghosts appeared in the bottom quadrant of his windshield, pesky little gnats waiting to be swatted. The computer counted down separate distances on all four planes—104 kilometers on the closest, a bit over 60 miles. Khan checked his airspeed, accelerating slightly. Though he was moving at 1.3 times the speed of sound, his fuel consumption was very light; the Leopard had yet to break a sweat. At this speed, the distance between himself and his targets closed by 23 miles a minute.

The HUD gave him a fire cue. Too anxious, Khan told the computer, watching it subtract the kilometers for another thirty seconds before opening the weapons bay and letting four Amraams go.

Each missile had to fire separately, rotating around on a giant rack dispenser that looked like the revolving blade of a farm thresher, made of specially treated plastics to conserve weight. Each Amraam was trundled into its position and released, the missile igniting a half second later as it fell slightly headfirst from the plane. This was a most vulnerable time, for Khan was just entering the range where the MiGs' detection systems might pick him up. He realized as he launched the third missile that he had not adopted the proper strategy to take advantage of the Leopard's stealthy technology, that he could have altered his flight path and made detection considerably more difficult. But it was too late to start relearning dogfighting tactics. He hit the switch on the armament panel to his left that closed up the weapons bay as the last missile left and rolled hard to head back toward the rendezvous point. His movements were jerky; despite the rush of blood and adrenaline and the excited messages from his brain, his muscles were still weighted with fatigue.

There was a distant contact climbing slowly to the north. No range—the radar couldn't get a solid read. But it must be one of the planes he was supposed to meet.

The CRT on the right side of his dash suddenly exploded with colors. There was all sorts of radar activity, Lisa or whatever it was getting closer.

TWO TARGETS DESTROYED, flashed the HUD.

Only two? More radars. The surviving MiGs, still coming on.

Khan's hand began to tremble as he took it from the throttle to punch up—to punch up what? The cockpit lay before him like a confused mass of an unsolved jigsaw puzzle. He began to experience vertigo, even though the horizon indicator told him he was flying steady and solid, climbing in fact, through fifty thousand feet.

The pilot was lost, his brain completely overloaded. His body floated in sweat. The plane itself jumped to five times its size, an immense, unfamiliar jumble of metal and plastic, out of his reach, much less his control.

Hir saved him. Khan's fiancée's voice seemed to magically whisper in his ear, telling him everything was OK. He took two deep breaths and refocused his eyes. He was at precisely 61,020 feet, his direction due north. The HUD painted two MiGs to his southwest in a trailing formation, one behind the other, with about a mile between them, heading straight for a small radar contact climbing into the heavens less than twelve miles away. The MiGs were either oblivious to him or ignoring him.

Khan leaned hard on the stick and opened the gates to the afterburner, supersonic air jumping through the intake as the power plants went ram and then some. He tucked the plane down in a thirty-degree angle toward the Indians' path. Within moments the trailing Fulcrum was in visual range.

Khan thumbed over to cannon mode and took a swipe just as the Indian plane lit its wick, going to afterburners to accelerate and escape the attack. The MiG ducked into a port roll and began angling away.

Khan turned his attention to the leader. He slid his radar back to air-attack and a pregnant triangle marked out his target. Two Amraams kicked out of the weapons bay just as his sensors warned that the second MiG was trying to catch him from behind.

Rocket Khan flicked his wrist and had the Fulcrum off his back easily.

Too easily. The fighter wasn't going for him at all.

The Amraams slammed home, a huge fireball replacing the first Indian plane.

The odd thing was that the MiGs seemed to be homing in on a small plane, a plane that couldn't be one of the Golden Bears. In fact, his threat identifier didn't see it as much of a threat at all—it claimed the plane was a Mush-shak, the same light observation type he'd flown in a few days before.

What was its pilot doing at 30,000 feet and still climbing? That wasn't exactly a good way to avoid a MiG.

Surely the Mushshak would have detected the approaching fighters by now. This pilot was either a fool for putting himself in such a vulnerable position, or a conscious decoy, trying to draw the MiG's fire.

In any event, Khan's duty was to his Golden Bears, not the observation plane. There might be another group of MiGs sneaking in right now.

What if it were Um, the enthusiastic pilot who had flown him to Islamabad. Could he just let him die?

Take the MiG out while you can, the voice that had calmed him before said. You have him right before you; it's easy.

It was bizarre, almost an aural hallucination—Hir seemed to be next to him, whispering in his ear.

Khan refocused himself, stared forward past the large rectangle of the HUD's ghostly projection screen. The MiG was right out in front of him, fat and outclassed. The Indian pilot didn't seem interested in attempting evasive maneuvers. He was concentrating on the Mushshak, beaming everything he had in that direction, ignoring the fleet black fighter closing off the trailing edge of his starboard wing. There was no way he couldn't know where Khan was. He was taking a suicide run.

Khan had two missiles left and a fat triangle engulfing the Fulcrum in the HUD. As he fired, the MiG jinked downward, trying at the last second to get away.

Khan continued over the Indian, which took a twisting plummet toward the earth. It fired off flares and tinsel, but the Amraams ignored them, strove in for the kill.

Not flares but missiles, coming around and picking up steam. Headed for the Mushshak.

Khan hadn't put this much energy into saving his little friend to let him go down now. He leaned on the throttle, goading the Leopard to put itself between the missiles and their target. Fortunately, he had an angle and they had to change direction; he pushed hard to cut in front. Everything in Khan's training had taught him how to avoid missiles; now he was trying to get hit by them.

Not hit, exactly. Just throw them off the scent. He swept into a turn and had the missiles dead behind. Poking his left wing over, he rolled out, sending a shower of chaff into the air.

Both weapons veered downward. One remained confused, plunging helplessly into the mountains and exploding. The other scratched its head, then decided to follow him.

Good work, he thought. Now all I have to do is save my own butt.

Khan took another roll, this one to his right, and let loose with more chaff. No dice; the Russian-made missile kept coming.

He couldn't outrun it. He had the throttle through the firewall and it was still gaining.

Chaff for one more try. It had to be something special, though.

Khan suddenly yanked the stick back, as if he were three times slower and trying to do a Cobra. The Leopard's computer flight controls did their best to follow orders, kicking out everything but the kitchen sink as the nose goosed itself upward. The plane became an unguided rock, unsure what it was supposed to do besides pull a wheelie in midair. So many g's hit Khan that he was just barely able to press the chaff button. He kept control, his body flatter than a pancake and the black edge of gravity swirling down the sides of his face.

As Khan pulled out of the resulting tumble dive free of the missile, he shot under a huge four-engined plane. Blacker than night, with wings longer than any he had ever seen, he realized it was flying where no turboprop ought to be, droning westwards at 45,000 feet. He climbed and looked over his shoulder at the plane, spotting a golden glow toward the top of the plane's fuselage.

He glanced down at the radar screen, and realized he'd found his "Mushshak."

In the Golden Bear. Apx. 9:10 A.M.

O'Connell steadied himself directly behind the pilot and copilot's seats, exhausted after helping Morena drag the bodies of the three dead crewmen out of the plane. The image of the last man falling through the round blue hole seemed burned into his retina; he closed his eyes and still saw it. The body tumbled head over heels, papers fluttering away, the wind ransacking his pockets.

Grasso reached up and put a plastic credit card over the last elliptical hole in the windshield left by the bullets. There was a sucking sound and a pop—the hiss of air stopped.

"We're maintaining cabin pressure now," said Greeley. "Looks like we can go all the way to sixty thousand feet—they've reworked this baby something terrific."

Greeley was doing a good job. They continued to climb, holding to a westerly course.

Keep going this way and they'd wind up at the airstrip where Renard was waiting.

He could land there and make five million dollars. Tell Grasso and Morena that there had been only one bomb aboard. Maybe they didn't need to know there were any bombs at all.

His head was too scrambled; it was letting him down. He turned and sank into the seat in front of the electronic warfare station, turning to the controls and trying to concentrate.

The others were practically giddy over the fact that they had escaped. Greeley launched into one of his talking jags, telling them what the air force had done to him.

"I got caught in the middle, right between segregation and integration," Greeley was saying. He had one hand on the wheel, the other draped back over the edge of the seat. He looked for all the world like an airline pilot gone slightly to seed—exactly the man O'Connell had imagined he was recruiting four days before. "There were a bunch of us who were being trained as pilots. We'd done like the preliminary tests. One day we're slotted to be pilots, the next there's orders breaking us up into new training sections. Everything got all mixed around, whether it was lost in the shuffle or what, I don't know. To make a long story short, I ended up in navigator school."

"Why didn't you complain?" asked Morena. She was sitting behind O'Connell on a small flight bench.

"It's not like I didn't say anything, but this was the fifties," said Greeley. "I was told—well, I ain't gonna tell you what I was told."

"There were black pilots in World War II," said Grasso.

"Sure, it was an emergency. Even so, they had to bust ass and prove themselves, in obsolete planes, most of the time. It wasn't easy—nothing works as smooth as they tell you in the history books. There were black pilots in Korea, too, even some of the best. But that didn't help me."

O'Connell found it more difficult to shut out Greeley's voice than the throbbing pain in his shoulder and back. He had seen extensive demonstrations of the equipment; it wasn't hard to operate in a couple of basic modes. Of the three multi-use displays in front of him controlling the radar masking system, the two on the left were dedicated to technical readouts of intercepted signals and the masked output. The third, larger than the others, displayed typed commands

355

and the radar's status. A set of white rocker switches with abbreviations next to them ran down the middle of the slanted panel directly below. The switch marked "Msk" was the only one in the row pressed down. These were radar profile presets; he didn't remember what Msk stood for (if he'd ever known) but it was a pretty easy guess that "Il-38 My" meant Ilyushin Il-38, a long-range Russian sea surveillance plane the Indians would be familiar with.

There was a red override switch at the bottom which allowed commands to be entered from the keyboard. A cheat sheet with some typical sequences had been taped to the small plastic desk space next to the keyboard. There ought to be a loose-leaf notebook somewhere with detailed coding commands—O'Connell ducked underneath the equipment ledge and practically fainted as the blood rushed to his head.

He had to struggle to get back upright in the chair. The large black display directly in front of him had one word on it, ACTIVE.

It was on. OK, that meant they'd been doing the preflight checklist.

No, that meant they'd finished it. They'd been ready to take off, pumping out the signals of an innocuous Pakistani plane in case any Indian interceptors were nearby.

O'Connell flipped frantically through the thick, plastic-covered sheets of the binder through the section covering the preflight procedure.

Activating the radar device followed arming the bombs.

Those suckers in the back were ready to go.

If his CIA briefer was correct, the bombs' primary detonation system would work on altitude. The expert had been present at the destruction of Pakistan's first generation of weapons, and though he termed them relatively primitive, he generally approved of the arming and fail-safe mechanisms, with one caveat. Once certain range conditions were met, the weapons did not have to be cut loose from the plane and its command systems to explode. "Just in case the guy gets shot down or goes unconscious at the last minute, they want it to go boom," he'd told O'Connell.

At least they were fail-safed until the plane reached a

predetermined altitude. Not only would that prevent them from exploding if there were an accident on takeoff, but the pilot's flight plan would probably call for him to fly low while still in Pakistan, rising to altitude only after crossing the border.

"Greeley—how high are we?"

"Forty-five thousand and climbing. I want to give that storm front plenty of room. Looks like a wicked one. Plane's got a hell of a climb rate, and we ain't even near the ceiling yet, according to this fancy dial. Now if this were the original—"

Once more the rush of blood from his brain as he jumped up from the chair left O'Connell dizzy.

"Are you OK, Michael?" asked Morena.

"I have to check something," he told her, pulling up on the ladder to the rear with his good arm. "Whatever you do, Greeley, you stay over those clouds."

After climbing the ladder, he pushed into the pressurized tunnel that connected the front of the plane with its bomb bay and rear sections. What was once the aft gunnery station was now stuffed with space-age electronics considerably more effective at warding off pursuers than the machine guns had ever been. The narrow crawl space that had once led to it was blocked off with a bolted access panel, but O'Connell wasn't going that far.

The refurbished bomb bay sat between the wings, only a few yards from the cockpit. Even in the dim light, the weapons were clearly visible through the scaffolding, two pregnant successors to Fat Man, the bomb dropped on Nagasaki more than fifty years before. As nuclear technology went, these bombs were not particularly impressive. They were only ten times more powerful than their American predecessor, and worked the same way—a high-explosive lens forcing fissionable plutonium to implode. But they were more than deadly enough.

A pair of thin cables slithered out of the crawl space and down to their roughened skins. On each weapon were three LEDs next to the small plug where the wires inserted. They were lit bright red.

O'Connell leaned over farther from the catwalk, grasping an aluminum strut for support. There ought to be a panel near the LEDs for the manual safe, but it was impossible to see from here.

He'd have to slide over to the end of the crawl space and stretch—maybe jump—to reach the access ladder down into the bay. No way he could do that with only one good arm. Even if he did manage somehow, he'd have to climb over the harness and stretch out over the bombs themselves to open the panel and turn the key. He'd need two hands.

He couldn't do it. But what was the alternative? The computer would not allow him to enter codes until he hit the right one. For all he knew, it might decide to detonate them there and then out of spite.

The envelope he'd seen flutter from the last body—was that the deactivation sequence?

"Michael! Michael!"

Morena's voice sounded eerie and desperate as it echoed in the plane's metallic hold. O'Connell started crawling backwards down the tunnel toward the greenhouse. He was halfway there when the plane shuddered with the sound of a muffled explosion. Moving more quickly, ignoring the surging pain of his wounds, O'Connell practically fell into the cockpit as the plane veered sharply to the right.

"There's a fighter out there," Morena said. "What are we going to do?"

Nizam's Compound. 9:15 A.M.

She had not watched them take the boy's body out. It was important to maintain her composure, and it would have been too difficult to see Jimale's limp arms drop roughly between the two soldiers, blood trailing along the floor. Instead, she went back to her quarters and changed into a more conservative *salwar kameez,* the loose trousers and tunic a dull green. Her chiffon *chunni* was the same color, furled around her neck, sedate and austere, though with a hint of defiance—it did not cover her head.

The man in charge of the assault, an army colonel who walked with the aid of a cane, told her politely that she was under arrest. The general, he added, without identifying which general he meant, would arrive shortly.

Nizam had survived other military power plays—she had once been detained for a week—but this was considerably different. If they meant merely to arrest her, they would have driven up calmly, not announced their arrival with a bombing run. Whoever was behind the coup was not overly prejudiced toward taking her alive.

There seemed little doubt that the takeover had been orchestrated by the general staff. She was not sure it would succeed; in fact, she suspected that officers in the military with whom she had some weak alliances would be maneuvering to outflank the coup leaders at this very moment. But their efforts were of little help to her.

Two guards were posted inside the door to her office. She had protested that men were not allowed in this part of the house, but the colonel only smiled apologetically, saying that these were discreet men who would do nothing to jeopardize her modesty.

In a small panel beneath her bed inside there was a long knife, reputed to be an assassin's weapon dating from the nineteenth century. Nizam was more interested in the sharpness of the blade than the historical accuracy of the tale attached to it. It was a last hope, a weapon she would use if circumstances allowed. For the moment, they did not; she kept it in reserve, a thin hedge against despair.

Murwan had given her the knife after her father's death. It had been most ceremonial, a touch of her father's flair and recognition of the need for ritual.

There were other things to think about than her aide's betrayal. The princess sat at her desk and began sorting through her papers. She assumed, she hoped, that there had been time to shred the most sensitive material in her offices at the other end of the complex. She had yet to destroy the contents of her small safe in the office. A small book inside contained the numbers of accounts that would give the military access to much of her wealth, but Nizam delayed dialing the combination that would initiate its destruction. The things inside that were truly valuable were her father's will and a few other documents relating to their now defunct state. Destroying them would be the final symbol that her family's quest had failed.

She pushed the papers on her desk aside and opened her drawer for some writing paper. One of the guards snapped to attention as she did so; she proceeded to lift the paper out slowly, staring at him the whole time. Without considering what she was doing, she began a letter to her mother, something she had hardly ever done when she was alive, let alone in the twelve years since her death.

"I wonder what you would think of my sitting here," Nizam began, and the words flowed, angry at times, more often philosophical, describing her present situation. It took several pages for the letter to become personal, for Nizam to address the woman who had held so little sway over her life. This part of the letter began with questions: Did you feel cheated of a daughter? Would you have been happier with a son? Were you proud of or repelled by my ambition?

"We were never close," Nizam admitted, and as she wrote the room filled with her mother's perfume, a scent from very early childhood, before the princess went to school or began spending every spare moment with her father. She was a lonely woman, her mother. It must have been an isolated, difficult life, governed by an ideal that could not be realized in her lifetime, an ideal that kept her husband and then her daughter locked away from her.

Nizam recognized the footsteps as soon as she heard them in the hall. She caught a glimpse of the guards snapping to attention and quickly looked back at her writing, defiant to the end.

At least she rated General Chenab himself.

"Princess," said the general as he stepped into the room, "I hope we haven't caused you too much inconvenience."

"Of course not," said Nizam, without looking up. "I've been catching up on my correspondence."

She could feel his greasy smirk examine her. The fat, self-important little man no doubt had some sort of deal to offer—her life in exile in exchange for a denouncement of the government and her family's birthright.

Better to walk with the ghosts.

"We've had to make new arrangements in light of the conflict," Chenab said. "The government has been streamlined."

"Who besides myself has been arrested?" Nizam asked, finally looking up. The general was dressed in a fresh uniform, with a full load of ribbons and battle decorations. His face was tired and, it seemed to her, troubled. He did not have the confident glare she thought he would.

"Have we arrested you?" The general turned to his guards as if they had the answer. "I don't believe you're under arrest."

"I'm free to go?"

"I didn't say that."

"How many of my people have you killed?"

"We haven't killed any."

"You bombed my house."

"The Indians bombed your house. A violation of the cease-fire. They apparently launched a plot against you," said the general.

"Your coup is failing, isn't it?" said Nizam.

"We are in control," said Chenab. He turned and with his head signaled to the guards that they should leave. "You, on the other hand, are not."

The general walked to the office door and closed it. He turned back toward her with his hands on his hips and gave her a look as if he had swallowed a dhole. The fierce eyes of the wild dog fixed her; its tongue slurped in anticipation.

The princess saw everything at that moment, knew precisely what would happen. A shudder passed through her body, a quick one. She recovered, and watched calmly as Chenab dug his fingers into his belt line.

"Why is it that someone like you has not found a man to tame her?" suggested the general. "Are you too proud for that?" He approached her in slow motion. "There are rumors, Princess, that you prefer girls."

Her nose filled with the pungent stink of jackal. She made her eyes hard.

"Have you ever even known a man?"

The spit welled in her mouth and propelled itself through the air on its own, acid dripping across his face. Chenab turned red, and brought his right hand around in a slap which she made no effort to duck. The blow sent her crashing back between her chair and a small table where she kept a fax machine. She rolled over, avoiding another swipe, but as she got to her knees Chenab's thick-soled shoe caught her in the side and she felt a piercing pain through her whole body. Still, she continued to struggle to her feet, and had almost succeeded when her head was yanked back by the hair and another blow struck the side of her face.

The punch sent the conscious part of her down a thick, defensive tunnel. From that hiding place it watched as Chenab yanked her up and slapped her twice. His hand was red hot, a poker just pulled from the fire. He dragged her from the office into the adjacent bedroom, pulling her across the floor and then draping her on the bed. Nizam's mouth filled with the metallic trickle of blood. Chenab tore her pants down, yanking at her underclothes, fumbling, awkward and uncoordinated in his rage. He pushed her blouse up and pulled at her bra, which did not want to give way; he had to use two hands and then managed only to twist it around, off her breasts. He left it at the base of her neck, the only piece of clothing on her body, a symbolic tourniquet that cut her brain off from the lower extremities.

He had to handle himself to complete his arousal. Nizam desperately turned over and tried to get out of the bed; Chenab grabbed first her leg and then her back, pulled himself on and then into her from behind. He grunted, the barks of an animal eating its prey, grinding himself against her buttocks.

The nauseating musk in her nostrils changed suddenly, becoming the light smell of flowers—a garden she remembered where the family had often gathered for parties when she was young. With the first breath she visualized the knife beneath the bed. With the second she relaxed, her body drooping as if it had surrendered. Chenab, his penis finally hardened, pushed her forward and continued to pound his way into her. Nizam threw her arms out, reaching over the edge of the bed. With every shove, she moved closer; it would be just a matter of time before the hole pushed her far enough to reach the knife.

How long it took she did not know. Her fingers felt the dust that hovered just above the floor, then the wood, then the fabric of the spread folded beneath the wood, the hard metal—

Chenab screeched, twisted pleasure snapped suddenly into pain, blood spurting from his side and then his chest, then his face as he rose, stunned. If Nizam had been able to think more clearly, she would have struck with the knife into his heart immediately, killing him before the commotion was heard. Instead she took another swipe at his face, the blade striding across in a diagonal, drawing a long gash through which the jackal in him escaped.

For a second, he stood before her, a pitiful man worried about his life. She saw him at his kindest, taking a moment from a cabinet meeting to share pictures of his grandchild. An instant later she saw only a white belly, a fat target for her knife. Nizam drove it home.

The general collapsed against her one last time. Nizam twisted the knife until she was sure he was dead, the blade severing everything it could reach inside the derelict corpse. When she got up, she was drenched in blood.

Whether they had confused the general's death groans with cries of passion or were out of earshot, his soldiers did not appear. They would break in soon enough. She stood looking at the body lying in its own blood in the center of the bed, and spit again on it. Then she walked to her office, leaned over and dialed the safe, immolating its contents.

Princess Ghazzala Hussain Raziyya Ali Nizam did not bother to watch the safe's destruction, nor to retrieve the unfinished letter to her mother on the desk. She walked slowly to her bath, the trail marked with Chenab's blood. She turned on the steam generator and raised the heater, then went into the water, walking straight down the steps, the slightly cool liquid cleansing her. With the knife still in her hand, she swam once across, then over to the side where she kept a basket of towels and soap.

Nizam washed the knife, cleaning it carefully, then placed it in the basket. She took a small rosette of imported soap, pulled herself up onto the edge of the bath and began with her feet. She lathered slowly, gently, covering her entire body, paying careful, delicate attention to her bruises. By the time she was done, the steam was heavy in the room and the water temperature had gone up several degrees. Nizam plunged to the bottom, touching the gems at the center one last time.

She was glad she had written the letter to her mother. Her father would not need a letter, nor her uncle. They knew her.

For a moment she hesitated, her eyes welling with tears. There were so many other things she could have done. She saw herself with a family, walking across the garden, a young boy in tow. But her stories would have filled him with dreams that could not be fulfilled. He would have died bitterly, cursing her.

She did not curse her father. She went to the side of the bath and took the knife. Floating toward the middle of the pool, she raised her wrist and then lowered it into water as warm as milk or blood, the ghosts rushing in around her.

In the Golden Bear. Apx. 9:20 A.M.

"Something was firing missiles at us," Greeley told O'Connell anxiously. "But it wasn't this guy here. He's been hailing us, like we're a flight he's supposed to escort."

O'Connell leaned against the Plexiglas side window panel, craning his neck backwards to see the black jet trailing them. Even from this distance it was obvious that it was something special.

Did it have a way to override the baffling system? Or did it just home in on the fake signal, realizing it was bogus? If so, he could jam and then change the signal, but it was useless while they were still in visual range.

"Take it down into the clouds," O'Connell said. "But go down easy. And don't get under eight thousand feet, whatever you do."

Greeley blanched. "You want me to fly through a storm?"

"Mr. Secretary, I need you to work this bench," said O'Connell. He practically pulled Grasso out of his seat. "Here, this sequence"—he jabbed his finger next to the neatly typed column of letters and numbers headed unimaginatively by the Urdu word for vanish. "You enter it on the screen exactly as it's written here. After Greeley gets deep into the clouds, push this button." O'Connell's finger hovered over the override. "But not until then. When he does that, Greeley, I want you to hit the gas."

"Hit the gas? We ain't going to outrun this guy."

"This is going to confuse him," O'Connell explained. "That's all we have to do. Take some turns, zag around a bit, then come back northwest." He turned back to Grasso. "After ten minutes or so, you can hit the presets again. Flip them on and off. These buttons—just don't push this one; that's the plane he's looking for, I think."

"What if it doesn't work?" said Grasso.

"It'll work," responded O'Connell with considerably more assurance than he felt. He motioned to Morena to ascend the ladder into the crawl space. "Keep it as steady as you can," he told Greeley. "Stay in the clouds, and don't go below eight thousand, whatever you do."

"What happens if he decides to shoot us down?"

"Tell him if he does he'll blow up half his country."

In the Snow Leopard. Apx. 9:25 A.M.

Khan leveled off at 60,000 feet, drawing his speed back and angling into a wide circle to come behind and above the plane he'd just passed. Everything about it was surprising and unexpected. How a propeller-driven aircraft managed this altitude he couldn't guess. More confusing, his computer stubbornly insisted it was a Mushshak.

There didn't seem to be anything wrong with his radar; its internal diagnostics checked out and it had, after all, just ID'd the MiGs. Assuming he wasn't hallucinating, this must be yet one more example of Kamra's magic. It explained General Dara's cryptic instructions to believe only his eyes.

Setting the Leopard up to fly into a tagalong position, Khan felt a twinge of patriotic pride that his countrymen could come up with something so bizarre and effective. But Dara had told him the plane would be headed directly to India, not flying westward. And where were the other two?

The pilot dialed into his contact frequency and gave the preassigned communications code. When there was no answer, he switched to one of the general frequencies used by Pakistani military flights.

"This is Major Syyid Khan to the Golden Bear flight," he said. "I am assigned to escort you."

There was no answer despite two more attempts to hail the plane. Khan couldn't tell whether its crew had a malfunction or just weren't paying attention. To make sure they knew he was here, he nudged his throttle and walked the Leopard toward the Golden Bear's right wing.

It was a long, long wing, coming straight off the fuselage like you'd expect for a propeller plane, but the portion beyond the engines was so tapered it reminded Khan of a sailplane. This was certainly no glider, however—two mammoth turboprops with heavily baffled exhausts sat inboard on each wing. A smaller box of pipe rockets was stuck like an afterthought toward the outside. Painted black like the rest of the plane, the wings were braced by a tubular webbing extending from the top and bottom of the fuselage, as if some giant spider had set its home there. Immediately above the wings was the golden-colored hump.

The front of the Golden Bear was made of glass panels, giving him a view into the cockpit as he passed. It was manned, at least.

Khan took the Leopard into another wide circuit, figuring to come up from behind again. Pulling parallel to the cockpit, he tried hailing the plane again, the computer switching through several frequencies.

"Major Khan, this is Golden Bear," answered the plane finally. "We have you in sight."

The words were all wrong. Though in English, the tone was off, the accent nothing like the sharp click of a Pakistani. It reminded Khan of his own horrible imitation of an American while he was refueling several hours before.

"Golden Bear, what is your mission?" Khan asked.

"Classified," responded the plane.

"I'm assigned to escort you," answered the major. "What is our course heading?"

"Classified," the plane responded in a scolding voice. "These are open communications."

True enough. And it was also true that the accent was anything but Pakistani. Khan took another pass over the plane, leaning to the side to get a better view into the cockpit. The copilot's seat was empty, though there were at least two people inside.

"Not so close," said a second voice as he passed. The Golden Bear started descending, perhaps buffeted by the Leopard's wash.

He cursed Dara for not telling him what the hell was going on. How could he ride shotgun for somebody if he didn't know where they were going? Khan, worried that getting too close might somehow damage the intricately constructed bomber, took his orbit deeper this time, straightening out five miles behind the plane, which had continued to descend. A range of cumulonimbus storm clouds were gathered ahead, the leading edge of the huge blanket Khan had skirted on his way to Gilgit. The prop plane seemed to be heading directly for the clouds.

He watched as the wispy fingers of gray slipped around the bomber. The clouds seemed to pull it inside, a lover opening the curtained door to the boudoir.

Khan's radar suddenly exploded in a rainbow of confused lines and colors. This was the work of a heavy-duty ECM, one even the Leopard's sophisticated black boxes couldn't fend off.

Cursing, he turned off the now useless unit and pushed forward in pursuit. Open radio or not, these bastards could have at least given him an idea where they were going. He lost them in the soup; even the FLIR couldn't seem to locate them because of the clouds and whatever thermal shielding had been done to reduce the plane's heat signature.

Either that, or the lumbering black plane had slipped through a hole in the universe. Khan opened the radio again, futilely asking the plane's pilot to acknowledge.

The thick storm clouds were like porridge; a visual sighting here was out of the question. Khan pulled up to 50,000 feet, unsure what to do next. His fatigue was returning. Waves of stiffness attacked his muscles, poking at his back and legs. He had the computer scan through the military radio frequencies, looking for any communication.

Only silence. It was as if the world had already been destroyed, and he was its sole survivor.

"Major Khan, this is Colonel Ali Hazan, speaking for General Dara."

The message came over the frequency he was originally told to use in contacting the Golden Bear. Khan started to acknowledge but the voice did not break.

"You are ordered to shoot down the Golden Bear. Repeat, shoot down the plane. It has been taken over by Indian agents. Shoot down the Golden Bear before it reaches populated areas."

Khan wanted more information—who had stolen it, why, where was it going, who was speaking to him? But the excited voice merely repeated his message as if it were on an endless tape loop.

Was this an Indian trick? Or did it explain why the plane had acted strangely? And why had that voice been all wrong?

Khan broadcast his own message—he wanted to talk to his cousin, Gen. Nur Khan. He went through every conceivable frequency, repeating his words without acknowledgment as he cranked the Leopard to the southwest, toward Karachi and the coast, looking for a break in the clouds below.

In the Golden Bear. Apx. 9:30 A.M.

There wasn't enough room at the end of the catwalk for her to turn around easily. Morena crunched her legs beneath her, twisting up and to the side. It was difficult to see; the small space was lit by a yellow bulb in a metal grille, and though it was only three feet from her head, it barely lit the interior below. But it was easy to guess what he wanted her to look at.

"Those are the bombs, aren't they?"

"They're armed," O'Connell said from behind her. "I need you to go down there and open a deactivation panel on each one. There's a key in there you have to turn."

"A key?"

"The fuses have an altimeter default setting. We'll blow ourselves and half the country up if we try to land."

"They can't be set to go off."

"They are," said O'Connell. "You see those lights? The crew can deactivate them from the cockpit, but I don't know what the code is, and we can't take a chance on just entering numbers in blindly."

"How do I get down there?"

"You'll have to climb over the rail—there's an access ladder screwed into the wall. See it?"

It looked thin and fragile, barely able to take even her light weight.

"There's a mechanical safe key in a panel near the lights. You'll have to look for it when you get down there."

"What if it's underneath?"

"It won't be."

As Morena stared at the weapon, her stomach suddenly dropped below her feet. She wondered if this was what death felt like.

"Hold it steady, Greeley," O'Connell yelled behind her. "Just hold it steady."

"I'm all right, Michael," she said, reassuring herself as much as him. She pushed backwards against him, her nostrils stinging with the smell of blood and raw, shot-up flesh.

"Move back and give me room. I want to take off my shoes."

O'Connell backed down the tunnel. Even with a few feet of extra room, there was no way for her to swing her legs around to unite the heavy jump boots, much less remove them.

"Undo them for me, would you?" she said, sticking them back toward his face.

"Geez, your feet stink," he said as he pulled off the first boot. Whether he meant it as a joke or not, she laughed.

Her feet free, Morena grabbed hold of the rail with her right hand and swung her legs over the side, easing her body down as slowly as possible. The airplane began to buck from another patch of difficult turbulence, and she was barely able to get her left hand on the rail. She had a vision of herself falling straight through the plane's thin metal skin.

"You all right?" O'Connell asked.

She began moving toward the ladder, working her hands together and then apart slowly. The rungs were nearly four feet from the crawl space railing—she braced herself as best she could with her left arm and then flailed toward it with her right. Something in the socket of her left arm snapped loudly; Morena realized she had ripped a ligament in her shoulder and quickly turned back, grabbing the metal brace and wincing as her left arm began to throb.

"You could have made it," O'Connell said.

"I pulled something."

"Screw that, Morena—my goddamn shoulder's in pieces and I'm not crying about it."

The hell with you, she thought, gingerly testing her arm. It seemed OK, but as soon as she let go with her right hand, the pain shot through so hard she yelped involuntarily.

"Are you OK?"

No way she would show weakness now. With a hard breath Morena swung her feet over to the ladder, managed—just barely—to hook the side of the rung, and in the same motion let go of the rail. Her body flipped downward and she crashed into the ladder, fortunately shielding her face with her good arm.

"Morena!"

"I'm fine," she grunted. Upside-down, but fine. She wiggled around and slid her good arm through a slot—this was like exercising on a parallel bar, wasn't it?

Except she'd never been too good at that.

Her heart thumping in her ears, Morena managed to work her way right-side-up and then down the ladder to the tail end of the bombs. They were suspended over the bomb bay floor by a set of metal struts that grasped their spherical bodies like bony fingers. Cushions separated the weapons from their holders, like jewels on display.

"There's a pair of manual release levers near your head—don't touch them!"

"What should I do?"

"You'll have to crawl out through the scaffolding on the bombs," said O'Connell.

"Crawl out on them?"

"They'll hold. You're not that heavy."

The bombs were about twelve feet long, including their fins. They were fat, more like bloated ovals than the thin cigars she expected. The black surface was not nearly as smooth as it had seemed from above; there was a seam where the outer casing had been welded together and dull impressions like faint pockmarks dotting the casing. Looking through the massive, rectangular fin section at the rear, she could see the small red lights distinctly—but still no panel.

"Michael, there are welding marks on the bomb—do you think they welded it shut?"

"There's got to be a panel on there somewhere, Morena. Go find it."

"This going to hold my weight?"

"Trust me."

What else could she do? Grabbing onto the ladder with both hands, she eased her legs onto the bomb assembly nearest her, pushing down—it moved, but the motion was solid, dampened by shock absorbers.

"Come on, Morena—I don't know how long Greeley can hold us level in this storm. If he goes too low we're going to be barbecued."

The weapons weighed a little more than a ton apiece; Morena barely a hundred pounds. Still, she felt very heavy easing onto the bracing. She pulled her arm up and lifted her feet over the fan tail—her foot slipped from the metal and then her arm slipped when the plane took a sudden lurch.

She fell face first onto the bomb.

Somewhere below the casing, below the packing and the high-explosive lens that waited to push it to critical mass, 7.442 kilograms of plutonium nestled calmly in its slumber, unaffected by the anxious breath of the woman who wanted to render it permanently inert.

The LEDs were the first thing Morena saw when she opened her eyes. She reached her right hand out toward them gingerly, feeling the surface of the bomb casing and sliding up slowly, as if her hand were working its way through a mine field. She found a neat slit just beyond the lights—the panel.

"I got it."

"Open it carefully," said O'Connell from above. "Come on, Morena."

"It won't come. Oh God, there's some kind of lock."

She eased a few inches closer. It was just a thumbscrew, something simple. If she'd had a screwdriver—Morena edged her nail into the shallow slot and turned gently. It wouldn't budge.

"Can you get it open?"

She pushed harder, wishing for once that she had longer nails. There was a click, and the mechanism sprung up heavy against her hand. She let the panel open all the way—the back of it was facing her; she'd have to sit up to see inside.

Morena held her breath as she hunched up her legs and shimmied forward. The shift of balance caused the assembly to rock gently.

"It should be a mechanical key, like you'd see in a windup toy," O'Connell shouted. His voice was hoarse.

"All right," she said. "Which way do I turn it?"

"If it goes more than one way, we're in big trouble."

Her fingers trembled as she reached for the switch. The

plane rocked just as she touched the metal—she yanked her hand back suddenly.

"Come on, Morena, for cryin' out loud."

Don't yell at me, she thought. You're the last one who ought to be yelling at me—you got us into this mess.

"Morena!"

"Relax," she said, reaching for the switch, a small, flat piece of metal sticking up in the middle of a caulked hole. It was ice-cold. Her fingers slid along the edge for a moment, caressing it, then she pushed hard on one end, felt it move and lock.

She had to shimmy back nearly halfway off the bomb before she could see for sure that the LEDs were off. She nodded to herself, confident now, and crawled back to safe the other weapon.

In the Snow Leopard. Apx. 9:45 A.M.

Khan had everything but his landing lights on and still couldn't find the plane. He kept hoping a squadron of fighters would arrive and help out, but his requests for assistance went unanswered. The Pakistani air force seemed to have gone into hibernation.

It was difficult even to guess the general direction the plane would fly in. Khan took a quick scoot toward the northern border, clearing the storm front. He found nothing. Accelerating southward—his one asset was speed—he pondered the radio message, which was still being broadcast, jamming out communications on that channel. Why was he to shoot it down before it reached a populated area? Were they only worried about a crash?

More likely, they were fearful the bombs would be used. Which city would be its target? The capital, Islamabad? No, the plane would have had to sneak back east past him, and he was fairly confident it hadn't; the fleeting contacts he'd had were all to the west of his original sighting. Lahore, much farther to the south? Too close to India, Khan reasoned; an Indian pilot would not want to strike so close to the border.

Multan? Karachi? There were so many possibilities. Khan watched the horizon creep up the left side of his HUD as he took a turn to sweep to the west. Perhaps he was best off not trying to outguess the pilot, just to trust that he would find him. Trust God to lead him.

The Muslim wished his beliefs were deep enough to do that. He especially hoped he was right about Lahore being too close to the border.

Perhaps Lahore was all he should care about. Protect Hir.

The radar bleeped. There was a plane ahead, a small plane in the mountains heading southeast. No, not a small plane, a MiG-29.

The radar flicked on and off the enemy plane, its signal barely adequate to give the pilot its direction. That was enough for now, though. His fingers cold despite the thick flight gloves, Khan pushed the stick and tucked the Leopard into a rolling dive. The MiG must have hooked up with the Golden Bear; find it and he found his target.

The white HUD altitude numbers had counted down past ten thousand feet when he lost the MiG in the mountain clutter for good. Khan continued on course, putting his plane closer and closer to the craggy peaks, seeking the same protection the fuzz provided the Indian. He switched from the radar to the FLIR, no longer encumbered by the clouds and wanting to keep surprise on his side as long as possible.

But the Leopard's gear failed him; it couldn't find even a hint of his prey in the air before him. Reluctant but determined to find the MiG and Golden Bear even if he had to make himself a target, Khan yanked back on his stick and watched the horizon bar jab downward. As soon as he flipped the radar on, it spit up an unidentified contact flying several miles to his right. The plane was low in the mountains, very slow, subsonic. Exactly what the MiG would do escorting the bomber.

Khan sliced to his left, his heart starting to pound. He pulled the control stick back to the right, then brought the Leopard over in a loop, rolling out at the top, his left hand pressing the throttle forward as far as it would go without reaching for the afterburners. At the same time he pitched into a dive back toward the Indian. The HUD put a shadow on the screen, marking out the plane as he came around. But once again his radar's fingers lost their stick and the contact disappeared.

Damn. Why was the radar suddenly so sloppy? But he ought to be within visual range. The sky blue fuselage should be easy to see against the brown and green backdrop of the hills; still, he couldn't spot the plane.

Out of the left corner of his eye he saw a contact flash once again on the radar screen. Unidentified. The automatic controls buried deep in the black boxes tweaked and twisted their transistors, trying to refine the signal while Khan put his own gear to work, straining his eyes and lodging his helmet almost on the glass as he stared out for a sighting. Finally he caught a glimpse of a bright yellow light hovering in a black shadow crossing the canyon floor.

The bomber.

Khan immediately slowed and instinctively checked the airspace around him, making sure he hadn't been suckered into the MiG's sights. Then he circled quickly to the right, dropping as he did, aiming to slip in behind the Golden Bear.

In the Golden Bear. Apx. 10:05 A.M.

O'Connell squinted into the display screen at the left end of the console, watching as it scanned the sky in search of the fighter plane's radar. It was clear, though that wasn't a guarantee of anything. He turned to the control panel and flipped the preset for the MiG back on, figuring it had some fright value. He could alternate between the presets and the fuzz.

"Cloud cover's breaking ahead," said Greeley, holding the headset off his ear to hear. "What do you want me to do?"

"Take it down to the hills, as low as you can go."

"We staying on this course?"

"I'm not sure yet," said O'Connell. He'd been so busy

worrying about getting the plane and then safing the bombs, he hadn't had time to decide where they should land. They could probably make the United Arab Emirates, though that would mean flying over a considerable stretch of Pakistan.

They could fly due north to Russia, but what if they were forced down in one of the republics? Or if the Russians decided to keep the plane?

He could always go west, over Afghanistan—and straight over southern Iran, where Renard was waiting for him with a five-million-dollar welcome mat.

There was a glimmer on the detection screen. O'Connell quickly hit the override, scrambling the radar.

"Get it lower," he told Greeley, tapping violently on his shoulder. "The clutter from the mountains and the hills will give us better cover. Don't worry about the bombs."

"I'm down pretty far already."

"There's a lot more room," said O'Connell, pulling off his headset. He stood and pointed over Greeley's shoulder into the high-rising plains that spread out before them in front of the Plexiglas nose. "Take it right into the hills."

Greeley began sinking the big plane lower. They slid down into a valley, nudging over small peaks that alternated red and brown rock tops with lush vegetation. If they hadn't been running for their lives, they might have thought about taking pictures.

"Wow, look at that." The secretary of state pointed out his bottom window, down at a sandstone canyon. A giant figure had been cut into the side of a hill, a huge, grinning Buddha. As they stared out the window, a dozen other figures were revealed, animals, saints, abstractions.

"Pilgrims used to travel through these mountains," Morena explained. "These glyphs are like religious billboards."

"Let me sit down a minute," O'Connell said to Grasso, motioning him to trade places. He stood and helped O'Connell slide into the seat.

The glyphs on the mountains were like a locator beacon—they weren't as far south as he'd thought. He flipped through the navigational computer, getting his bearings.

O'Connell's first touch of the buttons brought up the

course of the bombing raid that had been programmed into the computer before takeoff: east over Nepal and Bangladesh. The targets were Calcutta and Allahabad.

"They say the mountains are haunted," Morena told Grasso, pointing out the window at the hills below. "Thousands of religious people are buried here. When you're down there, you can almost feel it in the air."

"Imagine risking your life to cut that into the hillside," said the secretary of state as they passed a huge angelic figure cut onto the side of a cliff. "They must have been pretty hooked on what they were doing."

O'Connell's fingers tapped the nav controls anxiously—straight on the way they were going, give or take a slight mid-course correction or two, and they'd fly straight to Renard's strip. In the confusion of refueling, he could easily "lose" one of the bombs to the ground crew.

But he'd have to lose Morena, too, and the rest of them, if he expected to get away with it. Lose them, as in kill them.

"Michael?"

O'Connell turned to her suddenly, as if woken from a dream. Her deep green eyes were clear and penetrating, reaching for his.

One last temptation, wasn't it? But she was here to prevent him from giving in—even if his conscience would have let him trade a bomb to Renard in order to stay alive, it would never let him kill her.

And if she weren't aboard, if it were just him and Greeley, would he have gone on to Iran?

He could never do that, either. The bombs were too likely to be used somewhere.

So she was right then. He was responsible in the first place, sharing some measure of guilt for all of this. That was why he agreed to come back. He wanted to expiate his sin, not become rich or get revenge. There had been one final temptation—Renard. One more chance to go wrong; one more chance to redeem himself.

"Do you have the course?" Morena asked softly.

"Take a forty-five degree turn to the southeast here," he

said to Greeley as her eyes sank past his face, deep into his soul. "It's going to be rough, but our only hope is to go directly to Abu Dhabi in the Emirates. I'll have the exact coordinates in a minute."

In the Snow Leopard. Apx. 10:25 A.M.

Light splayed off the golden hump of the plane ahead, sharp long triangles marking his target. They were all alone. The MiG contact must have been another trick.

Khan's hard breath hissed in his ears as he closed the distance between himself and his target. His gun was loaded, charged, ready to fire. The little piper on the HUD gave him a fat cue. He kept coming, the distance narrowing from three kilometers to two. Khan was off the plane's tail twenty-five degrees, perfectly positioned in the killing cone. The bomber was completely defenseless, without so much as a machine-gun mounted in the back. No wonder they'd wanted him for protection.

And somehow the Indians had turned the tables on them. No matter; the protector was now the stalker, closing for the kill.

He popped his head back to check his rear one last time. Clean.

Khan was within a kilometer, the tail of the plane so close he could touch it. His heart skipped a beat as he pressed the gun trigger on his stick, leaving it there for a long burst as he gently nudged the Leopard first toward his left and then his right foot, a raking motion to spew bullets all through the Golden Bear's fuselage and wing section.

Except that nothing happened.

He pressed again, this time holding his position steady. Still nothing.

WEAPONS MALFUNCTION lit in the HUD. Khan caught up with the bomber and rode over its wing, cursing. The plane veered to the left as he rose to regroup.

What the hell was with the gun? The plane told him it

was ready to go, yet when he pressed the trigger, nothing happened.

Khan came around, slowing for another run. As he did so, he switched the radar that controlled the weapons through its different modes and back around to the air attack setting that worked the cannon on the unlikely chance that it had somehow locked out the gun. Still no result. He hammered the buttons on the master armament panel, flicked the trigger with three of his fingers, still couldn't get it to fire. He tried a few violent maneuvers, twisting as if he might shake the weapon awake. The cannon refused to work.

Keeping track of his quarry, at least, was no problem now. They were far from the clouds and there was no difficulty keeping it in view. He switched off his radar, thinking that perhaps the radar-fooling device on the plane had somehow snuck in and put the weapons system to sleep. This was such a turkey shoot he could take the Bear out with his eyes closed. But even on full manual the cannon remained dead.

There was radio traffic—the bomber was calling for help.

No, it was calling him.

"This is the American secretary of state to the Pakistani aircraft following us. By the authority of the United Nations I order you to escort us to international air under your country's safe conduct. International law provides that you must present me with diplomatic protection."

Khan considered clicking on the radio to claim that he was the premier of Russia. He had to admit that the Indian not only had balls; he was pretty good at mimicking an American accent.

But this was deadly serious; the bomber had nuclear weapons aboard. He had to take him down somehow. Khan accelerated over the Bear again, this time slashing directly in front as he passed. Its pilot reacted by climbing sharply back to the right, rising from the peaks, giving himself more room to maneuver. The fighter's wash seemed no more than a minor annoyance to the plane's reinforced airfoil.

Once more the plane called him. "We are carrying nuclear weapons," said the voice, a little more anxious than before, "if you shoot us down they will explode."

Perhaps, though Khan expected that the weapons were safed against accidental explosion. Even if they weren't, he surely couldn't trust them to put down without dropping them or setting them off. Anyone capable of stealing the plane would surely consider himself a worthy martyr.

They were still in the mountains; as horrible as a nuclear explosion would be, it would have considerably less effect here than over a city.

He'd have to ram the plane. Khan had been ready to die yesterday, and his cause was now even greater. But was it the only way to take out the plane? There must be other Pakistani fighters in the air by now.

"This is Major Khan to any and all PAF fighters and ground controllers in sector two-nine. Request immediate, top-priority assistance. I have a bomber in sight."

The radio remained silent as he closed the distance between his plane and the bomber. Khan's hands began shaking wildly as he neared. It wasn't a malfunction of the controls or the tricky air sucking up close to the mountains; it was nerves.

He yanked off, pulled straight up.

I have to do it, he told himself. I have to. And quickly—I may not have the guts if I wait too long.

"This is Major Khan to all PAF fighters in two-nine," he repeated, leveling off. "I am asking for assistance."

Not even static. If he did not sacrifice himself, surely millions of his countrymen would die. Already the plane was approaching a populated area as the hills settled into the high, fertile plains. Even if another fighter answered his call, it would be too late.

But as he reached for the throttle to accelerate, something seemed to catch his arm. Khan felt Hir come up behind him. Her voice whispered in his ear, telling him he must not bring down the plane.

"I am not a coward," he said aloud.

The plane was a huge black bird before him, fluttering its wings and magically dodging his aim. He maneuvered for a final, fatal plunge, Hir's voice loud in his ears, telling him not to harm the plane, not to sacrifice himself. No, he told her. You must let me go. This is my duty.

Syyid, Syyid, listen to me. Do not shoot down the plane. Do not attack the plane, little cousin.

It wasn't Hir, it was the radio. His cousin Nur.

"Did you hear me, Syyid? Break off the attack!"

"Where are you?" said the pilot, letting go of the throttle.

"Thank God I got you. I am on Command Two; I've been working with the Americans for the past half hour to find you. The conspirators are under arrest. The coup has failed."

"What about the bomber?"

"It is being flown by an American team. Haven't you heard its transmissions? The Americans are sending an escort. There will be peace after all, cousin. It is not too late. Do you hear me?"

Was it another trick? Khan realized that he had left his radar off. He switched it on to long-range scan, and caught what must be the command plane to the southeast. There was another contact to the west, two of them—a pair of American fighters hotfooting it in.

He rose to meet them. It was only as he leveled off that he realized tears were flooding his face mask.

In the Golden Bear. Apx. 11 A.M.

Grasso began doing a dance in the aisle as soon as the American fighter jet hailed them. The others looked at him with exhausted faces, but he didn't care if it didn't look dignified. He had a whole new perspective on dignity.

"Greeley still has to land this thing," said O'Connell. "Maybe we better hold off any dancing until then."

"I can land it."

"Without flipping us over this time."

"We ended up in one piece, didn't we?"

"Don't worry—I'll make sure they have a big bottle of Scotch waiting for us at the end of the runway as an incentive."

"No thanks," said Greeley. "That's the last thing I want. Especially in a Muslim country."

"I'll drink it then," said O'Connell.

The secretary of state slipped back onto the bench, leaning gingerly to avoid touching any buttons on the console. They were really going to make it now.

The blood from the men he had shot was smeared on the floor and on the rail across from him. Grasso had never killed anyone in his life; in fact, he'd always wondered whether he was capable of even adequately defending himself. It was part of a deep-seated insecurity, an anxiety that manifested itself in many ways.

It was gone now.

The first thing he would do after landing was call his wife. He'd speak to Tracy, too, eventually. She was a talented young woman, an asset to the department. It was time for her to be transferred.

"I'm going to put you all in for medals when we get back," he told them.

Morena loosened her grip on the ladder and flopped into the seat beside him. A few days ago the weight of her body would have sent his head spinning, and the arm he put reassuringly around her would have meant something more than the paternal kindness he felt now.

"You deserve one too, sir," said the young agent. "I think it was your ordering him to cease and desist that really did it."

Grasso laughed. The girl was so tired her eyes were almost closed.

"See if you can put this thing about thirty degrees to your right," O'Connell told Greeley, relaying directions from the air force plane. "He's going to try and line us up—all you have to do is follow his taillights."

"Assuming he can keep up with us," said Greeley.

O'Connell had a retort for him, but Grasso wasn't paying attention to them anymore. He'd begun thinking about how he was going to build on this cease-fire. If the coup had been suppressed and both sides knew about the nuclear weapons, perhaps everyone would be scared enough for him to work through a real, lasting agreement. It was a tiny opening, but if he pushed hard enough . . .

A Hospital in New Delhi. Noon.

There were two figures standing at the end of the bed, one black, one white. For a moment General Arjun thought they were more apparitions, representations of good and evil, haggling over his soul.

Gradually he began to understand that they weren't arguing. But they were talking about him.

"Shastri," he said as the darker figure, clad in khaki, came into focus. The men took no notice of him. "General Shastri," he said again, calling to his second in command. The men looked over, startled.

"The doctor was just telling me that you wouldn't be conscious for several more hours," said the brigadier. "And I was pointing out that many have underestimated you."

Shastri turned and whispered something to the doctor. The physician smiled.

"I will check on you a little later," he said, taking his leave.

Shastri shuffled forward to Arjun's side, pulling over the lone chair from the corner. It was an austere white room, the only luxury a large window, flushed with sunlight.

"How are the men?" Arjun asked.

"Everyone has done his job," replied the brigadier. "Had it not been for the cease-fire, we would have had Lahore in our control now. That was your real plan, was it not, to recapture the homeland of the Sikhs?"

Arjun nodded.

"It is too bad that you have not been able to succeed," said Shastri mildly. "Surely you would have. A hundred years of injustice might have been reversed."

"What happened to the men in the trailer?"

"They were killed in the explosion. There was nothing you could do; they died instantly."

"How many men have we lost?"

"Two hundred at most, including all the wounded. We have been lucky."

"Yes."

"We thought you were our greatest casualty. When we found your body it was almost completely drained of blood."

"You always exaggerate, Shastri."

"You were taken to a field hospital and then back here. It was very hazardous to move you, but there was nothing else that could be done. Our hopes were so slim."

"Where is this?"

"We are in New Delhi." Shastri smiled. "You didn't think I would leave you to the butchers in the provinces?"

Arjun nodded. General Shastri's face grew grave once more. His voice trembled as he continued. "General—"

"My leg is gone, isn't it?"

"Yes."

"Shiva told me," said Arjun. "We had quite a conversation."

"Shiva?"

"Don't worry, Shastri, I haven't converted to your religion." As he struggled to pull himself up with the brigadier's help, Arjun let his eye linger briefly over the covers.

"You may yet lose the other one, sir."

"No," said Arjun. "He would have used that to torment me, and he didn't."

Shastri gave him a puzzled expression before continuing. "They were very concerned that you would die. Several times it looked as if you had."

"There were a few times I despaired," replied Arjun. "But on the whole it was a remarkable experience. I did really have a conversation with the Hindu god Shiva."

"Yes, sir."

"It is interesting to find out what one truly believes," said Arjun. "Perhaps it is worth a leg." The brigadier looked at him doubtfully. "Come, come, Sattua," Arjun said to him, using his first name for maybe the first time. "Where is your normal cheer? Or perhaps some of your verse?"

"There is a report that the Pakistanis had nuclear weapons," said Shastri. He continued to use tones more somber than Arjun had ever heard from his mouth. Perhaps the weight of command had altered him. That would be a shame, thought Arjun—his philosophical nature was, all things considered, an asset. "Apparently the Americans stepped in to prevent them from using them."

"The Americans? No." Arjun shook his head, smiling. "It was not the Americans."

"Sir?"

"There is much you must learn, Sattua." Arjun felt his strength beginning to flag. But he could sleep now. There was time remaining to him.

"A great deal has happened since you lost consciousness. The American secretary of state was kidnapped."

"Yes, yes," said Arjun, waving him away. "We can discuss this later."

"General?"

He would have a great deal to do when he recovered. A man passes through four phases of life, discharging his proper responsibilities in each, first to his parents, then to the family he raises, next to the community or nation, and finally to his spirit or soul. Arjun had fulfilled the first three. New roads waited for exploration.

"I hope you like command," mumbled Arjun, drifting to sleep, falling backward into a shallow lake filled with gentle perfume and soothing oils.

EPILOGUE

The 1997 Indian-Pakistan War ended with a new round of agreements engineered by American Secretary of State John Grasso. Besides restoring captured Pakistani territory, the agreement reaffirmed the ban on weapons of mass destruction and established new compliance provisions. It also called for a new United Nations study of the Kashmir question.

With the help of several key families as well as army and air force officers, the Pakistani civilian government survived the coup. Democracy was strengthened in Pakistan. The breakaway nationalist movement championed by Princess Ghazzala Hussain Raziyya Ali Nizam floundered after her death, though a few diehards held out hope that the last remaining member of the clan, a young nephew of the princess currently studying in England, would some day return and aspire to the throne. All knowledgeable observers concluded that this was a futile dream.

Michael O'Connell turned down an offer of full restoration with the CIA. A month after the completion of the mission, he still had not decided whether to go back into business for himself, though the secretary of state had seen to it that the deposed DDO's promise of agency contracts would be honored. O'Connell was, however, continuing to see a lot of Morena Kelso, who had returned to Washington, D.C. Temporarily posted as a special assistant to the director, Kelso was rumored to be under consideration for deputy national security director.

Pierre Renard, the outlaw arms dealer living in Iran, was not pleased with what he came to see as O'Connell's deliberate deception about the bombs. Renard has survived by taking a philosophical view, realizing that everything works out in the end—even if you have to help some things, like revenge, along.

Major Syyid "Rocket" Khan was promoted to full colonel in recognition of his wartime exploits. He and his fiancée, Hir Ranjha, married as planned. After a brief honeymoon, they moved closer to the Sargodha air base, where his stealth fighter is now based.

And James Greeley? He returned home a proud man, though because of national security interests, the story of his role in averting a new nuclear war was never told in the press. He has almost made up for that deficiency himself by lecturing family members, grandkids especially, on the difficulties of flying a B-50 and the exotic pleasures of Pakistani food. Though the money he received from the government was enough to buy a new house, he has steadfastly resisted moving from the trailer. "Too much to remember here," he often tells his children.

A NOTE TO THE READER

African-Americans have played an important though often underappreciated role in the U.S. military since the revolutionary war. During World War II, black fighter pilots distinguished themselves in the 12th and 15th Air Forces, destroying a total of 261 enemy aircraft in the air and on the ground, according to Department of Defense records, even though they were often constrained to obsolete fighter types. Among other awards, at least 95 Distinguished Flying Crosses were handed out to African-American pilots.

The most famous group of black fliers was the 99th Pursuit Squadron, which trained at Tuskegee, Alabama, and came to be called the Lonely Eagles. The Eagles, like most but not all African-American airmen, served in an essentially segregated environment that was often less than equal. Despite their record of achievement, blacks continued to be discriminated against throughout the war and thereafter.

According to some military historians and the DOD, the

creation of the air force following the war gave that branch of the service a head start in recognizing and rewarding the talents of black fighting men and women. The air force was the first of the services to integrate, and the Korean War produced several well-recognized black pilots, whose abilities and records eventually propelled them to important command positions. It was the air force that produced the first 4-star African-American general; if the military was well ahead of the rest of society in integrating, the air force was well ahead of the rest of the military. But the process was slow and painful, with many now-forgotten victims along the way.

It is to the memory of those unsung heroes, their families and their dreams that the character of James Greeley is dedicated.

ABOUT THE AUTHOR

Jim DeFelice is a journalist and professor of communications who has long been interested in aviation and intelligence. He lives in Highland, New York, where he is completing his next novel.

A KILLING PACE
LES WHITTEN

"Gritty, realistic, and tough!"
—Philadelphia Inquirer

For George Fraser, dealing and double-dealing is a way
of life. But with the body count around him rising higher,
he decides he wants out of the espionage business. As a favor
for an old friend, Fraser agrees to take on one last job: just
running some automatic weapons—no big deal. Then the
assignment falls apart, and Fraser is caught in the sights of
terrorists determined to see him dead. Suddenly, Fraser is
on a harrowing chase that takes him from the mean streets
of Philadelphia to the treacherous canals of Venice. He is
just one man against a vicious cartel—a man who can stop
countless deaths and mass destruction if he can keep up a
killing pace.

_4017-4 $4.99 US/$6.99 CAN

EVIL INTENT

BERNARD TAYLOR

"Move over, Stephen King!"
—*New York Daily News*

John Callow hates the people of Valley Green. For years, Callow has waited while the townsfolk spurn him, insult him, cheat him. But with an ancient curse ripped from the bowels of hell, he'll visit misery on everyone who has ever slighted him. Death by grisly death, his neighbors will fall victim to a plague of ghastly suffering. And Callow's grim reaping will be stopped by neither heavenly prayer nor earthly weapon—only by an infernal power born in the same wicked domain as his evil intent.

_3904-4 $4.99